Stolen

Janet Durbin

Whimsical Publications, LLC

Florida

Stolen is a work of fiction. Names, characters, and incidents are the products of the author's imagination and are either fictitious or are used fictitiously. Any resemblance to actual events or persons, living or dead, is entirely coincidental.

Cover art by Vanessa Harper

Published in the United States by
Whimsical Publications, LLC
Florida

ISBN-10: 0-9787738-2-9
ISBN-13: 978-0-9787738-2-3

Printed in the United States of America

"Be careful there, young man, you don't want to hurt yourself."

"Who are you?"

"I'm an old friend of the family."

"Yea?"

"Yea." The big man squat low, resting one knee on the ground so he could be at eye level with the boy. "Who are you?"

"Joey."

The youngster gawked at the man. He had never seen anybody like him. Most people he saw were like his parents. This man was huge, his body all bumpy with muscles, and the sword on his back—wow.

"Joey, huh. Well Joey, how's your mom?"

"She okay."

"Her name's Shyanne, right?"

"How'd you know?" The boy's eyes widened.

"Remember—I'm an old friend of the family."

"Oh yea. You want to come to the house? Mom's inside, probably napping."

"Is your dad home?"

"Naw. He's gone right now. He had to go get some things from town. What's your name?"

"Ruben."

The big man extended a hand to shake Joeys. He made no attempt to come closer. Joey looked at it. He hesitated, not sure if he should shake it or run away. He remembered the few times his parents had had friends over and the way they had scolded him for not being polite, so he moved forward. He grasped the huge hand with his tiny one and pumped his arm up and down as he had seen his dad do when greeting other men.

Ruben could not believe his luck. He had been watching the house for some time, taking great steps to avoid the blasted cats ranging area, wondering how he was going to get the boy away from everyone long enough to grab him. Now, he was before him, alone, so innocent and trusting.

"Come say hi to mom. She'll be happy to see you."

The boy gripped the big hand and tugged.

"Joey, I can't stay. I've got to go to town myself." Ruben let go of the hand and started to walk away. He turned back toward the youngster after a couple of steps, "Say, did you want to come with me? We can meet up with your dad."

The boy's big hazel eyes lit up. The thought of going to town was wonderful. He had been there only a few times and remembered all the exciting things he had seen. Upset when his father had not taken him, he was going to get the chance to see them after all.

"Really? I can go with you?"

"Only if you think your mom won't mind."

"She won't care. I'll be with a friend, and they always said it was okay to stay with their friends."

"Well then, let's go." Ruben smiled as he reached out and took the boys hand in his.

Acknowledgments

This leg of the journey was completed with the help of some very important people. Editors Jim, Gene, and Bob kept the story on track and found boo-boos that this tired ole' brain managed to slip into the story. Without them, several names would be all wrong and scenes wouldn't make sense.

Vanessa Harper created a wonderful cover that still makes me wonder what I did to deserve it.

To all the people I work with at the hospital, I thank each and every one of you for putting up with my ramble on about my books. Your feedback encouraged me to continue.

And to my readers. Without you, this book would merely be words on paper and nothing more. Thank you.

Also by
Janet Durbin

Journey of Twins Series

AFTER
STOLEN
*VENGENCE**

Nature Kranderson Series

INNOCENCE TAKEN

———————

*Coming in 2008 from Whimsical Publications, LLC

Change is inevitable.

Whether we like it or not.

Synopsis of
After

The world in 2002 was a bustling time filled with modern conveniences like cars, subways, and all night fast food restaurants. It was also when twins Drayco and Shyanne were born. One had the complexion of her mother. The other looked a lot like his dad.

Their parents worked for the government, but not much of their work was discussed around the twins. They were more interested in teaching botany and camping and survival skills to their children than talking about germs that killed in the name of war or the genetic alterations of animals. The one thing their father had brought home from work was a humecat named Drizzle. He was a cub and one of the genetically altered mountain lion experiments.

As they grew into teenagers, Shyanne and Drayco joined the fencing team at school. Both excelled to the point that one had a hard time besting the other. After a particularly difficult match, Drayco was met at the door by his grandfather.

The elder man took him into the living room and presented him with a long wrapped item. It was a sword, but not just any sword. It was one handed down for generations. It was a samurai sword.

One day, the twins were doing their homework assignments when their dad came home early from work. He was sniffling and his eyes were red and bleary. They were informed to get ready for a camping trip the next morning. Sadly, the trip never happened. By morning, their dad had stopped breathing and was rushed to the hospital.

Their mother followed the ambulance after arranging with the grandparents to watch the twins. Drayco and Shyanne noticed that she had a sniffle and her eyes were getting red and bleary when she left.

That was when society as a whole fell apart. A virus created by the government escaped and infected billions, masking itself with cold-like symptoms. It killed a major number of people before running its course. Technology disappeared. The one who knew how to fix the machines died with the virus.

Only those with a high immunity survived. Fortunately, the twins were a part of the lucky bunch. Unfortunately, their genetic makeup was altered when they became infected. For one, it was manageable. For the other, it was a living nightmare.

The twins were forced to separate early on when Drayco lost control and almost killed Shyanne. The virus had altered him in such a way that he was forced to drink blood to survive. Shyanne, on the other hand, had another form of alteration: her aging process was slowed immensely.

By the year 2215, the world was medieval in nature. Technology was a thing feared by most because of the stories passed down through the ages. And because of the genetic monsters that roamed the countryside, especially after nightfall. The sword was the weapon of choice now. Survivors either learned to use it or died.

Shyanne missed her brother. She had not seen him in over 200 years and longed for the return of family. Thanks to the alterations to their aging and healing processes, she knew he was still alive. She followed lead after lead with her longtime companion, a humecat named Drizzle, trying to find him. Each time unsuccessfully.

Drayco had the same desire. He was tired of being alone, tired of needing to drink blood to stay alive, to stay young. But death was not an option. It was the easy way out and he had never done anything the easy way. With the inner sense of a twin, he started toward the one he sought, the one who loved him unconditionally: his sister.

In their separate adventures, they endured rizbaks, rats the size of medium dogs, infected wounds, Wanderers, and torture at the hands of two men. However, after they find one another, their most dangerous challenge was to find and face the Boss. To do that, they must get through Ruben.

Ruben was a mercenary hired by the mysterious Boss to locate Shyanne and bring her to his location. It seemed the Boss had discovered Shyanne's secret—her secret of long life—and wanted it.

Ruben and his band of fellow mercenaries destroyed an entire town in the search for Shyanne. They left no survivors, or so they thought. The twins discovered Joseph clinging to life. With their help, he recovered and tried to convince them to go after the mercenaries. They refused. In the cover of darkness, Joseph slipped away with Drizzle to seek revenge. The twins were forced to follow.

The mercenaries captured Joseph and Drizzle when they stumbled across them in some rocky terrain. On orders from the Boss, they were taken westward toward the town of Grandfield. Thanks to Drayco, Joseph escaped during a battle with spiderbats, but Drizzle remained a captive.

A journey across a vast flatland without animals to replenish his lack of blood, an injury, plus the burden of guilt caused by not freeing Drizzle forced Drayco to leave his sister in the arms of Joseph. He pursued Ruben alone and became a captive himself.

Ruben discovered the incredible healing powers that Drayco possessed when he forced the dark twin to drink the blood from an offensive, useless member of mercenary gang. He took him to the Boss, knowing full well that the woman they sought would follow.

The Boss was interested, but wanted Shyanne more. Through deception and pain, Ruben captured her when she entered the Grandfield inn looking for her brother and cat companion, and disappeared into a hidden underground facility.

Drayco, Joseph, and Drizzle discovered the entrance to the facility and followed. Technology from the past met them when they reached the bottom of a long flight of stairs. Layers of dust covered personal belongings from the previous occupants in every room. Every room, that was, except the main room where the generator was stored.

Unfortunately, a floating sentry guarded the place and almost killed the intruders before they found Shyanne. Drizzle became the bait. He lured the messenger of death away so the men could continue their search. They found her, but were unable to escape due to some medicine given to make Shyanne sleep. That and because of the machine used to help her breath in her unconscious state.

While trying to figure out how to free her, the Boss and Ruben discovered them. Joseph was knocked unconscious and a laser like device stunned Drayco. Just as the dark twin thought the end was near, Drizzle appeared, followed closely by the floating sentry. In a deadly crossfire, the Boss was sliced across the abdomen by the sentry and the stunning device used on Drayco zapped Ruben.

The Boss, as it turned out, was an ancient female who was trying to discover the genetic reason for Shyanne's long life so she could use it on herself. She died before Drayco could discover how to revive his sister.

Searching the computers that lined the room for a way to wake Shyanne, Drayco discovered the details for the virus. He used Joseph to smash the computers, thus preventing its return. Regrettably, while searching for information to help his sister, Ruben escaped.

The company destroyed the generator powering for the facility after awakening Shyanne and set fire to the inn to hide the entrance. They left shortly thereafter to start a new life, a life where Joseph and Shyanne married, and Drayco searched endlessly for the one who got away, Ruben.

One

Joseph guided the plow down the long open field. The horse, a dapple-gray, pulled at a slow, steady pace. The morning sun shined bright and hot, making the work that much harder. The fair-haired man thought about quitting for a little while, but knew the work had to be finished if they were going to have any food for the winter months. With a heavy sigh, he continued to follow the plow.

"Dad! Dad! Mom needs you right now!"

"But I'm not finished."

"Daaad! Come on!"

Joseph threw the guide reins to one side. He ran after his son, Joseph Jr, or Joey for short, who was already half way to the house. "What's the matter?"

The five year-old boy ignored his father. He was in too much of a hurry to get back to the house. Joseph increased his speed. He had to find out what was the matter with Shyanne. Both father and son reached the front porch at the same time. Joseph leaped up the step, threw the door open, and entered the main room of the single story dwelling ahead of his son.

The house was quiet—too quiet.

Six years ago, a man named Ruben had made life for Joseph, Shyanne, her twin brother Drayco, and their cat companion, Drizzle, a living hell. He had been working for a person called the Boss.

The Boss, as it turned out, was an ancient woman in

search of the fountain of youth via Shyanne's genetic makeup. The four of them had tracked her down and killed her. In the mayhem of the battle, Ruben got away. They tried to find the big man. They searched for months. It was as if he had vanished off the face of the planet. Drayco was still on the hunt, still looking for him.

Did Ruben find us? Is he here to take revenge for what we did to him? Shyanne, my love, I don't want to lose you, Joseph thought.

Joseph moved into the hall. He looked first to the right, into the bedrooms, then to the left. The rooms were empty. The kitchen was located toward the back of the house; he started in that direction. Before he made it half-way down the hall, an ear-piercing scream echoed back to him. Joseph ran forward, his heart pounding, wondering what was happening to his beloved wife. He skid to a stop at the doorway to the kitchen and looked around. Joey bumped into him, causing him to stumble further into the room.

Shyanne was kneeling precariously on top of the kitchen table, frantically looking around the room. Her strawberry blonde hair that was pulled back into a thick braid hung over one shoulder. Wisps of loose hair continually flew into her face. The fact that she was eight months pregnant did not help matters. It tended to make her as unpredictable as a grizzly bear in season.

"Shyanne! What are you doing? Are you okay?"

"Where is it?"

"Where is what?"

"The mouse!"

"The what?"

"The mouse! It was here a second ago!"

Joey looked around his father and broke into a giggle. Seeing his mother perched on top of the table afraid of something as small as a mouse was extremely funny to him.

"This isn't funny, Joey. Help daddy find the mouse for mommy."

"But mommy, you look so silly." The giggling increased.

The initial shock of seeing his wife on the table, not dying in a pool of blood, not giving birth, not being dragged away by Ruben, had worn off. A huge grin covered his face and a chuckle escaped.

"Don't you start, mister." Shyanne frowned. She did not see anything funny about the situation.

"Oh but honey—he's right. You do look pretty funny up there." A few more chuckles escaped.

"I don't care how it looks. Find that blasted mouse!" Shyanne slammed her palm hard on the tabletop.

One of the four legs was slightly shorter than the rest and the sudden motion caused the table to wobble and almost tip over. She grabbed the edges and held on for dear life. This action equalized the balance, which prevented the table from going over. Nevertheless, the sight of her face while she hung on was too much for the male family members watching.

They broke into a full out, gut-wrenching laughter. Joseph folded his arms over his stomach in an attempt to reduce the pain caused from laughing so hard. He leaned against the wall, tears rolling down his check. He knew he would pay for this dearly, but what the heck, he would enjoy the moment while he could.

"Ahhh—there it is! Get it—get it before it gets away!"

A small brown field mouse emerged from under a storage cabinet near the back door, wiggling its long whiskers. It looked at the frantic woman on the table and the males laughing at her plight. Unconcerned, it sat up on its haunches and began grooming itself, rubbing the pink nose with both paws.

Joey ducked around his father and ran toward the mouse. It darted to the right, away from the excited little hands trying to grab it—and straight for the table. Shyanne was terrified. She screamed.

"Ahhh! Don't let it get me! Kill it! Kill it!"

The spectacle going on in the kitchen was beyond his wildest imagination. Joseph slid to the floor, unable to remain on his feet any longer. He rolled onto his side, holding his abdomen as he tried to take a breath between the uncontrollable fits of laughter. He was in agony now.

"JOSEPH SR, THIS IS NOT FUNNY!"

Joseph continued to laugh uncontrollably while Joey chased the mouse around the kitchen. For a little tike, he was fast. One minute he was chasing it, the next he stood up holding the wiggling mouse by its tail.

"Mommy! I caught it! Seeee!" The proud little boy

held the dangling rodent out toward his mother. She backed away, nearly tipping the table over again.

"That's my boy. Now, can you please take it outside and across to the trees?"

"Sure thing, Mom!" Joey marched out the back door, grinning from ear to ear at the praise given. He flew down the back steps and across the large field, carrying the creature as if it was a prizewinner at the annual fair.

Shyanne climbed down from the table once the mouse was outside. She walked over to Joseph who was still lying on the floor wiping the tears caused by the laughter off his face, and shoved his legs with her foot. "That wasn't funny, Joseph. What if it had bitten me? I could have caught some kind of disease and died. The baby would have died too."

The fair-haired man looked up at his wife. He could barely see her face because her belly stuck out so far. He knew he should heed her words and take the situation more seriously, but the sight of her panicking over such a small creature would not allow it. He broke into a snicker and lost control again.

"Fine. If that's the way you want it, you make your own supper tonight."

Shyanne spun around and stormed down the hall toward the bedrooms. Joseph heard the door slam. He knew it would take her the rest of the day to cool off. Rising from the floor slowly, he managed to make it to a chair before flopping down again. He was exhausted from the plowing and the laughter.

The back door open and slammed shut. Joey came running into the room. "Mom! I took care of the mouse for you." He looked around the room when he didn't see her on the table. "Mom? Where'd you go?"

"She's in her room, son. I'd leave her alone for a bit. She's pretty mad at me right now."

"Why?"

"Because I laughed at her."

"But she was funny looking."

"I know. But she didn't think so."

"Will she come out soon?"

"I don't think so, not for a while yet."

"Why?"

"Because that's what girls do when they get mad."

"Oh..." Joey's smile faded. A thoughtful look replaced it as he tried to make sense out of what his dad had said.

"Hey kiddo...do you want to help me plow? You can ride Cloud and make sure he goes in the right direction. Wouldn't that be fun?"

The boys face brightened. "Yea!"

"Well then—come on."

Joseph stood and picked up his son. With an exaggerated groan, he tossed him into a sitting position on his shoulders and grabbed both legs to prevent the boy from falling off.

Joey squealed with delight. It was not often dad allowed him to ride the horses. He planned to do exactly what he was told, which was to keep Cloud going in the right direction. He wanted to make his father proud, like mom was earlier. Maybe then, he could ride more often. Maybe even learn how to fight with a sword like mom and dad did when they sparred, at least before mom became like she was, all fat with a baby and all.

Being an only child, his parents were overprotective. Joey was not allowed to stray far from home, and the town was too many miles away for the boy to go alone, so he had no friends. With no one to play with, that left only Drizzle. The cat was usually gone somewhere, which did not help the situation any. Now that the baby was coming, Joey knew he would have someone to play with. Until then, he would have to make due with what he had. And right now that involved riding Cloud.

Joey fell asleep in the stall next to Cloud while Joseph brushed the horse down. He had ridden for most of the afternoon, but became bored when it failed to veer away from the intended path. When Joseph questioned him about doing something else, the boy had not wanted to get off. Instead, he pretended to be on a long journey, a journey filled with adventures of rescuing damsels in distress, stolen from their families by bandits. Several times, he held up an invisible sword and swung it back and forth, as if he was in a battle. Joseph smiled to himself. The actions of his son reminded him of a not too distant past, a past where he had fought mercenaries for his own damsel in distress.

He walked to a stall opposite Cloud's and looked inside. Jack stood near the open window with his eyes closed. His tail swished at the flies biting various parts of his body. At the sound of the man's approach, he opened his eyes and moved over to the fair-haired man. He butted the hand resting on the rail with his nose, wanting to be scratched. Joseph obliged, moving his fingers up and down the forehead.

"How are you boy? It's been a long time since we've had an adventure together, hasn't it?" A wistful tone filled his voice. The horse butted him in the chest, trying to nuzzle inside his shirt. "I don't have any treats for you. I left them in the house."

Jack seemed to understand the words spoken to him. He turned away, returning to the window. This time, he leaned out and whinnied. He sounded as if he missed the open road and the vast plains as much as the man talking to him did.

A reply came, but not from outside. It came from the stall directly across from his. Cloud poked his head over his gate. He let out with another soft nicker. Joseph walked over to the horse and gave him a scratch as well.

"I understand. I wish we could go on an adventure too, but with a family to take care of—I can't."

Joseph gave the gray horse another quick scratch then began changing out the straw in their stalls. When he was done and the horses were fed and watered, he went outside to wash off.

A wooden barrel that collected rainwater from the roof stood next to the barn. A small cup of the same material, attached by a thin rope, swung in the gentle breeze.

He dunked his head in the cool water then threw it back. Droplets from his sandy colored hair that now hung past his shoulders sprayed everywhere. Water ran down his shirt, sticking it to his body. Joseph dipped his hands into the moisture and splashed it onto his face and neck, washing off the sweat and grime of the day. Before he could wash further, Joey emerged from the barn rubbing his sleepy eyes.

"Whatcha doin?"

"Cleaning the dirt off me. You should too." Joseph pulled several bits of straw from the brown mop atop his son's head. "See."

Both stripped and cleaned off as much dirt as they could. During the bathing process, a huge water fight ensued and Joseph found himself on the ground being tickled by a smaller version of himself.

"Stop! Stop! I give! I give!"

Joey stood up and crossed his arms in front of his chest. He wore a smug look as he glared down at his father, and said, "I win."

"Wow. What a powerful son you are. I only hope I grow up to be as strong as you." Joseph sat up suddenly and scooped the boy onto his lap.

"Daaad, quit kidding me." Joey grinned and punched him on the arm.

"If the need arises, do you think you can help protect your little brother or sister with that same kind of strength?"

"Of course, that's my job. I'm the man of the house when you're not here." The expression on his face was priceless. It was so serious.

Joseph smiled. "That you are, my boy. And a fine job you do. Mom says so." He bowed his head. "Thank you."

The words his dad spoke, about how good he was at being the man of the house, made him beam with pride. Joey had always been closer to his father than his mother, even though his dad didn't have much time for him because of caring for the farm.

Father and son had to rinse off again because of the water fight and tickling match. It was worth it though. After putting the same dirty clothes on, they made their way to the house. The smell of food cooking wafted to their noses as they approached the back door. Upon entering, both saw Shyanne by the wood burning stove. The skillet on top was filled with meat and vegetables.

She glanced over her shoulder, and smiled. "Supper will be ready in a few minutes." Frowning at their dirty clothes, she added, "You men go change."

Joseph looked at Joey then back at Shyanne then back at his son. He shrugged his shoulders. They made their way to their bedrooms, found clean clothing, and changed before meeting in the hall.

"Mom came out. Is she gonna to be okay?"

"I guess so. Women are so unpredictable, especially pregnant ones."

Joey smiled. He reached up and grabbed his dad's hand. "It's okay, dad. I still love her."

"Me too."

It was times like this that Joseph had a hard time remembering his son was only five years old. He acted far older. Yet, the recent situation with the mouse and the water fight kept things in perspective.

"Let's get back to the kitchen. We want to make sure she stays happy."

"Race ya!"

Joey took off at a run toward the back of the house. Joseph followed at a slower pace. His body was stiff from the long day of plowing. Even though he was only 29 years old, on days like today, he felt much older. He flexed his arm in a circle to work the shoulder out. He was still flexing it when he walked into the kitchen.

"Sore today?"

Shyanne was putting plates on the table as he walked in. Joey sat in his usual place, bouncing in the chair, a look of anticipation plastered on his face.

"Yes. I must have slept wrong last night or pulled something. Usually the plowing doesn't bother me." He moved across the room, pulled out a chair and sat down.

She walked over and started massaging his shoulders. He stretched his arms across the table and leaned his head forward. A sigh escaped. His wife had the most beautiful hands in the world. They were not soft and dainty like most women. Calluses covered them, making them rough and scratchy. Right now, rough or not, they felt like heaven.

"Oh honey, you are divine..."

The next thing he knew, an arm wrapped around his throat and he was pulled sideways. The chair tipped out from under him and he fell to his knees. His neck felt like it was in a vice grip. Air was becoming harder to take in and the world started to go gray. He tried to force the arm off, but it was strong, muscular, and unyielding. Just as he thought he was done for, knuckles rubbed him hard on the top of his head.

"Noogie! Noogie! Noogie!"

The grip around his throat relaxed and air rushed in. He fell forward onto his hands and knees and gasped deeply several times before attempting to speak. He glanced up at Shyanne, and asked, "What—the hell—did you do—that for?"

Shyanne stood over him with her fists resting on her hips, grinning from ear to ear. There was no humor in the smile. Joey stopped bouncing and stared wide eyes at his mother. The room became as quiet as a tomb until Shyanne broke the silence.

"I wasn't going to let you get away scot-free, mister. I had to get even for earlier." Her smile faded.

"By nearly killing me?"

"But it looked funny, your eyes all bugged out and all."

Both parents glared at each other, Joseph kneeling on the floor and Shyanne standing before him. A smile crept onto Shyanne's face. A chuckle followed. Joseph tried hard to continue the glare, but failed. He broke into a smile and laughed with his wife. Joey jumped out of the chair and joined his parents, hugging both tightly. Joseph stood up. He looked at his wife while hugging her close. He was a foot taller than her short 5' 2" frame.

"Love you, wife."

"Love you, husband."

"Don't forget me!" Joey tugged on his parents clothing to remind them he was there.

"Love you too, son," both parents piped together as they pulled him into the center of their hug.

After the evening meal was finished, the dishes washed and put away, along with Joey tucked into bed for the night, the parents relaxed in their own bed holding one another close. Joseph smiled at his wife. She must have sensed it with that uncanny sixth sense of hers because she glanced at him.

"What?"

"You. The woman who has lived far longer than most human beings, except for one; who has taken on monstrous creatures and lived to tell; who fought mercenaries, and who survived the Boss—afraid of something as small as a mouse."

"Hey." She punched him in the arm, "It could have been riddled with diseases. The baby could have been hurt—or killed." She rolled onto her back and rubbed her swollen abdomen.

"Not with you around, you She-Ra." Joseph rubbed his neck. He could still feel her strong arm around his throat cutting off his airway.

"Seriously, though." Shyanne frowned. "I don't want any of my family to suffer. Not like before."

Joseph felt the change in her mood. He rolled to his side and propped his head up on his hand. "What's bugging you, Shyanne? You've been so touchy lately. Is it the pregnancy?"

"No." She hesitated, then blurted out what was eating at her. "I've been having these weird dreams lately. I keep hearing someone crying and my name shouted over and over. I search everywhere but can't seem to locate where it's coming from. It sounds like Joey, but when I attempt to focus on the voice, it fades."

Joseph watched the woman lying next to him as she spoke. He saw her anguish, her concern. "Don't worry, my love. He's safe here with us. Nothing will happen."

"I know he's safe—but those dreams are so real. And Ruben's still out there."

He put a finger over her lips, "Shyanne—shhh— everything will be fine. I promise you."

Shyanne kissed the finger before moving it out of the way to brush her lips against his. Afterwards, she curled into a fetal position with one arm tucked under the pillow and the other draped across her belly. Joseph lay back. He placed his hand on her swollen belly and felt a kick in his palm.

Must be a girl, I keep getting kicked when I get too close. Joseph smiled at the picture of a smaller Shyanne swinging a leg at him from inside the womb. Still thinking about what Shyanne had said, he drifted off to sleep.

Little did either know how true Shyanne's dreams was about to become.

Two

Drayco entered the small town and headed toward the inn located in its center. Survivors had built a thriving community close to what was left of Wichita. Occasionally, the townspeople ventured into the ruins to retrieve anything usable from the past, but not often. Things of unspeakable horror lived there now. Things created by man over 200 years ago, during the time before the virus.

In the beginning, many men entered the concrete refuge looking for items to make their survival easier. Only a handful returned, rambling about tales of terror and horrible deaths. Drayco had encountered some of the creatures and their mutated strains in his long lifetime. He did not want to do so again any time soon.

He found the inn and dismounted. The establishment had a small stables attached to it in the back. He led Bravaro around the side of the building and handed the reins to the boy who met him at the doorway.

"Take good care of him. Two gold pieces await you if you do a good job."

"Yes sir!" The day had been a complete washout before this moment, and he had almost given up on making any money. "Don't you worry about a thing, sir. I'll make sure he's taken good care of."

Drayco flipped a coin toward the boy. He caught it with one hand. "One for now, another later."

The boy brightened. "Thank you, sir!"

The gold piece disappeared into a tattered pair of pants and his horse was led into a stall where the bridle and saddle were removed. A brush started across the muscular body. He and the horse had been together since the twins killed the burley man who rode him six years ago. He was not about to let the partnership end through carelessness. Satisfied, the dark man went around to the front of the inn and entered.

A man stood behind the counter. Drayco had a momentary flashback, a flashback to a time six years ago when he was a captive of Ruben's. He shook it off immediately. The man behind the counter was not thin or proper looking, like Louis. He was short and stout; a moustache covered his upper lip.

"What can I do ya for, young man?"

"I need a room for the night, and some information if you have it."

"I can supply ya with tha room, but I don't know about tha information."

"I'm looking for a big man, a man with a deep tan, muscular build, and long dark hair. He's a little taller than I am. I heard he might be in this area. His name is Ruben."

The clerk shook his head, "Don't seem to remember seeing a man by tha description around here. Sorry. Now—how about tha room?"

Drayco asked for a room located in the back of the building. The dark man did not want any unexpected guest to drop in. He wanted quiet, not excitement. He'd had enough of that lately.

"If ya're hungry, there's an eatery down the road that serves great food. They might also have an answer to that question of yars," the man said as he handed Drayco the key.

"Thanks, I'll keep that in mind."

Drayco went up the stairs and followed the narrow hall to room 215. He unlocked the door and stepped inside. Dim light shined in through the window. The sun was going behind the building across the way, but its intense rays managed to brighten the room enough for the dark man to light the candle sitting on a table by the entrance. He closed the door and locked it behind him. The room was scarce of furnishings. The only items present were a bed, a table by the door, another by the bed, a chair, and a small wash door, another by the bed, a chair, and a small wash barrel.

"Better than sleeping in a blanket on some god for-saken hard ground out in the cold," Drayco muttered as he put his pack on the floor.

The world was far different than it was 200 years ago. Technology was gone. Genus minds in the government had created a virus, a virus they thought they could control. It proved to be fatal. The population of the planet was nearly obliterated in a matter of weeks. Only people with high im-mune systems survived, people like Drayco and his twin sis-ter, Shyanne.

At first, survivor's eeked out a living in the big cities. But, as time went on and the food supplies became critically low, most left to begin new lives. A good portion of the survi-vors were young. They did not have any technical knowledge or skills yet. Because of this, when the machines quit work-ing, no one knew how to repair them. Out of necessity, fire replaced electricity, the horse for the automobile, and swords replaced bullets. Life became a struggle. Many died during the first couple of years.

Drayco remembered all this because he was there. He was one of the survivors. He had endured the loss of his par-ents and his way of life at the tender age of thirteen. Now all he had was existence, 219 years of it. That was because the virus had altered both him and his twin sister in a way they never imagined.

Of the two, Shyanne had been the lucky one. The vi-rus only slowed her aging process; it did not have a price. Drayco, on the other hand, had to drink the blood of a living being, be it animal or human, to stay alive and young. To not do so caused a painful and agonizing death. He knew this fact all too well. He had almost died on several occasions.

The sun disappeared behind the building, sending out a final glow of reds and pinks before slipping into darkness. Drayco sighed. He stood by the window and watched it as it continued on its journey. A frown crept onto his face. He was tired, tired of his own long journey, tired from lack of sleep. Mostly, he was tired of killing for the sake of living.

Tonight I will have to kill again. Tonight, another per-son will have to die so that I may survive. Drayco bowed his head, his hands clenched into fists. His thoughts continued, *Damn the virus. Damn the people who caused it. Why? Why did this happen to me? All I ever wanted was to settle down and raise a family. But I'm not allowed to do even that.* His shoulders sagged.

He almost had what he wanted 25 years after the virus ended so much. Allison came into his life when some crazies injured him. They fell deeply in love. She found out about his affliction and accepted it without hesitation. She had not looked at him with horror or fear like so many people had since.

Everything was great and he was happy until a man named Sam shattered his world. He killed Allison because of some fanatical religious idea and would have killed Drayco except the dark man got to him first. Since that time, he had not found another woman he wished to share his life with. He was not sure if he wanted to go through having to watch his partner fade with age while he stayed young, like his sister was doing with Joseph.

I guess I'd better get something to eat. Maybe someone there will know about Ruben.

After locking his room, he returned downstairs and went out the front door. Stopping on the porch, he looked toward the direction indicated by the clerk earlier. The road was dark. Only a few shops remained open, their lights glowing faintly. He stepped off the porch and disappeared into the gloom.

The darkness enveloped him as if he was family. His long dark hair, dark tan and dark clothing made him hard to see. The only thing that stood out was the streak of gray hair above his left eye.

He made it to the bar without encountering anyone and went inside. An empty table was in a corner near the back of the room. He went to it and sat down, repositioning his sword so it was within easy reach.

An elderly woman came over, took his order, and left quickly. The air around the dark man felt ominous. She wanted no part of it.

Drayco watched her go. He saw the fear in her eyes and knew why she had hastened away instead of staying to talk. A short time later, she returned with his mug of ale, setting it down near the edge of the table. She left before he could thank her or ask her any questions.

Drayco shrugged his shoulders. He knew it would not

be the last time something like that happened. He picked up the mug and brought it to his lips. After a long pull of the drink, he sighed. It had been a long time since the taste of this fine beverage had hit his tongue. It was exactly as he remembered. He upended the mug and signaled for another round. The elderly woman nodded her head to show she understood. A slender young woman with chestnut hair brought the next drink. The older woman refused to go near the dark man.

"Thank you. You are an oasis to a man lost in the desert."

The woman smiled. She was used to hearing words like that from the men in town. It was nice to have it confirmed by a stranger.

"What's your name?"

"Arbor."

"Arbor, what an unusual name—but a nice one. It suits you."

"The smile broadened. She liked this man, even though there was something about him that unsettled her. The local men were dull and predictable. This man was new and exciting.

"You're not from around here, are you?" She stated the obvious.

"No. I'm passing through."

"Would you like some company?"

"Why not. I haven't spoken with a pretty woman in a while." Which was true in a sense. The last time he had spoken with his sister was over a year ago.

Arbor sat across from Drayco. She rested her chin in her palms, and stared. This man fascinated her. She wanted to know more about him.

"What's your name?"

He lied. "Brenth."

"Well, Brenth, what brings you to this small town?"

I'm trying to find someone."

"A woman?"

Arbor hoped the disappointment she felt inside was not evident in her voice. She wanted the man before her to spend some time with her. That would not happen if he were looking for another woman. It had been a while since she had had any fun in this dreary town and she wanted to have some tonight.

"No. I'm looking for a man. His name is Ruben. Have you heard of him?"

"Oh, what a relief." Arbor's face turned a lovely shade of pink after she realized what she had said. "I mean…I'm sorry but I don't know him." She sat up straight, averting her eyes from his. Her smile faded.

Drayco reached over, covering her hands with his. "It's okay, Arbor, I'd like to spend some time with you too."

She looked up at him, hope shining in her eyes. "Really?"

"Really."

The smile returned.

They talked for hours about anything and everything. When the meal was brought to the table, he shared a portion of it with Arbor. More ale was ordered and drank by both. The elderly woman frowned, but said nothing. The bar was not busy right now and the girl was enjoying herself, which was something that did not happen often. Another hour passed. Laughter echoed periodically from the dark corner.

The elderly woman returned, "It's closing time. I need to clean up."

"Aww Mally, I'm having such a good time."

""I need to be going anyways," Drayco said.

"Awww, do you have to?"

Glancing in Mally's direction, he said, "Yes, I must." Drayco stood and started toward the exit.

Arbor stayed where she was, watching him move across the room. After a moment's hesitation, she stood and followed him. "Would you like some company? I've enjoyed our conversation immensely and want to continue it." She folded her arms around his.

Drayco knew what she really meant. He may be drunk, but he was not dense. What the hell, a little frolic would be nice. "Sure, come on."

Arbor was just as drunk. She was not used to drinking so much ale, even though she worked in a bar. When he indicated for her to lead, she turned around and almost fell over one of the tables. Drayco wrapped an arm around her waist, preventing disaster by steadying her. He guided her arm around his own and together, they staggered out the exit.

Mally watched the couple leave. She shook her head, frowning. She knew she ought to say something about her ill feelings toward the stranger but kept quiet instead. It was a decision she would later remember with regret.

Drayco guided Arbor up the stairs toward the room, shushing her as they walked down the hall. He had a hard time getting his key out of his pocket, but he eventually accomplished it. The door opened with a twist of the wrist and they stumbled into the dark room. He closed it and engaged the lock once the candle was lit.

"Nice room," Arbor said. She immediately spun around and fell into Drayco's arms, pulling his head down so she could plant her lips on his.

She had no intentions of continuing their earlier conversation. She wanted to make love to him...not talk. The ale helped. It lowered her defenses, making it easier for her. She normally tolerated the words of the local men at the bar but never went home with them. This man was different. He was mysterious, dark, and nothing like what her parents would have approve of—if they were alive to say so.

"Brenth—Brenth—Oh Brenth," she said between kisses, her hands exploring his body.

The need in Drayco responded. He had not been with a woman for many years. To have one so inviting and so willing was exciting. He guided Arbor toward the bed. When they were next it, he sat her down. Looking down at her young face, he smiled. She smiled back, then pulled her top over her head. Drayco kneeled in front of her and kissed each breast.

Arbor sighed with pleasure. She leaned back to allow the dark man better access to her chest. He moved from one side to the other, cupping each in a hand, kissing them both. Amber pushed him away as she sat straight. She reached for his sword belt and started undoing the buckle then yelped with pain. She had snagged her finger on a jagged piece of the metal. A small drop of blood appeared.

"Poor baby, let me kiss the pain away."

Without thinking, Drayco put the finger in his mouth. He realized too late that it was a mistake. The taste on his tongue caused his other need to take over, the need to drink blood.

He was no longer in control of himself. Instead, his animal instincts took over. He moved to Arbor's lips. With his lips locked on hers, he forced her back on the bed. His body pinned her underneath him.

Arbor had no idea that the lover to be was no longer in control, she was too drunk to realize the danger she was in. The dark stranger kissed her face in several areas before moving to her neck. She arched her head off to the side, eyes closed, enjoying the feeling of his lips on her skin.

Suddenly, a sharp pain registered in her foggy brain. She opened her eyes wide as she realized the man on top of her was not trying to make love. He was biting her neck, hard. She tried to say something, to get him to stop. Before she could utter a sound, a hand covered her mouth. She started to panic, to fight, but could not. The weight of the mysterious dark man's body prevented it.

She felt her head pulled farther to the side, exposing the neck even more. A whimper escaped as she saw the man known as Brenth shift his position. Blood ran from the corner of his lips. Her blood. He lowered his face. The pain intensified. She felt sick to her stomach when she realized that the wet sucking sound she heard was from the stranger as he drank her lifeblood.

The last thing she remembered thinking about before death took her was that her parents were right. She should have listened to what they had said when they were alive. She should have found a nice local boy to settle down with.

Drayco woke some time during the night. The candle still burned, its length greatly reduced. He could tell from the size, several hours had passed. He had no idea what had transpired during that time. Arbor lay next to him, resting on her side, facing away from him. She was partially nude. He reached over to nudge her awake, the skin under his hand felt cold...too cold. A rush of dread washed over him.

"Arbor? Are you awake?" No reaction. "Arbor?"

Drayco slowly rolled the woman over. The gaping wound on her neck became evident. Her eyes, wide with fear, met his. They were glazed over from death.

A sob escaped from the dark man's throat. He now

knew what had happened during the lost time. He hid his face with his hands and wept. He had taken another life for the sake of his own. When was the torture going to stop? When was he going to have peace?

After he recovered from his initial shock, he placed Arbor on her back, closed her eyes, and pulled the covers up to her chin. She looked so peaceful, like she was sleeping instead of dead.

"I'm so sorry Arbor. I had no idea what I was doing. If I could take it back, I would. I hope you will forgive me."

The words sounded stupid, especially since they were directed at a dead woman. He could not hold them back. He had to say them. He only hoped she heard them in the here-after.

Drayco gathered the few things in the room quickly. With a single glance at the woman lying in the bed, he blew out the candle and left the room. He made his way to the main floor, set his key on the counter, and walked around to the stables.

The lad from earlier was still there. He was sleeping on a cot in a small area located in the stables. The dark man left him alone and went to the stall holding his horse. The bridle and saddle were in place before the boy stirred.

Eyes still heavy with sleep, he said, "What's going on?"

Drayco led Bravaro down the walkway. He tossed a coin in. "Here's the other coin I promised you. Thanks for the fine care you gave my horse."

The boy caught the coin as he had done many times before, with one hand. "Your welcome, mister." A huge yawn escaped.

The dark man smiled as he watched the boy lie back on the cot and pull the blanket up over his head. Guiding Bravaro outside, he got into the saddle. With a final glance at the inn, he rode into the blackness of the night.

Drayco rode steadily east for five days. He had skirted past the town once known as Chanute, avoiding contact with the people and creatures living there. Both were in disarray. Man because of the hardships endured since the virus, creatures because of their genetic makeup.

Scientist from before the virus had attempted to play god. They spliced together several different species' genetic makeup, trying to make new ones. Some, like Drizzle, worked. Others were horrible creations. They stalked and killed anything that moved, including man.

What had been the Missouri borderline was crossed just after sunup. It was close to noon now, and he was drawing near to the town of Sheldon. Even though the people kept the name, it no longer looked like it had.

It was filled with rundown buildings and run down people. Some smiled when he rode down the main street. Most averted their eyes. Post virus people tended to be suspicious of any strangers, even 200 years after the mass mayhem ended.

A bar stood to the right. He guided Bravaro to it, dismounted, and tied the reins to the post near a watering trough. The horse lowered his nose and drank deep. Smiling, Drayco gave the animal a pat on the neck before going inside.

The room was small, like the town, but clean. Several patrons sat small tables located throughout the room. They stopped what they were doing to check out the newcomer when he entered. When nothing exciting happened, they returned to their drinks and conversations.

Drayco moved to the bar located to the left of the entrance. He pulled out a stool and sat down. The barkeep walked over.

"What'll you have?"

"An ale please."

"Coming right up."

He walked a couple of paces away, picked up something, and pulled the handle attached to a barrel located on the back ledge. The glass mug, a rare treat these days, filled quickly. The barkeep returned and motioned for the payment before setting the mug down.

"That's one gold piece."

The dark man pulled his moneybag out from under his shirt. He poured several pieces on to the bar and slid two across the counter toward the waiting man. "One for you and one for payment."

The barkeep hesitated. He was not sure if the dark stranger was joking or not. On previous occasions, others had left money for him, only to yank it back, laughing. When he reached for the payment and nothing happened, he relaxed. The dark man picked the mug up and took a sip.

"That's some good ale." He took another drink, a longer one, savoring the smooth flavor as it washed over his tongue.

"You been traveling long?"

"Longer than you could possibly imagine," Drayco said with a sigh.

"What brings you to theses parts?"

"I want to see family again. I want to go home for a while." He stared at the mug cupped in his hands.

"Well, I wish you a safe journey. Moving on right away?"

"After a couple more of these fine drinks."

Drayco moved two more pieces of gold across the counter. The mug in his hand was almost empty. He wanted another ready and waiting when it was.

The barkeep set another glass mug next to the dark man before he started around the room. He went to each table and took their orders. Due to the size of the establishment, a waitress was not needed. He stopped at the last table and talked to a pair of rough looking men. A couple of times during their conversation, they glanced at Drayco. He was in a world of his own and did not notice. A minute later, the barkeep left to fill the orders given to him.

Drayco was thinking about home. *I wonder how Shyanne is doing. Joseph and little Joey too.* Realizing the mug in his hand was empty, he picked up the full one. *I keep getting these feelings about her. Feelings of her being in trouble or hurting. I hope she is okay.* Taking a drink from the mug, he drained it halfway before setting it down. A smile creased his face. *With Drizzle around, though; I don't think I have to worry about her. If for some reason Ruben were to show up, that cat would show him the errors of his ways.*

The dark man stayed for two more drinks. When he stood, he wobbled a little. That was because he was tired, not because he was drunk. Repositioning the sword on his side, he moved to the door leading outside.

"Come again anytime, mister." The barkeep raised a hand in salute then returned to washing the glasses.

Drayco threw an arm up as he exited. When he was out of sight, the barkeep glanced at the two men still sitting at the table. A slight nod passed between them. The pair got to their feet, slinging packs over shoulders. They gave Drayco enough time to get on his horse before following.

On the landing outside, they watched as the dark man started out of town. As casual as possible, but with a touch of urgency, they hurried to their horses.

"Did you see him? He's drunk. He'll be easy pick'n for sure."

"Just make sure you do it right this time."

"Hey, that last one wasn't my fault."

"Shudup and get on your horse."

Once in the saddle, they raced out of town in another direction, a direction that would intersect the trail Drayco rode.

Drayco kept Bravaro's pace to a steady walk. It was not that difficult because both were tired. Besides, no matter how badly he wanted to get home, the dark man would not do it at the expense of his horse.

He was taking in the beautiful scenery of green grass dotted with yellow and white flowers, intermingled with tall majestic trees, when he heard the sound of horses coming his way. They were coming fast. Looking in all directions, he tried to locate where the sound was coming from. Suddenly, he felt something hit his left shoulder, knocking him off his horse. Pain shot through him as he landed awkward, taking his breath with it.

While trying to recover his breath, he saw an arrow shaft sticking out of the area between his shoulder and neck, near the collarbone. It had equal parts showing from the front and back. He looked up as a pair of horses came into view. Two men jumped off when they reached him.

"Aims off a bit like always, Rayne."

"Hey." The man holding a bow shrugged his shoulders "Practice makes perfect."

One of the men came over and grabbed Drayco by the front of his shirt, half lifting him off the ground. He back-handed him hard across the face, causing blood to well in the corner of his mouth where his teeth had cut the inner lip. The movement caused the arrow to shift. The dark man glared at them, showing no sign of the pain he was experiencing.

"Ohhhh, we have a strong one here," Whit said as he

tossed Drayco back to the ground.

Rayne chuckled. "Finally. A challenge."

Drayco remained silent. He gave no indication of what was running through his head. Because of the arrow sticking out of his flesh, his left arm was useless. But his right arm, well, that was an entirely different matter.

Both advanced on the fallen man. Plans of stomping the hell out of him were written all over their faces. Rayne reached him first.

The thief was caught off guard when Drayco leaped to his feet and pulled his sword out in one fluid motion. Before he could get out of the way, the sword lay buried in his chest. He fell to his knees, a look of surprise locked in place as he died.

Whit gasped and skidded to a stop when he watched Rayne die. He turned and ran toward the horses. The bandit wanted to get away from the man standing there as if the arrow through his shoulder was not bothering him in the least, as if he was not feeling any pain.

Drayco allowed Whit to almost make it to the horses before he reached down and withdrew his boot knife. With a flick of the wrist, the blade flew across the open space and embedded itself in the back of Whit's right thigh. The bandit went down in a tumble of arms and legs, stopping just shy of his horse. He was struggling to get to the animal when the dark man reached his side.

"Where do you think you're going?"

Whit lay on his back, hands held up as if he was giving up. "I wasn't going to do anything. It was all Mac's idea. Honest. I was just along for the ride."

"Sure Whit—Whit isn't it?" Drayco squat down next to the fallen man. "Sure. I believe those words about as far as I can throw my horse."

To Whit's astonishment, the dark man reached up and pulled the arrow out of his shoulder, never flinching once. "Who's Mac?"

"He's the one who gave you your drinks."

"Ahhh, now I remember you. You two were the ones he chatted with last." Drayco understood what was happening now. "What were you after, Whit?" He knew the answer, but wanted to hear it from this scum.

"The gold you carry."

"All this trouble for gold—will people never learn?" Drayco said mostly to himself, shaking his head while he spoke.

Whit watched him, thinking the man insane, and wishing he had never gotten involved with Rayne or Mac. He inhaled sharply when the shirt covering the area where the arrow had been shifted. The wound underneath was almost closed over. The bleeding had stopped.

That arrow was only just removed. Who—or what—is this?

Drayco looked first at the man then where he was staring. He rolled his eyes skyward. "Aww—now you've gone and done it. Now I can't let you go—you know my secret."

Whit focused on the dark eyes looking at him that seemed without end. The blackness he saw inside made him shiver.

"I—I promise. I won't tell anyone what I saw."

"Whit, you know better than that. I bet you've heard those same words a thousand times from other people. You know they won't work." Drayco followed his words with several tisking sounds and a wave of his pointer finger in front of Whit's nose.

"On my honor—I won't say a thing to another living soul." Whit was pleading now.

Drayco leaned over, grabbed his knife and gave it a tug. The blade slid out easily. Whit yelped with pain.

"Shut up, you lousy piece of stinking rizbak. Who gave you permission to make any noise?" The yelp ended abruptly as the dark twin slapped the open mouth.

Whit put a hand over his bleeding lip, palm facing outwards. His eyes widened as he saw the blade come closer. Drayco inched it toward the exposed throat. At the last minute, he wiped it off on the bandit's shirt and put it back in its sheath.

"Bet you thought I was going to kill you with it, didn't you?"

Whit nodded his head.

"No, my friend, I have better plans for you. Even though I recently drank, I can't pass up a gift handed to me."

Whit had no idea what the man meant. What did drinking have to do with killing him? Unfortunately, he would soon find out.

Drayco leaned over and ran his tongue up Whit's chin. Blood coated his mouth when he pulled back. He ran the tongue over his lips, savoring the taste.

"My—what a lovely flavor you have grandma." He answered himself with a smirk. "The better to drink you with my dear."

He grabbed Whit's head, twisted it quickly to the side, and sank his teeth deep into the exposed flesh. The answering blood flowed fast and strong. It tasted so sweet. Drayco savored every ounce.

When I kill like this, for this reason, the feeling is better than anything I experienced before.

The anguish he experienced when he discovered what had happened to Arbor vanished. It was replaced with a stronger, more satisfying emotion, almost as if he was a superhero from the past. One from the comic books he used to read. He had defeated the villains and reaped the benefits. Once the blood flow ceased, Drayco leaned back and roared. The sound was filled with undeniable pleasure.

He sat there relishing the feeling of energy flowing through his veins. When it diminished from a level of intense pleasure to a more manageable level, he dropped the body and stood. He flexed the healed shoulder as he walked over to his horse. A smile creased his lips as he got into the saddle and indicated for Bravaro to move toward home, toward his sister, to Shyanne.

Several hours later, a traveler stumbled upon the bodies lying near the trail. He had not stayed long. The looks of surprise and terror locked on their faces told him enough. If whatever had left the gapping hole in one man's neck was still around, he had not wanted to be there when it made another appearance.

He stopped at the nearest bar, thinking the alcohol would calm his jittery nerves. The traveler's hands shook too much when he attempted to drink from the mug in his grasp. Part of the ale splashed onto the bar. When the barkeep came over, scolding him for making a mess, the traveler told him of the horrible sight he witnessed.

Mac listened. He remained silent, rubbing at the hairs rising on the back of his neck. He had a feeling he knew who the men were. Rayne and Whit had not returned yet. They would have by now. He also had a feeling he knew who the killer was.

After the story was completed, he thanked his lucky stars that the dark stranger had not come back to finish the job. He poured himself a drink to steady his own nerves, praying that his luck would continue.

Three

Joey ran around Drizzle's sleeping form, laughing and giggling. Occasionally, he would reach out and tap on the cat as he ran past.

"Tag! You're it," echoed across the open field.

Drizzle ignored the bothersome child for a few more passes until he could not take any more. "Will you stop? I'm trying to sleep."

This only enticed the child more. He ran past several additional times, smacking the humecat on the ears, nose and rump with each pass.

As Joey made another swipe at his body, the cat reached out and snagged the youngster's pants with a claw, causing him to fall. Joey landed with a huff, the smile wiped off his face in an instant.

"I told you to stop."

Joey's hazel eyes filled with tears. He yelled, "I only wanted to play! I don't have any friends to play with, you big meanie!"

Drizzle looked at the pint size version of Joseph. The boy glared at the cat with open defiance, the same as his mother used to do as a child. Both held their stares. Finally, a chuckle escaped from the cat.

"You know, you may look like your father but you're a carbon copy of your mother when it comes to attitude—won't back down from anything."

A growl emitted from deep in the cat's throat. It was

neither threatening nor serious. The tail started swishing back and forth in a rapid fashion. Suddenly, Drizzle pounced on the boy. He play wrestled with him, pretending to bite him but never doing so. This was the part Joey loved best. He never fully understood what the cat meant by the other stuff, but he always loved the playing that followed each time they argued.

Shyanne watched from the window in the kitchen as Joey and Drizzle played this game out like so many times before. A smile crept onto her face when the pair ran off toward the woods. This part of the game was over. Now, the hide and seek part began. She returned her attention to the task at hand.

Material lay spread out on the table. Several pieces sat off to the side already cut out, waiting for her to sew them together. She picked up the scissors once more. Holding them up, she stared at them, remembering the time when she and Joseph had found them in some rubble. The metal was protected from the elements by a carrying pouch and it was shear blind luck that they were found at all. Shyanne had tripped over a chunk of stone and nearly smashed her knee on them. Since then, they have been a useful addition to her life.

A low humming sound emitted from her as she eyed which way to cut next. It was a pleasant song from long ago, though she could never remember the words.

First, I'll go this way, then that. And in no time, I'll have another outfit ready for the baby.

Some clothes were available from when Joey was little. However, if this one was a girl—what then? To make sure she was ready, either way, she embroidered several touches to the jumpers. A flower here, a hummingbird there. Joseph simply shook his head whenever he saw her embroidering. He knew better than to tell his wife not to do it.

The soft material cut easily with the sharp scissors. An hour later, she straightened up. With a groan, she arched her back as far as her swollen belly would let her. Her pregnancy was going along without any difficulty, just like the first one. She was happy that she had not experienced the nausea and swelling most women experienced, or any other problems for that matter. Now, it was almost over. The only thing that bothered her was an ever-present tiredness. A nap usually resolved that.

The chair scraped across the wooden floor as she slid it back. Going to the window, she looked for her son and Drizzle. They were nowhere in sight.

Drizzle was a godsend. With his ability to think and speak like a human, hence the designation humecat, he kept Joey well occupied. The cat was created by her father's workplace before the virus, a virus that escaped its creators and wiped out a major percentage of the humans on the planet.

Must be off on another adventure. Those two are hopeless together. Shyanne stretched again. An eye-scrunching yawn accompanied the stretch. *I'm going to take a short nap. Drizzle will keep Joey safe.* As she moved down the hall, she thought, *I hope Joseph gets home soon; I sure could use a back massage.*

The bed looked so inviting when she entered the bedroom. Pulling back the covers, she crawled under them and turned onto her side. She snuggled her head deeper into the feather pillow and drifted into what she hoped would be a restful nap.

Joey ran into the woods to hide from the cat chasing him. They played this game of hide and seek a lot. It usually ended with him hiding somewhere in the house and the cat finding him. The boy remembered the times he had hid in great places, only to be sniffed out by Drizzle's highly sensitive nose. He found better places now, places the cat could not sniff.

Once he had rubbed onions all over his body to mask his scent. When he presented himself to his parents later that evening, they held their noses and tried to wash the smell off. Nothing worked. His skin was raw after so much scrubbing and he stunk for about a week before the scent finally dissipated.

This time he wanted to try something new. He watched as Drizzle ducked into the trees then ran with all the speed his little legs could muster back to the house. He made it without being spotted. With a snicker, he darted inside, ran quietly to his room and crawled out his window. He crept around the house to the cellar doors. Reaching out, he touched them then backtracked to his window.

Furball will think I'm hiding in the cellar. Ha! Let him, he thought as he crawled inside.

Joey ran back to the woods, sprinkling some of the precious spices he took from the kitchen to cover his tracks. His parents may be overprotective and, in his opinion, too busy to play with him, but they had at least taken the time to teach him how to cover his tracks if he was hunted. And they had taught him how to survive if he got lost in the woods. At the young age of five, he knew more about how to stay alive in the wilderness than most grown men did.

Let old furball try and find me now. He'll sneeze and sneeze and sneeze. Maybe I'll hide so I can see it. I bet it'll look real funny. Joey hid a giggle behind a small hand.

He entered the dense undergrowth and began looking for a good place to hide so he could watch the fun. He did not see the tall man with dark hair watching him until he almost bumped into him. With boyhood innocence, and a little bit of suspicion, he stared up at the stranger.

"Be careful there, young man, you don't want to hurt yourself."

"Who are you?"

"I'm an old friend of the family."

"Yea?"

"Yea." The big man squat low, resting one knee on the ground so he could be at eye level with the boy. "Who are you?"

"Joey."

The youngster gawked at the man. He had never seen anybody like him. Most people he saw were like his parents. This man was huge, his body all bumpy with muscles, and the sword on his back—wow.

"Joey, huh. Well Joey, how's your mom?"

"She okay."

"Her name's Shyanne, right?"

"How'd you know?" The boy's eyes widened.

"Remember—I'm an old friend of the family."

"Oh yea. You want to come to the house? Mom's inside, probably napping."

"Is your dad home?"

"Naw. He's gone right now. He had to go get some things from town. What's your name?"

"Ruben."

The big man extended a hand to shake Joeys. He made no attempt to come closer. Joey looked at it. He hesitated, not sure if he should shake it or run away. He remembered the few times his parents had had friends over and the way they had scolded him for not being polite, so he moved forward. He grasped the huge hand with his tiny one and pumped his arm up and down as he had seen his dad do when greeting other men.

Ruben could not believe his luck. He had been watching the house for some time, taking great steps to avoid the blasted cats ranging area, wondering how he was going to get the boy away from everyone long enough to grab him. Now, he was before him, alone, so innocent and trusting.

"Come say hi to mom. She'll be happy to see you." The boy gripped the big hand and tugged.

"Joey, I can't stay. I've got to go to town myself." Ruben let go of the hand and started to walk away. He turned back toward the youngster after a couple of steps, "Say, did you want to come with me? We can meet up with your dad."

The boy's big hazel eyes lit up. The thought of going to town was wonderful. He had been there only a few times and remembered all the exciting things he had seen. Upset when his father had not taken him, he was going to get the chance to see them after all.

"Really? I can go with you?"

"Only if you think your mom won't mind."

"She won't care. I'll be with a friend, and they always said it was okay to stay with their friends."

"Well then, let's go." Ruben smiled as he reached out and took the boys hand in his.

They walked to another clearing a short distance from the house where a black horse with a white blaze on its forehead grazed on the grass.

"Is that your horse?" Joey was awestruck by the size of the creature. It was huge, like the man standing next to him.

"His name is Wind Racer."

"We're going to ride on him?"

"Are you afraid?"

Joey stammered, "N–n–n—no."

"It's okay, Joey." Ruben leaned over closer to the boy. "To tell you the truth, I was a little afraid when I rode him the first time."

Joey glanced sideways at the big man. "You're teasing me—aren't you?"

"No way, I would never do that to you." Ruben held up both hands.

The youngster smiled. "Does he go fast?"

"As fast as the wind. That's why I called him Wind Racer."

The horse must have heard Ruben's voice because he looked up at the two standing near the edge of the woods. With a nicker and a toss of his head, he trotted over to them, his mane flowing like silk, the tail held high. Joey hid behind the big man. He had never been this close to something so massive before. It was scary, but at the same time, thrilling. Ruben reached up and gave the animal a firm pat on the neck.

"Joey, let me introduce you to my horse. Wind Racer, this is the young man who is going to accompany us on our journey."

The horse looked at Joey and seemed to bob his head in understanding, or at least that was what it looked like to an excited five year old.

"You ready to go?"

When he bobbed his own head yes, Ruben picked him up and placed him in the saddle. Joey watched as the big man, who said he was a friend of his parents, got up behind him. He grabbed the saddle horn when the horse shifted his weight from one foot to the other. The ground seemed so far down.

"Don't worry, Joey, I won't let you fall."

The youngster gave the big man a sheepish look before he peered at the horse again. "I'm not afraid. I think he's wonderful."

"He's my best friend," Ruben replied. "He'll take good care of us."

Ruben gripped the reins with one hand, hugged the child close to his body, and tapped Wind Racer in the sides. The horse responded immediately. They flew across the clearing, and in a short amount of time, they were on a dirt road heading east. Joey was having so much fun he failed to notice that they were heading in the opposite direction, away from the town where his father was located.

The dreams haunted Shyanne during her nap, making the rest she sought impossible. The crying was so faint she felt herself straining to hear it. Tossing back and forth, she finally decided to get out of bed. Judging by the angle of the light shining in the room, she must have slept a little before the nightmares started. The baby kicked when she sat on the edge of the bed.

I think Joseph's right. This must be a girl. Joey was never like this. She rubbed her swollen belly. The active child inside calmed.

After struggling to get up off the bed, she moved down the hall to the kitchen. The tired feeling was still there, but it was not as strong. Upon entering the room, she noticed the back door stood open. She walked over and stepped outside. Her cat companion was sprawled on the porch. Joey was not in sight.

"Worn out already? Where's Joey?"

"I don't know. Hiding somewhere I guess," grumbled the cat.

"What do you mean you don't know?"

Drizzle knew he would get no more rest today. He rolled onto his belly and looked up at Shyanne. "The last time I saw him; we were playing our usual game of hide and seek. This time he was sneaky, he used pepper to cover his trail. I sneezed like crazy when I ran across it."

"But WHEN was the last time you saw him?" The silence was starting to bother Shyanne. It was quiet, too quiet for an active five year old.

"Maybe an hour ago. Or two. I'm not sure."

"WHAT! You mean to tell me you have not seen him for that long and haven't gone looking for him? Drizzle!"

Shyanne stormed back into the house. "Joey? JOEY! Young man! Where are you?"

She hurriedly searched each room but found no trace of her son. Drizzle remained on the porch. When she returned, she was madder than a disturbed hornet's nest.

"Where was his scent last?" She demanded.

Drizzle saw the frantic look in her eyes. "The cellar, I

lost it from there."

Mom and cat raced around the building to the cellar doors. Throwing them open, Shyanne ran down the stone steps. Drizzle could hear her calling out for her son, but no reply answered her.

Returning outside, she turned on the cat, "Dammit Drizzle, you were supposed to keep an eye on him!" She stomped the ground with her foot while she spoke, her arms stiff at her sides, the hands clenched into tight fists.

It had been a long time since the cat had seen Shyanne this angry. It had also been a long time since she was this scared. He remained silent, enduring her harsh words better than any human would have.

Tears welled in the corners of her eyes. "Please, Drizzle—please—find my little boy." Her body held the stiff position, but her eyes filled him with sorrow, wrenching the heart inside his chest. "Find little Joey and bring him home."

Their eyes locked. With a nod of his head, he turned toward the woods. He knew where he had to go. He had to follow the trail of pepper. Where it went, so did Joey. He glanced back at Shyanne before entering the woods. The woman stood with her face buried in her hands, her shoulders shaking. She was crying.

"Because of my laziness, a little boy is lost. Don't worry, Shyanne, I'll find him and bring him back to you." He whispered more to himself than to anyone in particular.

Drizzle sniffed at the ground. Almost immediately, he found Joey's scent and began to follow it.

Drizzle had gone only a short distance before he knew what had happened to Joey. He sniffed at the ground to confirm what his nose told him.

The cat followed the trail to a clearing next to the one by the house. He noticed horse droppings in the field. The smells of Ruben, the horse the big man rode—and Joey—were strongest here. Sniffing around, he discovered the scent went to the east.

"Damn!"

Drizzle ran back to Shyanne. She was no longer in the yard but inside sitting at the table. She looked up expectantly when she heard him enter. The look fell when she saw him alone.

"Did you find him?"

"I found his scent and followed it. The trail led to the east."

Shyanne could see he had more to say. "What else?"

"He wasn't alone."

Shyanne felt the bottom of her stomach fall out. The feeling of dread she recently experienced when discovering Joey was gone, returned to her full force. "Who was with him?"

The cat turned his head and spat out one word with such hatred, it made Shyanne flinch. That word was, "Ruben."

The very name caused Shyanne to freeze. Every nerve ending in her body was going wild, though. She wanted to scream, to cry, to thrash out irrationally, or any combination of the three. What she did was remain calm.

"Can you tell how long ago?" The words came out barely above a whisper.

Drizzle bowed his head. "Somewhere between one to two hours ago."

The silence that ensued was worse than any ranting could ever be. The ranting he could handle. This—this was more than he could bear.

"Shyanne, I'm sorry. I…."

A hand shot up, silencing the cat before another word was spoken.

"Drizzle," she hesitated, "I shouldn't have put so much responsibility upon you."

Drizzle started to say something else, but the hand moved again, emphasizing silence.

"But I am going to put a lot on you now." She watched the cat walk over and sit next to her before looking down at her hands. "I'm asking you to find Joseph and tell him what happened. I need you to bring him home. I need you to do that as quickly as possible. That ass already has a good head start on us—we don't need to let it widen." Shyanne met the cat's eyes. They were as calm and determined as her soft voice.

Without hesitation, he said, "Consider it done."

Drizzle left without allowing Shyanne to remind him again of the importance of time. He had already done enough to shatter her trust in him. At least by doing this, he could try to rebuild.

He ran across the field and onto the road. It was the same road taken by Ruben a short time ago.

Stopping to look east, he snarled, "I will make sure you pay for this Ruben." Drizzle paused a moment longer before he ran to the west, toward the town of Fount.

The town was several hours away by horse back. That was if you were walking the horse or if it was pulling a wagon. The cat was running full out, thus reducing the distance at a steady ground-eating pace.

The sturdy bridge build by Joseph when they first settled here allowed Drizzle to continue without having to swim the stream flowing under it. The rough road was wearing down the pads on his hands and hind paws, so he moved to the side where the grass grew in patches. Several time he winched with pain as a sharp stone cut into him. He disregarded it. It was the price he deserved for letting Ruben get his hands on Joey.

Fount came into sight in just over an hour. The cat was panting hard as he made his way toward the shopping area. He paused for a moment to catch his breath then went to look for Joseph. Drizzle knew better than to look for him in the many stores. Instead, he looked for the horse Joseph rode to town.

Jack stood in front of the nonperishable goods shop. He whinnied and touched noses with the big cat once he was close enough. Drizzle looked at the building. He knew he was not supposed to go inside, but this was a special case. He had to if he was to alert Joseph.

Twisting the doorknob with his stubby hands, he shouldered the door open and slinked inside. A brass bell tinkled above, alerting the shop owner of a customer entering his establishment.

The owner looked toward the door. When he did not see anyone standing there, he returned his attention to the pile of things on his counter. Joseph stood across from him, making sure his calculations and the owners matched.

After he finished, the owner said, "If I calculated right—the total is 50 gold pieces."

"I only counted for a total of 48 gold pieces."

The owner glanced at the pile again. "These things

here and the ones out back are a total of 50 pieces. I know my prices, Joseph."

"Gif, I know them too. This is four pieces, this is...." Suddenly, he felt something tug on the back of his pants. "What tha..."

He glanced over his shoulder. Drizzle stood there, his hand gripping his pant leg. "Drizzle—you know you can't come in here."

The cat looked at both men before he focused his attention on Joseph. "I have to speak with you."

"Drizzle, I'm busy now."

The owner leaned over the counter. "Drizzle, you know you're not supposed to be in here."

The cat ignored the owner. "I have to speak to you—now."

"I'll be through in a minute. We'll talk then." Joseph turned his attention back to Gif. A sudden shooting pain from his calf area reminded him of who was behind him.

Joseph had to hop on one leg as he was pulled toward the exit. He dare not yank his leg away because of the claw buried in his calf.

"Ow—oww—owww! Drizzle! What are you doing?"

"I said now."

Joseph found himself outside before the claw was removed. As he knelt down to inspect his torn pant and bleeding leg, Drizzle sat back on his haunches.

"What is so important that you had to do this?" Joseph was not happy and his tone indicated it.

"I screwed up. Because of it, you need to go home—now. Shyanne needs you."

The mention of his wife's name caused him to look up sharply. "What happened? Is it the baby?"

Drizzle paused. He dreaded this moment, but knew he had to tell of his failure to protect Joey. "No." He took a deep breath then continued. "Joey was taken."

"What did you just say?"

"Joey's been taken. You need to go home so we can go after him."

Joseph started toward his horse. "Why didn't you say so instead of clawing me?"

"You wouldn't listen."

"I am now. Do you know who did it?" He could not

imagine who would want his son.

He untied the reins and was beside Jack reaching for the saddle horn when he realized Drizzle had not answered. He glanced back to see the cat still sitting where he was, silent, avoiding eye contact.

"Drizzle?"

Joseph could tell by the cat actions, the news was bad, very bad. He could feel the pit of his stomach start to sink. With the next words, it fell like a lead weight.

"Ruben took him."

"Ruben."

Joseph was stunned, unable to believe what he had just heard. Ruben—the man who had made their lives a living hell; the man who had almost killed Shyanne and her brother six years ago; the man who had worked for the Boss—was back. Now this same man had his son.

"I'm sorry, Joseph. I failed to keep him safe."

Joseph recovered from his initial shock. As he gripped the reins and got into the saddle, his face looked like it was made of granite. A jerk of the reins brought the horse sideways.

"Let's go."

He kicked Jack in his ribs harder than he should have, but, right now, he was not concerned about that. All he could think about was getting to Shyanne and finding his son. The horse responded by leaping forward. Joseph had a firm grasp on both the reins and mane, preventing him from being unseated by the animal's power and speed. In seconds, man and horse were racing out of town.

Drizzle remained where he was for only a second before getting up to follow. Joseph had showed remarkable refrain. Instead of yelling at him, he simply left. Drizzle would have felt better if the man had yelled. He ran from Fount with a heavy heart, hoping the two people he loved most would one day be able to forgive him.

Froth was coming out from under the saddle and Jack's sides were heaving from the race to get home by the time Joseph rode up to the house an hour later. He ran inside to locate Shyanne. She was sitting in Joey's room holding his pillow close. Her eyes were red and bleary. The moment she saw him, she jumped to her feet and ran into his arms.

"Oh Joseph—it was Ruben—he took Joey." She started to sob.

"Shhh, I know, Drizzle told me." He guided the distraught woman to the bed and sat down with her.

Shyanne buried her face into his chest. Her shoulders shook as she released all her pent up anguish. Joseph held her close, whispering meaningless words of comfort as she cried. When she was able to bring herself under control, she looked up at him. The fear and hopelessness he saw before was replaced with determination.

"Joseph, we have to go after him. We have to go before they get too far ahead."

"Do we know where to go?"

"Drizzle was able to track them to the road behind us, the one that goes east."

"Shyanne, do you think it's wise for you to travel with your pregnancy so far advanced?" He knew what her answer would be. Under the circumstances, it was necessary to remind her.

She looked at him, her eyes hard. She stood. "I can't believe you just asked that." She stormed out of the room and went toward the kitchen.

With a sigh, Joseph rose and followed her.

"The only reason I asked is because I don't want to see either of you get hurt in any way."

I'm not going to be left behind like some poor little house woman, unable to manage just because she's pregnant!"

"Shyanne, please, the journey may be long and hard, think about it."

"I have." She crossed her arms in front of her and glared at her husband.

Frustrated, he sighed, "All right then. Have it your way."

Shyanne's posture relaxed a little. "Really? You're not going to try and stop me?"

"I know better than to argue with you, woman. You'll make my life a living hell."

Shyanne smiled. She came to him, allowing herself to be enveloped in his outstretched arms. As she looked up into his serious eyes, she had only a moment to realize he was up to something before a fist slammed across her jaw. She slumped over in his arms, unconscious.

"I'm sorry, Shyanne, but I can't allow you to risk both yourself and the baby. I hope you'll understand when you wake up."

After making sure she was not seriously injured, he picked up Shyanne and carried her to their bedroom. He placed her on the bed and pulled the cover over her. Drizzle sat in the doorway when he turned around. The cat watched his movements intently.

"What do you intend to do now?"

"I plan on finding my son."

"I'll help."

"I was hoping you'd say that."

Joseph went outside and led Jack into the stable where he removed the saddle and bridle. The thought of not using the horse ate at him, but after the long hard ride, he knew better. He saddled Cloud instead and led him to the back porch. After securing the reins to the railing, he disappeared inside to get the necessary supplies for the journey. He was not sure how long it would take to find his son, so he prepared as if he was not coming home for a while.

In less than ten minutes, Joseph was riding after Drizzle, toward the east, to find the much-hated man named Ruben who had taken his son.

Four

Ruben rode for the better part of the day before he pulled Wind Racer to a stop. The boy had fallen asleep during the ride. He stirred awake when the continual motion of the horse ceased.

"Have we gotten there yet?" Joey asked as he rubbed his sleepy eyes.

"Not yet. I have something better to show you first."

Ruben slid off the horse and made his way to a clump of bushes. He smiled before grabbing a section and pulling them off the thing they covered. A frown appeared on the young face as he looked at the contraption sitting before him.

"What is it?"

"This is something wonderful, Joey." The big man walked over and helped the boy off the horse. He grabbed his small hand and led him toward a battered metal object. "I found it during my travels. Want to see what it does?"

At first, Joey was afraid. He had never seen anything like it before. The excitement on the big man's face was the only thing that made him reconsider running away. If this man who was bigger than anybody he knew was not afraid, then he should not be either. He looked up at Ruben and inched closer to the metal object.

Both stepped onto a flat rubbery surface secured on top of the metal at the same time. In pre-virus time, the contraption would have looked like an oversized treadmill.

Ruben let go of Joey's hand and grasped his shoulders, steering the boy ahead of him. When they stood in front of a console covered with weird knobs and buttons they stopped.

"This is something I think you'll really like." Ruben lowered himself to eye level with Joey. "See these buttons...push this one."

Joey looked at the button then back at the big man. The grin on his face was infectious. The boy smiled. A small hand slowly reached up until a couple of fingers rested on the circular button. With a slight push, the button disappeared into the console.

The platform under their feet started to vibrate. Joey's eyes jerked open wide with fear and he would have panicked had Ruben not grabbed him and hugged him against his body. When nothing attacked, when nothing leaped out to tear him apart, the boy relaxed.

A soft hum accompanied the vibrations. Joey looked down. The platform had not changed one iota. The smile returned when he looked up at the man next to him.

"What is it?"

"It's a flying machine."

Joey gave Ruben a cockeyed look. "You're trying to fool me, aren't you?"

"Like I said before, little man, I wouldn't do that to you. We're friends. Friends don't do things like that to friends."

Joey liked being called little man. It made him feel older, like he was finally being recognized as the lad he thought he was. His father never called him that. He always treated him like a little boy.

"No, friends aren't supposed to do that."

Ruben smiled. Over the years, the mercenary had manipulated all kinds of people and he was quite successful at it. He knew how to work the boy so that he wanted to do whatever was asked.

Everything was going along as planned. In minutes, he would be flying off toward his hideout, and no one, not even that damned cat, could track him then. He would have the ultimate revenge: the taking of that blasted woman's son.

The console lit up when the power button disappeared. Green, blue and yellow lights glowed brightly. Joey watched them with childlike fascination. Electricity had ended over 200 years ago. All these wonderful colors were a new and amazing sight.

"How does it work?" Joey bent over to look under the console. The only thing there was the support pedestal.

"It's powered by these panels. See?" Ruben pointed to a set of dark rectangle shaped objects running along both sides of the machine. Arm rails prevented the occupants from stepping on them and breaking them. "I learned about these things from a friend of mine."

"Wow! This is so great!" Joey kneeled down to take a closer look. He jumped to his feet, excited. "What else does it do?"

"Hang on tight and I'll show you."

Ruben wrapped his hand around a stick poking out from the center of the console and pushed it forward, causing the vibration to increase in intensity. Joey grabbed the console and a side rail next to him quickly. His fear returned full force as the metal platform began to lift off the ground. He kept it hidden from the big man next to him, though. He was a little man, after all, and needed to show that instead of quivering like a little girl.

Swallowing his fear, the boy watched in awe as the ground receded. Fascination took over after they hovered a minute or two.

This is way better than riding that dumb ole horse back home, he thought.

Ruben guided the machine around the area where Wind Racer grazed. The horse never flinched when the pair flew inches above him. He was used to it. Joey giggled with sheer delight as they dipped and climbed, twisted and turned, before they settled with a soft thud onto the ground. No towns or cities were close so the antics of the flying machine went unobserved.

"That was tons of fun. Can we do it again?"

"Now?"

"Yea!"

"Aren't you getting hungry? I am."

"Well..."

Joey was having so much fun that he hadn't realized how much time had passed since he last ate. He was hungry.

The thought of food caused his stomach to remind him of its existence.

"We can fly to my camp and get something to eat there. What do you think?"

Joey was thrilled. He had never been asked for his opinion on anything before, only told what to do. "Well, okay, we can do that."

"I just have to start Wind Racer on his way home." Ruben stepped off the platform and walked toward the horse.

"Can't he ride on this?" Joey pointed at the flying platform.

"He's too heavy, little man."

"But, won't he get lost?"

"Not this horse. He's a smart one. He can find home from anywhere. He might even beat us there."

"He is fast." Joey remembered the ride from earlier. That was when he remembered his mother. "What about mom? Shouldn't we let her know where we'll be?"

"I'll send her a message after we get there. Don't worry, I won't let her fret too long." The big man gave the boy standing next to the railing a comforting smile.

"Okay. I guess that will be okay."

Ruben turned his back toward the boy. A grin flashed across his face as he thought, *How easy it is.*

After removing some jerky from the saddlebag, he told the horse to go home and gave it a swat on the rump. Wind Racer took off at a slow easy trot in a southeasterly direction. The pair had performed this particular feat many times until the horse had gotten it right. The big man knew without a doubt that they would meet again at the camp. He returned to the flying machine and handed a slab of dried meat to the boy.

"This will hold us until we get to the camp."

With a gentle touch of the stick, the flying machine lifted off the ground. Both man and boy started in the general direction taken by the horse, each enjoying the meat and the flight with the same enthusiasm.

*   *   *

The cat was several horse lengths in front of Joseph with its nose close to the ground, sniffing at it like a bloodhound. The picture would have been funny if it was not for the gravity of the situation. Darkness would soon be showing its head and the fair-haired man knew they had to find shelter before then.

They had been riding for just over four hours and Joseph was sore. He was used to riding Jack. The recent hard ride from town forced him to use Cloud instead. He was finally getting used to the animals awkward stride when Drizzle caused him to pull the horse up sharply.

"What? Is it Joey? Are they ahead of us?" he whispered.

The cat held up a digit, indicating the need for silence. Joseph could not see what lay ahead. Whatever it was, it sure had the cat's attention. As he watched, Drizzle flattened himself close to the ground and laid his ears back. A silent snarl appeared.

Joseph wondered what could cause the humecat to react like this. *Surely, it can't be Ruben. If not him, then who—or what?* As if to answer his questions, a creature stepped onto the road ahead.

"Oh man," Joseph gasped. "And I thought the rizbaks were ugly."

The thing before them was a cross between a rizbak and a shar-pei. It was called a grosbark, an offshoot from the mating of a rizbak, a genetically altered creature from a lizard and a wolf created before the virus, with wild dogs. The results were pretty gross, hence the name.

It was hairless and covered with wrinkles. Two tails extended from the body. The lower jaw was wider and a bit longer than the upper jaw. Long fangs pointed skyward near the end and smaller sharp teeth filled in the rest of the mouth. Most of the body resembled a dog except for the eyes. They were above and below the jaw line. Four eyes regarded the man, horse, and cat.

"Drizzle, can we get past it?"

"No. As you can see, it effectively blocks the path ahead."

"You know what I mean."

"This beast is extremely cunning. If we are to get past it, we have to do so very quickly, before others join it."

Before either could move, noises came from several areas at once. More grosbarks appeared to the right, left, and from behind. Ribs showed on all the animals. The new arrivals were part Shepard, part retriever, and others were part collie. The combinations, along with the rizbak green lizard scales, gave Joseph the willies. The travelers were surrounded. He knew they were in big trouble.

I should have known the others were already here; they always run in packs. The one in front must have been a distraction so the rest could get into position, the cat thought.

"What do we do now?"

"We fight!" The humecat jumped up and ran toward the one in front. "Go after the one ahead of us. It's the leader!"

Joseph kicked Cloud in his sides. The tired horse started forward, but immediately shied to the right when one of the grosbarks leaped at it. He was almost tossed from the saddle by the unexpected maneuver. A frantic grab of the saddle horn with both hands prevented him from falling. Fortunately, he retained possession of the reins. Once Cloud straightened his stride, Joseph was able to pull his sword free of its sheath.

He sliced at the closest grosbark. The collie-mix ducked away before he could hit it. A Shepard-mix grosbark slipped in under the swinging blade and bit the left hamstring, making the horse scream with pain. Cloud kicked and bucked at the creature biting him.

This time, Joseph was not able to remain in the saddle. The frightened horse threw him over its head, causing him to land on his back. His breath whooshed out with the sudden landing. As he lay on the ground, gasping, a group of eight grosbarks ran around the bucking animal. One broke away from the pack and came at the downed man.

In true fighter fashion, Joseph managed to keep ahold of his sword. He brought it upward just as the grosbark leaped. The blade buried deep into the animal's side, killing it instantly. As it flew past, the forward momentum wrenched the weapon out of his hand. He was still trying to catch his breath when another grosbark broke away and came toward him.

His sword was just beyond his reach, stuck in the body of the dead animal. Joseph rolled over and began crawling toward it. Before he reached it, a heavy weight landed on his back, shoving him down on the ground again. A deep growling filled his ears and hot breath blew on his neck.

Joseph covered his neck with his hands, hoping to prevent his throat from being ripped apart while he came up with a way to get the nightmare off. Just as he was building for a battle, the weight flew off him.

Drizzle stood between it and the man lying on the ground, snarling at the dog-thing as it rose to its feet and shook itself. Both animals faced one another: one a successful creature created by scientists a long time ago, the other a nightmare creature inadvertently created by those same men.

The humecat had long bleeding marks down several parts of his body. None looked life threatening. Joseph glanced back where he saw the pack leader last. Its torn dead body lay in the grass. He returned his attention to the creatures facing each other just as the grosbark decided the cat was too strong an adversary. It ran over to help the other dog-things bring down the horse. At least the horse was easy prey, unlike the big cat.

Joseph watched as Cloud was finally brought down by the sheer weight of the animals on him. The shrill screams from the terror-filled horse filled his every fiber. The sound was cut off abruptly when a gurgling sound replaced it. He rose to his feet and pulled his sword from the dead grosbark then ran away from the grisly scene as fast as he could. He had no desire to stick around to see what happened next.

Drizzle joined him as he ran down the road in the easterly direction taken by Ruben. They both slowed when the sounds of growling and barking were no longer evident.

"That didn't turn out so well." Drizzle stopped and sat down to lick at the wounds caused by the fight.

"It shouldn't have ended like that at all." Joseph was mad at the loss of the gray. He flopped down beside the cat. "How come you didn't know they were there?"

"They were very clever. They stayed where I couldn't smell them and they hid the sound of their approach by causing us to focus on the leader." Smugly, he said, "Now they need a new leader."

"And I need a new horse." Joseph's face was grim. "Without Cloud, Ruben will get farther ahead, to the point that we'll never catch up to him. We'll never find Joey if that happens."

"We won't as long as you sit there pouting about a lost horse." The cat rose and started east. He glanced over his shoulder. "You can sit there and wallow in self-pity if you want. I'm going on."

Joseph got up and ran after the cat. "At least I was able to salvage the gold for the house." He patted the breast of his shirt. A clinking sound followed.

"Then you'll be able to get a new horse, now won't you."

"Drizzle, horses, especially good ones, aren't cheap. I wanted to save some of the gold for the house. Besides, Cloud was a good horse. He didn't deserve to die like that."

The cat stopped. He faced the man following him. "Are you forgetting something? Huh? Are you?" He was tired of hearing about how he had supposedly failed again. "Which is more important to you—the house, that horse—or your son. You tell me." While he glared at Joseph, lightning bolts filled with anger seeming to shoot from his eyes.

Joseph's mouth fell open. He could not believe what he just heard. "Has anyone ever told you you're a sarcastic son of a bitch?"

"Shyanne tells me all the time." The cat relaxed. His angry words changed to ones full of amusement. "I do think you'll be getting a sample of hers when she sees you again. Especially after what you did to her."

Joseph winced. He knew he was going to be wiped all over the face of the planet when he returned to his wife. He hoped dearly his son would be with him by then to soften the blow.

"Let's get moving. Hopefully the next town we run into will have a horse I can buy."

The cat sniffed at the ground to make sure they were still heading in the right direction then started walking again.

After a few steps, Joseph said, "Drizzle?"

"What is it this time?"

"I want to thank you for saving my life."

"If you had died, I would never hear the end of it from Shyanne." He glanced back. "And I don't know about you, but I don't like it when she rants on and on and on."

Joseph did understand. "Anyway—thanks. I owe you

one."

Drizzle hesitated. He watched the man for a few seconds without comment before continuing eastward, muttering to himself as he went. "At least I'm good for something."

With the carnage left far behind, they moved down the road, each hoping to find their stolen family member before Ruben hurt the lad. Or worse.

It was slow going for the man left on foot. His food and supplies were gone. They disappeared with his horse, Cloud. He had had no time to get them off before the grosbarks killed it. Fortunately, fresh water was easy to find. Food, on the other hand, was another matter. Drizzle went looking for game, only to return a short time later with nothing but a squirrel. It was scrawny, but it was better than nothing. The problem for Joseph was his fire-starting things had also been in his pack. If he wanted to eat, he had to eat the meal raw.

"The area seems hunted out," Drizzle said while they rested. "I think those stinking dog things must have killed anything they could find, whether they were hungry or not." The cat sat on his haunches, glancing sideways at the man sitting on the rock nearby. "You know, if you weren't so picky, you'd have something in your stomach by now."

"True. But unlike another member of the family, I don't have a particular fondness for the taste of blood." Joseph paused to let his words sink in before he snickered.

"The cat looked at him. "Did you just say what I thought you said?"

Joseph shook his head yes, grinning.

The cat rolled his eyes skyward. "Over a thousand comedians inhabited this planet once upon a time and I have to be trapped with a wannabe."

A thoughtful frown replaced the grin on Joseph's face. "What's a comedian?"

"A person who thinks he's funny."

The words rolled out with such sarcasm that Joseph had to wonder whether the cat was joking or not. He never moved. He never blinked.

Finally, Joseph sighed. "I had to do something to relieve the tension. Everything has gone wrong to this point. I feel so absolutely frustrated." Joseph stood and started to pace back and forth, his hands clenched into fists. "First Joey was taken, then, for the first time since we met, I had to hit my wife—and now—Cloud was killed by a pack of mangy, flea bitten, man-made creatures from hell! What am I supposed to do—break down and rant?" His face was beet red by the time he stopped and glared at Drizzle.

A smile, or the closest thing the cat could do for a smile, crept onto his face. "You know, you're absolutely adorable when you're mad."

That broke Joseph's concentration. Shocked, he realized what he was doing and started to laugh so hard he fell to the ground holding his gut. Once he recovered, he raised his head, resting it on an upraised arm, "Like I said before, that sarcasm of yours is amazing."

"I do my best."

Joseph rose to his feet. "I guess we'd better get going. Too much time has already been lost." Dusting off his clothes, he moved again toward the east. "Do you know how much farther to the next town?"

"No. I've ranged all over, but not so far in this direction."

"Just keep us going in the same direction as the ones we seek. I want to see the look on that sorry louses face when we catch him—before I kill him."

Drizzle remained silent. He understood what Joseph was going through. He had experienced it once before when the big man had taken Shyanne six years ago. This time, he was going to make sure Ruben did not get another shot at any of his family again.

If Joseph doesn't kill him, I will.

Drizzle and Joseph walked on through the day without encountering another human being. Birds flew overhead, though none came close enough. Without a means of bringing them down, the winged tormenters mocked the hungry pair.

Several times, they heard rustling in the trees, which caused both man and cat to glance around. Nothing was visible except an occasional bird. Even squirrels were missing. As they continued to walk eastward, they had the feeling they were being watched. The uncomfortable feeling followed them while dusk started to cover everything with its grayness.

A break in the thick growth ahead showed a vast open field. Joseph increased his pace and was about to leave the cover of the trees when the rustling sound suddenly increased in intensity. The hackles on Drizzle's back rose and his upper lip curled into a snarl. Joseph stopped and glanced toward where the cat stared.

Red eyes appeared in the growing darkness. It looked as if thousands of them were watching them.

"What are they?" Joseph whispered.

Instead of answering, Drizzle crouched down and an angry rumble emitted from his throat. He but did not stay there long.

Leaping to his feet, he yelled, "RUN!"

Joseph watched as the leaves shook and little shapes dropped from the trees so fast he was not able to see what kind of creature they were. He did not have to though; Drizzles response was enough for him. He turned and ran as fast as he could, trying to stay ahead of what ever followed them.

Drizzle looked over his shoulder to make sure Joseph followed. He was, but the movement in the grass behind him was catching up fast. Too fast. He knew the man was not going to make it unless he helped. The cat spun around and started back.

As he passed the fleeing man, he yelled, "Keep going, I heard the sound of running water ahead. It will slow these creatures down long enough for you to get away."

Joseph hesitated. He was not going to leave the cat alone. His stride became shorter and he would have stopped. A yell from Drizzle made him speed up again.

"You stupid fool! Do you want to see your son again? Get moving—NOW!"

Joseph increased his stride to a full out run. The fear in Drizzles voice told him that whatever was behind them scared even something as strong as the cat.

The silence of the creatures was unnerving. Of all the animals he encountered in his travels since the death of his town and his mother, none was like this. All had made some kind of noise to drive paralyzing fear into their prey. He hoped Drizzle knew what he was doing.

A high-pitched squeal sounded, causing the hairs on the back of his neck to rise. It was followed by a high-pitched yowl from Drizzle. The sounds continued back and forth until a sudden fury of noise arose. Joseph pulled up sharply, turning around to see what was happening. He could not see a thing; it was too dark. The sounds stopped abruptly. Several pairs of red eyes appeared in the distance. The fear caused by those eyes returned full force. He started running again.

The stream, or what appeared instead to be a river, came into view. It was wide and he could not see the other side. Joseph hoped it was not too deep or strong because he was exhausted after his sprint across the field. He knew he would have a hard time with the current if it were.

Joseph stopped at the bank to recover some of his wind and faced inland to look for Drizzle. The cat was nowhere in sight. The red eyes of the mysterious creatures were closing the gap between him quickly. He was turning around to jump into the river when a solid object hit him square in the chest, knocking him backwards into the water.

Claws sank into his shirt, dragging him under. He fought to get free from whatever clung to him. Water ran into his nose. He started to panic. He needed air. What little air he was able to take in before going under was all but used up with his struggles.

The weight on his chest kept the much needed air out of reach. The weight of the sword on his back did not help matters either.

The river's undercurrent grabbed him, taking him further offshore into deeper waters. His feet were no longer able to touch the bottom. All sense of reason disappeared. He tried to knock loose whatever had ahold of him so he could surface before the enveloping blackness swallowed him completely.

In what felt like hours but was only a couple of minutes, Joseph felt a tugging on the front of his shirt. His face broke the surface and the wonderful stuff his lungs screamed for was there.

Air—beautiful air.

Joseph breathed the sweet fresh air in deep and started coughing. The water that had run into his nose was now exiting, abruptly. He felt something move next to him and clung to it like a life raft while he vomited.

"I told you to run, not stop and gawk."

The voice was the best thing Joseph had heard all night. When he was able to speak, he croaked, "Drizzle, you are amazing."

The fair-haired man was not able to continue. His breathing was still too short from being under water for so long, and more coughing and retching followed until he thought his insides were going to be floating beside him soon.

"I don't know how you survived this long. Can't seem to take you anywhere without you getting into trouble," Drizzle said.

Joseph smirked. He would have laughed if there were enough strength to do so. It was taking every ounce he had left just to hang on to the cat's powerful body.

Drizzle started paddling downstream, angling toward where land was located, he hoped. The current was strong, but manageable. No moon glowed to help light the way. It made it that much more difficult to tell where the water ended and the shore began.

Joseph passed out sometime during the journey. Because of the awkward way he held the cat's body, Drizzle was having a hard time keeping him from going under or drifting away.

The strain of hauling Joseph and continually having to fight the current was starting to take its effect on the cat. After a dozen weary strokes, Drizzle noticed the twinkling of lights to the left.

Finally. This big galoot is becoming almost too much to handle, he thought. *Damn gold and sword. Without them, you wouldn't be so stinking heavy.*

When he drew nearer, he saw the lights were flickering candles covered with circular glass globes. Their brightness made it easier to see the shoreline. A single two-story building stood in the distance. He angled away, not wanting to be noticed until he knew whether they were friend or foe. With Joseph out, and him exhausted from the effort of swimming, unfriendly types would easily overpower them.

Drizzle dragged the unconscious man toward the shore. He wanted to sigh with relief when his paws hit solid ground, but couldn't, not until they were safely on dry land.

Keeping a grip on the shirt, the cat crawled out of the

water and pulled Joseph on to the firm surface. He looked around and saw a path near their location. If anyone walked past, the tall grass covering the shores edge and the darkness of the night would hide them.

A noise sounded close to him.

The cat spun around with his lip curled into a snarl and his teeth bared. His eyes nearly bugged out of their sockets and his mouth fell open in shock when he saw what created the noise.

It can't be.

What stood before him was something he never thought he'd see in his lifetime. He sat on his haunches and looked into the golden eyes staring at his. Amazement was written all over his features.

Five

Two weeks of steady riding had brought Drayco closer to Shyanne's home than he had been in a while. The town of Fount was long gone, passed more then half an hour ago. He was tired. His horse was tired. Both their heads hung low. Blood from a recent kill flowed through his veins so he knew this tired was an honest one.

During his journey, he kept having the feeling that something was wrong with his sister. The feeling was an ever-present prickling, like thousands of ants crawling all over his skin. As he drew closer to her home, it grew in intensity.

Their bond was a strong one. It was the bond of twins. It kept him moving eastward, only resting when the horse would have dropped without it.

In his exhausted state, Drayco began to second-guess himself. *Maybe I'm imagining things. Maybe everything is okay and I'm just sick of this never-ending hunt for Ruben.* Drayco frowned as his thoughts roamed to the big man. *Since the night he got away, I have not been able to stop. I have to make sure my sister and her family stay safe.*

Bravaro walked across the bridge built by Joseph just before midday. The sound of his hooves hitting the wood brought a smile to the dark man's face, forcing him out of the reverie he had slipped into during the long ride.

He was close now.

The horse felt the change in its rider and picked up

speed. A walk became a canter, a canter to a trot, and a trot to a gallop. By the time they skid to a stop in front of the house, both man and animal were covered with sweat.

Drayco jumped off and ran up the step to the front porch. He was exhilarated from the fast ride and the thought of seeing his sister again. A grin covered his face, something that did not happen often nowadays. He paused. The grin disappeared. The house was too quiet. Something was wrong.

He pulled his sword out of its sheath and entered.

Light shined in the windows, making it easy to see that nothing moved in the front room. With his back against the wall, he moved down the hall toward the rear of the house. Each open doorway he passed showed an empty room beyond. Nothing looked out of place. The kitchen was another matter. Someone was there.

"Shyanne?"

His sister sat at the table with her hands clasped together. Her eyes stared at nothing and her hair was unkempt, her clothing rumpled. It looked like she had not moved in days. Drayco rushed to her side.

"Shyanne? Are you okay?"

Words barely above a whisper came from the woman at the table. "Their gone. They're all gone. I've lost them all."

Drayco strained to hear her words. "Shyanne? Who's gone?" He lifted her chin, forcing her to look at him. A bruise with yellow edges appeared on her lower jaw line. "Shyanne—what happened? Who did this to you?"

The eyes stared, no recognition, no conscious thought, nothing. He edged closer and wrapped his arms around her. Her swollen abdomen became apparent. It had been hidden from view by the table.

She's pregnant. No wonder she's acting so strange. With Joey, she was an absolute terror. But this, this is so not like her at all. She's a fighter through and through. I wonder what could have happened to make her like this."

"Shyanne, can you hear me? What happened?"

He kept talking in a soothing tone, trying to get through whatever wall she was hiding behind. He wanted to investigate the rest of the property, but did not want to leave his sister's side. Where could Joseph be? Joey too. The house was too quiet.

A shuddering brought his attention back to Shyanne. Her body was shaking in his arms, her eyes closed, her cheeks wet with tears. Joseph knew the soothing words were finally getting through.

"Shyanne? Shyanne—what happened?"

D–D—Drayco? Is it really you? Am I dreaming? Are you really here?"

"I'm here, little sis. I'm really here."

"I haven't lost everything then. He didn't take everything from me." She fell into his arms, sobbing. "You really are here. I'm not alone anymore."

"Shyanne—who—who are you talking about?"

She continued to sob uncontrollably. Drayco knew he was not going to get anything more from her right at present. She was in shock. Holding her close, he rocked her back and forth until the sobs lessened and she relaxed. Looking down, he saw she had fallen asleep.

Drayco rose to his feet gently so as not to wake his sister. He carried her to the bedroom where the blankets lay crumpled, as if someone had gotten up in a hurry. He put her down and watched Shyanne curl over onto her side. Grabbing the covers, he pulled them over her sleeping form then returned to the doorway.

Looking back at Shyanne, he pondered, *What the hell happened here? Where are Joseph and Joey? Where is Drizzle? And who is this person she spoke of?*

He left the room and retraced his steps to the kitchen. Standing with his hands on his hips, he looked around. Dishes were piled in the sink. The stench of rotten food filled the air. The place was a mess. Something had tossed his sister for a loop. She was usually meticulous about her cleanliness.

Drayco went out the back door and covered the distance to the stables in seconds with his long strides. The only horse he saw after opening the door was Jack. He reached over the stall's railing and nickered when the dark man entered. Drayco walked up to the horse and slapped the broad neck. That was when he saw the deplorable condition of the stall.

He opened the outer gate and released the horse into the field beyond. Jack ducked his head and ran the entire length of the field as fast as he could before stopping, his head held high, nostrils flared to smell the clean fresh air.

"Now I know something bad happened here. Shyanne loves that horse almost as much as her family."

Drayco watched Jack bend his head down and begin to graze before he returned to the stall. Shaking his head back and forth, he grabbed a wooden shovel and cleaned out the many layers of muck. He used a wooden wheelbarrow to cart it to the edge of the tree line.

Clean straw covered the floor and the food and water buckets were filled before he returned outside once more. A large barrel with a battered cup swinging from it stood near a drain. He took advantage of the cool water and cleaned the grim of the road and stall off.

With a start, he remembered the horse left in the front of the house. He brought Bravaro around to the stable and removed the saddle and bridle before releasing him into the field with Jack. The horses nosed one another in recognition once they met. Drayco smiled when they began running across the open space side-by-side, play biting at each other.

He made his way back to the kitchen. With a sigh, he picked up a rag and began to clean. In short order, the place was neat and tidy. His stomach made funny noises, reminding him of the absence of food after so much work. Rummaging around the cabinets, he found enough foodstuff to make what he considered to be a decent meal.

One more thing to be thankful for—the ability to cook and clean. Mother would have been proud. A faint smile creased his face with that thought.

The smell of food and the sound of activity filled the small area quickly, making it feel more like a home instead of the tomb he encountered when he first arrived.

Shyanne opened her eyes, turned over in the bed, and looked around. She was in her room with no recollection of how she had gotten here. The last thing she remembered was taking the saddle off Jack and putting him away in his stall before returning to the kitchen. Everything from then on was a blur.

The sun shined bright in her eyes, causing her to squint. It brought back memories, memories of the time when she stayed at an inn with a rearing stallion painted on its sign. It also reminded her of how she had been hunting endlessly for Drayco—only to find him at last.

A noise in the back of the house caught her attention. Shyanne sat up abruptly, causing the room to swim. She closed her eyes with the hopes of getting the world to become stable once more. She assumed the lightheadedness was from the lack of food and drink and not from the pregnancy. When she opened them, Drayco stood in the doorway with a tray of food in his hands.

"Nice to see you again, sleepyhead."

"Drayco!"

Tossing the covers back, Shyanne scrambled out of bed and ran up to him. He barely got the tray up out of the way before she wrapped her arms around him, hugging him as tight as she could due to her swollen belly.

"Drayco! I've missed you so much." She started to cry. "I thought you were just a dream—but you really are here. You really are…." Sobs wracked her body, cutting off her words.

"All this for me? My, my, little sis, what a slushy you've become."

Drayco propped his chin on his sister's head. The tray was held in one hand while the other smoothed her hair. Words of encouragement echoed across the room as he tried to calm her. When the sobs lessened, he maneuvered her back to the bed. The tray was placed on the bedside table before he sat down beside her.

Shyanne, what's going on here?"

She kept her head lowered, refusing to look him in the eyes.

"Shyanne?"

"We became complacent. We let our guard down."

"Who—you and Joseph?"

"Because we were soft, we made it easy for him."

"Little sis, what happened?" The anguish in her eyes when she finally looked at him made his heart wrench. "Shyanne—what happened?"

"He's gone, Drayco, and I don't know if we'll find him before its too late."

The frustration Drayco felt due to her lack of making sense flared. "Goddammit, woman, what happened!"

The angry tone in his voice caused Shyanne to rouse

from her stupor. Her expression remained one of anguish, but hatred edged into her eyes.

"Ruben was here."

Those three words hit Drayco like a fist in his gut. He felt his breath vanish. It rushed back in after what seemed like an eternity.

"When?"

"I'm not sure. Joey and Drizzle were playing when I decided to take a nap. He was gone when I awoke. Drizzle found Ruben's scent in the same area he found little Joeys. That's how we knew he had my son. After Drizzle brought Joseph home, I wanted to go with him to find Joey. He hit me, knocked me out, and left. After I realized what he had done, I sank into a depression." She bowed her head. "I don't know if he left yesterday or three days ago. I just don't know."

"Jack is still here."

"He went after Ruben on the dapple gray—him and Drizzle."

"Shyanne, I need you to tell me everything."

Shyanne looked up at her brother. His already dark appearance seemed to have a new level of darkness to it. If she had not known him like she did, she would have been very afraid.

She told him everything, everything from before the kidnapping to when she phased out in despair. Drayco remained silent until she finished.

"What are you thinking," she asked softly.

"About how much I hate that man. For the last six years, I've searched all over this god forsaken land for him. This land filled with unspeakable horrors and hardships, only to have him show up here. I should have known he wouldn't have given up so easily." Drayco shook his head with disgust. "I should have stayed close, anticipated this. Now your son is paying the price of my stupidity."

It was Shyanne's turn to comfort her brother. She covered his clenched hands with hers. "Drayco, we should have been on better guard. Time made us forget. Time made us complacent. Time was all he had."

Shrugging her hands off, Drayco stood. "I'm going after them."

"I'm going with you." Shyanne rose to her feet.

"Do you think that wise with your advanced pregnancy?"

"Brother, if you try and stop me, like Joseph did, I'll kill you sure as you're standing there."

He had no doubts in what she said. Her body language emphasized that she meant every word. The dazed look that covered her face when he first found her was gone. One of angry determination replaced it.

"If you slow me down, I'll leave your ass behind."

"Like that will ever happen."

They glared at one another, each trying to intimidate the other into buckling to his or her will. Suddenly, a fist shot out and hit the dark man on his upper arm, almost knocking him off balance.

"Oww, what was that for?" Drayco shouted as he rubbed his arm.

"To let you know I mean business." The glare softened with a slight smile. "And to let you know I can still handle myself, even though I'm fat as an ox."

"Well...can you handle this?" He leaped at Shyanne and started tickling her. He did not let up until tears of laughter and the threat of wetting her pants was screamed at him.

Panting from the exertion, Shyanne reached up and stroked the streak of gray hair over Drayco's left eye. "Brother. Thank you."

"For what?"

"For being you. And for bringing me back."

"That's what I'm here for—to annoy the heck out of you. It's what brothers do best."

Shyanne moved toward the door. "We better get moving."

"Eat first. I've been here since yesterday and you've slept the entire time. You need food"

"But Drayco..."

"Shyanne—another hour or two won't make a bit of difference. If I know Joseph, he and that cat will have found Ruben long before we reach them."

Her shoulders sagged. She knew he was right. She had to eat. If not for herself, then for the baby inside. She sat on the bed, pulled her legs up, and crossed them in front of her. Drayco picked the tray up and placed it on her lap.

"Everything is probably cold by now."

"That's okay. I'm so hungry, it won't matter." Grabbing the fork, she stabbed a large clump of scrambled eggs and shoved it into her mouth.

"I'm going to get the horses ready. When you're done eating...and I do mean after you're done," he wagged a finger at her, "get some things together. We may be gone for a while so pack accordingly."

She saluted him with her fork. After she swallowed the bite, she said, "You know—you sounded a lot like dad that last night—remember?" As if chasing away the horrible memories of his death, she crammed another large chunk of egg into her mouth. Her cheeks bulged out like a chipmunks when she smiled at him.

He shook his head. "You're hopeless. You know that?"

Drayco turned and walked down the hall, through the kitchen, and out the back door to the stables. Two horses reached over their gates toward him. The dark man had returned them to the clean stalls to feed them some grain prior to coming inside.

"Feel better boys?"

By way of greeting, the dark horse with a white speckled backside shoved Drayco in the chest, almost knocking him off his feet.

"I guess that means yes."

Drayco remembered the time when Jack would not let a man near him. Shyanne's loving care, plus the close association with Joseph, had calmed the animal down greatly. He gave him a pat on the neck. Bravaro stretched his neck as far as he could, but was not able to reach Drayco. To show he was not happy with his rider showing so much attention to another horse, he let out with a high-pitched whinny. The sound echoed in the small area, causing the man to wince.

"Jealous are we?" He moved across to Bravaro. "You know I love you, you silly beast." Drayco hugged the outstretched neck.

His horse was the only thing he truly felt close to. His sister was important to him, but she was human and could turn away at any time. She almost had shortly after they reunited. Only one other time had he allowed himself to get close to someone. It had cost him dearly.

Allison, a survivor of the virus that killed so many, had helped Drayco recover from a vicious attack. During his convalescence, they fell in love. He was happy for the first time since the loss of his family, since the mutation that made his life a living nightmare drove him away. The happiness had not lasted, though. A maniac killed her just as they discover she was pregnant with their first child. Since then, he had not felt that kind of trust or love.

With a heavy sigh, he whispered, "We'll be going soon."

He grabbed Bravaro's halter and led him out into the breezeway. Securing him, Drayco readied the horse to ride. He did the same for Jack once he finished. In just under fifteen minutes, he led both horses to the back porch and tied their reins to the banister. Each one received another pat on the neck before he stepped up onto the porch and entered the kitchen, intent on urging his sister to hurry up. She was a girl, after all, and he remembered how long it took her to get ready for anything, especially when it involved leaving the house.

Shyanne stood by the sink. She was washing the dishes and placing them in the drainer next to the sink. Packs sat on the table and her sword was leaning against a chair.

"Now that's the Shyanne I know."

"What's that supposed to mean?"

"We're about to go hunting for a madman who took you son and your doing the dishes." He leaned against the wall, arms crossed in front of his chest as he watched her continue.

"We may be gone for a long time." She glanced over her shoulder. "I don't know about you, but I'm not coming home after a long journey only to have to clean up some smelly mold-covered dishes." She grabbed a small towel and dried her hands. "Besides, I'm finished."

Drayco walked to the table and grabbed one of the packs. Shyanne came over to his side. She was wearing a long pullover shirt, which covered her expansive belly, and soft leather breeches. In one smooth motion, the pack and her sword were off the table and their straps flung over a shoulder. She started toward the door. When she reached it, she turned around. She had not heard him following.

"Well, brother—are you coming or not."

"Shyanne—you are truly hopeless—but I love you

anyways."

Several strides from his long legs brought him to her side. Together they left the house. Shyanne stopped and pulled the door shut. With a heavy sigh, she glanced at Drayco, smiled, and strode over the Jack. She secured her pack before getting into the saddle. It took a little effort, but she made it up on her own.

"This should be interesting." She shifted her hips to a more comfortable position. "I haven't ridden in a while.

Drayco stood beside Bravaro securing his own pack. He stopped while Shyanne was getting up on Jack, just in case he needed to help her. Once she was settled, he got on his own horse.

"Like I said, little sis, if you slow me down, I'll leave you ass."

"And I say again—like that will ever happen. I said this would be interesting—not impossible."

"Then lead on McDuff. You know which way they went."

Drayco tugged Bravaro around to face away from the house. Shyanne guided Jack toward the field beyond, toward the east. With a gentle kick, the pair moved to catch up with Joseph or Ruben, whomever they met first. Drayco hoped it would be Ruben.

*   *   *

Joseph lay still, his eyes closed, listening. He had no idea where he was. The last thing he remembered was the horrible experience of not having enough air in his lungs. He heard the sound of movement coming from somewhere to his left. Suddenly, he remembered the river and almost drowning and Drizzle helping him.

A wet tongue licked the side of his face. He jerked his head to the side and reached up to wipe his cheek. Opening his eyes, he saw a cat standing next to him.

"Drizzle, what do you think you're doing? Are you trying to drown me again?"

No answer.

"Drizzle?"

Joseph took a better look at the cat next to him. It was a humecat, all right, but smaller. His jaw fell and his eyes opened wide as he stared in shock. The cat sat down on its haunches and locked eyes with him. The staring contest ended when it raised a paw-like hand and the tongue that had drenched him a second ago, now bathed the upraised arm instead.

The fair-haired man sat up abruptly, intent on finding out where he was. The sudden motion caused the room he lay in to spin and a coughing fit to start. He leaned over the edge of the cot when the force behind the coughs made him throw up. The only thing that came out was liquid, nothing solid. It burnt the back of his throat like a hot iron. When nothing more came up, dry heaves followed, wracking his body further. He lay back after his body calmed down, gasping for a breath, his eyes closed, tears running down his cheeks. The rough tongue returned to his face. This time he did not object. It felt cool against his hot skin. He tried to relax as best he could.

I must have a fever. It would make sense since I hot as an oven and feel like total crap.

He heard the sound of someone entering the room, but was too tired to look. The tongue left his skin.

"Chikara, that's enough cleaning for the time being."

The voice was soft. Joseph did not recognize it. He opened his eyes and turned his head slowly toward the sound, curious. A young woman stood next to him with towels in her hands. She had long black hair and some oriental features to her face. She looked to be in her mid-twenties.

"I heard you throwing up and thought you'd need these when you were finished." She placed one of the damp cloths on his forehead.

A sigh of relief escaped from his lips. He ached everywhere. Suddenly his body was shaking uncontrollably. His teeth started chattering and goose bumps broke out.

The woman tossed some dry towels onto the mess next to the cot to soak it up. She reached over and pulled the blanket up under his chin, covering his body. It had fallen down around his waist when he had sat up. It was thin, but helped reduce the chills, though not fully. He wished he had more. His teeth continued to chatter and his body shake. Joseph felt the material on his bare skin. It felt like thousands of tiny pins. That was when he realized he was naked. He should have been embarrassed, but did not care, not with the way he felt at the moment.

"You have a fever, as you have probably already deduced. The river is filled with nasty things not meant for breathing. Some of it got into your lungs when you tried to do so."

Bending down, she wiped up the mess. "I'll be right back." She picked up the towels and walked from the room, only to return a few minutes later with a cup of something in her hand. Steam wisped from it. Grabbing a three-legged stool, she carried it over to the cot and carefully sat down.

"What is that?" he asked.

"An herbal tea. It will help with the fever."

She guided the cup to his lips. He struggled to help her hold it, but his hands shook too much. Some of the warm fluid spilled over the edge. Instead, he lay back and let her support his head. He sipped at the contents, barely taking any in.

"It's kind of bitter. What is it?"

"Hyssop."

"Hys-what?"

"Hyssop. It will help with the fever and any congestion you might have. I have a feeling you have developed pneumonia, or are trying to."

"That would explain why I feel so lousy."

"Sit up and drink the rest. You will sweat, but that is expected. I will try to keep you dry."

With her help, Joseph rose slowly to a sitting position. After finishing the tea, he said, "I don't know your name?"

"Hana."

"Hana, that's a beautiful name. Does it mean anything?"

"It means flower."

"I'm Joseph." He pointed across the room. "Does your cat speak?"

"Is she supposed to?"

Joseph stopped. Did he truly hear what he thought he did? He stared at the cat bathing itself. *A female humecat. I didn't know one existed. Boy will Shyanne be surprised. Drizzle too.*

To Hana, he said, "My wife has a cat just like her, only he's a he." The statement sounded stupid, but he could not help himself.

Hana did not appear to be surprised by his words. Her face remained calm as she said, "You mean Drizzle?"

"Yea, that's him. Where is he?" Joseph tried to reposition himself higher on the cot but another coughing fit took over.

Hana rest a hand on his shoulder as he leaned over the edge, his face red from the effort. This time he kept the liquid down. When the coughing fit subsided, he flopped back, panting for a breath.

"Drizzle is enjoying the warmth of the sun outside."

Joseph was thankful for her calmness, her gentle touch, and her soft voice. Sweat broke out on his forehead, probably from the medicine and the illness. Hana replaced the damp cloth that had fallen off with a new one.

"How is it you know so much about how to help me?" he asked when he was able to speak.

"My grandfather was a healer. He taught me a lot about herbs and their medicinal uses."

"Thank you grandfather," Joseph muttered. His eyes were getting heavy, but he forced them to stay open.

"Don't fight the sleep. Your body is telling you it needs rest."

"But I have so many questions." His eyes closed. He jerked them open.

"There will be plenty of time when you wake. Right now...sleep."

She reached up and closed his eyes with her fingers. This time they stayed shut. A soft snoring followed shortly afterward. Glancing at the cat, she said, "Chikara let me know when he gets too wet." Chikara looked at the woman and dipped her head in understanding. She returned to her bathing. Hana rose once she was sure her movement would not disturb the sleeping man. A large humecat met her in the room beyond.

"Will he live?" Drizzle asked.

"He will."

"Good. He has a mission to complete."

"He may be down for a while," Hana said. "I added passionflower to the tea to calm him and help with his pain."

"If I know Joseph, he won't stay down long. He's trying to find his son."

"He strikes me as a man full of nintai: perseverance."

"Lady, you have no idea." Sarcasm was thick in his tone.

Hana smiled. A noise behind her drew her attention away from the cat. Chikara was in the doorway. A nod, almost too slight to perceive, occurred.

"I have to go. Chikara tells me Joseph is wet."

Drizzle remained quiet. He understood the bond between humecats and their human companion.

Hana grabbed some extra cloths and bed linens before returning to Joseph. Drizzle watched the small woman. Her movement was fluid, calm and precise. Even thought she was a smidge shorter than Shyanne, the cat was sure she could handle herself if the need arose. With that assurance, he settled down next to Joseph's room to wait.

Six

The twins rode through what was once the state of Kentucky. The land was still beautiful. The grass a lush shade of green. The sky a pale blue with wisps of white blended in. Shyanne looked up and watched as a bird soared on the air currents high above. A kick in her belly returned her attention below.

"You're an active one, aren't you? I think you'll be a hard one to keep up with whenever you get out into the world." She smiled as she rubbed her swollen abdomen, calming the active child inside.

"What do you think it is?" Drayco asked.

"I think it's a girl. This pregnancy is totally different from the last."

"What will you call her if it's a girl?"

"I like Molly. It's such a pretty name."

"Molly—that fits. What if it's a boy?"

"Raymond—for dad."

The mention of his name brought back all the memories of their camping trips, the family outings, and those special times when just the two of them went for a walk. The loss still gripped Drayco's heart whenever he saw a father and son together.

"I miss him. Mom too."

"Me too, little sis."

"Why did this virus thing have to happen? It messed up everything." Shyanne's smile faded.

"A bunch of power hungry idiots in the government decided to play god," he answered, scorn making his words harsh.

"So because of them, we have to suffer. Just like the government, always thinking of ways to mess stuff up, even though they think they're helping."

"At least they died early so they couldn't mess up what's going on now." Drayco was glad for the change in subject. He preferred to talk about anything other than the loss of his father.

"Yea. Saved us a lot of hassles. We don't have to listen to them bicker about everything."

"Like a bunch of cackling old hens." Drayco added.

Shyanne folded her arms, placing her hands in her armpits, and flapped them like wings, "bawk—bawk—bbaaawwwkk!"

"God, what I would give for a bucket of hot wings right now." Drayco's tone was so pitiful. He made his lower lip quiver as if he was about to cry.

Shyanne giggled like a little school girl, hiding her mouth behind her hand. "You nut-ball!"

"What! It's been a long time since I had any. Don't tell me you don't miss them too. I remember how many you ate in one sitting."

"No. What I miss more is the convenience of fast food. A burger from McDonalds or a frosty from Wendy's...that would be wonderful. You have no idea what a pain in the backside it is to cook in a wood-burning stove." Shyanne rolled her eyes. "And to have indoor plumbing—that would be a real treat."

Drayco chuckled. "Yea, those outhouses do get to you on a hot summer day." He crinkled his nose as if he smelled what he was describing.

"Little Joey always hated having to go after his dad. Joseph would leave some whopper smelly ones that took hours for the odor to go away."

At the mention of her family, Shyanne fell silent. Drayco looked at her. A tear formed in the corner of her eye. It ran down her cheek. The happy face of reminiscing was gone. One of sadness took its place.

His heart wrenched in his chest. "We'll find them, Shyanne, alive and well. You'll see. We'll find them."

They rode for several more hours, keeping the pace slow and steady due to Shyanne's advanced state of pregnancy. By the time they stopped, Shyanne's back was killing her. Reaching her arms up, she arched backward then forward to stretch out the tired muscles. It had been a while since she had ridden for this long a period. A sigh of relief escaped when she dismounted.

"Wow, am I sore."

Drayco dismounted and let Bravaro's reins drop. The horse moved into the open area to graze. Jack followed. The dark twin watched to make sure they would not wander off too far before moving to the shady area under a tree. He flopped down on the grass, almost as exhausted as Shyanne. He had had little rest before arriving at her house, and none since. A light breeze blew from the west, bringing with it the scent of flowers.

Shyanne eased herself down next to her brother. She inhaled and exhaled deeply a few times, stretched out her legs and leaned back against the trunk with her eyes closed.

"This is one of those times I don't miss technology. All these wonderful smells would have been overpowered by the smog and pollution."

Drayco breathed deep. He smelled the flowers, but something else as well, something that perked his interest. He sat up and looked around. The wind had shifted; it was now coming from the east.

Shyanne was still leaning back with her eyes closed. She opened them when she heard Drayco get to his feet. "Everything okay?"

"I smell something. I'm not sure what it is." He gazed toward the east, following the road as far as he was able to before it disappeared. He saw nothing out of the ordinary.

Shyanne remained where she was. She was interested, but too tired to follow.

"I'm going to check it out."

"I'll wait for you here."

Drayco walked a short distance away from the tree. When he still didn't see anything, he decided to get Bravaro. Walking to his horse, he told Shyanne, "I'll be right back. I want to locate where that smell is coming from."

"Okay," she murmured sleepily. Shyanne had lain down, resting on her side, her arm under her head like a pillow.

The dark man had a feeling he knew what caused the smell. He wanted to make sure before he said anything to Shyanne about his suspicions. Hopping up on Bravaro, he urged the horse into a trot. Just over a mile down the road the stench grew so powerful, he had to cover his nose with his shirt to reduce the intensity and prevent himself from throwing up.

He found the source a short distance farther up the road.

Bodies in various stated of decay lay about the area. He urged Bravaro forward. The horse resisted. He wanted nothing to do with what lay ahead. Drayco tried to make him move, but the horse turned away. He gave up and got off, covering the rest of the distance on foot.

A dark mound lay before him. As he drew closer, the blackness moved. Flies took to the air, uncovering the body underneath. It was a dog-like creature. At first, he thought it was a rizbak. It was different, though. Parts of another body lay beyond. At one time, it had been a horse. Now all he could see were the legs, the head, and some gore covered bones between the two.

This time Drayco could not hold back. He turned away from the carnage and threw up. When the heaving stopped and he had himself under control, he returned.

There were a total of three bodies: two small ones and one larger one. Millions of flies covered each. Moving around the two closer ones, he inched toward the third one. Dread filled him at the though of what...or who...he might find. Fortunately, it was another dog-like creature. He heaved a heavy sigh of relief.

At least it's not Joseph, he thought.

Moving back to the horse, he was able to see a saddle mixed in with the remains. Grabbing the only part he saw without decay on it, one of the stirrups, he pulled it away from the body. The movement caused the stench to increase and the flies to swarm again. Holding his nose, gagging, he dragged it several yards away from the disgusting mess. Bending over, he inspected it. Scratch marks and gore covered most of it, but bits and pieces of the design were still visible.

This is Joseph's saddle. I remember him showing it to me the last time I visited.

Drayco stood. He walked the perimeter of the attack area. He found nothing else of importance, only the three bodies.

At least I don't have to tell Shyanne I found her husband lying here.

At the lack of a body, another idea came to the dark twin. He searched the area once more. This time, he located the footprints of a man and a cat leading toward the east. The prints indicated both were running.

He must be okay. If he wasn't, these creatures would have brought him down and I would have found his remain along with the others.

A snort from Bravaro brought his attention back. The horse stood with his ears pointed toward the north. Drayco looked, but nothing was visible. He decided to return to Shyanne before something did appear and blocked his way. Leaping into the saddle, he spun around. No urging was necessary. Bravaro raced back the way he had come as if he was thrilled to .leave the area. Drayco understood, he was thrilled as well.

In their haste to depart, neither saw the grosbarks as they emerged from the forest.

Shyanne lay on her side, sleeping. Sweat covered her brow, her head thrashed back and forth. Her body shifted from one side to the other. Something disturbed her, making the restful sleep she needed impossible. It was the dream, the dream that had haunted her for many months.

She woke with a start and sat up abruptly, her heart racing, a scream locked in her throat. Fleeting images of flying and of her son crying blurred together into a jumbled mess. When she tried to remember what it was about the dream that had scared her so badly, she could not. The images faded too fast. Her heart slowed as she lay back, looking up at the white clouds mingled with more and more gray floating above.

Rain clouds are moving in. If that happens, we will lose Joseph's trail for sure.

With that in mind, plus an impatience to get back on the trail of her family, she rose to her feet. A whistle brought Jack to her side. She was getting into the saddle when she heard the pounding of hooves coming in her direction. Sitting as straight as her condition allowed, she pulled her sword free, holding it ready.

Jack let out with an ear-splitting whinny, nearly making Shyanne jump out of her skin with its suddenness. A reply echoed back. Drayco rode into view. At the sight of her brother instead of an unknown rider, she let out the breath she had been subconsciously holding. She returned her sword to the sheath resting across her back.

"Did you find anything?" The look on his face told her more than his silence did. "What was it—was it Joseph?"

"No. But I did find a dead horse and some dog-like creatures."

"A horse? What kind of horse?"

"I couldn't tell. The only parts with flesh left on them were the head and legs. It had grayish-white hair," he paused, "like a dapple gray."

Shyanne felt her heart skip several beats. Joseph was riding our dapple horse. From the way her brother acted, she could tell there was more; more he did not want to tell her.

"What else?"

"When I dragged the saddle free, I recognized it. It was Joseph's." Before she had time to say a word, he added, "I didn't find him, though. Him or Drizzle."

"I have to see."

"Shyanne, it's pretty bad. The stench is horrific."

She ignored him as she swung her heels hard into Jack's sides. The horse leaped past him before he had time to stop her.

"Shyanne! Don't!" His words fell on deaf ears. He spun Bravaro around and raced after her.

Drayco watched in admiration as his sister rode ahead of him. *Even with her pregnant belly, she manages to stay neatly in her saddle.* He wished it were for some other reason than the death scene that lay ahead.

The bodies were coming into sight when he saw movement in his peripheral vision. He turned and saw several of the dog-things running toward them.

"Shyanne! Don't stop! Keep moving!"

He wasn't sure if his shouting had reached her, or if she saw the creatures dart from hiding. Either way, it didn't matter. What mattered was she swept past the carnage without stopping.

Thunder rumbled in the distance. Thick dark clouds sped in the same direction as the fleeing pair, almost as if they were racing. A flash of bright yellow shot across the sky. More flashes, followed by long rumbles that vibrated everything, sliced through the growing darkness above.

Drayco glanced over his shoulder. The dog creatures continued to run after the twins, their barking intermingled with the thunder. They were catching up. Hunger made them desperate, and with desperation came speed. He leaned closer to the saddle and urged Bravaro into a faster pace. The horse answered, but he was tired from the long ride. A break in the trees appeared. A large open field lay ahead.

Shyanne rocketed down the road, flying past the stench of death when she heard Drayco's shout. Her belly screamed at her with pain because of the abuse it was suffering from the ride. She wrapped an arm around it, leaned forward a little and hugged herself tight to keep it from bouncing so much. It eased the pain some, but not all the way. When she glanced over her shoulder, she saw the grosbarks were catching up.

Drayco remained ahead of the pack, but he was loosing ground fast. If she stopped to help, she and her unborn child would surely become leftovers for the pack. She also thought about slowing so she could help if Drayco was caught. She discarded that thought when small red eyes appeared. They were in the trees, under bushes, and recessed in the shadows. None was on the road ahead.

"Drayco! Move your ass!"

The tiny red eyes paralleled them on either side. She could not make out what was behind the eyes because of the ever-increasing darkness caused by the approaching storm. When she broke out into the open field beyond the tree line, they hung back.

She was half a mile away from the forest when she heard a horse scream. She pulled hard on the reins, causing Jack to skid to a stop and spin around.

Drayco had just made it out of the woods before the grosbarks caught him.

Several of the dog-creatures were running around the pair, trying to nip at Bravaro's legs. The horse screamed again and lashed out, hitting one in the side that was too slow. It went reeling into a tree and lay unmoving.

The red eyes which had followed them, gathered at the edge of the tree cover. Drayco's attention was focused on the dozen or so beasts darting around him. He failed to see what was happening beyond.

A chill ran up Shyanne's spine, causing her shoulders to shake. It wasn't the grosbarks that caused her blood to run cold. It was the things hidden in the forest. Something about those red eyes bothered her. They seemed to glow forever, never blinking. They also seemed familiar, like something from the past, but she was not able to remember what.

As she watched, they disappeared. She stood up in her stirrups, looking all along the tree line, trying to locate any sign of the mysterious creatures. Every last red glow was gone. That made things worse.

A yelp brought her attention back to her brother. Another grosbark attempted to bring Bravaro down, only to meet with Drayco's sword. The dog-thing limped away, leaving a bloody trail behind it. Movement in the tall grass beyond the forest, close to the fighters, made her gasp. The red eyes reappeared. They were almost on top of the combatants.

She cupped her hands around her mouth, and shouted, "Drayco! Move! NOW!"

Her shouts caused Drayco to look her direction. She waved her arms for him to come toward her immediately. He hesitated. His path was blocked by one of the nightmarish dog things.

Suddenly, a ball of black fur jumped from the cover of the tall grass and landed on the back of the canine. Drayco heard hissing and growling. More balls of various color combinations landed beside the black one. The dog-thing began twisting its body, jaws snapping, in an attempt to get them off. It was no use.

He was unable to see what happened next because Bravaro reared unexpectedly, almost throwing him out of the saddle. When the horse dropped down, a tiger-stripped creature clung onto its rump near the tail. Bravaro responded in the only way he could—he bolted toward Shyanne.

Drayco managed to grab a handful of mane before the wild ride began. With one hand full of horsehair and the other clutching his sword, he bent over to reduce the strength of the wind trying to knock him off. He glanced over his shoulder to see the creature still clinging behind him.

A cat face with slit eyes, pink nose, and whiskers sat on a ball of orange striped fur. Claws extended from the tiny feet visible beneath the hunched body. They were embedded into the horses flesh. It hissed when it noticed him looking at it. In the distance, Drayco saw more of the cats attacking the dog creatures. All were quickly overcome by the sheer number of felines.

Shyanne gasped as she watched the grosbark pack disappear under a sea of writhing fur. She saw one land on Bravaro. The horse took off, coming her way, fast. His eyes were rolled back with only the whites showing. The furball held on. As Drayco flew past them, she wondered how she could help. Holding her swollen belly with one arm, she urged Jack to follow.

Drayco saw his sister as they flew past. Shock and concern was written all over her face. He focused his attention back on the clinging ball of hissing fur. It was moving. Intelligence shined from the slit eyes. With every few bounces, it released one set of claws then sank them in before the next bounce. Each time the claws went in, the horse responded with more speed. The dark man knew he would be in trouble if he did not do something, anything, soon.

He tried to sit up, but the wind pelted him, almost knocking him into the spitting ball. Leaning forward again, he thought about what else he could do.

A flash of lightning shot across the sky. Thunder boomed on its heels. The light reflected off the blade in his hand, causing him to squint at the sudden brightness. An idea came to him. Watching the mass of fur, he stayed in his hunched over position and twisted his upper body around, gripping with his knees to maintain his balance. Raising his arm, elbow pointed toward the cat, he swung it backwards.

The hissing creature flattened itself against the horse. The blade missed it by a fraction of an inch, slicing just over its head. Before Drayco could get his arm out of the way, a paw came up and raked the exposed skin.

"Ouch! You flea-bitten furball! That hurts!"

He did not have time to examine the wound; the cat was on the move again. He tried once more to hit it with the sword, but the angle was wrong. And the cat was too close. He did not want to hit his horse with the blade by mistake. Another tactic was in order. Because the ride was too rough to allow him to sheath it, he tossed his sword aside. He would return for it later.

Drayco opened his hand and slapped at it. The cat ducked, avoiding the hits. With his third swing, the dark man struck pay dirt.

He caught the cat square in the face, but it remained firmly attached. Several more hits in rapid succession yielded the same results. He could tell the cat was furious now. It wanted to kill the man thing in front of it. Drayco held back, watching for an opportunity. It came quickly.

The cat raised a paw, fully intent on moving forward. Drayco's hand lashed out and struck its side. With only one set of front claws buried in the horse's flesh, it almost worked. The beast rocked back and forth, swatting at the hand swinging at it, leaving gouges in the skin. Ignoring the sting coming from the wounds left by the sharp claws, the dark man beat at the cat until it finally went sailing off the horse. He watched as it landed in typical cat fashion: on all four feet.

Before it had time to move out of the way, pounding hooves closed in on the cat. Jack trampled it as he flew past. Shyanne turned away. She did not want to see the end results. She loved cats, but these were feral creatures. Since the passing of the virus years ago, they had became extremely cunning, along with very dangerous.

Shyanne sped after Bravaro and her brother. She hoped Drayco got the horse under control soon because her belly was killing her. She prayed the rough ride was not doing any damage to her unborn child. When she saw the pair ahead slow, a sigh of relief escaped.

Once the cat and its painful claws were gone, Bravaro slowed his pace. Drayco was able to reach forward and grab the reins. He pulled back and tugged them to the right so the horse turned around. Shyanne came up to them holding her stomach.

"Are you alright?" he asked.

"Just a bit winded. I'm not used to riding like this, remember?"

"You're not going to deliver now, are you?"

"No—not right now. I just hurt—that's all."

Drayco watched her as she grimaced with pain. "Are you sure you're not going into labor?'

"Drayco, I'm sure. I have done this before...though not under these circumstances. Remember?"

"You're sure..."

"Drayco!"

"Okay. Just checking." Looking past her, he said, "I'm going back for my sword. I had to get rid of it when I was trying to get that damned thing off my horse."

"I saw it. It's not too far back." She grimaced again but relaxed as the spasm eased.

He rode back the way he came during his wild ride, passing the trampled body of the striped beast with hardly a glance. He was more interested in retrieving his sword. A bolt of blue white lightening struck close. An ear-splitting rumble, which caused the dark man and his horse to jump, followed almost immediately.

We need to find shelter quick, or else. Drayco thought. *Moreover, Shyanne needs to rest longer than a half hour, especially after that last ride.*

Even though it was late afternoon, the storm clouds above made it seem like it was dusk. Drayco found the weapon leaning at an angle with the point imbedded in the dirt. He jumped down, pulled it free, and returned it to its sheath. He inspected the claw marks in Bravaro's rump. Tiny blood-filled holes were evident, but they were not deep. Neither were the scratches on his arm or hand. After returning to the saddle, he backtracked to Shyanne.

"We have to find shelter or we are going to get really wet. I don't know about you, but I don't want to become a crispy critter from the lightening that's hitting the area."

Shyanne pointed toward the north. "Maybe we can find a cave or overhang in those hills over that way. Plus, I hear the sound of fast moving water off to the east. Maybe it's a river."

Now that she pointed it out, he could hear it also. He looked up. The thick black clouds appeared ready to drop their load of moisture any minute.

"Shelter first, then the river."

Shyanne nodded her head in agreement. Both turned toward the north, prodding their tired horses into motion. They were a short distance from the hills when fat drops began to fall. By the time they found a cave large enough to hold them and the horses, they were drenched.

Seven

Ruben stared at the pink and red rays shining across the darkening sky. Night was coming. He would have to land the flying craft before that happened. It worked great when the sun was out, but quit when the light disappeared or when thick billowy storm clouds blocked it. He knew the panels on the machine were called 'solar' panels. Beyond that—he had no understanding.

His association with the Boss had taught him much about the machines from long ago. A few were easy to understand while others were beyond his comprehension, like the flying machine.

Joey stood beside him, his face split with a huge grin. He was enjoying the ride. Ruben draped a hand onto the child's shoulder, pulling him close.

"Having fun?"

"Yea! This is way better than riding some dumb old horse!"

We're going to have to stop soon."

"Aww." The boy looked up. "How come?"

"It has to rest at night, just like we have to."

Joey looked at the colorful streaks etching their way across the sky. His saddened face made Ruben chuckle.

"It's okay, little man, we'll be flying again soon enough."

The words 'little man' and 'flying' brought the smile back.

Ruben spied a break in the trees below. Beneath the break, a gently sloping hill emerged and ended at a drop-off. Dirt and rocks of various sizes littered the downward slope. He knew this part of the country was riddled with caves and decided to see if his hunch was correct.

"Hang on tight." A glint of mischief filled his eyes.

He waited for Joey to grab the siderail with both hands before letting out an ear-splitting yell. The big man pushed the control stick forward, causing the flyer to drop from the sky like a rock. Joey yelped in terror. His eyes opened as wide as they could before he slammed them shut. The casual grasp on the rail became a white knuckled death grip.

Ruben looked at the child and chuckled at the sight of his face. Squeezing the small shoulder to reassure him, the big man eased the stick backwards, reducing the speed and angle of the drop. The boy's grip remained tight, but he managed to open his eyes once they leveled out.

Guiding the flying machine to the right, Ruben noticed a dark opening in the hillside. *So there is a cave as I had hoped,* he thought. *What luck, especially since storm clouds are building.*

He landed the machine near the opening, but not too close. He wanted to make sure it was unoccupied before he allowed the boy to venture inside. He told Joey to stay where he was. The boy nodded, unable to speak for the moment, his throat still constricted from his earlier fright.

Ruben stepped off the platform and withdrew his sword. He advanced on the opening slowly. When he reached it, he flattened his back against the cold stone, listening. No sound came from within. He took several deep breaths. The cave had a fresh earthy smell; the smell of animal occupation was not present. He ducked inside to make sure, emerging seconds later, satisfied at their good fortune.

He walked back to the craft with the sword still in his hand. Joey remained where he was, as if he was unable to convince his hands to release the railing yet. At least the look of terror was gone from his face. This made the big man happy. Dealing with a whiney frightened child was not something he wanted to do.

Joey's eyes were glued on the sword in complete awe. He remembered the first time he first saw it. He thought it was great then. But this, this was awesome! The sword was huge. The blade shined bright, even in the cloudy, dusk shrouded light. He watched reluctantly as Ruben returned the sword to the sheath on his back.

"That was a great ride, don't you think little man?"

The memory of the hair-raising event, which was forgotten by the sight of the sword, returned. "I—I guess."

"I love doing that. Makes my stomach feel like its going to explode out my mouth." The grin on Ruben's face was infectious.

Joey smiled in return. "Mine too."

Turning his head slightly and leaning close to the boy, he asked in a conspiring tone, "Want to do it again tomorrow?"

Not wanting to disappoint the man standing before him, Joey stammered, "O–o–okay."

The more Joey thought about it, the more he realized it was fun. The ground rushing toward him and the wind whipping past his ears had caused him to think he was going to crash. Remembering how well his new friend had handled the situation, and the fact that they had not become a bloody pile of mush, helped him look forward to doing it again. The big man's voice brought Joey's thoughts back to the ground.

"Little man, I need your help. How about it?"

Joey stared in disbelief. He was asked for his help instead of told what to do. This was something new for him. "Sure!"

"I need you to help gather firewood. We need as much as possible." He looked up at the cloud-filled sky. "A storm is coming and I want us to stay warm tonight."

Joey's shoulders sagged. All Ruben wanted was firewood. That was something he was told to do as a chore at home. He had hoped it would be something different, something exciting, like being asked to stand guard, or asked to start the fire. Something other than the same boring thing he already did.

Seeing the disappointment on his face, Ruben added, "Afterwards, you get to move the flying craft closer to the cave."

The boy straightened. "Do you really mean it? I can fly this?"

"Only if we get the wood gathered before dark."

That was all it took. In under half an hour, a huge pile of broken dried wood and twigs was stacked inside the cave. Ruben leaned against the wall, thinking, while the lad raced around. *This kid isn't so bad. He's nothing like his parents. They were nothing but a huge thorn in my side. Instead of killing him like I planned, maybe I can turn him against them. That would be an even sweeter revenge.*

When he finished, Joey ran up to the big man. His eyes gleamed at the prospect of moving the flying machine all by himself. The gleam diminished some when he saw Ruben step onto the platform.

"Don't worry, little man. I'm only here to make sure you do it right, that's all."

Joey brightened and leaped onto the platform. He reached the console in two large hops instead of the several steps required to reach it by the bigger man.

"Remember which button to push?" Ruben asked when he stepped up behind the boy.

Standing tall, he glanced at the various buttons, "This one. Right?" He pointed at the round one in the center.

"That's correct. I always knew you were a smart one." Ruben reached up and jostled Joey's hair. "Go ahead. Push it."

Joey mashed it in harder than necessary. The machine responded by humming to life. He grinned at the big man standing next to him, waiting for more instructions.

Ruben looked at the sky. Dusk was blanketing everything with its growing darkness. "Best hurry, before we lose the light all together." He returned his gaze to the boy. "Now, grab the stick and move it back slowly."

Joey reached up and wrapped his fingers around the stick. He tugged it toward his body slowly, as instructed. The machine responded, though it was sluggish because of the lack of sunlight. It rose off the ground. The boy squealed in delight and let go of the stick. The craft teetered wildly in response to the sudden loss of guidance, almost throwing both people off. Ruben quickly brought the craft under control.

"Whoa. Now that's what I call taking fun to extremes." He grinned at the boy, "If you don't mind, can we save the rest of the antics for tomorrow?" He indicated for Joey to take over the control stick again.

Joey reached for the stick, surprised that he was

asked to take control again. Instead of shouting and taking over like his parents did when he messed up, Ruben trusted him and let him have another go at it. He guided the craft upward, his brow furrowed in concentrated. This time, the ride was smooth. With a gentle tap, he spun it around, nose pointed toward the cave.

"Now you have it, little man. Great job. Guide it over there and set her down." Ruben pointed to where he wanted Joey to go.

Joey obliged. He wanted to smile, to look up at the man standing beside him. Instead, he kept his eyes focused on the landing site. He did not want to repeat the craziness of a few moments ago. Ruben might not let him complete the task if that happened. When the craft set down with a teeth-jarring thud, the boy sighed. He knew what came next; it always did, especially since mom got pregnant with his brother or sister. Cringing, he peered up at Ruben. What the big man said next surprised him even more.

Ruben faced the boy. He placed his hands on his hips, frowning. The frown disappeared and a huge grin replaced it. "That's something we're going to have to work on. Can't have you jolting something loose with those rough landings of yours. Might mess something up." He reached up and ruffled Joey's hair again.

"You're not mad at me?"

"Why? Should I be?"

"Dad would have been. He would have sent me to my room. Maybe even without supper."

"I'm not your dad. Besides, it would be silly to send you to your room; you don't have one here…not yet at least." The thoughtful pose he assumed, fingers rubbing both sides of his chin as if he was actually contemplating where to put a room, caused the boy to giggle.

"You're goofy."

"Isn't that better than being a grumpy ole bear?" He leaned over and spread his arms wide, growling, pretending to be an angry bear.

Joey giggled harder.

He straightened. "Not scary huh?"

"Nope."

"Well then I guess we'd better go make a fire instead. Are you hungry?"

On cue, a rumble sounded from the boy's stomach. He wrapped his arms over his middle and said, "Starved."

Ruben moved to the back of the platform. He pushed a small button located to the right. A hidden door popped open. Reaching inside, he pulled out a pouch filled with foodstuff, some more jerky, and another pouch filled with water. "All the things a growing body needs. I keep these handy...just in case."

"What are we going to cook that in?" Joey asked.

Ruben moved to the other side and pressed a similar button. Another compartment opened, revealing a small pan inside, "One pan coming up." Setting the foodstuff in the pan, he said, "Come on, little man, let's get started. I'm starved."

Reaching down, the big man took the tiny hand in his and led Joey inside the cave. In no time, a roaring fire brightened the area and food filled their empty bellies.

*   *   *

Joseph felt the cool wet cloth placed on his forehead. Within seconds, he heard water splashing and another cloth touch his upper body. He kept his eyes closed, savoring the coolness on his hot skin.

"Shyanne—mmmm Shyanne, that feels wonderful."

He reached up and ran his fingers over the hand holding the cloth. It was small, smaller than the one that belonged to his wife. Opening his eyes, he immediately shut them again. The light shining from the candle located next to him was bright, too bright to tolerate. Trying again, he opened them into narrow slits, allowing as little light as possible in.

Darkness shrouded the rest of the room. Night was visible through the window. When his eyes adjusted to the candle, he opened them full. A woman of oriental decent sat next to him, a wet cloth in her hand. He could not remember who she was or how he came to be here, wherever here was. Suddenly, the memories rushed in. He sat up abruptly.

"Joey!"

He threw a hand up, palm flat against the wall, to try to steady the wildly spinning room, to no avail. Gentle but firm hands pushed him back onto the cot.

"Do not try to move yet. You have been down for several days."

"How many?"

"Four. I was beginning to think you were not coming back."

"Four!" Joseph sat up again, causing the world to go on another wild ride. He lay back on his own this time, exhausted. "I have failed him. He could already be dead by now." He threw an arm over his eyes to hide the tears. It only helped the moisture flow down his cheeks. He didn't care. This was his son, for god sake.

Hana spoke in a calm voice as she placed her small hand gently on his shoulder, "I am sure he is not dead. What would be the purpose?"

"He took him to get back at us!" Joseph flung the arm away from his eyes and glared at her. "What better way to do so than kill him?"

"If this man wanted to kill him, why not do it immediately. Why take him?"

"To make us suffer over and over." Joseph covered his eyes again. More tears flowed down the sides of his face, crisscrossing the previous tracks. The gentle hand wiped them away.

"I have a feeling your son is not dead. You will find him—this I believe."

The words were so confident, so reassuring, they helped Joseph to bring his emotions under some measure of control. Moving his arm away, he looked at the woman sitting next to him.

"Hana—it's Hana right?" She nodded her head yes. "I hope you're right. I really do."

"I'm going to get you some broth. You need it to regain your strength before getting up. Some tea as well."

"Is it going to have more of that medicine in it?" Joseph remembered the taste of the last tea. He had grimaced like a baby tasting a lemon for the first time.

Hana smiled. "The tea will. It will help you relax and sleep. The broth will be just that, broth alone."

"I'm not hungry."

"Every little bit you take in will help you recover that much faster," she said as she rose to her feet. "I'll return in a moment."

Joseph stared at the ceiling. All he could think about was his son. What if Hana was right, what if he was still alive. He hoped so. He did not know what he would do if Joey was gone from him forever.

There are so many things I want to say to him...how much I love him...how proud I am of him. While he thought of his son, the tears began anew. *I have been so wrapped up in the farm and Shyanne's pregnancy that I brushed off the many things he wanted to do. When I find him, that will never happen again!*

He tried to sit up. Again, he was unable. The effort and the spinning room started another coughing fit. He rolled onto his side, curled into a tight ball, and coughed and coughed and coughed. When Hana returned with the tea and broth, he was gasping from the exertion.

"These will help sooth your ravaged throat."

She helped him onto his back and brought the cup holding the brown liquid to his lips, pouring a miniscule amount of its contents into his mouth. The broth was warm and, as promised, soothing. He finished it eagerly. Afterwards, he was able to sit up and hold the cup of tea on his own.

"This tastes different," he said after taking several tentative sips.

"It is. It is a combination of skullcap, passionflower, chamomile, and lemongrass. It is called a calming tea." Hana sipped at the cup in her hands.

"It's doing the job alright." He relaxed against the wall and drank the warm liquid until it was gone. Hana took the empty cup from him and set it on the small table.

A noise at the door caused both people to turn their heads in that direction. Drizzle walked in. The cat came over to the bed then sat back on his haunches.

Drizzle! Am I glad to see you!"

The big cat remained silent. Something was bothering him, Joseph could tell. Finally, he could not take the silence any longer.

"What is it?"

"I went back to the place of the attack, near the rivers edge," the cat began. "I found the picked over bones of the dog things and some of the small furred cat things as well. I also found traces of Jack and Bravaro."

"What of their riders?" A feeling of dread replaced the elation he felt only moments ago.

"I found nothing. Their trail was washed away by a strong rain. I was unable to locate which direction they went."

"But you didn't find any bodies?

"No, only the bodies of the cat and dog things. I did find one separated from the rest. It had been trampled by a horse."

"Wait...did you say Bravaro?" He sat up straight. This time, the room remained stable.

"I don't believe I stuttered." The cat stared at the man on the cot as if he was a complete idiot.

"That means Drayco is with Shyanne. Well I'll be damned. I guess he finally decided to come home." He leaned against the wall again, "About time. Wish it was under better circumstances, though."

Hana picked up Joseph's cup and left the room. She returned a breath later with more tea. "It is late and you need more rest. You have a son to find and strength is required to do so."

"With Shyanne and Drayco looking, we should find him in no time." Joseph took a large drink of the steaming liquid. He spit it back into the cup immediately. "Wow is that hot!"

Moving toward the door, Drizzle muttered, "Imbecile. Only an imbecile would drink from a cup before checking how hot the contents are."

"I heard that—I'm not deaf you know!"

"I know," the cat said before he disappeared out the door.

"Stupid cat." Joseph sipped at the tea, this time taking in a small amount instead of a full swallow.

"On the contrary, I find him quite intelligent. Chikara is but an infant to him."

"How old is she?"

"From what I've been able to ascertain, she is 113 years young."

"How do you communicate with her if she doesn't speak?" A yawn escaped from Joseph. The sedative in the tea was kicking in.

"It is almost like she senses what I am thinking and

vice versa."

"But…"

"No more tonight, you need to sleep." She took the cup out of his hands.

There were so many questions he wanted to ask. To find another humecat, a female one to boot, was something he never thought he'd do. Before he could think another thought, his eyes closed and the world vanished into the realm of dreams.

Joseph woke to sunlight shining bright through the window. He was lying on his side, curled into a ball, facing the wall. When he rolled over to look around, he discovered a nose mere inches from his own. Flinching back, his head hit the wall.

"Oww! That hurt!" Rubbing the aching area, he looked at the cat sitting so close. It was Chikara. "You startled me, young lady."

The cat continued to stare at the man on the bed.

"Now Chikara, it's not polite to stare."

The voice came from the door. Hana entered carrying a tray laden with food, "Time to eat." At the suggestion of food, his stomach growled.

"Betrayed," he said with a grin.

This morning, he felt like he had an appetite. He sat up slowly and folded his legs before him on the bed. The simple move left him winded, but it felt good to sit up after lying down for so long. Hana set the tray on the cot beside him. She picked up one of the cups before moving to the stool. Chikara slid gracefully to the little woman's side and settled to the floor. She returned her gaze to the man once more.

Two plates were covered with eggs, sliced ham, and biscuits with flour gravy. Joseph picked up one and consumed everything on it with a zeal not felt in a while. He picked up the second when his appetite was not sated with the first. After both plates were empty, he realized the small woman was not eating. He hoped one had not been hers.

Embarrassed, he asked, "Was one of those yours?"

"No, I ate earlier. I knew you would be hungry so I prepared everything for you." Hana brought the cup to her lips and sipped at the contents.

He wondered if she was telling him the truth, but did not say so aloud. "Thank you. It was delicious."

He picked up the other cup and sniffed at its contents. It smelled different from the previous ones, the ones with the medicine in them

"What is this?"

"Green tea with a touch of mint. It is soothing to the soul." She raised her cup again.

Joseph sipped at the light colored tea. He felt its warmth flow down his throat and deep into his stomach. It warmed him inside, but did nothing to ease the uptight feeling that was there as well. He felt he had wasted enough time with his illness, especially after hearing how many days he had been unconscious. It was time to find his son. Setting the cup back on the tray, he moved with slow determination to the edge of the bed. By the time he had his feet on the floor, he was breathing hard and sweat covered his body.

"You need to allow your body to focus on digestion first. Then it will have the strength to do what you want."

"I need to start moving. I have to find the man who took my son before something happens, if it hasn't already."

Joseph pushed off the bed with his arms until he was standing in a hunched position. His legs felt like they were made of rubber. He wasn't concerned. With determination the likes of his, they would hold. Stretching his arms out to either side like a balancing artist on the high wire, he straightened. A triumphant smile broke out. It evaporated quickly when the floor rushed up to meet his face.

"Something happened," Hana said. She remained seated, sipping at her tea with a straight face.

"That's not funny."

"Am I laughing?"

"Maybe not on the outside," Joseph said as he struggled into a sitting position. Reaching an arm toward her, he asked, "Can you help me up?"

"No."

"Why not?"

"You insisted on getting up—now you are down. Since you did not listen to me, you must find a way to help yourself now." She rose and walked to the door. "I need more tea. I shall return shortly. Chikara, please come with me." She turned her back on the fallen man and left the room.

The humecat stared at the man sitting on the floor with her golden eyes. They appeared to be saying, "You should have listened." Without blinking, she turned and followed the little woman out.

"Damn woman," he muttered under his breath, angry. "Who does she think she is? I'm not some invalid in need of pampering. I can do this one my own. I'll show her."

Joseph rolled over onto his knees. After several attempts, he managed to rise to his feet. His legs were just as wobbly as before he fell. Not sure how long he could last, he moved with stubborn determination toward the door through which Hana had disappeared. He fell to his knees, gasping, once he reached it. In the room beyond, Hana sat at a small table. She was watching him.

"It is good to see you did not give up. It shows what kind of character you have."

He struggled to his feet and made his way to the other chair pulled away from the table, facing his direction. Flopping down, he gasped, "Did you have this ready for me?"

"Yes."

"How did you know I'd come?"

"You strike me as shitsukoi."

"What does that mean?"

"A person who is persistent...stubborn."

"Shyanne, my wife, tells me the same thing."

"She is a very wise woman then."

Joseph quieted. He stared at the wall but did not see it. His thoughts were on his family. *I wonder where were they are. It's been almost a week since I last saw them. I hope they're still okay.* The idea of never seeing his son and wife again tore at him.

"It's about time you got your lazy butt out of that bed," Drizzle said as he walked into the room. His tone was full of sarcasm, his tail swishing back and forth. "I was wondering how you were going to keep all those manly muscles you built up by sleeping all the time.

Joseph jumped at the sudden words. Recovering quickly, he watched the cat make his way toward him. "I love you too, Drizzle."

"You okay?" Drizzle asked when he was close to Joseph's chair.

"Yea."

Looking at Hana, he repeated, "He okay?"

"He is well."

"Will he be able to travel soon?"

"Ask him yourself." She nodded her head toward Joseph and gave him a slight smile.

Joseph listened to the exchange between the two. A frown settled on his face. He was upset that Drizzle had not asked him directly, as if he was a simple child instead of a person able to speak for himself. "I'll be ready to leave soon enough."

"I wanted to make sure with the healer. I know how human males can overestimate themselves."

"Oh—and you don't huh."

"I'm not a human."

"Part of you is."

Drizzle focused his eyes on the fair-haired man. "First you nearly drown yourself. Then you whine about getting sick. Now you insult me. I'll give you one day—one day. After that, I go find Joey on my own." The cat walked back the way he came. Before disappearing, he snarled, "I've wasted enough time waiting for you."

"I'll be ready—you'll see." Joseph crossed his arms in front of his chest.

"One day. Remember that," Drizzle said over his shoulder and left the room.

Slamming his fist down hard on the table, Joseph shouted, "The nerve! Like I planned on being attacked! Like I planned on nearly drowning! Like I planned on getting sick!" He rose to his feet and had to grab the table to steady his wobbly legs. "I'll show him!" He started pacing. He made it only a few steps before having to stop to catch his breath.

"Come sit down, Joseph," Hana said softly.

The soft voice gave him something to lash out on. "And do what! Haven't I done enough of nothing already?" He could feel the frustration rising in his throat. It felt like he was going to choke on it. "My son is in the hands of a killer— my wife is eight months pregnant—on horseback—instead of at home resting." His legs buckled under him, causing him to land hard on his knees. "I can't keep doing nothing—I have to help my family." He hunched over, covering his eyes with his fists.

Hana rose to her feet and moved next to Joseph. She kneeled in front of him. "You need to rest. I know you want to go, but your body is not strong enough yet." She wrapped her arms around him, hugging him close. "I know these are not the words you want to hear, but they are all I can offer at the moment."

Joseph wrapped his arms around the small woman and buried his face in her shoulder. Sobs echoed from between their bodies as he released the pent up frustration. He knew she was right; he was not strong enough yet. He hated the feeling of helplessness running through him.

"Why? Why did he have to take Joey? Why did he find us? Why do we have to suffer like this—why?" The last word was barely a whisper.

Hana said nothing. She held the despairing man and rocked him as she would a child.

*   *   *

Drizzle sat outside the room, listening. He knew what Joseph was going through and was sorry for the cruel words spoken during the heat of the argument. He knew the man wanted to find his son. Unforeseen circumstances prevented him from doing so.

"This I promise to you, mate to my companion. I will find your son and bring him back to you. And, I will kill the one who took him, thus ending any more suffering at his hands."

The cat slid out of the house and started east.

Eight

The twins huddled in the cave, waiting for the rain to cease. It had been pouring non-stop for many hours. Both were cold, wet, and miserable. And both had not gotten much sleep during the early hours of the night.

"If I ever see another raindrop—I'll scream!" Shyanne shook her fist at the moisture cascading from the sky.

"Please don't. My ear is right next to you. I don't want to become deaf." Drayco pulled Shyanne close, trying to help her stay warm. The rain made the surrounding wood too wet to use for a fire.

Shyanne remained silent. She glared at the water dripping from the overhang to the cave entrance.

"Little sis, it will be okay."

"Will It?" She pulled her knees up as close as she could, given her swollen belly.

It was Drayco's turn to remain silent. He did not know what he could say that would make things better. Her body shivered under his arm.

"It will be hard to follow their trail now. The rain has washed everything away.

"Hard, but not impossible—remember that." He grabbed her face, pressing his fingers into her cheeks. "We've been in worse situations that this and made it through. We will make it through this one too."

"Drwaco, pwease wet go of my phace." Her words came out wrong due to his fingers squeezing either side of her mouth.

He shook her head back and forth playfully. He wanted to take her mind off their present situation, even if only for a second. "What if I don't wanna—huh—huh?"

"Drwaco..."

"Go ahead, make me little sis, if you can."

Before he had time to think, she grabbed his hand, rose up onto her knees and twisted it to the right, forcing his head toward the ground. His arm was effectively pinned behind his back. Her other hand held his head against the cave floor.

"Oww, oww, let go." The hand pinning his arm felt like a vise grip.

"Make me."

The dark twin saw his sister was not smiling. She was angry. "Dammit, Shyanne, all I wanted to do was get you to smile."

She released her hold on him. Remaining silent, she rose to her feet and stormed to the mouth of the cave, crossing her arms in front of her when she stopped just inside the entrance.

Drayco followed, massaging his sore shoulder. When he reached his sister, he hesitated before taking a chance and wrapping his arms around her.

"I'm sorry, Shyanne. I just wanted you to smile, that's all."

She reached up and covered one of his hands with hers. "I know. I'm sorry too. I should not have reacted like I did."

They both stared into the darkness beyond, watching the falling rain.

"I miss my son. I miss my husband. And I miss my quiet life."

Drayco wished he had the things Shyanne mentioned. He knew he never would, though, because of his affliction. "We will find them."

She turned around and hugged her brother close. "I love you."

A kick from her belly made him flinch with surprise. "I see that one doesn't like to share."

Shyanne looked down at her belly and rubbed it gently. The much-desired smile appeared. "No Molly doesn't.

She kicks Joseph all the time." The mention of her husband's name caused the smile to fade a little.

"Come on. It's almost sunrise and we need to get some sleep before we move on."

He guided her to the back of the cave. Once she curled into her blanket, he lay down next to her to help keep her warm. Eventually both slept, though neither felt rested.

*   *   *

It took Ruben three more days to reach his destination. Cloud filled, rainy skies made travel difficult for the machine they operated. It needed sun to fly. In those three days, he had established the beginnings of a bond with the child taken from his parents. Joey never questioned why he was away from his family for so long. He was too busy having fun, soaking up all the information given to him like a sponge. It was Joey who guided the flying machine as the thick growth of trees separated, allowing the cave entrance to come into view.

"That's our destination."

"The cave?"

"Yup. Set her down close to the entrance, little man."

The landing of the craft was smooth. Joey beamed as the big man complimented him on how much he had improved in so short a timeframe. *Dad never talks to me like this,* he thought. *All he ever does anymore is yell.*

He thought less and less of his parents because he was having too much fun and did not want it to end. He did not want to go back to the boring farm with its many chores and no one to play with except Drizzle. Letting go of the guiding stick, he waited to see what Ruben wanted to do next.

"We need to push the air ship into the cave. I don't want it to be seen. It scares people due to the fact that they don't understand what it is. Do you think your muscles are up to it?"

The boy marched up to one of the side rails and grabbed it with both hands. He knew the huge man did not need his help, but that mattered not, he was being asked to help. Ruben smiled. He moved to the other side. Together, they hid the floating platform: one pushing with ease, the other trying with all his might.

"Thanks, little man. That was a big help."

Ruben liked the boy. He was not a whiner like some he had seen whenever he went into town. Always crying. Always wanting their mommas. This kid had spunk. He reminded him of himself when he was younger.

"Now what?"

We go inside and I show you around. This place is bigger than you think."

Before either moved, a loud crash sounded from within the trees nearby. Snapping sounds followed. Ruben shoved the lad behind him and slid his sword out of its sheath. Crouching low, he held it with both hands, ready to kill whatever danger came at them.

Joey stared at the huge sword instead of the trees. He was scared, but because of the size of the sword, he knew nothing would get past the man before him. Eyes open wide, some tall bushes close to the edge of the clearing drew his attention when they shook violently.

"Stay behind me, Joey. No matter what. Okay?"

"Y–yy–es sir." Joey was embarrassed at the quiver in his voice. He was a man, after all, at least in his young mind he was. And men don't show fear.

More shaking closer to the clearing caused Ruben to grip the sword tighter. Suddenly, then big man straightened. He was laughing. Joey was not able to see around the body in front of him.

"See what we were afraid of, little man?"

Joey peered around to see the head and front part of a horse step into the open. He smiled.

"I forgot about Wind Racer." Ruben put the sword away before moving toward the horse.

"You were afraid? Even with that big sword? I didn't think you would be afraid of anything."

"It's okay to be afraid. It shows you're smart enough to understand consequences."

Joey was not sure what 'consequences' was. All he knew was this man was the best. He did not yell. He allowed him to do thing his father never would. And he treated him like a grownup. Helping Ruben guide the horse inside, he dreamed that one day he would have a big sword like Ruben and of wielding it as good as he did.

Several days later, Joey marveled at the chisel marks in the wall. To him, it was a huge feat to make a big hole in the mountain. Especially one as large as this one. Holders with torches shining bright were scattered throughout the tunnel. He had explored every aspect of the manmade part of the cave. Another entrance led into the natural part of the cave. It was too dark for him to explore and no torches lit the passageway. Moreover, Ruben had told him not to go in there. He said the boy would get lost forever if he did, and he did not want that to happen.

A noise drew his attention to the room on the left. Wind Racer reached his long neck over the wooden railing to his enclosure, trying to get to the barrel of grain stored next to it. Joey walked over, pulled the lid off, and scooped up a handful. With his arm extended, he slowly advanced on the horse. A first the animal was hesitant, but the smell of the grain overcame any opposition. Joey giggled as the horse's lips tickled his hand.

"He likes you. That's an honor."

Joey spun around, startled, and dropping the grain. He had forgotten about the big man.

Ruben was leaning against the doorway, arms crossed. He walked into the room to stand beside the boy. Together, they watched the horse work his head through the rails to clean the floor of the spilled grain.

"He's an exceptional animal. Always loyal. Never wants to leave." The big man placed a hand on Joey's shoulder.

Joey saw the frown on his face. He sensed that something was not right. Ruben had left him alone for several hours while he went on a restock trip, only just now returning. "Is something the matter?" the boy asked.

Ruben did not answer. He pulled his arm away and started toward the door. "We need to unload the flyer."

The boy stared at the retreating back. He did not understand. Running after him, he asked, "Did I do something? How come you're so sad?"

Ruben remained silent. He walked to the junction of the tunnels close to the entrance. Sunlight brightened the outside world with its rays. The manmade tunnel was to one side, the natural tunnel to the other. Joey remembered the warning given to him the first day there, the warning about never entering that area alone. He did not want to get lost forever.

"Ruben? What's the matter?"

The big man stopped at the opening to the outer world. The flyer sat close, a deer on the platform, other bundles located next to it.

"I heard from your folks."

"Really?"

"They sent me a message."

"Do they miss me?" The child's face lit up at the mention of his family. He realized that he missed them and wanted to see them again.

"No."

"No?" That one word hit him like a stone, taking his breath away.

Ruben squat down next to the lad. He pulled him onto his lap. "They have another mouth on the way, remember? Since you've been gone, they realized it was far easier to plan on the care of one instead of trying to manage two."

"But—I don't eat much."

"I know that, little man. But they don't want to worry about how to feed two. Or even how to take care of two for that matter."

"But..." Joey remembered how his father did not have much time for him anymore. Not since mom became 'pregnant' as he called it. The water fight was the first time they had done something together in a while. "But..."

Ruben watched the tears well in the lad's eyes. His chin began to quiver. He was trying hard not to cry, to be a man. As he pulled the child against his chest, something wrenched inside. He knew he was lying to Joey. He wanted to hurt his parents. The boy, on the other hand, was something else. He liked him. He hated hurting him.

Joey did not want to believe Ruben's cruel words. He was their little boy. How could his parents not want him? He wasn't any trouble. Or was he? He remembered all the times he ran off, wanting to find someone to play with. All the times he gave his parents a hard time about doing his chores. He was five years old. To him, chores were for the kids seven years or older.

Maybe it is true. Maybe they don't want me. Maybe they haven't wanted me all along.

"I'm sorry Joey. I can't make them love you or want you." He smoothed the child's hair, holding him close. "But if you'll let me—I'll be your father."

The word sounded good as it rolled off his tongue. It was something he never thought would happen to him. He had remained a loner since the death of the Boss, only being around others when he had to, or when he killed them.

Father.

The more he thought about it, the better he liked the idea. He hoped Joey would like it too.

"What do you think, little man?"

Joey pulled back from Ruben. He stared into the larger eyes, looking for any signs of teasing. There was none. "Do you really mean it?"

"I do. I've always wanted a son—someone to teach how to use a sword, how to ride a horse, to pass all my knowledge on to."

"You won't get rid of me if I give you a hard time? If I wander off?"

"Not a chance."

"Even if I don't do chores?"

"Even if you don't do chores. However, I will need your help once in a while. I can't do everything by myself."

Joey threw his arms around the big man's neck. He could not believe what he was hearing. One second he was alone, facing the world unwanted and unloved by his parents. The next, he had someone who wanted him. It did not matter that he knew so little about this man; he wanted him. That was enough.

Ruben hugged Joey back, then released him and said, "Okay, little man, we still have to unload the flyer."

The boy jumped off his lap and ran toward it. "When do I get my own sword?"

"When we finish our work. The deer meat needs to be cured, the supplies put away."

Joey's shoulders sagged. "That sounds like chores."

"But I promise fun stuff will follow. Besides, I have a surprise to give you."

"Really? What!"

"Not until after the work is finished." Ruben picked up

the deer carcass and tossed it over one shoulder. "Come on, let's get this done."

He handed a sack to Joey. Whiffs of flour flew into his face, causing him to sneeze several times. The big man chuckled as he moved into the cave. The flyer was emptied in record time.

*   *   *

Drayco and Shyanne rode into the small town, tired and hungry. They had ridden north for close to a week, trying to find Joseph's trail. They were unsuccessful.

The local townspeople said the inn was on the east side of town. When the twins saw it, they groaned.

"That's the inn? What were they thinking?"

"Drayco, this is a small town."

"Yes—but this? This is more like a house than an inn."

"It kind of reminds me of a bed and breakfast place."

The building was little bigger than a cottage. It had a well-maintained yard with a quaint little garden beside it. As they drew closer, an old man stepped onto the front porch.

"You two young people look ready to drop." He stepped off the porch and came alongside the horses. "Come on down off of there and bring yourselves inside. I have a nice warm fire waiting for company."

"What about our horses?" Shyanne asked as she dismounted. Her body ached everywhere.

"Young man," he said to Drayco as soon as his feet hit the ground, "put those fine looking animals in with Betsy. She won't mind."

He pointed to the side of the building opposite the garden. In their tired state, both had missed the enclosure standing there entirely. Drayco grabbed the reins from Shyanne just as the old man grabbed her arm. He guided her up the steps and onto the porch.

"Come with me, little lassie, the missus will be happy to have some female company for a change." A grin covered his face, exposing the few remaining teeth in his mouth. "She gets tired of listening to ole' Kilan all the time, likes to have new people to talk to."

Shyanne smiled and waved at her brother at the same time that Kilan towed her through the front door.

Drayco walked the exhausted horses around the side of the inn. The greeting he received when he opened the doors and led them inside surprised him.

Hhheehhawww—heeehaaww—heehaw—heehaw.

The sound grated on his tired nerves, like fingers scraping along a chalkboard, but he had to smile. What stood before him was the smallest donkey he had ever seen. The animal looked to be a cross between a burro and a donkey rather than pure donkey, though.

"You must be Betsy—pleased to meet you." He tipped his head toward the little creature.

Drayco pulled the much taller horses into the empty stalls located next to the occupied one. While he removed the saddle from Bravaro, Betsy reached her nose up toward Jack. They touched. The horse jerked back before snorting a greeting.

The size of the enclosure surprised Drayco. From the front, it seemed small, but once he was around the building, he saw it in its entirety. It was huge.

"The animals have more room than we do," he muttered under his breath.

After removing the saddle and bridle from each animal, he gave them a quick rubdown. With a departing pat for Bravaro, he returned to the front of the inn and walked through the front door. He was immediately handed a cup of hot cider by the wife of the old man.

"My, you are a handsome one, aren't you?" She glanced up at the gray streak in his dark hair. "And so mature looking too."

Blushing with embarrassment, Drayco accepted the cup. "Thank you."

"And has manners to boot. Not many young people have those these days." She smiled, causing the corners of her eyes to crinkle. Reaching up, she grabbed the hand not holding the cup and pulled him toward the fire. "Come, sit by the fire. Come...come."

Making sure the contents of the cup did not spill; he obliged her, allowing himself to be towed toward the fire and a seated Shyanne. A plush worn stool sat next to the high back chair occupied by his sister. He sat on it. Shyanne held a cup in her hands. She shrugged her shoulders and grinned when he glanced her way. The old woman disappeared after making sure he was comfortable.

"Well?" she asked.

"The horses are fine. They have a great companion—a little donkey named Betsy."

"I remember him saying something about Betsy when we arrived."

"Cutest little thing I've seen in a while."

Brother and sister sat in front of the fire sipping at their cider, quietly enjoying a moment of silence while watching the flames dance.

"Do you smell something?" Shyanne asked a short while later. She lifted her nose higher and took in a deep breath.

Following suit, Drayco said, "I do, but I'm not sure what it is."

"I think I know—I haven't smelled it in a long time."

Just as she was about to say what she thought, the old woman walked into the room with a large platter in her hands. Drayco set his cup down, rose, and took the heavy item from her.

"Oh thank you, young man. My arms just aren't what they used to be."

Small triangle sandwiches sat in the middle with sliced fresh fruit and, to Drayco's delight, oatmeal cookies on either side of the plate.

"Shyanne, look!" He balanced the plate on one hand and held up a cookie in the other.

"I haven't seen one of those in forever." Her eyes lit up like a child opening presents on Christmas morning.

He brought the food over and sat down on the floor, placing the plate on the vacated stool between them. They both bit into a cookie at the same time.

"Whoa—that is fabulous!"

"MMMmm–mmm–mmm–mmm–mm," was all Drayco could manage. His mouth was full of cookie.

The old woman stood with her hands clasped together, watching them, smiling. "I'm so happy you're pleased. It's good to be able to bake for others again."

"Thank you so much Mrs.—Mrs.—" Shyanne stammered.

"Oh my, did I forget to introduce myself?" She moved closer. "I'm Minificent, Mini for short."

"Mini, these are wonderful. I haven't seen, much less tasted anything like them since our mother made them."

The mention of their mother caused the smiles on the twin's faces to fade.

"Oh, I'm sorry, dearies. Has it been a long time since you lost her?"

"You have no idea," Drayco said.

"It seems like an eternity," Shyanne added.

Mini bent over and gave each one a hug. "Then I hope I've brought you some good memories to chase away the bad ones."

Shyanne whispered to the older woman as she hugged her, "You have, Mini—you have."

"If you don't mind my asking," She pulled back and placed a worn, wrinkled hand on Shyanne's abdomen, "when are you due?"

Shyanne had forgotten all about her swollen belly. Giving it a pat, she said, "soon." The child inside responded with a firm kick.

"Then let me get you some warm milk instead of that cider." Mini moved toward the kitchen. "The baby needs that more."

"Mini—please, don't. The cider is good enough." Her words went unheard; the woman was already gone.

"Just give up, sis. She's going to do it anyway." He picked up another cookie and bit half of it off. "These are heaven."

"Just like moms." Shyanne stared into the fire. The mention of her mother reminded her of the task they were trying to accomplish, to find her own son and bring him home.

As if reading her mind, Drayco said, "We'll find him, Shyanne. We will bring him home." He knew he was repeating himself. He hoped it would encourage her to believe in what he said. Picking up a sandwich, he continued. "First, though, we have to rest. We are both exhausted."

"But Drayco—the longer we take, the colder the trail becomes." Despair filled her voice. "I want my little boy in my arms again." A tear ran down her cheek.

"We'll start out first thing in the morning. Who knows, maybe this couple, or someone in this town, has seen or heard of Ruben and little Joey."

"Do you think so?" Hope replaced the despair as she wiped the wetness off her cheeks.

"We won't know unless we ask. Right now, you need food and rest." He handed her a small sandwich.

She took it from him, hesitated, then took a bite. The flavors of the meat and vegetables inside the hard bread made her mouth water. Without realizing, she finished it and three others off before she knew it.

"What about you?" She asked sheepishly after seeing him watch her eat.

"There's plenty. Mini's a wonderful hostess."

At the mention of her name, Mini strolled into the room holding a mug of the promised warm milk. Her husband followed behind her, another plate laden with more sandwiches and cookies in his hands. She gave the cup to Shyanne then eased herself into the easy chair opposite the one the twin was sitting in.

"These old bones just aren't what they used to be. They ache even when it's warm outside."

Kilan handed Drayco the plate before he pulled up another worn stool and sat next to his wife. "Don't let her fool ya, young man, she can keep up with the best of em." He winked at the dark twin. "She just likes to groan sometimes. Makes her feel better."

"Oh papa," Mini grabbed the hand resting on the arm of the chair arm and gave it a squeeze.

Drayco felt the love emanating from the old couple. It made him realize how lonely he was, how he wished he could find someone to care for, someone who would not be afraid of him. He stared into the yellow flames flickering in the fireplace. A hand touched his shoulder. He looked up at his sister and saw the concern in her eyes. He covered her hand with his, giving her a faint smile at the same time.

"What brings you two out this way?" The old man asked as he picked up a sandwich.

"We're looking for a man, a man who has a five year old child with him," Drayco said.

Kilan asked, "What you want with this man with the child?"

"He has my son," Shyanne said. The words were so soft. "He took him and I want him back."

"Oh dearie, that's horrible. Do you know where this

man went?"

"No."

"Papa, have you seen who they're talking about?"

"I don't know, mama. I don't know what he looks like."

"Oh—silly me." She smiled sheepishly at her husband.

"He's tall with long dark hair," Drayco started. "He has a strong face, is muscular, and has a dark tan."

"That sounds like Ruben." Kilan rubbed his chin, his face scrunched in thought.

Both Drayco and Shyanne leaned forward abruptly, their eyes focused on Kilan. Simultaneously they demanded, "You know him?"

"Not sure if it's him. Never seen him with a child."

"But you've seen him. When was he here last?" Drayco asked.

"He comes into town about every 14 days. Is that right mama?"

"Yes papa, he always has a kind word for us."

"When will he come again?" The words sounded like a plea to Shyanne.

"It's been about eight or nine day now—I think."

Drayco turned toward Shyanne, "I know I said we'd leave in the morning, but we need to stay. Rather than searching the countryside aimlessly for him, we'll let him come to us."

"I'm not sure he's the man you're after," Kilan warned.

Drayco turned back to the old man. "We'll find out shortly, won't we."

Nine

He knew Joseph would be mad at him for leaving the way he had, but that was not important. What mattered was finding Joey before anything happened to him. Drizzle continued his eastward trek.

A twinkling in the trees ahead caught his attention. When he drew closer, he saw it was a pond. With the taste of a recent kill still fresh in his mouth, he felt a drink would be refreshing. The cat hesitated before entering the pen area surrounding the body of water. Something was not right. It was too quiet. Holding his nose upward, he sniffed at the air.

The pungent odor of grosbark was thick, though it was not fresh. The scent of other recognizable creatures was present as well. Yet, like the grosbark, they were not fresh. Only one scent remained strong. It was the sweet smell of decay. It permeated every aspect of the clearing.

Why didn't I smell that before? He crinkled his nose in disgust. *That reek should have been obvious miles away.*

While he pondered how he could possibly have missed such a stench, a huge beast lumbered into the clearing. Its body was hairless except for the long growth hanging from its underbelly. Four arms protruded from the upper torso, each with wicked claws extending from the hands. Two stocky legs carried its bulk. Drizzle marveled at the quietness of the animal. He crouched lower to the ground to avoid detection by the many eyes scanning the area.

Satisfied that nothing waited to snatch its prize, the

beast waded into the pond. It bent over and groped into the murky depths. When its arms reemerged, the bloated, waterlogged body of a man came into view.

Drizzle suppressed a gag. He knew zindrell's were scavengers, but this was a bit much. He wanted to leave, horrified fascination kept him glued. He watched as the creature put an arm in its mouth and bit down with its many sharp teeth. The appendix came off easily.

The body wore the remains of a dingy colored red shirt with a no longer white sash around the waist. One boot was still on, but the other was gone. The cat recognized the clothing as that of a Wanderer, a roving gypsy type person.

His fascination fulfilled, he moved to leave the area. No drinkable water was to be found in this pond. The slight sound of his movement caught the zendrell's attention. He froze. It halted in its feeding and looked around with its many eyes. Drizzle hoped he had not been seen. He was not so lucky.

The zindrell emitted an ear-piercing whistle as it threw the remains of the body back into the water and charged toward the cat. Drizzle laid his ears back, baring his fangs in a hiss. He did not have time to waste battling the charging beast. It was defending its feeding ground and the cat wanted no part of what it defended.

He fled through the undergrowth with as much haste as the thick undergrowth would allow. A path worn by the passing of many feet appeared before him, allowing him to increase his speed. He left the pond with its horrible contents far behind. The zindrell did not follow. Fortunately, the cat was still heading east.

Drizzle stayed on the trail until it branched into several directions. Putting his nose to the ground, he caught a faint whiff of a scent he remembered from the farm: the scent of Ruben's horse. It reaffirmed that he was heading in the right direction.

The age of the scent told him the horse passed this way some time ago. It disappeared after a few paces. He weaved from side to side until he found the scent again, and continued with this method of tracking, finding the scent, losing it, finding it again, for miles. He knew the only way he would stop, especially now, was when he found the man and boy he sought.

Drayco heaved another bundle of straw into the freshly cleaned stalls. Gnats swarmed over his head, biting him whenever they could, making the job miserable. Hot and tired, he stopped to wipe the sweat from his brow. He saw Kilan leaning against the fence rail, watching. A bit of straw hung from his mouth. Drayco smiled at the sight. It reminded him of the farmers from long ago.

"I want to thank you again, young man. It's nice to get a break from this job."

"I can understand."

"Betsy thanks you too."

Drayco looked at the little donkey standing next to the old man. The horses were in the field behind the stable; their long necks bent low, their teeth chomping at the tall grass.

"My pleasure. Besides, it kills time while we wait."

Shyanne walked around the corner of the house carrying a tall mug in her hand. "I brought you something wet, compliments of Mini." She stopped a short distance away from her brother and waved the mug back and forth, singing, "You're gonna love it."

Drayco watched her antics, his eyes focused on the mug. "You know, sis, if you keep that up, I'll shrivel up like a raisin." He suddenly grabbed at his throat with both hands, and shouted, "Oh no! Too late! Shriveling process begun!" He fell to his knees and rolled over onto his back. Just as suddenly, he went limp, as if he had passed out.

At first, the old man looked concerned. He quickly realized the dark twin was only playing and not really hurt. Shyanne made a dramatic show of rushing to his side. She kneeled down beside him in the awkward way pregnant women do when their belly is huge. The mug tipped in the process, spilling some of its contents on Drayco's face. His tongue licked at the moisture close to his mouth. He opened his eyes.

"Lemonade—and sweetened at that." He propped himself up on an elbow and tried to take the mug from Shyanne.

She jerked it away from his outstretched arm. "Say

please."

"Please."

"With sugar on top."

"With sugar on top"

"And plum pudding on the side."

"Shyanne…."

"And raisins in the pudding."

"Shyanne…."

"And…."

"Shyanne—enough! Give me the mug—please!"

"Not until you say all those things," she pouted.

Drayco caught the mischievous twinkle in her eyes. Rolling his eyes skyward, he said, "Please with sugar on top and plum pudding with raisins on the side." He held his hand out for the mug.

"Okay, here you go." She handed it to over, handle facing toward him.

"Thank you."

"You're not welcome."

Gulping down more than half of the tangy, yet sweet contents, he smacked his lips afterward. "This is fabulous." He finished off the rest in one drink.

"Man, you can be such a pig sometimes."

"Thank you, your majesty." He rose to his feet and bowed deep to her. "Do you think your highness can get this lowly pig another?" He extended his hand to help her up.

Grasping the offered hand, Shyanne groaned as she struggled to her feet. "This belly is driving me crazy. I can't wait until she comes out."

"Let's not rush things, your majesty."

"Drayco—you're a goof." She reached up and ruffled his hair. "Give me that mug so I can get you some more."

"You are too kind to take such wonderful care of this unworthy pig." He bowed to her again.

"Don't you forget it, mister." With a swirl of her dress, she turned and retraced her steps into the house.

Drayco smiled as she walked away. *It has been a long time since Shyanne had this much fun. It was good to see.* Picking up the rake, he began to throw the straw around again.

Kilan shook his head. It was fun seeing the antics of the brother and sister played out. It reminded him of when his children were still young and living at home. They were all grown now, moved on with their lives. Holding the bit of straw in his mouth, he walked into the house to check on the women folk.

*   *   *

Sweat from the workout with his sword ran like rivers down Ruben's exposed upper body. Joey sat on a rock a short distance away, watching in awe. The boy held a smaller version of the sword in his hands, given to him after the chores were finished.

"What do you think, little man? Do you want to try?" He stepped back from the chipped and well-used sparing post in the center of the room.

"Can I?'

"Of course. Come on over."

Joey leaped off the rock and rushed over to the post. Grabbing the sword's handle with both hands, he swung it as hard as he could. It bounced off the hard wood and flew from the boys hands. Joey's eyes widened. He looked sheepishly up at the big man, expecting the yelling to start at any moment.

Ruben stared at the blade lying on the ground then at the boy cringing near it. Putting his hands on his hips, he leaned back and roared with laughter.

Joey could not believe his eyes. Instead of being screamed at, the man was laughing at him. That would never happen with his dad. He would have been furious and taken the sword away as punishment.

"You're not mad?"

"That was the funniest thing I've seen in a while. The look on your face was priceless." Ruben wiped a tear out of the corner of his eye. "But do me a favor next time—try hitting it with a little less force. You might have better results."

Joey scurried over to the sword and picked it up. With a determined look on his face, he returned to the sparing post. Gripping the weapon firmly, he swung it, though not as hard as before. The sound of metal slicing into wood echoed throughout the cave. The lad's face broke into a broad grin.

"Now that's the way to do it. You'll be an expert in no time."

"You really think so?" Eagerness filled Joey's voice.

"If you keep practicing, and take good care of the sword...then yes, I do."

The child ran over to Ruben and hugged him tight. "You're the best!"

"Be careful, little man. I don't want to become your first victim."

"Oh...sorry." He Yanked the hand holding the sword away from Ruben's body, again looking sheepish.

"It's okay. Now, what do you say we take a little break and eat something?"

"Do we hafta?"

"We need to stay strong to fight. To do that, we have to eat."

Right on cue, the boy's stomach growled loudly. He covered the traitor with his empty hand. "I guess we have to."

Placing a hand on Joey's shoulder, Ruben steered him toward the doorway. The big man was pleased with the bond he was building with the boy. If by some chance the parents did find the cave, he hoped it was strong enough to keep him at his side. He liked the feeling of being a father and did not want it to end. Returning to the main room, they enjoyed a meal fit for a king.

*   *   *

Joseph strode into the kitchen, moving toward Hana. He no longer wobbled when he walked; his endurance had increased greatly with the passing of time. A ruddy color filled his cheeks as he straightened the pack on his shoulder.

"It has been a week since Drizzle left. I can't take this inactivity any longer. I'm going after him."

Hana glanced up from her needlecraft, "You are better, that is true. Do you require food for the travel?"

Joseph was glad she had not objected. "Only if you can spare some." He already owed her so much.

Hana set her work on the table, rose to her feet, and moved toward the cabinets. "I have plenty. This year was good for growing things."

She pulled down several items and placed them on the countertop, then moved to another storage area where she grabbed a pack. Returning to the previous spot, she placed the items inside.

"I have a pack. I don't need another."

"This is not for you."

Picking up the pack, she moved to the opposite side of the kitchen. She looked at the small pouches stored there. After a minute, she pulled out several and placed them inside as well.

"What do you mean...not for me?"

"This pack is not for you." The tone was matter of fact.

He realized what she meant and frowned. "You're not coming. I won't allow it."

"It is not for you to decide. Only I can say what is allowed for me." She flipped the top over and tied it shut. Picking the pack up, she moved toward the exit.

That was when he realized she wore riding clothes instead of her usual flowing dresses. "Wait. What about this place? You can't just go away and leave no one here to care for it."

I anticipated your leaving and sent word to someone I trust. He is already here. He will care for the animals."

"I haven't seen anyone."

"You have not been looking. You have been preoccupied with the thoughts of finding your son."

"Hana—I can't take you with me. It wouldn't be right."

Ignoring him, she went outside. Exasperated, he followed. They walked to the stables: one without hesitation, the other with great reluctance. Inside, Joseph saw two horses saddled and ready to go.

"You planned on coming with me all along, didn't you?"

"Yes."

"Why?"

"You may feel better, but you are still not well." She emphasized the last word. "Plus, your son may need help. This way it will be there instead of delayed."

Joseph saw her logic. Yet, he still did not like the idea.

She grabbed the reins of one of the horses. Locking her gaze on his, she said, "You can either continue to stand there doing nothing, or you can follow and find you son." She waited for his next move.

He remained silent, lips pressed tight. A second later, he nodded his head. Joseph moved to the other horse, secured his pack behind the saddle, grabbed the reins, and pulled it toward the door. He was almost to the exit when the horse flicked its head in a nervous manner.

"Chikara, I need you to stay. I will return as early as possible."

The cat came into view. She sat on her haunches and locked eyes with the speaker, her eyes glowing in the gloom-filled interior.

After what seemed like an eternity to the waiting man, Hana said, "Chikara, please."

Chikara's tail jerked back and forth in rapid successive movements. Suddenly, she left without looking back. Sadness filled Hana's eyes as she stared at the spot recently vacated by the cat. She knew Chikara was angry about being left behind, but the horses were afraid her. They became unmanageable each time she drew close. This lack of control was not an option for the journey ahead. With a heavy sigh, she pulled her horse outside.

"Is everything okay?" Joseph said once they were out in the open.

"Yes."

He waited to see if she would say anything else. When she did not, he got into the saddle. He looked over to see her settling into hers.

"Drizzle and I were heading east before the incident with the river. I think that is the direction we need to go now."

"Then that is the direction we shall take." Hana nodded her head toward the road. "We should start there."

The road was a main thoroughfare into the area and wide enough for both to ride side by side. While they traveled in silence, Joseph glanced at the woman next to him several times.

Finally, he asked, "Hana how is it that you have a humecat?"

"I don't have her." Hana faced Joseph. "Chikara decides to stay on her own. And for as long as I can remember, she has always been with me."

""Do you know if there are others?"

"There may be, though I have never seen one before Drizzle. One should never rule out such things."

"Has your family always lived here?"

"My parents died a long time ago." Her look became distant. "I was raised by my grandfather."

"I didn't see him. Is he still around?"

"So many questions, Joseph. What is it you seek?"

"I'm sorry. I'm running off at the mouth again. My wife accuses me of driving her crazy with it." The mention of Shyanne caused Joseph's voice to fade into silence.

"Where is she now?"

"I left her at home. But I'll bet she's not there anymore." A slight smile creased his face. "She's eight months pregnant with our second child. Joey is our first."

"I heard you talking about them when you were sick. Is Joey the one you are seeking?"

"Yes. Him and the man who took him." The words were thick with hatred. "I have an old score to settle with Ruben, an old one and now a new one."

"Why would Ruben want to hurt your son?"

The questions continued in this fashion: Hana asking, Joseph answering, as they rode toward the east in a slow steady manner. He never realized how effectively she had redirected the conversation off herself and on to him.

Later, when the sun was just above the treetops, gradually making its way behind them, Joseph asked, "Hana, do you know of someplace around here to stay?"

A traveling hut is just up the road. I warn you, it may be occupied, it is well known."

"I don't care, so long as whoever is there doesn't cause any trouble." He reached up and touched the sword riding in the scabbard on his back.

Hana smiled. She saw the stooped posture of exhaustion, the dark circles under his eyes. The illness suffered from the near drowning had taken it toll on Joseph, though he refused to admit it.

"There it is."

A shamble of a building came into view. The walls looked sturdy enough to keep unwanted thing out, though. No windows broke its smooth surface.

"I don't see any signs of others staying here. No horses."

"The horses are stored inside to keep them safe."

"Stay here. Let me check it out first." He prodded his horse into a faster pace as Hana drew hers to a stop.

Joseph halted outside the door and jumped down. He almost crumpled to his knees because of the growing weakness that was gaining control of his body. The hand gripping the saddle horn was the only thing that kept him upright. He glanced over his shoulder to see if Hana had witnessed anything. Her gaze was directed elsewhere. With a determination driven by pride, he strode to the door, making sure his steps were straight.

The door was slightly ajar. Pulling out his sword, he pushed it open with the blade. Light from the setting sun shined through the doorway into the room beyond. Nothing moved. A few chairs and a table were all he noticed. He stepped inside and saw a fireplace with wood piled next to it against one wall, an opening to another room opposite it. Behind the main entrance, he discovered sleeping mats rolled up and hanging on pegs.

He ventured into the other room. It was the storage area for the horses, like Hana mentioned. The pungent smell of dropping hung in the air. Moving back to the fireplace, he found warm embers. Joseph used a set of tongs to light several candles positioned throughout the room. He returned to the main door and waved to Hana, indicating it was safe for her to approach.

"The place is empty, but it hasn't been that way for long."

"It is well known and used often," she said as she dismounted.

Both took their horses inside, fed them, and bedded them down for the night. Joseph lit the fire. The smoke slid up the chimney, leaving the living area clear. While he set up the sleeping mats, Hana started the meal. In short order, the wonderful aroma of spiced meat filled every nook in the place.

"I bet the previous occupants didn't eat as well as we will," Joseph said as he inhaled the wonderful scents deeply.

"It will be finished in a few minutes."

"I can't wait."

The door to the building swung open abruptly and two large, dirty men stepped inside. Joseph and Hana jumped when the door slamming against the wall.

"Neither can we."

Hana composed herself quickly. "There is plenty. Please have a seat. The flat bread will be ready soon."

Joseph watched with open suspicion as the men moved across the room to the table. They pulled out chairs and flopped into them.

"Boy, am I beat," one said.

"It's been a long ride since the last town." The other glanced over at Hana while he spoke; his eyes traveled up and down her slim body. "Is it very far to the next?"

"Not far, a short distance to the west."

Hana tossed the flat bread over in the pan. One of the men rose and walked toward her. Joseph bristled.

"It's okay, little man. Rajan won't hurt your woman. To us, married women are sacred."

"She's not my woman." The words were out before he could stop himself.

The looks on the men's faces changed. They no longer saw a woman who was untouchable. They saw a plaything. Joseph attempted to rise to his feet, but the man sitting next to him backhanded him across the face. He tumbled over the chair and landed hard on his side, knocking the wind out of him. While he lay there gasping, he watched in anguish as the men advanced on the little woman.

Hana remained where she was, calmly watching the advancing intruders. "This is a safe house for all. If you wish to disturb the sanction of the place, please do it somewhere else." Both ignored her.

"Did you know this was a sanctuary Lyon?"

"Nope, you?"

"Nope. Guess that means its okay then."

She's defenseless—without a weapon—and I can't help her. Joseph thought as he tried to suck in a breath. *Damn this weakened state!*

Before either man reached her, Hana raised an arm, exposing an opening in the flowing fabric of her sleeve. She grasped the object hidden there and brought it out. The sound of metal clanking against metal echoed across the room. A wooded rod was in her hand while another hung from a short bit of chain.

"What's this—a little toy to play with? I prefer the

fleshy kind myself." Rajan ran his tongue across his lips in anticipation.

"Me too, partner." Lyon made a crude gesture toward Hana.

The little woman stood her ground, rod swinging back and forth in front of her. No emotion showed on her face. Rajan moved as fast as lightning to force himself on her, but she was not there.

SMACK!

The rod landed hard on one of his extended arms, breaking the bones underneath with a resounding crack. Rajan bellowed with pain as he went down. Snarling, Lyon lunged at her. In the blink of an eye, he was bouncing off the wall, a red line planted across his cheek. He fell to the floor, dazed.

Joseph's mouth hung open in surprise. Did he really witness what just happened? One second ago, Hana was being attacked, the next, she was in complete control of the situation.

What kind of weapon is it? He stared at the rod swinging in her hand, forgetting he was short of breath.

"Since you gentlemen decided to tarnish this place, I would appreciate it if you left."

Rajan looked at her, his eyes filled with pain. "Lady—is you crazy? It's dark outside."

"You should have thought of that before acting. Now you must pay the consequences."

"But—it's not safe."

Joseph rose to his feet, his breathing back to normal. "You heard the lady. It's time to leave!" He pulled his sword out to emphasize the words.

Raja inched his way to his companion's side. "Hey—hey Lyon—let's go." Shaking a shoulder, he tried again. "Hey—Lyon, let's go!" He glanced at Hana to make sure she had not moved. Lyon shook his head, trying to clear it. It didn't work. "Come on, get up!" Rajan tugged the man to his feet, dragging him toward the door.

"There's an inn about twenty miles down the road. If you're quick enough, you might make it," Hana said.

After the door was closed and the bolt latched, Joseph turned to the woman, "You directed them to your inn."

"Quite the irony, isn't it? They try to hurt me, and instead, I make money off of them." She touched a pointer finger to her lips, her brow furrowed, "that is if they get there." she shrugged, "Oh well, I believe I got the better end of the deal."

He smirked. "You surprise me. Here I think you are defenseless and I'm unable to protect you. Then you kick the snot out of them." He directed his gaze to the rods gripped in her hands. "What are those called?"

"These are called nunchaku. An old weapon of sorts," She flipped open her sleeve, revealing a holder on her arm. "I love them for their simplicity." When the weapon was out of sight, she said, "Now how about that meal. I hope the bread isn't burnt."

Joseph shook his head as he moved back to the table and sat down after picking up the chair. *This is going to be an interesting journey.*

Ten

Drizzle lost track of time, his concentration was focused on searching for the ever-elusive horse scent. For many days now, the scent was getting stronger. Tall hills covered with thick trees surrounded him. Caves dotted the countryside.

If he's hiding in one of those caves, I will find him. I owe it to Shyanne—and to Joey.

With the stubborn determination he was born with, he started into a valley. After an hour of weaving through undergrowth, along with investigating the various caves he found, Drizzle located fresh horse prints in the dirt. He knew he was close.

I have to be cautious now. I don't want Ruben to see me before I see him.

Moving with the silence of his breed, he slid from one patch of growth to another, checking the area ahead each time before moving. He froze when a rustling noise sounded close to his position. A bush swayed as if something brushed against it. He was downwind so he was unable to scent whatever was there.

The cat ducked down just before the branches parted. A small female deer stepped into view, causing his stomach to respond with a growl. No food had entered the cavity for days and it was expressing an opinion about the idea. Drizzle cursed the creature before him.

The cat watched as it grazed, its tail flitting around

rapidly. He decided to kill it when it was close enough to do so successfully, thus shutting up the void for a while. In his favor, the wind had changed directions. It now blew his scent away from the deer. Waiting until it came up beside him, he lunged at the exposed throat.

He nearly had it.

The deer sensed that a predator was close and suddenly leaped sideways, throwing his aim off. Drizzle's claws sank in to the soft tissue of its shoulder, but not deep enough to bring it down. The deer shook off its attacker, leaving gashes where the claws once held. It fled into the trees before the cat could get another try at it.

Damn.

He remembered his mission and, again, cursed to himself. *I hope that blasted creature doesn't run into Ruben. If he spots it, he might put two and two together.*

What Drizzle did not know was that Ruben was nowhere in the area. He and Joey were off on a restock mission.

* * *

Ruben watched with pride as Joey guided the flying machine to the designated landing site, a small clearing with tall grass and even taller trees surrounding it. The craft set down without the slightest bump.

"That was great! You don't need my help anymore."

The boy beamed at the taller man. "Can I take it out on my own sometime?"

"Not just yet. I need to make sure you can fix her if she breaks down."

Joey's enthusiasm deflated like a released balloon.

"Don't worry, little man—at the rate you're going, that will be in no time." Ruben placed a hand on the boys shoulder and squeezed it.

"I'm glad you let me stay, Mr. Ruben."

"You're my son now, remember? Or do you not want me to call you that any longer?" Ruben put just the right amount of hurt in his tone. "Do you want to go back to your family instead, the one that didn't want you?"

Joey opened his young eyes wide; a look of shock filled them. "Mr. Ruben, I don't want to go back. I want to stay here. I have more fun with you!" He wrapped his little arms around the big waist, stretching them as far as they would go. "Please don't make me go back."

The words made Ruben's heart swell. He had achieved the ultimate revenge on the people whom he felt had ruined his life. Moreover, he had gotten a son in the process without having to endure the nagging of a woman.

"Do you think you could start calling me dad? We've been together for a little while now and I would really enjoy that a lot." He squat down and lifted the child up onto one leg.

Joey hesitated. The feelings he had about going back to his father were strong, but the fear of rejection was stronger. He threw his arms around Ruben's neck and said, "Dad."

"Thank you, son." Ruben hugged him tight before standing up. "Now, I need you to stay with the flying platform. Can you do that for me?"

"Can't I come with you? I promise to be good and stay out of the way."

"Little man, what I ask you to do is a very important job. If someone were to find this and wreck it, we would have to walk all the way home. That's a long way."

"Yea," Joey replied, his face frowned with concern.

"Can you make sure it stays safe for me?"

Joey stood erect with his arms straight at his side, his face full of seriousness, and said, "Yes sir!"

I will be back in an hour or two. Use your sword if you must—don't be afraid to kill. And don't leave the craft for any reason, understood?"

Joey pulled his sword out of its scabbard and held it up high. "You can count on me!"

Ruben returned the lad's salute with his own sword. "If you do a good job, I'll bring something back for you." A smile broke the serious look for only a moment. He kept his own smile hidden when Joey began to march back and forth.

The big man turned and disappearing into the trees. He had the boy land a couple of miles from the town to avoid being seen by the locals. Like Joey was when he first saw the machine, they would be fearful of it. And of the one who rode it. He could not afford that. He enjoyed this town and the comforts it provided, both materialistic and human.

His usual route into town took him past the inn. He liked the old couple who ran it. They reminded him of the grandparents he remembered but knew so little about. Like his parents, they died when he was little. Raiders looking for things to benefit their lives, the easy way, killed them. He escaped and learned to live by the law of the street. It was that or die. To him, that was not an option.

He hit the jackpot when he met the Boss. She paid him well until those bastard twins ruined everything. It took him more years than he cared to admit to come anywhere near the lifestyle he was used to. The anger at the injustice done to him smoldered inside. Most times, he kept it under control. When he felt it growing out of hand, he found something to kill.

On a good day, he found a lone man or a man with his family traveling alone and killed them all. Men, women, children—it didn't matter. The rush he felt with the release of their blood was better than a soft female body in his arms, especially if they screamed for mercy long and loud. The growing pressure inside told him he needed to find a release soon. The only thing that kept it in check currently was the boy.

The store he used came into view. He entered confidently, looking around at the faces inside. None was new. He strode up to the counter, placed his order with the owner, and handed him his empty bags before moving into the eating area. Ruben knew to return in half an hour to pick up the goods. It was a ritual performed many times over the years.

As soon as he crossed the threshold, a woman shouted at him.

"Ruben!"

"Baby!" He never could remember her name.

The woman who looked to be in her mid thirties dressed in a low cut white shirt and flowing skirt rushed over to the big man, arms opened wide. He enveloped her in his huge arms and grabbed her firm bottom with both hands. She planted a kiss full of suggestions on his lips.

"Are you staying long?" She asked after they separated.

"Can't this time."

"Aww, Rubie—I missed you." She leaned close, her flowing mane of curly brown hair cascading over her shoulder. "I'll let you tie me up again."

"Baby, you don't know how you tempt me" He moved a hand to one of her breasts and squeezed.

The local patrons were used to the open display shown by this pair; they had witnessed it many times before. Almost as one, they rolled their eyes and looked away.

Ruben bent over and kissed each breast. "See you girls later."

He walked over to his table and sat down. If other patrons occupied it, they left when he towered over them, glaring, his tall muscular frame intimidating them into moving. If they did not, he helped them to leave the hard way.

"You want the usual?" Erika asked. She had followed him to the table.

"Yea. And bring me an ale." He smacked her bottom as she walked away.

She returned with the drink and set it on the table. Ruben grabbed her around her slim waist and pulled her into his lap. She giggled as he nibbled on her neck.

"Did you really mean it when you said you'd let me tie you up again?" His breath was hot on her neck.

"Only as long as you don't get mean or rough like the last time. I almost couldn't work."

"I promise to be more gentle." He reached under her shirt and rubbed her bare skin. She stifled herself by kissing him.

"When?" She whispered after moving her lips to his ear.

"Tomorrow—I'll come for you late in the evening."

"I'll wait for you out back, like the last time."

"Baby—you're too good to me." He pushed her off his lap and shoved her toward the kitchen. "Now go get me my food, woman—I'm starved."

"I bet you are," she said as she blew him a kiss. "And it's Erika, remember?"

He threw his hands in the air and shrugged his shoulders, grinning like a kid caught with his hand in the cookie jar.

Half an hour later, when the food and drink were gone and the bill paid for, Ruben returned to the store. His bags sat next to the counter, ready.

"Here you go Ruben. How are you paying this time?"

The big man pulled out ten gold coins. He placed them in front of the owner. "Like this, Lentril." He put two more beside the others. "Buy Whittney some of that fine fabric you have over there, some of that shimmery stuff."

"You know I don't have to buy it for my wife. If she wants some, she can get it anytime."

"If you don't want it, I can always take it back." Ruben reached for the extra coins.

Lentril scooped up every coin on the counter before Ruben could touch them. He tucked them away just as fast.

"On the other hand, I did see a bolt of fabric during my travels that I know she would love."

Ruben smiled.

The owner liked the big man, especially for the money he brought into the store. But he wished he wouldn't smile. It had the quality of a hungry beast ready to tear its next meal apart. "See you in about two weeks?"

"About then," Ruben answered as he shouldered his bags. He grabbed a carrot from a bin standing close to the door, waving it at Lentril as he exited. "For Betsy."

Lentril waved. A huge sigh escaped when the big man disappeared from sight. He was glad to do business with Ruben, but also glad the visits were short. Something about him caused the owner to feel lucky he remained alive every time they parted.

Ruben started back the way he came, twirling the carrot between his fingers. He whistled a catchy tune he remembered hearing in his travels while he walked. Several boys ran past him, yelling about who would catch the biggest fish. Each carried a fishing stick tight in their grasp. Thoughts of Joey entered his mind. His feelings for the boy grew stronger with each day. He hoped they would stay so, especially after the test he planned for tomorrow.

I think I'll get some of Mini's cookies when I give Betsy her carrot, he thought. *Joey will love them.*

He followed the road until he saw the inn. Instead of going up to the door, he went around to the back. No animals were in the field because it was later in the afternoon. He knew the elderly couple would be sitting in front of the fire warming themselves, as he had seen them do on other occasions.

He opened the doors to the stable and stepped into the darkness beyond, halting long enough for his eyes to adjust to the gloom. Once he could make out the objects surrounding him, he moved to where Betsy was kept. The little donkey met him at the rail. She nuzzled his outstretched hand. It was empty. Smelling what used to be there, she moved down to his waist. The carrot poked out of his belt. She bit the floppy bit of green stem and jerked her head upward. It slipped out with ease. With another jerk, the carrot flew into the air and landed in her mouth.

The sound of crunching echoed as she chewed, her eyes closed in contentment. Ruben scratched behind one of her ears. Another sound caught his attention. It was the sound of something big moving around. He looked toward the back of the building, trying to find the source. Darkness shrouded everything. Leaving his bags with the donkey, he moved to get a better look. What he saw made his blood boil with rage.

A tall bay colored horse with a white blaze on its forehead stood next to a dark horse with a speckled butt. Ruben recognized the beasts immediately; they belonged to those bastard twins, the ones who ruined his very profitable life.

"How did they find me?" he whispered as he glanced to the right and left, making sure no one was in the stable watching him. His guard up, he thoroughly searched the building. He found no one except the animals. Standing next to his bags, He pondered what to do.

"Joey."

The thought of Drayco and Shyanne finding and taking the boy from him flooded the big man with dread. He picked up the bags as if they weighed nothing and backtracked to the side of the inn. He paused, listening. Before he could move, someone stepped onto the front porch.

Shyanne walked outside, no longer able to take the stuffiness or the inactivity. She grabbed the railing surrounding the porch and leaned onto her arms, watching the distant glowing ball as it made its way over the tops of the nearby trees. She didn't really see the view. Her thought were far away. Drayco moved up behind her. He rested his hands on her shoulders.

"He'll show soon, sis. I know he will."

"Are you sure? Are you really sure?" she asked. "Because he hasn't yet. It's been so long already."

"Yes," he replied, his tone confident. "Mini said he would."

Ruben knew they were talking about him. For the first time since he knew the couple, he cursed the old woman.

"How do we know she isn't senile? She seems a bit out of sorts at times."

"Kilan agreed with her."

Again, Ruben cursed silently.

"But Drayco..."

Drayco spun his sister around, "Shyanne—I'm the one who doubts everything—not you. What's really eating at you?"

"Do you really need to ask?" Her words were full of emotion.

"Yes. I know you. If I don't push, you clam up."

She hung her head, "I miss Joey. I want him home." She sighed heavily. "I miss my husband and that silly ole cat—and my quiet life." She looked up, tears running down her cheeks. "I want them all back. I want them back before the baby is born. I want my family complete again." Her hands moved to her swollen belly.

Hugging his sister against his body, Drayco said, "We will find them, little sis. You and your family will be back together in no time."

Drayco did not say what was really on his mind. He knew that no matter what, even if he had to hunt day and night, he would find the man who stole Joey. He would find him, kill him, and bring the boy back to his family— whether his sister was with him or not.

"I love you, big brother."

"Love you too, little sis."

Throwing an arm over his sister's shoulder, Drayco walked Shyanne back inside the building. Ruben smiled. It was the smile Lentril hated, the smile of death.

He waited a few minutes more before starting toward the hidden flyer. He knew he was having an impact on the twins, wearing them down. He also knew the group was separated. Now all he had to do was figure a way to end the local problem quickly before seeking an end to the rest of the problem.

He continued toward his destination with a smile locked on his face, his step bouncier than it was when he arrived.

Joey sat on the edge of the floating thing looking at the clouds above. The sword given to him by Ruben lay across his lap. The first half hour, he marched from one end of the flyer to the other, making sure nothing bothered it. When nothing did, he became bored. There was only so much attention span inside an active youngster. Sword practice with a sapling helped pass more time. After a while, that grew tiresome too. Now all he wanted was for Ruben to return.

He thought about his mom and dad. The thought faltered when he remembered the words told to him. The ones about them not loving him anymore. Those words hurt. He knew Ruben wouldn't stop loving him. He promised. And Joey knew he would keep his promise, he had so far. However, deep inside, he still loved his parents. He wanted to call the big man dad. It felt awkward, though. Maybe it would be easier later on.

He moved the sword beside him and stretched out on the platform, using his hands as a pillow. That was where Ruben found him, asleep, curled into a ball on his side. The big man smiled. It was not the smile of death; it was the kind of smile given by a loving parent.

Moments like this caused the raging anger inside to calm. Because of it, he wanted more than ever to keep Joey at his side. Killing Joseph and Shyanne, along with Drayco, was the only way he could see to accomplish that. The boy satisfied a burning need, the need for someone to love and trust. Two things he had not done for a very long time.

"Joey. Wake up Joey."

Kneeling next to the platform, Ruben reached out and touched a small shoulder. Joey jumped away from the touch, leaving his sword behind. His eyes barely open, he searched for whatever woke him. Ruben's face came into focus. The boy lunged forward, wrapping his arms around the large neck.

"You're back! I knew you'd come back!"

Startled by the suddenness of the boy's reaction, he grabbed the railing to prevent himself from toppling over. He pat on the small back, and said, "You didn't think I'd leave you, now did you? Family doesn't leave family." Ruben picked up Joey and tossed him over a broad shoulder. "You're my son now, you're family."

Joey squealed, "Yeah!"

Ruben exaggerated the up and down motion of his steps toward the discarded bags, causing Joey to huff with each bounce. "I have something for you—a surprise."

"What is it? What is it?" Joey yelled, kicking with delight. "Can I have it?"

"I won't be able to show it to you if you kill me with those flying legs," Ruben said with a laugh.

Joey froze. He lay as still as possible, except for the bouncy steps taken by the big man. It had been a long time since anyone had given him a surprise and he did not want to mess things up, especially since this was the second one in so many days. As they closed on the bags, he no longer found himself resting across a shoulder, but rolling toward the ground at breakneck speed. His mouth hung open in shock when his feet plopped on the ground and he remained in an upright position. The hands under his arms helped. A giggle crept up his throat. It exploded from him when he recovered from the fright.

"That was fun! Can we do it again?"

"Why not."

In an instant, Joey found himself back in the big man's arms rolling downward again. The process was repeated several times. Each time, the boys face lit up like a shiny coin.

"More! More!" Joey shouted, bouncing on his toes when Ruben was forced to stop.

"What about your surprise?"

"Oh yeah!"

Joey watched with wide-eyed fascination as Ruben opened one of the larger bags and reached inside. Concentration covered the man's face as he groped around the interior.

"Ow—ow—oowww!"

Suddenly, Ruben flung his body back as if he was trying to get away from the bag. It seemed like he was unable to break free from whatever had his hand.

Joey stumbled backwards. He had no idea what was in there. The only sounds heard were the moans coming from Ruben. *Whatever has him must be bad. I have to free him if I can.* He glanced over his shoulder at the forgotten weapon. By the time he returned his gaze to the big man, Ruben was laughing.

The trapped arm emerged from the bag. No bite marks covered it. No blood dripped from the fingers. Instead, a small brown package materialized in the hand. "This is for you."

Joey wasn't sure if he wanted to take the package. Looking at the injury free hand, he moved his eyes to the big man's face and realized he was being teased.

"Why you…."

He snatched the package and shredded the paper covering, revealing the contents inside. A pair of soft leather boots, exactly like the ones worn by Ruben, fell out. The boy stared at them in disbelief.

"Well—you going to put them on or just leave them there?"

Joey flopped down and ripped off his old worn shoes. They went flying into the nearby bushes. He picked up one of the new boots and flipped it into the air, about ready to shove his foot inside when something shiny fell out, barely missing his other foot. A small boot knife stood tip down in the ground.

"Watch out there, little man, you don't want to cut off any toes."

Joey looked up, his eyes large as saucers "Is that for me?"

"It's too small for me. Besides, my son needs a knife if he's to learn sly combat tricks from his ole' dad."

"Wow!"

Joey put the boot down and carefully picked up the knife, turning it this way and that, causing the sunlight to reflect off both sides of the blade.

"It goes like this." Ruben lifted his pant leg and showed the boy where his knife was located in his boot. "See inside yours? That's where you put it when wearing them. Keeps it hidden and handy."

"Wow," Joey said again.

Ruben lowered his pant leg and looked skyward at the sinking sun. "Put the boots on, son. We need to head back before it gets too dark for the flyer to work.

The boy yanked the boots on quickly and shoved the knife in the holder. He jumped to his feet and ran to the control panel, shouting. "I get to fly! I get to fly!"

Ruben followed, shaking his head. After he had the bags stowed away in the compartments and was standing beside him, an excited Joey pushed the button to start the flyer. Like a pro, the boy maneuvered it out of the hiding spot. He started east, as instructed. Several miles passed before he turned in a southeasterly direction toward the cave.

What both failed to see during the takeoff was the old man standing close to a tree, watching everything.

Eleven

Drayco was sitting on the porch enjoying the warmth brought by the gentle breeze, his chair leaning back on two legs when Kilan came into sight. The elder man was shaking his head, a bewildered look on his face. The dark twin heard him muttering under his breath as he drew closer.

"Damndest thing I ever seen." His eyes were focused on the road before him. "Maybe I'm going senile. I am 73 years old, after all." He tisked his tongue against the roof of his mouth several times. "Mama will be so disappointed—but then again—maybe not. Won't have to put up with my ranting on about things." Kilan knew better. They had been together far too long for that to ever happen.

Drayco set the legs of the chair down and rose to his feet. Moving to the steps leading up to the porch, he waited for the man. Kilan, not paying attention to where he was going, nearly plowed him over. Drayco caught him before he could fall down the steps.

"Oh—sorry there, young man."

"What's the matter?"

"Not sure. Might just be me is all."

Drayco waited in silence. He saw that Kilan wanted to say more, but he hesitated, as if formulating how to say what he wanted. After a moment of consideration, he moved to one of the chairs and sat down, indicating for Drayco to follow. When the dark man was seated next to him, Kilan continued.

"Ever seen something that made you question your ability?"

"Ability?"

"Yea—ability." Kilan tapped his temple with a finger.

"Oh, that ability. Not in a long time." Drayco's eyes took on a distant look before he refocused them on the older man. "Why do you ask?"

"I think my old age is finally catching up to me." He eased himself back in the chair and crossed his legs in front of him.

"Kilan, what's got you so worried?"

"I'm not sure I want to say. You might think me nuts before I really am."

"I won't—I promise."

Kilan glanced at the twin sitting next to him. All he saw was concern: no smile, no smirk, no laughter in the eyes watching him...only concern. With a nod of his head, he decided to trust Drayco and tell what he saw.

"I was walking around in the forest, like I sometimes do." Kilan picked up a twig blown onto the porch by the last storm. "I thought I heard voices so I went to check it out." The twig twirled between two fingers. Drayco could tell he was nervous.

"Most times, the voices I hear turn out to be kids out for a jaunt." He winked at Drayco. "If you get what I mean."

Drayco listened to Kilan droned on about the townspeople and some of their, in his opinion, annoying habits. He had almost phased out like he used to when his father lectured him when a couple of words brought his attention back with a snap. One was the word flying and the other was Ruben. He shot to his feet, startling the man next to him.

"Did you just say you saw Ruben?"

"Weren't you paying attention?" The older man looked up at Drayco in amazement. His gaze fell and his head started shaking back and forth as he muttered, "Wants me to tell him about my thinking I'm going nuts and don't even listen while I'm tell'n it." He crammed the end of the twig into the corner of his mouth, letting the man next to him know how frustrated he was by his lack of attentiveness.

"Kilan—please. Tell me what you said."

Kilan glared at Drayco. The desperation in the dark eyes staring at his helped the older man relax. He sighed.

"All right, I'll say it again." He spit the twig out. "I had to stop and relieve myself when I heard these voices. I snuck up, expecting to see a couple of kids doing the he-she thing. Instead, I see Ruben. He was talking to a boy. I don't remember seeing the kid before. Figured he was here visiting family or something. Anyways, I see the kid take a pair of boots out of a package and put them on. He seemed really happy."

Drayco kept the excitement from his voice. "What happened next?"

"He tossed a perfectly good pair of shoes into the brush. Young people these days...don't know how to save a thing."

Before the older man could go off on another storytelling event, Drayco asked, "Can you describe the boy?"

Kilan scrunched up his face, thinking. "He was about this high." He held his hand up to about where Shyanne described Joey's height to be. "And he had brown hair with hazel eyes."

This time, he could not keep the excited tone from his voice. "When they left, did you see which direction they went?"

"That's the funny part." He glanced up at the dark twin. "I saw where they went, all right; but my old eyes nearly bugged out when I saw how they went." He emphasized the word how. "I saw this thing they were stand'n on go straight up into the air and fly off like a bird, only it didn't have wings. The boy grabbed a stick poking out of the tall part near the front; he seemed to be telling it where to go with that."

"Are you sure?" The excitement of finding Ruben and Joey shattered after Drayco heard Kilan's words.

"I told you you'd think I was nuts. You may not be say'n so, but I can tell you think so." Kilan lifted his bottom and shifted his position in the chair. His old bones were not used to sitting in one spot for too long.

"I don't think that, not in the least."

"At times like this, I wonder myself." He steepled his fingers and gazed off into the field beyond the house.

"Don't. You're fine, I'm sure of it." Drayco moved to the door. He stopped before going inside. Remembering his previous unanswered question, he asked again. "Can you remember which direction they went?"

Kilan raised his arm. "That way." He pointed toward the east. "I lost sight of them quick because of the sun was glaring in my old eyes."

"Kilan, thanks, you helped a lot." Drayco stepped inside and shut the door.

The old man wiggled a foot, a nervous habit he had tried to break over the years. It annoyed Mini. For the most part, he was successful, except in times of stress like now. He was not sure if the young man believed him or was just humoring an old man. He sure acted like he did, but a nagging doubt still filled him. Rising to his feet, Kilan made his way to the stables.

A long bray met him. Betsy extended her neck, trying to find the carrot he usually hid in his clothes. She found it in his pocket. While she munched contentedly on the treat, Kilan swore he would never tell the story of the flying contraption again. He pulled out another carrot and leaned against the railing. The sound of crunching, from both man and animal, echoed throughout the enclosure.

Drayco found Shyanne rolled on to her side in the bed curled into a tight ball. Her arms were folded over her stomach. She looked like she was in agony.

"You okay?"

She clenched her teeth together, unable to answer. Sweat covered her brow. Her hair was drenched with it, as well. He moved quickly to the bed and kneeled beside her. Finally, the spasm passed and she relaxed her tense position.

"God that was a bad one."

"Are you in labor?" He hoped not. He knew how important it was to her to have the family reunited before the birth.

"I don't think so. I'm still a couple of weeks away from my due date." She uncurled her legs slightly. "Besides, this pain is different from when I had Joey. I hope it's just false labor. If it isn't, we'll find out soon enough." She brought her hand up to his face and cupped his cheek, smiling weakly.

He covered the smaller hand with his. "Shyanne, I think you need to stay here." He put a finger against her lips when she started to protest. "If you are in labor, false or real, you don't need to be on a horse. You need to rest. This is the best place to do that."

Shyanne jerked her hand out from under his and struggled into a sitting position. "I told you before, Drayco, I'm going to find my family. I won't be left behind like some sniveling helpless female." She slammed her fist on the bed. "I won't!" She held his gaze. "Promise me you won't leave like Joseph did. Promise me," she pleaded.

"Shhhh, it's okay. I promise not to leave you." He held her close, reassuring her even though he was not sure if his words would remain true. If she was in labor, he would stay until the birth then go find Ruben. "But I do need to check something out. It's here so I don't have to go far. That way you don't think I ran off without you." He leaned back, looking into her blue eyes. "Do you trust me, little sis?" He purposely held back the information obtained during his conversation with Kilan, about her son and Ruben. Now was not the time to discuss it.

Piercing him with her gaze, she said, "Yes, brother, I do trust you." The waves of pain that wracked her earlier appeared to have finally passed. She eased herself against the headboard, holding her swollen belly just in case.

Rising to his feet, he moved toward the doorway. "I promise, I'll come right back." He disappeared with a wave.

The chair used by Kilan was empty when Drayco left the house a short time later. He crossed the porch by means of several long strides and reached the road through several more. From their earlier conversation, he knew Ruben had Joey stashed somewhere close while he restocked his supplies. He turned left; toward the direction he remembered Kilan coming from and walked with a determined step. He was going to find where that hiding spot was, and what he was looking for: Joey's shoes. He wanted to make sure the boy was actually the missing child, and not some other boy.

Drayco followed the road leading out of town, looking for any indication that someone had cut into the trees. He found one after another and painstakingly tracing them until he was certain it was not the right path. He was between two to three miles away from the house when he halted in frustration. He kicked a stone. It skipped across the road, bringing back the memory of a little girl he met once, a little girl so much like Shyanne.

He watched it until the stone rolled to a stop. It was partway down another trail. A couple of the tall weeds were bent over, broken by the passing of something. As he drew closer, a small object came into view. He stooped and picked it up. It was a piece of straw. He glanced around to see if a field of the stuff grew nearby. Nothing but trees and swaying grass was in sight. He turned toward the trail again. Farther down, he spotted another piece of straw.

His heart raced. He knew with certainty that he was finally on the right path. Picking up speed, he followed it to a small opening in the trees. The opening was wide enough for something that flew to fit.

The grass was flattened as if crushed by something heavy. Drayco knew what had done it. He moved to the middle of the landing site and looked all around on the ground. Nothing showed. Raising his eyes, he scanned father out. Tall grass surrounded him, mingled with trees of various sizes. Again, nothing came into sight. He walked to the outer perimeter and started around it, keeping his eyes locked on the ground before him.

He was halfway around when he noticed something partially hidden under some large ferns. A worn brown leather shoe attached to an equally worn and scuffed sole stuck out. Drayco bent over and grabbed it. Bringing it into the open, he recognized Joseph's handiwork. He knew it was his work because Drayco still wore a pair of boots made by Shyanne's husband. *This was Joey's, all right.* Glancing around, he found the other one a few feet away. Gripping them firmly, he ran back to the house.

He met Mini in the hallway outside Shyanne's door. She was shutting it behind her. A couple of wet cloths were draped over her arm.

"Is everything okay?"

Hooking her arm into the younger man's, she directed him away from the door and into the sitting area with the fireplace. "She's fine, young man. Just needs a bit of rest is all."

"She's not in labor, is she?"

"Aww no. She's just tired. Those pains of hers can take a lot out of a person." Patting his arm in a motherly way, she added when she saw his worried look, "Don't worry, it's not labor. It's just the baby letting us know the time for introductions is near, that's all." After making sure he was not going to disturb the resting woman, she left him to wash out the cloths.

Drayco held the small shoes in his hands tight. He looked down the hall leading toward Shyanne's room. He knew he could not show her what he had found, not now. It might cause her too much stress. It might start the actual labor. He was not going to do that. He wanted the rest of the family here to greet the baby when it came into the world. Instead, he walked to his own room and hid the shoes in his wardrobe under a pile of clothes. Shutting the doors, he rested his forehead against the solid wood.

I know I promised not to leave you, but I also warned you that I'd go on without you if the need rose, he thought. Straightening, he turned around and leaned against the wardrobe. *I want this problem solved. I want your family with you when the baby arrives. I can think of only one way to do that and it doesn't involve sitting here waiting. I hope one day soon you will forgive me for what I'm about to do. If I can find Joey, you might be able to.*

He picked up the pack he had readied it prior to hunting for the shoes. He already knew he was going to leave, with or without Shyanne. As Drayco passed his sister's door, he paused and put a hand on it, feeling the wood grain beneath his palm. With a sigh, he moved on to the back of the house.

Mini was standing in the kitchen by the wood stove. She glanced at the dark twin when he entered, raising an eyebrow at the sight of the bag slung over his shoulder. Before she could say anything, a noise echoed down the hall. It was the sound of a door opening. Drayco took the pack off and tucked it into the pantry. The older woman kept her expression bland when Shyanne entered, a hand resting on her lower back. She waddled to a chair and plopped into it then glanced at her brother and smiled.

"I expected you to be missing." She arched her back, trying to stretch tired muscles. "I'm glad you kept your promise and stayed here."

Drayco remained silent. He slid behind her and started rubbing the annoying site. Shyanne sighed with relief.

Mini returned her attention to the pot of stew. She

gave the wooden spoon a twirl to help the vegetables inside keep from sticking to the bottom. The aroma of spices wafted past the noses of everyone in the kitchen.

"Oh, Mini, that smells fabulous," Shyanne said, her eyes closed, savoring both the smell and the massage.

"Thank you, dear. It's an old family recipe handed down to me by my mother, god rest her soul."

The back door suddenly opened and slammed shut, causing everyone in the room to jump. Turning as one, they saw Kilan standing with a sheepish look on his face. "Sorry about that. Have to fix that one day." He moved behind his wife and peered over her shoulder. "Mama, my nose tells me you've outdone yourself again. When's supper gonna be done?"

"In a few minutes. Papa, why don't you escort these young people to the main room. I'll bring supper to you for a change."

"You're too good to me." He hugged Mini before moving to Shyanne. "Young Missy, would you be so kind as to give this old man the pleasure of your company during the long walk?" Kilan extended a hand to help her up.

Shyanne grinned as she grabbed the offered hand. "Why of course, fine sir. I'm glad to see manners do still exist." She struggled to her feet and hooked her arm in his. Before disappearing from view, Drayco saw her tongue stick out in his direction. The corners of his mouth rose into a slight smile.

Before he followed, he walked up to the older woman standing by the stove. "Thanks, Mini, for not saying anything."

Not missing a spin of the spoon, she said, "I understand. I see the restlessness stirring inside you. If I were in your shoes, I don't know if I would have waited so long." Tapping the spoon on the rim, she continued, "If you do decide to go missing, don't worry about your sister. I'll make sure to take good care of her. She doesn't need to be on a horse right now anyway. That baby is going to come real soon; I can feel it in my bones."

Drayco stared at Mini with newfound respect. He wrapped his arms around her, and whispered, "You're the best." Letting go, he followed the others out of the room.

Mini smiled while she pulled four bowls off the shelf.

The tall dark man was so like her son, the son she had lost when she was younger. Maybe that was the reason she felt so close to the pair. They felt like they were family. And family always took care of family. Tugging the stew off the flame, she ladled large amounts into the waiting bowls. Shortly thereafter, the group enjoyed its simmered flavor, relishing every bite before the warm fire.

When the meal was finished, Mini stood to take the dishes to the kitchen. Shyanne moved to help her but a spasm overtook her. She fell back into the chair, holding her stomach with both hands. Drayco rushed to her side, hovering, afraid to touch her. Kilan stood and took the tray from his wife. He turned and handed it to Drayco, forcing the dark twin's attention away from his sister. Grabbing an elbow, the older man guided him out of the room. Mini kneeled next to Shyanne. She placed a comforting hand on her swollen belly.

"It's okay, work your way through this. It's not time yet."

The whispered words of encouragement helped Shyanne ride through the worst of the spasm. When it eased, she wondered if anything was wrong with the baby. She hadn't experienced these with Joey. Why was she having them this time? She voiced her concerns to Mini.

"Dear, each baby is different, just like each pregnancy is different. This one is fine, I can feel it."

"Do you really think so? How can you be so sure?"

She gave Shyanne a warm smile. "Child, I've delivered more babies than you are years old."

"I doubt that Mini, I really do." The smile faded as another spasm wracked her.

Shyanne never knew when the wet cloth hit her forehead or how she reached the bed. All she knew was the pain. If this was not labor then she was not looking forward to its start. A cup of liquid touched her lips. She drank greedily. Opening her eyes, she saw Mini sitting next to her. The calm mannerism of the older woman enabled the pregnant woman to lie back, knowing she was in good hands. If something were wrong, she would have seen it in her eyes.

"Feel better?"

Reaching out with her senses, she examined her body. The pain was gone, though her abdominal area still felt like it had been put through a marathon of sit-ups. "I think so. How long was it?"

"Not long." She grabbed the hand resting on the bed, "but I bet it felt like it was forever."

"God yes." Shyanne threw an arm over her forehead. She pulled it away suddenly when the pressure caused water from the cloth to run down the sides of her face and onto the pillow. She tried to sit up, but hands forced her back down.

"Don't worry about it, it's just water. It will dry. And you do not need to sit up right now. Right now, what you and the baby need is rest, and lots of it."

"But Mini…."

"Don't 'but' me, young lady. If you want that baby to be healthy when it's delivered, you'll do as I say." Mini waved a finger at her to emphasize her words. She rose to her feet and started toward the exit. Over a shoulder, she added, "From this point on, you're on bedrest. If you make a move to get up for any reason except to relieve yourself, I'll tie you to the bed." She stopped before leaving. "And don't think I can't do it. I may be 71 years old but I've had lot of experience on making people follow instructions." She smiled to soften the words. When Shyanne gave her no argument, she left, leaving the door open so she could hear when Shyanne called out.

Taking the wet cloth off her forehead, she sat up and flipped the pillow over so the dry side faced upward. As she was lying back, Drayco peeked into the room.

"How are you doing, kiddo?"

"I've been pinned to the bed. If I make a move to get up, Mini will not allow a repeat." Shyanne rolled her eyes and sighed, crossing her arms across her belly.

"I heard." He came in and sat on the edge of the bed. "I can tell you think she's a pain, but I think she's wonderful. She took good care of you when those spasms were forcing you to curl into a tight ball. Kilan and I had to help bring you in here. You weren't able to make it on your own.

After that, she shooed us out so she could tend to you." He glanced furtively over his shoulder and leaned close. "I snuck in here to make sure you were okay. She told us you needed to rest for a bit before we could see you. But, you know how I am about listening." He gave her a sly grin.

Shyanne reached up and ruffled his hair. "Just like when we were kids—always sneaking into each others room when we were supposed to be going to sleep." A faint long-ing smile edged onto her face. Her blue eyes met his dark ones. "Oh Drayco, I don't want to go through this birth alone. I'm scared. Something might be wrong with the baby. Mini may not be telling me the truth for fear of upsetting me." She leaned against him and hugged him around the waist. "Something might happen during the birthing and I might not see my family again. I want you here, just in case."

Drayco felt her tears drop and ran his fingers through her hair. "You're going to be fine. Mini is the best. She will make sure you both come out of this all right. You'll be show-ing off a beautiful baby once everyone is together again."

"I don't know. I've been having these terrible dreams, dreams about a child crying, all lost and alone. I can't ever find the child. What if it's because I'm not here. What if it's because I'm in another plane and others are mourning my loss?"

Drayco leaned back from her. He gripped her arms, and said, "Shyanne, are you listening to yourself? Are you?" He was angry, and a little frightened. "That's stupid talk, a bunch of what ifs. Are you going to live your life by those what ifs, giving up before you've tried? Or are you going to fight, to live like the sister I know and love."

His harsh words made her winch. She knew she was being irrational. Hearing it from another only emphasized the fact. It also helped her see the silliness. She pulled him close, not ready yet to look into his eyes.

"I think Mini's right, you need to rest. It's been a long hard day and it's late." He kissed the top of her head and pushed her back on the bed. "Love you, little sis. I'll see you in the morning." He got up and walked to the door.

Before he left, Shyanne pleaded softly, "Please don't leave me, brother. Please be here for the birth. Please. I love you."

Drayco bowed his head. He glanced briefly at Shy-anne then continued out the door.

Shyanne lay back on the bed. She knew in her heart Drayco was leaving. She saw it in his eyes, in the way he carried himself. In fact, she was surprised he was still here. That spoke volumes about his character. Resting a hand un-der her head and the other on her belly, she lay awake far into the night, listening for any sounds of movement. She fell asleep from exhaustion before any occurred.

Drayco peered in on Shyanne. She was laying in the bed, asleep, her head turned slightly to the side. He watched her for a second, smiling a ghost of a smile. His earlier statement still rang in his ears, the one where he said he would see her in the morning. He knew it was a lie when he said it. He knew he was going to leave, to go find her family. The episode from yesterday with the spasms and their conversation finalized his decision.

The dark man slipped into the kitchen and retrieved his hidden pack. Something lay on top of it. He smiled when he realized what it was. Tossing the strap over a shoulder, he walked out the door and across to the stable. He held out the carrot left by Mini to keep Betsy quiet once he entered. The donkey reached over the railing and took the offered treat before emitting the loud bray characteristic of her breed. She was happily munching as he moved farther into the gloom. A faint nicker told him Bravaro was waiting.

He saddled the horse as silently as possible and guided him outside. The sword given to him by his grandfather over two centuries ago rested on his hip. He held it to keep it from clanking while pulling Bravaro away from the inn. A mile down the road, he stopped and sprang into the saddle. With a final glance toward the house, Drayco pointed the horse's head to the east and tapped his sides. He moved briskly in the same direction taken by his most despised enemy, a mercenary named Ruben.

Twelve

Since his failure to bring down the deer, Drizzle had only caught sight of a small squirrel. It had its nose buried under some mulch made of fallen leaves and did not scent the cat until it was too late. He leaped on it and brought it down as it tried to escape up a tree. The welcome meal disappeared in two bites.

His belly echoed with its opinion of the extended fast, making his already sarcastic disposition that much worse. The fact that he had not found the blasted horse yet had not help either.

The scent trail grew harder to find with the passing of time. Other animal scents crossed its path occasionally, but he never saw their source. If he had, they would be in his belly by now.

The horse had followed a little used path that headed toward the northeast, into a mountain range. Drizzle worked his way through the trees, avoiding the occasional drop off and, once or twice, had to detour around a gap too large to jump across.

The openings for caves littered the hillside. He thought about exploring them and hopefully finding something that he could eat holed up in one, but he wanted to find Joey. He had wasted enough time. The journey to track him down had lasted weeks instead of the days it should have taken. The longer it took, the angrier he became at himself.

If I had only paid more attention to the boy. If I had

only been more tolerant. If only.

He missed the change in direction due to his internal ranting. The unconscious tracking of the scent helped him realize it before he was too far off course. Muttering under his breath, he backtracked and started after the elusive scent once more.

When ten miles had passed under his weary paws, the smell of the horse grew so strong that the cat crouched and observed any opening in the tress before crossing it. He knew he was close. After another mile, he caught sight of a clearing before a cave. It was a big one, the mouth large enough to accommodate a horse the size of Ruben's. Droppings lay near the opening and hoof prints, mingled with human ones, crisscrossed the area. One pair of footprints was small enough to be that of the child. He moved under a thick group of bushes to hide and observe.

This was the cave; the hiding spot of Ruben, he was sure of it. He lay too far for his nose to confirm it, but what he saw said volumes. No sounds echoed out to him. He continued to wait. If he went in now, before confirming where the mercenary was, Ruben might discover him and kill the boy.

A faint humming started. The cat hadn't noticed it at first, it was so subtle. As the noise drew nearer, an annoying tickle teased the base of his spine and worked its way up to his head. He looked all around; trying to find what caused the disturbance. Something moved in his peripheral vision. An object came into sight. It landed in the open area, in front of the cave.

Drizzle saw what appeared to be a floating platform. If the sight of it hadn't caused his heart to race, the two people who stepped off it did. One was someone he despised intensely; the other was someone he loved dearly. Suppressing the urge to snarl, he watched Ruben and Joey gather things from hidden compartments and take them into the cave.

Joey looked happy. That was something he had not expected. He expected to see him tearful, to see him fighting, screaming, yelling—something other than what he was. Instead, what he saw was a bouncy young child with a huge grin on his face, following Ruben like a puppy dog. He stared in disbelief when he saw the boy come out, alone, hop on the platform and guide it into the dark opening of the cave. He made no attempt to flee.

Drizzle pondered the event he had just witnessed. *What could Ruben have done to make the boy so cooperative? What could he have used, what could he have said?* He had to get to Joey to find out. He'd have to wait until the blanket of darkness settled over everything before he tried to enter. Until then, he'd do his best to ignore the empty rumble of his stomach.

Ruben brought the supplies into the main room. The boy was right behind him, his arms full as well. Joey heaved the heavy stuff up onto the table then twirled around afterwards to face the big man.

"Do I get to bring the flyer in?" He danced from one foot to the other; hoping permission followed the request.

"Because you did a real good job bringing us home," he said, putting the stuff in his arms down, "you've earned the right to bring it in."

"Yiipppeee!"

Joey darted out of the room, his small arms churning as fast as his legs. Ruben listened to his footsteps as they faded down the passageway. He grinned while he put their purchases away. The feelings rolling through him were wonderful. He planned to make sure they continued. He planned to kill the mother lodged with the old couple, the mother and her blasted twin. He remembered the encounter with Drayco at Grandfield, the encounter that ended so much. Yet, it began so much more, like now with the boy he called son.

The sound of running feet, mingled with a whinny from farther down the hallway, brought him back. Joey skid to a stop just inside the room. He waited, the grin still plastered on his small face, his chest heaving from the run.

"Did you have any problems?"

"No sir!"

"Then maybe we should go tend to Wind Racer. What do you think, son?" He extended his arms to the boy.

Joey ran up to Ruben and leaped into his arms. Hugging his neck, he asked, "Dad, can I ride him out?" It was getting easier to call the big man dad. It didn't feel as weird saying it. Instead, it felt right, like he had been saying it for some time. Memories of his real dad surfaced periodically, but they were being replaced with the fun ones occurring now.

"Absolutely." Grabbing one of the arms holding him, he squeezed it. "Those muscles can handle him."

"Come on! Come on! Let's go!" He bounced up and down excitedly.

"Hang on tight"

Ruben bounced in time with the boy as he stepped out of the main room and into the passageway. Between the two of them, every bit of metal on them clanked so loud that their laughter was lost in the noise. When they entered the enclosure for the horse, Wind Racer's ears were darting beck and forth and he paced anxiously. He let out a loud whinny. The sudden loudness of the sound deafened the ears of the people next to him.

"Boy, he's anxious to get out." Joey stared in wide-eyed wonder at the tall animal.

Putting Joey down, Ruben said, "He loves to run. Maybe tomorrow we can take him on an outing and let him burn off some of his pent up energy. Think you're up to it?" The big man ruffled his hair.

Joey loved the way he was included in the decision process. At home, he was told what to do, never allowed to have a say in anything. Here, his opinion mattered. It made him feel very important. It made him happy to stay. Ducking away, he moved several paces off and mimicked the big man's previous pose. "Absolutely."

"Why you..." Ruben crouched low and raced after the fleeing child. He caught him before he escaped from the room.

The tickle match that followed, first led by Ruben, then by Joey, left both lying breathless and teary-eyed. Their swords lay off to the side, crisscrossing each other, just like the people who carried them.

Joey rolled onto his side and hugged the big man as tight as his small arms allowed. He couldn't remember having this much fun in his whole life. He never wanted it to end, not ever. "Dad, you're the best. I don't ever want to leave you."

"Joey, son, you don't have to worry about that. If someone, even your mom and the man who sired you try to take you from me, I'll make sure they understand the mistake they're making."

The mention of his original family caused the smile to falter. It returned when the big man picked him up, rolled onto his back and tossed him into the air, catching him before he fell to the ground.

Bringing the boy down to a rest on his chest, Ruben said, "We better get some sleep little man. We have an adventure to undertake tomorrow." Hugging him against his body, the big man rose to his feet. "We'll let Wind Racer out then."

"Dad, instead of sleeping in my room tonight, can I sleep with you?"

"Only if you promise not to kick me in the middle of the night."

"Daaad, how can I do that when I'm asleep?"

Assuming a thoughtful pose, he replied, "Maybe I could roll over and pin you under me."

Looking at the big man's rolling muscles, Joey answered, "But that would squish me."

"You're right, that would make a squishy mess. And, I don't know about you, but, I kinda like you the way you are."

"Yea. Me too."

"I guess we'll just have to try it. You up for the possibility of being squished?"

"Yea!"

"Then hang on tight, we're going to make a dash for it!"

Ruben bolted from the stable area, into the passageway, down to the main room, and ran around its circumference several times before he ran into the sleeping area. Joey cackled with absolute joy during the entire run.

He flopped onto the sleeping pad and Joey curled against his side. Sweat covered him; it was a good kind of sweat. It was the kind earned with family. Lifting his head, he kissed the top of the small head. "Love you, son."

He could not remember the last time he had said those words and truly meant them.

"Love you back, dad."

They drifted to sleep, one making sure not to 'squish' the other, the other dreaming of the wonderful new life he had, missing his previous family less and less.

Drizzle lay under the thick growth trying to ignore the grumbling of his stomach as well as the pouring rain. Neither helped his disposition, neither looked like they were going to end any time soon.

He thought about going into the cave to try to locate Joey but vetoed that idea. With the horse inside, and him not knowing where it was, he might stumble upon it. One whiff of his scent would cause it to go crazy and alert the people inside to his presence, ending any chance of getting Joey out quickly and quietly.

No, at this point, he needed stealth, not excitement. He remained in the pouring rain, enduring the torture of so much wetness, and grumbled as much as his empty stomach did while he watched the entrance of the cave for any sign of movement.

Sometime during the night, Drizzle curled into a tight ball and covered his face against the rain with part of his front leg and hand. He dozed lightly, one ear cocked toward the entrance, listening in case the occupants decided to go somewhere. Just before the coming of dawn, the rain finally let up. It became a light sprinkle then stopping altogether as the rays of the sun made the tops of the trees glow.

The cat uncurled and rose to his feet, shaking the water off in the process. He stretched out in typical feline fashion, arching his back and spreading the fingers of his hand like paws wide, extending the claws to their fullest at the same time. At the peak of the stretch, he yawned. His fangs were displayed for all watching to see, which at the present was only the birds hiding in the upper branches of the trees. The jaw snapped shut and the claws disappeared as the cat sat on his haunches to look at the cave.

Again, he pondered about the event of yesterday. *I wonder what's happening in there. Why didn't Joey try to escape when he had the chance? What did Ruben say that kept the child there?* These thoughts ran round and round in his mind. *And why did Joey look so happy when he should have been miserable?*

As if in response to his silent questions, the mercenary appeared. He stood in front of the dark opening and looked around the clearing, arms resting on his hips. His sword lay across his back, within easy reach. Drizzle froze. It was too late to drop to the ground. The movement would attract unwanted attention.

Fortunately, the bush he had slept under was in front of him, making it difficult to spot him. His tawny fur mingled with the green foliage and the brown branches holding them. Unless one knew where to look, they would miss him entirely, which is what Ruben did. Drizzle watched the big man's eyes rest on him for a brief second then move on around the clearing.

Ruben sensed something was out of place, but saw nothing out of the ordinary when he scanned the area. He waited, listening. A long time ago, he learned to trust the inner feeling that had alerted him to so much. It saved his life on many occasions. Nothing unusual echoed back to him. Shrugging his shoulders, but knowing he would stay alert to his surroundings, Ruben returned the way he came. He had a horse and a son to get ready for an adventure. That thought brought a smile to his face.

Drizzle released the breath he was holding and lowered himself to the ground, never taking his eyes off the entrance to the cave. Minutes passed. When Ruben returned, Joey and the horse were with him.

The mercenary guided his horse into the open, scooped up the boy, and tossing him into the saddle. Joey squealed with delight, clinging to the animal's mane as he bounced his legs up and down. Ruben had a foot in the stirrup when a puff of wind brought the cat's scent into the clearing. The only one to notice was the horse.

It spun around, head held high, eyes wide. Ruben held on to the saddle and reins and hopped with the animal as it danced in a circle. He quickly threw his leg over and positioned himself behind Joey, wrapping his arms protectively around the boy to prevent him from falling off.

Wind Racer feels it too.

Again, he scanned the area for the cause of the disturbance. Again, nothing stood out. He tugged on the reins and cooed to the horse. At the sound of his voice, Wind Racer calmed. But his ears still flew in every direction.

"What's the matter, Dad? Is Wind Racer going to be okay?"

"He's fine. He's excited about leaving the cave and

running, that's all."

Glancing over a shoulder, Joey asked, "Can I hold the reins this time? I can handle him."

"I know you can, little man." Knotting them together so they could not fall is Joey accidentally lost them, he handed them to the boy. "Here, they're yours."

Joey took the offered gift, unable to believe they were truly in his hands. With his other dad, the one who never seemed to find time for him, this would have never happen. He would have been told he was too young. In fact, he had been told that very thing many times. With his new dad, the one who wanted him, he had yet to hear it.

"Thanks, Dad." Joey squeezed the arm holding him tight. "I'm glad you're my dad."

"That's the best thing I've heard all day." Ruben kissed the top of the head sitting in front of him. "Now show me what you can do with Wind Racer." He grabbed a handful of mane and braced Joey and himself for the wild ride to come.

"WAAHOO! Let's go, Wind Racer!"

The boy flung his legs out and kicked the animal's sides. The horse hesitated, unsure if it was okay to go. Ruben gave him a gentle nudge with his heels. That was all he needed.

Bunching his back legs under him, the horse shot forward like an arrow. He weaved through the trees on a trail that led in a westerly direction, almost hitting the towering monarchs before turning away at the last possible moment. The sound of laughter bounced from tree to tree for a long time, eventually fading as they distanced themselves from the cave.

Drizzle could not believe what he had heard. *Joey called him Dad. Now I understand why he's not afraid. That idiot has brainwashed him into thinking he's the child's father, not Joseph.* The cat knew the news would not be accepted well.

Before leaving to find Shyanne and Joseph, he wanted to scout the layout of the cave. This way, when he returned, he would know where to lead them. He crept around the edge of the open area until he stood next to the opening. Hearing nothing, he slid inside.

The flyer sat near the entrance. Several steps beyond

it, the passageway branched into two paths. Drizzle moved a short distance into the left branch and lowered his nose to the floor. Joey's scent was present, but it was very faint, as if much time had passed since the boy last came this way. The cat glanced farther down the darkened path. The keen night sight of his breed showed him nothing but natural cave. He backtracked to the path on the right.

The scents of both the humans and the horse were strong on this path. The cat raised his lips into a snarl at the stench of the mercenary. The snarl disappeared with the smell of Joey.

Unlike the left passageway, this one appeared to be man-made. Chisel marks worn with the passing of time etched the walls. As he went farther into the cave, the walls continued with the same pattern.

Drizzle marveled at Ruben's ability to find functioning pieces of technology from the past. First, he associated himself with the Boss. The Boss—a marvel herself—living far beyond imaginable with the aid of machines. She had tried to use Shyanne's genetic makeup as the fountain of youth, but they thwarted her plans before irreparable damage was done. Before they escaped, they destroyed the generator that powered her underground complex, rendering it useless.

Now, the mercenary had found a floating platform and this bunker. The cat wondered what else awaited him. The only way to find out was to press on into the cave.

With no idea what lay before him, Drizzle moved cautiously down the passageway. Another one of those floating balls of death could materialize out of nowhere, like when they searched the underground facility for the Boss so many years ago. Although, he was relatively certain that if it were here, it would have found him by now.

A large dark outline took shape ahead on the right. He was able to make out the gap of a doorway due to the light that flickered from the end of the passageway. Drizzle believed a fire caused it and raised his nose and confirmed his suspicion. It was a fire, but how was the smoke kept from filling the cave? It was a mystery to be answered shortly, he hoped.

Inching forward, he peered into the room. This was where the horse was stabled. The thick smell of straw and dung hung heavy in the air. He ignored it and moved on. He would find nothing of use in there. He located two more rooms, both used for storage. Again, he ignored them. What he sought lay in the room with the flickering light; he was sure of it.

The circular room was vast. It had been cut out of the surrounding rock also, but, unlike the passageway, these walls were covered with a smooth material. Near the top was an opening. The soot from many a fire had turned the domed ceiling black. Drizzle assumed it led to the outside, thus explaining the lack of smoke. The fireplace stood in the middle, under the opening. Its warmth circulated throughout the room. Drizzle had a feeling the occupants would be comfortable even in the coldest of winters because of the insulated walls.

Walking around the room, he discovered an alcove with bedding tucked in it. Joey's scent covered everything. A short distance away, the cat found where Ruben slept. He refused to go inside the tiny room. He did not want that stench clogging his nose when he raced to find Joseph and Shyanne, or Drayco for that matter, whomever he found first.

He thought about laying in wait for Ruben and attacking him when he returned. The more he thought about it, the more the idea felt wrong. Too many factors could cause it to fail. And if it failed, what would happen to Joey. No, he had to get help; he had to let the others know where to find the boy.

With that, he exited to cave and started toward the northwest. That was the last place he knew to look. That was where he had found evidence of Shyanne, and of her twin brother Drayco.

His belly reminded him that he had not eaten yet today, or for the last couple of days for that matter. He would have to feed soon. Until then, he would cover as much ground as possible.

Wind Racer cleared the forest a couple of hours after leaving the cave. The constraints of so many trees had required his movements to be slow. At the sight of so much open space, the horse tossed its head with a snort and flew across the field. Both occupants on his back leaned forward to reduce the buffeting wind that tried to unseat them. Both had huge grins plastered across their faces. Finally, Ruben told the boy to pull up on the reins and slow the horse. Reluctantly, Joey did as he was told.

Ruben wiped the wind driven tears from his eyes, and said, "You did good, little man."

The boy looked up. Streaks of dried moisture crisscrossed his cheeks, giving him the appearance of having lightning bolts drawn on his face. "That was fun! Can we do it again?"

"We have to let the horse cool down. See the wetness showing in front of you?"

"Yea."

"That means he needs to slow down. If he doesn't, he could get sick or die."

Looking at the head bobbing before him, Joey said, "I don't want him to die—he's wonderful."

Ruben reached up and pat on the muscular neck. "I think so too." He noticed a stream running through the field on to the opposite side of the open area. "How about we walk him that way? We can camp for the night by the water."

Joey peered across the field toward where Ruben pointed. After spotting the water, he tugged on the reins and started the animal toward it. When Wind Racer picked up his pace, he pulled back as hard as he could, preventing him from doing so. Ruben smiled.

When they reached the gentle flowing water, Ruben jumped off and helped Joey down. He loosened the saddle and removed it, carrying it as if it weighed nothing. Joey marveled at how easy the big man made it seem. He decided to do his share. Walking over, he tugged at the wet saddle pad until it fell off the horse and onto him. It was heavier than he thought; he buckled under the weight.

"Need some help there, little man?" Ruben set the saddle down and faced Joey. His hands were resting on his hips and his appearance showed concerned, but he was not overly worried.

"Nope. I can do it," Joey huffed as he shoved the weight off him.

"Let me know if you need my help." He returned his attention to the saddle, but kept an eye on the boy just in case.

Joey continued to be amazed at Ruben. The fact that he let him handle the pad instead of taking over, thus treating him as if he was a grownup and not a baby, said volumes. It made him more determined than ever to succeed. Scrunching his face in concentration, he bent over and tried to pick up the pad. It was too heavy. Discarding that idea, he tried several others, each with the same results. The pad remained where it had fallen. Frustrated, he stood with his arms crossed before his chest, thinking.

Ruben refrained from laughing, or even smiling. He knew that would be the worst thing he could do. He sat down on the ground and leaned back against the saddle, supporting his head with his hands. He waited for Joey to make his next move. The boy surprised him with his next idea.

One moment Joey was standing beside the moisture filled pad, completely frustrated. The next, he had a corner in his small hand and flipped one side onto the other. He grabbed the edges and began dragging it behind him until it sat next to the saddle. With a huge grin on his face, he heaved it up to stand in a vee shape to dry.

"I knew you would find a way to do it." He grinned at the beaming child. "Now that that's done, I think I need to wash up. How about you?"

The stench of wet horse rose to greet Joey's nose. Holding the front of his shirt away from his body, he answered, "I don't think I need a bath, I know I need a bath!"

"Let's go then!"

Ruben scooped the boy up and lunged into the water, ignoring the fact that they were still dressed and their swords were still on their backs. The child let out a surprised yelp when he suddenly went underwater. When the big man surfaced, Joey came up sputtering.

"Dad! What ya try'n to do—drown me?"

"You said you needed a bath—I helped."

"But do ya hafta drown me?"

That's what makes it so fun."

With that, a huge splashing battle broke out. The larger hands of the big man gave him an advantage over the smaller ones of the boy. But, Joey's younger age gave him better speed and quickness when it came to darting around to splash back. By the time they stopped, both were soaked and exhausted, but at least both were clean.

"Let's get out of these wet clothes." Ruben removed his sword from the wet sheath and laid it on the ground next to him. Joey followed suit. Minutes later, wet shirts and pants hung from nearby branches, drying in the mid afternoon sun.

The big man removed the blankets from the pack and spread both out side by side. Naked, he sprawled out on one and indicated for Joey to join him. The boy curled into the crook of Ruben's arm and closed his eyes.

Before he slipped into slumber, he opened them and asked, "Dad? Do you think I'll get muscles like yours?"

"If you work hard and practice—yes, I do"

"Can we practice when we get up?

"We can practice now if you'd like."

"Naw, I'm pretty pooped right now."

"Me too. We'll practice later then."

"Okay dad. Love you."

"Love you too, son."

Their eyes closed simultaneously and the warmth of the sun on their bodies lulled them to sleep.

Ruben woke with a start, feeling that something was not right, that something felt out of sorts. He kept his eyes shut, listening. *There—that sound—the sound of someone stepping lightly in this direction.* That was when he remembered his sword resting on the ground near his clothes, and silently cursed his stupidity. *I'm an idiot. My sword's too far away for me to grab.*

Something very sharp poked the shallow pit near the base of his neck. He slowly opened his eyes. Surprise registered in them.

Can it be? Can it really be them?

"Hello Ruben—long time no see. Who's the kid?"

A tall man with shoulder length, dirty blonde hair held the sword at his throat, smiling. A woman stepped into view. She rested her hands on the man's shoulders and admired the body lying exposed before her.

"You're still looking good—I see." Her gaze moved up and down his body, hesitating at certain areas before moving on.

"Honey, how come you never talk to me that way?" The man pulled the sword back and wrapped an arm around the woman's waist.

"I do, sweetie, every chance I get." She nibbled on his ear.

Ruben chuckled as he slid free of Joey's sleeping form and sat up. "Like I've said many times before—you two need to get a room." The pair flashed wide grins at those long forgotten words. "Andrew, Sheena—good to see you again."

Thirteen

Drizzle could not believe his luck. He had been running for what seemed like forever when he stumbled upon a deer drinking from a small stream. He killed it quickly before it could dart away, not wanting a repeat of his previous encounter with its kind.

It was near morning, so he dragged the body away from the waters edge and into hiding. He was close the last known site for Drayco and Shyanne, in the territory of the cat things that had almost cost him and Joseph their lives at the start of their journey. While he ate, he listened for the intruders that were sure to come. Halfway through the meal, a rustling noise sounded off to his right. It was echoed on his left. More rustling started in the leafy growth overhead. He saw many beady pinpoints of red staring back at him and knew it was time to leave.

Moving slowly, he inched away from the carcass. Once he was in the clear, he fled the area before the creatures behind those eyes could attack. He made it to the river's edge without incident. The feral cats had not followed. They were more interested in the meal he had left behind.

Drizzle paralleled the river to where he had found traces of the twins while he waited for Joseph to recover from his near drowning. A small pile of scattered bones was all that remained of the cat trampled by Shyanne's horse. Continuing in the same direction, he discovered the cave where they had taken refuge. He knew that too much time had passed for him to track Shyanne and her brother, but he tried anyway, unsuccessfully. He could only guess at which direction they had gone. The obvious choice was north. South would have led them back to the cat things. The twins may be a bit of a pain, but they were not stupid. He started north, hoping his decision was the correct one.

Hours later, he came upon a small town. Sounds of activity echoed from many of the buildings. Drizzle watched the people as they went about their business, unaware of his presence. Listening, he tried to locate any signs of the twins in the bustling activity. He found nothing. The cat was about to move past a house with a stable behind it when he caught a whiff of something familiar, something that halted him in his tracks. It came from the stables.

Before he could investigate, the back door to the house opened and an older woman walked onto the porch. She held a bowl full of long string beans in her hands. Another bowl was underneath it. He watched her set them on a table next to a chair and gently ease herself into it. She plopped the empty bowl into her lap and grabbed a handful of beans. With the ease of much practice, she snapped them in half and dropping them into the bowl before scooping up more.

One of the side gates to the stable opened and an elderly man, presumably her mate, stepped into the sunlight. Drizzle watched him step up on the porch and pull a chair over next to hers. He put a foot up on the railing and leaned back. A bit of straw hung from his mouth.

"Papa, you shouldn't do that. You might fall." She never looked up from her task; her hands never skipped a beat.

"I know, Mama. I just forget is all." He set the chair back on all four legs, but his foot remained on the railing. Taking the straw out of his mouth, he twirled it as he asked, "How's she doing?"

"She'll be fine. That baby is due any day now."

"I wonder why her brother left knowing she wanted his help."

Drizzle perked up. He knew instinctively the pair was talking about the twins, even though their names had yet to be mentioned.

"He's got a restless soul. He knew she was in good

hands and wanted to find Ruben and that poor boy. She wants that too, you know. He's just trying to help her that way instead of waiting around wringing his hands with inactivity. If you were a bit younger, you'd have done the same thing." She paused and gave him a warm smile.

He returned her smile. Reaching over, he grasped her hand and squeezed it. "You're right, mama, I would have." Staring across the field, he said, "She sure was mad when she found him gone. Thought she was going to deliver right then. Good thing you calmed her down."

Her hands resumed their work.

"Best get those stalls mucked out before supper. I don't want to be late for that wonderful meal you got planned." With a groan, he rose to his feet and moved back to the stall vacated earlier. "Miss having that young man around to help though."

Drizzle had heard enough. He knew the dark twin was on the move. He had left recently so he would be easy to track. He also knew that Shyanne was inside the house, and in her present state, of no use to his current mission. All he would do was upset her further. He decided not to alert her to the fact that he was here.

Without knowing which way to go, he had to wait until everyone left the immediate area to search for a scent. He chafed at having to do so; it seemed like an eternity. Finally, she finished her chore and returned inside. The man was still in the stable. Drizzle heard him rustling around while he continued to clean. Easing his way around the building, the cat found traces of Drayco's horse immediately.

He tried to stay out of sight in case Shyanne came outside. He made it to where Drayco turned east without being seen. Taking the same trail, he started after the dark twin, determined to overtake him as quickly as possible.

*   *   *

Joseph and Hana had been traveling for over a week. The fair-haired man was exhausted. He could not understand why his traveling companion still looked so fresh. It made him almost jealous—almost.

Their meager supplies were all but gone and they had not encountered a town of any kind where they could replenish them. Except for ruins. They avoided those as much as possible. Things of unspeakable horror took refuge in them. The last one they were forced to pass through reminded them of that. The horse he rode bore angry scratch marks from the rat creatures that had ferociously attacked them.

Hana rode in front of him, her shoulders bowed ever so slightly. It was the only sign he saw of her level of exhaustion. Her stance straightened and she stopped once she topped the slope. He understood why when he rode up beside her.

A town lay at the base of the mountain. It was small, but smoke rose from several of the buildings, showing them to be occupied and not abandoned.

He hoped the people were not so superstitious about strangers. Many were, especially the ones that did not see many travelers. Eying the mountains surrounding them, he doubted many made it here.

"What do you think?" he asked

"It does not matter what I think. It matters that our supplies are almost gone."

"Good point. But what if they aren't happy to see us, what then?"

"Then we move on as quickly as possible." She urged her horse over the top and down the tiny winding path toward the town.

With a weary sigh, he followed.

Close to midday, they emerged from the trees and started down the dirt road leading into town. A few men and women stopped what they were doing and stared. Their clothes were ragged, their skin filthy. Haunted looks filled their eyes. Others had an almost hungry look to them. Joseph could tell this town was different; it had an ominous feel to it. He wanted to continue, to bypass it completely and get their supplies somewhere else. Hana had other ideas.

She stopped next to a woman, and asked, "Is there an inn or a store in this town?"

The woman only nodded her head no and scampered away quickly. She glanced over her shoulder to make sure the strangers were not following her before she ducked out of sight around a corner. Hana shrugged her shoulders. Joseph echoed hers with one of his own.

Other people close to where the woman had stood darted glances at the strangers then down the road. They disappeared before they could be questioned. A few, mostly younger men, stood with their arms crossed in front, watching the pair intently like a pack of wolves.

There will be no resupply here. We might as well move on, Joseph thought. He was about to say so to Hana when she prodded her animal into motion.

The horses had gone only a few steps when a tall man with a slim muscular build and gray hair at the temples walked out of a building. It sat a little distance on the right, away from the others. He halted them with an upraised arm.

"Strangers—what is it you seek?" His stature was different. An air of authority surrounded him.

Hana spoke first. "We seek a place to rest for the night and supplies for our travels. We have money to pay for what is given."

"There is no inn here. Our town is not well known enough for one. Instead, I insist that you stay at my home for the night and not out in the open in these cold mountains." He extended his arm sideways. "My fair wife will make you food. Merna? Come join us, please."

In contrast to the tall host, a tiny bit of a woman emerged. Her mouse brown hair was in a tight bun and her dress covered all but her hands and face. One hand rested on her swollen abdomen while the other reached for her husband. She looked more like a child herself than a woman old enough to bear one. Joseph could see from the look on her face that she adored the man before her. He felt a momentary pang. He missed Shyanne dearly.

As they drew closer to the house, the man introduced himself.

"I am Jacob, the head prefect for our fine little town." He fanned his arm out to include the surrounding buildings. "Most of the people have lived here for generations. Occasionally, someone like yourself rides in and after staying a day or so, decides to remain because they like it so much. Maybe the same will be said of you two." He stepped back and allowed Hana and Joseph room to dismount. They guided the horses to the side of the porch where the hitching post was located and secured the reins.

"Thank you very much for your hospitality, Jacob," Joseph said. "It is good to finally have a firm roof over our heads for the night." Turning his attention to the small woman beside the man, he added, "and the prospect of a warm home cooked meal, Mrs..."

"Merna, call me Merna." She tucked herself against Jacob and giggled.

The odd feeling returned. He kept it from his face, not wanting the couple before him to see the turmoil rolling around inside. He would talk to Hana later, in private. Indicating for the little oriental woman to lead the way, he followed Jacob and Merna up the steps and into their home.

"I'm Joseph. And this is my wife, Hana." The incident at the travelers hut taught him not to deny her as his wife. He hoped Shyanne would understand.

The wondrous smell of ham wafted past their noses when they stepped into the main room, making the house seem less ominous and more inviting. Comfortable furniture surrounded the hearth with its warm fire. Jacob guided the pair of travelers toward some chairs.

"Please sit and make yourselves comfortable. I'll bring something to drink and check on how long it will be before the meal is ready." As he turned away, he gave them a measured look then moved toward another part of the house.

Joseph watched the tall man depart before moving next to Hana. She was already settled into a plush chair located close to the heat. "I don't like it here. I get a bad feeling, a feeling that all is not what it appears."

"I sense nothing of what you feel."

Before he could explain, Jacob returned with the promised drinks. He handed one to Hana and the other to Joseph. He did not have one for himself. Alarms went off inside Joseph's head. *Why does he not have a drink? It customary for the host to toast with the guests.* He eyed the mug in his hand, sure that it held something else mixed in with the liquid.

Hana brought the mug to her lips without hesitation and sipped. Her eyebrows rose in surprise. "Lemonade. Where did you get the lemons?"

"We grow them here. We grow all our food here, and all the produce is shared equally amongst the entire commune. Makes life easier for everyone, no need to venture far."

"How convenient. Is that why the others you mentioned have stayed?" She took another sip, savoring the tartness.

"Life is very difficult now. With the safety of numbers and the security of firm walls, many do not want to venture out. They have fought long and hard to survive and want something different; they want a chance to rest. We give them that."

"Is there a price for all this safety?" Joseph had yet to sample the drink in his hand.

"None."

Merna entered the room with two mugs in her hands. She gave one to Jacob and kept the other.

He held it high, and said, "A toast. To our guest—may you enjoy your stay and wish for more—or—may your journey be a safe one should you wish to move on." With that, he took a long pull from the mug, eyeing the guests to make sure they drank with him, as well.

Joseph knew he had to drink now. It would be considered an insult not to. Putting the mug to his lips, he tilted it enough to get only a small amount of the liquid in his mouth before lowering it. He swallowed. If anything was in the lemonade, the tartness masked it.

The host raised his drink once more. "And a final toast before we eat. May your thirst be quenched and your hearts be full." He drained the contents and placed the mug upside down on a table beside Joseph, indication he should do the same with his.

Joseph looked at the man then at the drink he held. He knew it was a challenge. He knew it by the gleam in Jacob's eyes. He wanted him to finish the lemonade, but for what purpose? For what reason? If he refused to drink, what would happen then? Remembering the haunted, scared looks on some of the people's faces when they entered the town, he had an idea what would happen. For Hana's sake, he downed the contents.

The drink had the usual tartness of unsweetened lemonade, until he reached the bottom. That was where it became very bitter, causing him to sputter and cough. Joseph glanced up and saw the triumphant look on Jacob's face. It was replaced with one of concern by the time the women focused their attention on him. He knew now beyond any shadow of a doubt that something was in the drink. He only hoped that whatever it was, it was slow acting so they could get away before it kicked in.

Once the coughing was under control, he said, "Dear, we forgot to take care of the horses." His step was purposeful when he walked toward the door because his legs were beginning to feel like they were made of lead weights. Hana hesitated. Seeing the way he moved, she rose to her feet and followed.

Somewhat to Joseph's surprise, the horses still stood where they had been left. He expected to see them missing. He stumbled across the porch and down the steps, nearly falling to his knees. His breath came in ragged gasps. Whatever was in the drink was faster than he hoped. Hana hurried to his side.

"Joseph, what's the matter?"

"There was something in the drink. I tasted it at the bottom, something really bitter."

"Mine tasted fine. Do you think it was a bad lemon?" She wrapped an arm around his waist to prevent him from falling.

"No." The porch started to sway to the right. Each step became an effort. "Help me onto my horse; we have to leave before it's too late." He had a feeling it was too late already.

Instead of arguing with Joseph, she helped. Her association with him during his illness and recovery showed him to be an honest, fair man. If he said something was wrong, then it was so. She managed to get him into the saddle before Jacob emerged from the house. His facial expression was one of shock. It turned to anger at the sight of them attempting to escape.

Before the tall man could reach them, Hana kicked her animal's sides hard and forced it to spin back the way they came. She kept a firm grasp of Joseph's reins as both horses were running through the town at full speed.

People scattered out of the way. One man foolishly tried to grab her horse's bridle, only to wind up trampled under hers and Joseph's hooves. She shot a glance back to make sure Joseph was still with her. He was, barely conscious, hanging on to the saddle with all his might.

Hana kept their pace fast, wanting to put as much distance between the townspeople and themselves as possible, in case of pursuit. And in case there was something in her drink as well. The more she thought of Joseph's description of the taste, the more she suspected what was given. She only hoped Jacob knew what he was doing when he made it. Otherwise, it could be deadly for the fair-haired man, and possibly her as well.

They had reached the hilltop and was heading down the other side when Hana began to feel a lightheadedness settle in. She urged the tired horses to continue. So far, she had not heard the sounds of pursuit. That could change at any moment. Sensing her awareness slipping, she secured Joseph's reins to her saddle to prevent losing them. Joseph had passed out many miles back. He was draped over the horse's neck, an arm hung over either side, his head rolling with each step.

Day became night, night became day. She had no idea how far they had traveled or for how long. Her world was reduced to staying in her saddle, and making sure that Joseph stayed in his.

When she finally came to her senses, she found herself curled into a ball in a field of grass. She was alone. Sitting up abruptly, she had to close her eyes and lean forward until the queasy feeling in the pit of her stomach faded. She raised her head and looked around afterward, trying to see where the horses were.

They grazed a short distance away. Both saddles were empty.

Where's Joseph? Did Jacob find him? If so, why are the horses here? Those would have been a great prize...along with us. She panned the area slowly. *If they're still here, that means Joseph's here too. I only hope he's alive.*

Hana rose to her feet, causing the little bit of control she had gained over the nausea to be lost. She vomited until it felt like her stomach would explode out of her mouth. Dry heaves echoed across the area when nothing solid remained. She cared not. All she wanted was to stop. The heaves finally ended, but not until tears covered her cheeks and she was back on her knees.

Once more, she rose to her feet. This time her stomach behaved.

She stumbled toward the horses, her body shaking from the effort of being sick. With their strong legs instead of her wobbly ones, they were her best bet to find Joseph. Her breath was ragged and sweat caused her eyes to burn by the time she reached the animals, but she had made it without falling. That was a feat she was especially proud of considering her weakened state.

Looking at what appeared to be a mountain of an animal, Hana knew she was not going to have the strength to pull herself into the saddle. Instead, she grabbing a handful of mane to steady herself and glanced around. All she saw was tall grass waving in the gentle breeze. She did not see Joseph.

A trail of the beaten down grass led toward a small opening in the trees. *That must be the way we came. If I follow it, I might find Joseph.*

She gripped the mane with one hand and the reins with the other before clucking her tongue to get the horse moving. At first, it walked too quickly. She was dragged several feet before she managed to pull back on the reins, slowing its forward progress. They reached the trees without further incident.

Hana stopped the horse at the edge of the tree line and allowed it to graze while she peered into the gloom. Rays of light pierced the interior, showing her bit and pieces of what lay inside. Tall ferns extended their arms upward. One such arm was bent over and broken. Underneath it, a mound darker than the surrounding darkness became evident.

"Joseph."

She let go of the saddle and stumbled into the trees. As she neared the mound, the shape of a man materialized. Joseph had fallen off the horse and lay sprawled on his back, his arms and legs resting in different angles. A patch of fern acted like a pillow for his head, cushioning it after the abrupt landing. Only a small cut over the left eye showed the roughness of the landing.

The last of her strength gave out as she reached his side. Hana collapsed to her knees and placed a hand on his chest. It rose and fell. Bowing her head with relief, she moved her hands up and down the rest of his body. Even though he had landed awkwardly, nothing appeared to be broken, for which she was thankful.

As she sat back, Joseph moaned. His eyes fluttered open and an arm rose to his head. "My god, my head is killing me."

"I don't wonder. Between the drink and the bump you received when you fell out of the saddle, I suspect it will for a while."

"That's right!" Joseph sat up suddenly and fell back just as quick. He rolled onto his side and vomited. Hana comforted him, knowing what he was experiencing. She had done the same thing not that long ago.

He rolled gingerly onto his back when the retching subsided, keeping his legs bent to reduce the pull on his abdomen. His arms covered his eyes against the bright rays of light twinkling down through the waving leaves.

After a few deep breaths, he managed to say, "Where are we?"

"I'm not sure. I was affected like you, but not to the extent you were. Probably because I didn't finish all of the lemonade."

"What was in it? Do you know?"

"I think it was aconite—monk's hood—though I've never heard of it in this part of the world. Jacob must have found some and learned how to prepare it. That's the only explanation as to why we're still alive. If not done right, it can have deadly consequences."

"I feel like I died. My gut and head are killing me."

"It will pass. In the meantime, we will rest here." She leaned back against the tree trunk. "I have not heard the sounds of pursuit. Even if there were any, I do not think I would have the strength to do anything about it."

"I know what you mean." His words sounded sleepy. In moments, she heard soft snoring coming out from under the arms.

Hana smiled. "Rest, my valiant companion. When we awaken, we will continue on the journey to find your son." With that, she curled against Joseph and fell asleep.

In the field recently vacated, two riders pulled up sharply when they spotted the other animals grazing ahead. One of the riders was tall; the other was shorter by a foot and had a stocky build.

"Is those their horses?"

"They are." Jacob answered. Getting off his horse, he scanned the area for any sign of the missing pair. They were nowhere in sight. "Remember, Mead, I want the female unharmed so we can use her to replenish our people. She looked young and fertile. She will bear us many fine children. The man, you can do with him as you please."

Those words brought a smile to the shorter man's sun wrinkled face. "Anything?"

"Anything."

"Are you sure they're still here? They could have left their beasties and went on foot."

"They're here. After I challenged him, Joseph drank the full cup. It had enough sedative in it to knock a horse over. And Hana, well, she sipped enough to affect her as well. I'm just surprised that they made it this far." Moving into the area to search, he said, "Come on, let's look for them. I'm sure they're sleeping it off somewhere close by."

The stocky man got off his horse and followed Jacob, attempting to look in all directions at the same time. He was honored when the tall man had asked him to go on this mission. Other travelers had gotten away before this, but this was the first time he went to hunt for them. And he wanted to make sure not to disappoint Jacob. That way he could go on future missions. He also wanted to help the commune in any way he could, even if it meant fathering a child. He smiled at that prospect.

Hidden from view in the woods, Joseph and Hana slept, unaware of who was coming their way.

Fourteen

The cat poked his head out from the underbrush and scoped out the scene ahead. In a very uncatlike fashion, his tongue hung out of his mouth. He was hot; he was tired; and he was ready to kill a dark twin.

Damn! Is he ever going to stop? He has to rest sometime!

Drizzle was frustrated at his inability to catch Drayco. He was sure he would have done so by now, if the man had stopped. Two days later, he was closer, but still not there. The scent of the horse was so strong; he would have thought Bravaro was standing right in front of him. Yet, he wasn't.

Knowing Drayco's need for blood to stay alive, Drizzle knew he would stop soon. He had to or else he would die. And that wasn't his purpose, at least not on this present mission.

There he is...finally, Drizzle thought. *About time too*

The gray blanket of Dusk was settling in, covering everything including the silhouette sitting next to a horse. Drizzle crept out of the brush slowly. He wanted to make sure it truly was the dark twin before he announced his presence.

Drawing closer, he smelled the coppery stench of blood. Drayco had made a kill. In response, the cat's stomach rumbled with its emptiness.

"I knew you'd be along shortly, so I saved this for you." Drayco tossed a rabbit carcass in Drizzle's direction.

The cat stared. He never understood how Drayco always seemed to know when he was there. It was as if he had eyes in the back of his head. He picked up the offering and carried it several paces away. Settling down, he said, "Many thanks."

Drizzle had not given Drayco much trust over the years, having lost it when he almost killed his sister so long ago. Since then, the dark twin had done much to restore it, though not to the level it once was.

"Where's Joseph?" Drayco glanced over a shoulder at the cat.

"I'm not sure. I left him when it took him too long to recover."

"Recover from what?"

"Too much water."

"Shyanne and I found his horse. It was killed by the grosbarks and shredded."

"Fortunately, the man on its back wasn't. He just forgot how to swim. I helped him to relearn." Drizzle ripped a large chunk of meat off and began to chew. When it disappeared, he continued. "I found where Shyanne is staying."

"Did she see you?"

"Don't worry; I have no plans on upsetting her further. I want the family together for the birth, same as you." He resumed his meal.

"Good. My leaving was bad enough." He fell silent. A couple of minutes later, Drayco asked, "Drizzle, why are you here? I sense a purpose, not random wandering."

Damn. There's no fooling this one. He has grown much in the past five years. "I found Joey."

Drayco slowly faced the big cat. "You what?"

"I found Joey."

"And why has it taken you so long to say so?" The tone coming from the dark man was low and menacing.

"Because Ruben has done something to him. The boy now calls him dad, as if Joseph no longer exists." He sat up on his forelegs and met the dark eyes glaring at his. "If I had told you the information right away, you would have raced to him. You would have snatched him and possibly damaged the boy beyond repair. We need to find out what Ruben has said or done to turn the boy away from his family."

Drayco thought about what the cat said. It made

sense. Then again, it didn't. Joey was a smart kid. Once he was with his family and saw the true nature of the man he was with, the boy would come willingly, he was sure of it. He did not express these thought to Drizzle, though. He needed to know where Joey was first before deciding what his next move would be.

"Tell me everything."

Drizzle recounted the events that transpired, including the joy seen on both when Ruben and Joey were together.

"That puts an interesting twist on things."

The darkness that replaced the dusk made it difficult for Drizzle to see Drayco's face. His dark tan, hair, and clothing did nothing to help matters either. That, plus clouds were rolling in. Rain was on the horizon; its smell was thick in the air, hiding any light from the moon above. His cat vision was good, but only as good as the light around him allowed.

"They left on horseback the day I came hunting for you. I do not know where they went. The only thing I overheard was some mention of an adventure."

"How long do you think it will take to get there?"

"A couple of days steady riding."

"Then we will leave at first light. And hope the coming rains will not drown us in the mean time." He rose to his feet and walked to his horse, removing the sleeping blanket attached to the saddle. Unrolling it, he wrapped it around his shoulder and lay down close to his horse.

Drizzle watched the dark form settle down. *He's up to something. What it is, I don't know. But something. I can tell by his manner. Years ago, he would have blow up, ranted and raved. Now he's reserved, calm. I think I liked the other way better. At least then I knew what to expect.*

He returned his attention to the half-eaten carcass, not sure when the opportunity for another meal would arise. When he finished, he carried the remains into the forest where scavengers would take care of the rest.

He curled into a ball when he returned to where Drayco slept. With one ear listening for any movement in case the dark twin tried to sneak away during the night, he closed his eyes

You have come far in my trust of you, dark one. But I will not underestimate you as I have done in the past.

That thought locked in his mind, the cat slept.

The day was overcast and wet. Both man and cat were miserable. Both had no desire to talk. The steady plodding of horse hooves through the puddles was the only thing to break the silence.

The storm that threatened during the night held off until the first rays of dawn attempted to reach across the sky. At that moment, the thick clouds unloaded their moisture in a heavy downpour, drenching both thoroughly. The blanket draped over Drayco's body did little to stop it. It now lay bunched up behind the saddle.

They had been traveling south since early morning. No creatures stirred. The rain kept them hidden in their warm dry burrows. Drizzle wished he were in a warm dry cave right now. Even the birds failed to sing.

He glanced back at the man on the horse. Drayco's shoulders were hunched and his head leaned forward, causing his wet hair to fall over his face. He had the appearance of someone not paying attention to where he was going. Instead, he appeared to be focused on inner thoughts. If Drizzle had not known the twin like he did, he would have thought he was in need of blood. Fortunately, he drank yesterday.

Was it only yesterday? It feels like it's been months.

A glimpse of movement brought his attention back to what lay ahead. He saw something off to one side. A black shape darted behind a large tree trunk. It was matched by another a short distance from the first.

Damn this rain. It masks all sound with its never-ending drip. He halted his forward progress.

Drayco came out of his reverie instantly. He pulled on Bravaro's reins, keeping him from stepping on the cat. Instead of asking what the cat was doing, he remained silent. He stared at where the cat's attention was directed and saw the dark shape dart from one bit of cover to another. He also saw that it was not alone. The sound of metal sliding free from its sheath sounded.

The rain not only masked any sound, it covered any scents as well. Drizzle had no idea what was out there. More and more dark shapes darted through the trees. Drizzle saw they were in deep trouble. Whatever was out there was on the hunt, and he felt certain they were the meal.

The cat knew he could outrun the creatures, but he was not sure if the horse could. The path they followed was narrow and windy. It would slow the animals speed, thus making in an easier target.

"Drayco, we are forced to make a stand here. If we try to run, you will be taken down quickly." Eying Bravaro, he added, "Try to stay in the saddle. It will give you a height advantage. And don't worry about anything getting behind you; I will prevent that from happening." The shapes darted around the pair on all side now.

Drayco gave the cat a wry smile. "Just make sure to stay out from under his hooves. He tends to throw them around when provoked." He gripped the sword handle tighter and shifted his position in the saddle. "Luckily, the trees which block our view also prevent them from rushing us all at once."

A loud crash ended all conversation. The man and cat saw a bulky black hunk of fur emerge from the trees and rise up to its full height. It towered above Drayco, even though he was on a horse. Intelligence radiated off the creature.

To his surprise, he saw it was a black bear; a black bear larger than any he had ever seen before or since the outbreak of the virus. Remembering what his father had taught him during one of their many outings, Drayco shouted, "Drizzle—black bears usually run away when confronted. Try lunging at it and see what happens. I'll try shouting and waving my arms."

The cat flattened his ears back and let out an ear-piercing yowl. He bared his teeth and darted toward the bear, swatting at it with a clawed hand. Drayco bellowed as loud as he could and flailed his arms wildly over his head. The bear stayed where it was, unmoved by the display.

Drayco quieted. What they were doing wasn't working. Drizzle followed suit. While he pondered what to do next, the rest of the dark shapes moved closer. They were all black bears, only smaller.

I wonder why it didn't scare off. Black bears usually avoid confrontation when possible. If they feel threatened, they usually bluff-charge then run away as quickly as possible. Something is different with these.

"Drayco! Watch out!"

The sudden shout brought Drayco back to the situation at hand. He spun around just in time to see one of the smaller bears charge. He yanked on the reins so that he faced the charge instead of having it behind him. Bravaro, already nervous because of the close proximity of so many predators, responded immediately.

When the bear was almost upon them, Bravaro reared unexpectedly. The dark twin grabbed the saddle to keep from tumbling backwards. He managed to keep both himself and his sword from hitting the ground.

Bravaro let out with an ear-piercing scream when he thrashed with his hooves. The bear avoided the flaying limbs, moving with a speed and agility unusual for the breed. Black bears were fast, but not that fast.

It lunged under the horse's upraised hooves and came at the man on its back, ignoring the exposed underbelly of the horse. Before Drayco had time to react, teeth sank into the arm holding the sword. He bellowed with surprise and pain.

The attacking bear tried to pull the man out of the saddle. Drizzle was on it before it could succeed. The cat sank sharp claws into the soft flesh, leaving several open gashes on both flanks. The bear let go of the dark twin and bawled in pain. It spun around to face the cat and never saw the hooves coming at it. Bravaro sent the creature reeling into the trees. When it stopped rolling, it rose and shook itself.

Blood flowed from the many puncture sites on his arm. Drayco ignored it because the big bear was on the move. It dropped to all four and came around to the injured bear. Sniffing at the wounds, it licked them clean. The other bears stayed where they were, watching the big one. They were waiting. For what, Drayco could only speculate.

A loud deep-throated pulsing echoed through the forest. Both man and cat looked in every direction, trying to locate it. Their eyes stopped when they reached another bear a short distance from the wounded one. The creature lowered it head and charged.

The animal was larger than the first, but not as large as the apparent leader. This time, Bravaro cooperated; he held his position. Drizzle hissed. It had no affect whatsoever.

The bear kept coming. It appeared to want him, not the animals. Crashing through the trees, it stopped just short of the dark man and started making a blowing sound. It slapped a paw on the ground a couple of times.

Drayco knew these were traits of an uneasy bear. What was different was that there were so many together when they usually ran alone, and that they were not afraid when he threatened them. Moreover, like the bigger one, a glint of intelligence radiated from the eyes.

Never taking his eyes from the display before him, Drayco said, "Drizzle, I know you think Bravaro isn't fast enough—but if we stay, we will die. These bears are playing with us. Once they've finished, they will come in for the kill."

The cat saw another bear moving in. It began making the same blowing sound, followed by the paw slapping. Then another and another and another joined them until all were making the same sounds and actions. If the situation wasn't so grave, it would almost be comical.

He glanced at the man before focusing on the direction they had to take. Three bears blocked the way. "I think you're right. I can dispatch two of them. Do you think you can take out the last?"

"If I can't, then I deserve what I get."

Laying the reins across the base of Bravaro's neck, he slowly lifted his leg and removed the boot knife hidden there. The arm holding the sword throbbed from the bite so he switched it to the opposite hand. With both hands now filled with lethal steel, he nodded to the cat that he was ready.

Drayco pressed his leg against Bravaro's side to signal the horse to turn around. The slow movement caused the bear display to increase in intensity. Squeezing hard with his thighs, he leaned forward. That simple action caused Bravaro to shoot toward the bears blocking the path ahead.

Drizzle was there first.

He raked one across the nose, leaving deep gouges in his wake. It flinched, bawled, and ran away. The other bear took advantage of the noise and attacked. It swung a paw at the cat. Catching him off guard, he flew into a tree and landed hard, the wind knocked from him.

Drayco saw the bears closing in on the cat and charged. He brought the sword down across the back of one and buried the dagger up to the hilt in the shoulder of another. He lost his grip on the dagger when the bear jerked away.

The dark man jumped from the saddle and ran to the cat. Blood ran from several small slashes created by broken branches. Otherwise, he seemed unhurt. "Can you move?"

His breath recovered, Drizzle snarled, "You fool! What are you doing out of the saddle. Get back into it before those bears get you."

"If you sit around arguing with me about a saddle, then yea, they will. You mind shutting up and moving instead."

After making sure Drizzle could move, Drayco ran toward the horse. Before he reached it, a bear darted between them. It let out with a knife-like bellow, causing the dark man flinched. All of a sudden, his world went topsy-turvy. Another bear had come up behind him and rammed into him.

Just as the first bear reached him, he brought the sword up and sliced into the outstretched paw. It jerked back, tumbling into the one who had knocked him down. Seeing his opportunity to escape, Drayco rolled onto his feet ran toward Bravaro. This time he reached him.

He heard the sounds of a battle behind him. The sudden yowl of a cat was followed by a deep bellow. There was no time to check out what was happening. He had to get in the saddle before the bears regrouped and attacked again. As he was throwing a leg over the back of the horse, teeth sank into his right leg. The pain almost caused his to fall from the horse. Swinging blindly with his sword, he felt it meet something solid.

Instead of letting go, the bear bit down harder. Drayco heard the bones snap.

He screamed. Through the haze of pain, he saw it was the lead bear. It no longer sat idle next to the injured one. It had his lower leg in the huge mouth and it intended to pull him from the saddle with it.

Drayco lashed out with the sword, losing count of how many times he struck before the bear let go. He continued to swing at it until the sudden forward motion of the horse forced him to hang on.

Drizzle had witnessed the big bear bite Drayco. He could do nothing about it because he had to dispatch the ones in front of him before he was able to help the dark twin.

Several swipes of his sharp claws cleared the way ahead. He raced over to Drayco and drove Bravaro a short distance down the path, digging a claw into the horse's flank when he slowed.

"Are you able to hang on?" Drizzle shouted.

Drayco's eyes were squeezed shut; his teeth clenched in pain. Unable or unwilling to speak, he nodded his head yes.

Bravaro needed no further encouragement to move. He sped down the path with the cat before the bears could recover and give chase.

Drayco clung to the saddle with every ounce of strength he could muster. The pain intensified with each pound of the hooves. He forced himself to stay conscious, to not give in to the pain and succumb to the increasing darkness closing in. He managed to win for a while. Eventually, the enveloping darkness won and he passed out.

When he awoke, he was lying on the ground partially covered by a blanket. He had no idea know how much time had passed. The dreary overcast sky was gone and sunlight way too bright for his newly opened eyes replaced it. A crude brace surrounded the break on his leg. The pain still nagged at him, though not to the point of being unbearable. He rolled his head over and looked around, trying to figure out where he was.

Bravaro grazed a short distance away with the saddle still on his back. Drizzle lay close, observing him through slit eyes. His tail gently lifted and flopped onto the ground.

"About time you woke up, sunshine."

Drayco remembered the bears and sat up quickly. It felt like every muscle in his body protested the action at the same time. A gasp escaped and sweat broke out on his brow. He managed to remain upright through sheer determination. After taking several deep breaths to calm his racing heart, the muscles relaxed their protest.

"Where are we?" he wiped the sweat off before it ran into his eyes and began twisting his upper body slowly, trying to loosen the tautness.

"A day's ride from where we encountered the bears. We're close to Ruben's hideout."

Drayco froze, one arm held over the opposite shoulder. "Excuse me? Did you just say we're close to Ruben?"

"When did I stutter?"

"Dammit Drizzle! I'm fed up with your smart remarks! A boy is in the hands of a killer, a killer who is brainwashing him, and all you can do is make snide remarks." Struggling to his feet, the dark man grimaced at the pain it caused. He limped toward Bravaro. "If you want to continue with the stupid remarks, then stay here. I don't need you." He reached the horse and leaned heavily against the animal's body. The injured leg was cocked to take the weight off it.

Drizzle watched the dark twin struggle to walk. He waited until he was beside the horse before moving. "I know you want to find Joey quickly. But in your present condition, you won't be able to take on Ruben."

"I don't care."

Drizzle remained silent, waiting.

"Blast it all to hell!" Drayco hit the saddle with a fist, causing Bravaro to shift his position out of reach. The dark man teetered off balance then fell, landing on his injured leg. The only sound to escape from him was a sudden intake of breath.

His head leaned forward, the face hidden by his hair, he asked, "Drizzle....I need to drink from something. It will help me to heal faster. Can you help me?"

Drizzle knew how proud the dark twin was. For him to ask like this showed how desperate he was to find the boy. His voice was filled with such anguish, the words pleading, that the cat felt compelled to help him. He nodded his head and raced into the forest to find what Drayco needed.

A half hour later, he returned with a small rabbit. It was the only thing he could find in such a short amount of time. Drayco took the offering and turned away. The sound of tissue ripping and sucking filled the immediate area. Drizzle left before the sounds stopped. He had to find more for the incredible healing powers to be useful.

Several hours later, he returned with another struggling rabbit and gave it to Drayco. The scents of many animals were everywhere. Their trails led in several directions, yet they remained elusive, enough so that he was not able to locate them. The rabbit was the only one to misjudge and fall victim to the cat.

"Thanks, Drizzle." The dark man hesitated, as if building up for his next statement. "I'm sorry I snapped at you earlier. I'm just tired of all the complications. I'm tired of living like this, forced to take blood from others to stay alive. I want my life to be like it was." He released a shaky breath. "Like it was before the virus."

"I understand. Unfortunately, we can't go back in time, we can't bring back what was lost." He gave the best wry smile his cat face could offer. "As your father used to say—if wants were pennies, we'd be millionaires by now."

An air of sadness settled over Drayco as he looked first at the carcass lying a short distance away, then at the rabbit cradled in the crook of an arm, its nose wriggling up and down. He ran a hand over its smooth fur.

"Still, I wish I did not have to do this to survive." He failed to say how he felt deep inside when the blood rushed through his body, making him feel more alive than ever, making his wish for more, almost like when an addict wished for drugs.

Frustrated at the change in Drayco's demeanor, Drizzle spat, "Would you get over yourself! I'm tired of listening to you wallow in self pity. Don't you think I get tired of killing? Don't you think we all get tired of killing?"

Drayco's hand halted its petting motion. He stared at the cat, unblinking, listening.

"If I didn't think you were needed, that you were important, do you think I would have wasted my time looking for something for you to drink from? Do you think I would have risked saving you from the bears?" He glared at Drayco with his golden eyes. Rising to his feet, he started pacing back and forth, never taking his eyes off the man before him.

"When I left the first time, you were all set to take on Ruben, hurt leg or no hurt leg. Now all you want to do is whine about things from the past. Would you figure out what you want to do and do it?" He halted his pacing. "Which is more important to you—that rabbit in your arms or the boy in the hands of a conniving killer?"

Drayco grimaced at the last words; they stung like a branding iron. They were too close to the truth. Usually he had better control. For some reason, his emotions were all over the place. *Maybe my connection with Shyanne is affecting me. Maybe because her emotions are a mess, due to the pregnancy, it's carrying over to me.*

Holding the cat's eyes a moment longer, he turned

away and said, "I'll finish quickly; you can have the carcass afterwards."

"This one is plenty." He walked to the discarded rabbit and picked it up in his mouth then moved several paces away from the dark twin. Lying down, Drizzle said, "By the time you're finished, I will be too."

He could tell by the cat's tone and mannerism that he was still angry with him. Shrugging his shoulder, knowing the cat would get over it; he held the head over and bit into the tiny neck. The rabbit's struggles ended after a few swallows, as if it knew resistance was pointless. Eventually, the pulse ended as well. As he wiped the blood from his lips, Drizzle came up to him.

"Well?"

"Well what?"

"Did the blood help any?"

Flexing his leg and flinching at the pain it caused, Drayco said, "Some. I can tell it's still broken, but at least it's not as painful." He raised the dead rabbit. "Sure you don't want it? Shame to waste it."

"Like I said before—when did I stutter."

Drayco caught a glint of humor in the cat's eyes. With those words, their conversation had gone full circle. From calm to angry and back to calm again. Drawing back, he threw the unwanted carcass as far as into the trees as possible. It ricocheted off one and fell into some brush.

"I have to redo this splint." Looking at the supports, he saw they were flat pieces of wood. "Where did you find these?"

"They were part of a small hut we passed. I knew you would have need of them so I grabbed them."

"Bet that was awkward to run with." The dark twin snickered at the sight that came to mind and began untying the rope holding the boards together.

"You have no idea." The words dripped with sarcasm.

The leg was various shades of purple where the bear had bit him. Thanks to the healing powers of the blood, and the genetic alteration from the virus, the holes where the teeth sank in were no longer open; they were shiny with new skin. Gently touching along the shin, Drayco located the break. The surrounding area was swollen and the bones felt slightly out of alignment. He hoped it wasn't too late to set them straight, that the bones had not started to mend due to the blood.

Frowning, he thought, *I'm so stupid. I should have done this way before drinking that blood.* Aloud, he said, "Drizzle, I need you to do something for me. I need you to hold the leg...hold it no matter what. Okay?"

The glint of humor was gone, replaced with one of understanding. He nodded his head and moved forward, grasping the ankle firmly with both hand like paws.

Before he had time to think about it, Drayco settled back onto his elbows, dug his other heel into the ground, and pushed away from the cat as hard and fast as he could. He felt the bones shift, causing pain to flash through his body like lightning. Unable to help himself, he leaned his head back and screamed.

The sound bounced from tree to tree, echoing across the surrounding area. Drizzle hoped they were far enough away from the cave to avoid being overheard. If they were, he knew Ruben would take Joey and run. It was something he refused to think about right now.

The dark twin collapsed onto his back, tears streaming down the sides of his face. He covered his eyes with an arm, breathing in and out slowly to try to reduce the pain. It helped some, but not a lot.

"Drizzle, do you think you can find something else, something larger...please?"

"How about a bear?"

He was unable to laugh at the cat's lousy humor; the pain was too intense. "Please?"

"I'll do what I can. Do you want me to resplint the leg first?"

"No, let it be. I'll do it later."

After the cat left, Drayco lay there until he felt able to move. gritting his teeth, he sat up and guided his fingers over the break again. The alignment was better, but a bump under the skin showed him it was not complete.

I'm too late. I waited too long to do this. Damn!

He flopped back onto the ground, angry. He was angry at the bears, angry at his leg, angry with himself for allowing this to happen, angry at the virus for ruining his life. Mostly, he was angry with Ruben. If the mercenary had not reentered their lives, he and Shyanne would still be together, not gallivanting all over the blasted countryside trying to find loved ones. He slammed his fist against the ground several times, unable to do anything else to relieve the tension.

By the time Drizzle returned with a stunned buck, darkness had settled in. Drayco was calmly sitting next to a small fire with his leg splinted, staring into the flames. Bravaro stood a short distance away. The saddle was removed and the dark man had it behind him, using it like a backrest.

He dropped the buck close and nodded his head in the direction of the horse. "Hard to get off?"

"Some. Had to do it, though."

"How are you doing?"

"I'll manage."

Drizzle looked at the man. Drayco's eyes were fixed on the buck. At first, the cat thought he saw pleasure wash over the twin's face. In a flash, the look was replaced with one of disgust, as if the deer were a diseased thing instead of a life giver. It happened so fast that he wondered if he had truly seen it.

"I'll take the first watch. You drink then sleep. I hope that by morning your leg will be able to support you without pain. Then we can go on to the hideout." The cat rose and started toward the wooded area.

"Drizzle—I owe you."

"You owe me nothing. We're doing this for Shyanne...and for Joey." He disappeared into the cover of darkness.

Drayco returned his gaze to the buck. He stared at it for a short time before leaning forward and biting deep into the neck. The blood from the wound poured into his mouth. Closing his eyes, he swallowed. The thrill of the rejuvenation blood coursed through him, almost taking him over. He fought to maintain control, and won, almost wishing for the pain instead.

The blood stopped shortly after the heart did. Drayco pushed the buck away. He rolled onto his side and fell asleep within minutes.

In the woods, Drizzle watched. *I hope he isn't losing control again. If he is, I'll have end that threat. That would be a shame because I'm finally starting to like the man.*

The cat sighed before fading into the surrounding

area.

Fifteen

In her dreams, Hana heard the rustling of the fallen leaves. She heard the faint whispers of voices echo through the trees. They were growing louder. She wanted to tell the speakers to be quiet. She wanted to tell them she needed more sleep. Her head hurt.

A loud snap brought her awake. She remained motionless, listening.

"I think I see them. They're over there."

The whispered voice was not one she recognized. The harsh whisper that answered was. It was Jacob. They had found them.

"Silence—or you'll wake them."

While she slept, her hands had cupped together. Thankful for her body's choice of sleeping positions, she moved her right hand closer to the opposite arm. She hoped the approaching men would not notice. Fortunately, they missed it.

The wooden handle of the nunchaku felt good in her grasp. *At least this way I have some way to defend myself.* She thought about waking Joseph; the sound of the approaching footsteps was too close.

"What do we do now?" the mystery speaker whispered.

"They must still be under the effect of the drug. Let's tie them up, just in case they wake on the way back." Jacob spoke normally. "I don't want this prize to get away again."

"Do I still get to do what I want to the man?"

"Of course, whatever you want."

Hana heard the sly tone in Jacob's reply and knew they meant Joseph ill will. She waited until she heard the sound of someone kneeling next to her before she moved. Pulling the nunchaku out from her sleeve, she swung it in a wide arch. It landed with a thud, followed by a cry of pain. She rolled away, getting to her feet as quickly as possible.

Jacob stood back a short distance, his mouth hanging open. A short stocky man was bent over where she once lay. His arms covered his belly. Hana heard him trying to recover the breath she had knocked out of him with the hit. Before either realized what was happening, she advanced on the winded man.

Moving with the speed of a humecat, she brought her foot up against his head. Mead tried to turn away before the hit landed; he was too late. He flew against a tree trunk and rolled off, falling face first to the ground. He didn't move.

At least I took one out. Now the odds are more even. Let's hope Jacob is more of a talker than a fighter. She eased back on one leg, ready to move in an instant.

"Well, young lady, I see you dispatched Mead in a hurry. You surprise me.

Hana remained silent. She glanced quickly at Joseph. He continued to sleep off the drug.

"He will not help you. He drank too much of the sedative."

"Was it Monkshood?"

"Again—you surprise me. How did you know?" He circled around her, trying to get closer to Mead.

"I'm familiar with its uses." Hana kept the prefect in front. She had no desire to have him behind her. The only problem was Joseph was now between them, along with the unconscious Mead.

When Jacob reached the unconscious Mead, he stooped and felt for a pulse. Straightening, he said, "I'm afraid you killed him, my dear."

"That is too bad. Life is precious and should not be wasted so."

"You will not find me as easy a victim. I'm the head prefect for a reason; I can handle unruly ones like you—and tame them nicely. Just ask Merna." He eyed Hana's slim frame, his gaze pausing in inappropriate places. "She was once like you. Rough around the edges, yet moldable. I showed her the errors of her ways and she came around to adore me. I look forward to our lessons with the same eagerness." He lunged at her so suddenly; he almost succeeded in catching her off guard.

She stumbled backward over a fern. Catching herself, she ducked under his outstretched arms and hit him in the ribs with the end of the wooden handle. He grunted with the impact, but did not go down.

He jumped away instead of grabbing at her. While they circled one another, he rubbed the spot where she had landed the hit. "Tisk, tisk. That was not very ladylike."

"It is not very gentlemanly to force a woman to do what she does not want to."

"I'm not forcing, my dear, only redirecting thoughts."

"Of course. That is why Merna is pregnant at such a young age."

"Of course."

Jacob gave her a smile filled with meaning; it held no warmth. It made her sick. *I have to be careful; he is so much larger than I am. However, that is only a hindrance, not an obstacle. If I watch his body motions, I might be able to judge when he is going to attack. Then I can find his weakness and take advantage of it.*

Hana watched Jacob reach around to his back and pull out a small whip. He uncurled it with a flick of the wrist, trying to intimidate her. It didn't work.

The tiny woman crouched low while moving, making herself as small a target as possible. Jacob twirled the whip in ever tightening circles. Suddenly, it shot toward her. She rolled out of the way before it struck. She had seen the muscles in his shoulder bunch and knew he was about to use the weapon. It hit the fern close to her instead.

Jacob jerked the whip back. He twirled it again, waiting, playing with her. He didn't think the mere woman before him stood a chance against his superior intellect.

The whip shot out several more times, each one missing her, but not by much. His aim was getting better, though. He was starting to understand how she moved. She knew it was time to act. If she did not, Jacob would win in the end. That was something she would not tolerate.

"Why linger the inevitable? Why not embrace the future that awaits you? I will take good care of you. Better than this man would have." He pointed to the prone figure of Joseph.

The whip snapped at her again. This time, it hit. She was distracted by looking at Joseph and missed the arm motion. It hit her left shoulder, causing the material of her shirt to rip open. A small trickle of blood oozed from the wound.

"See? I will win. I will take you home with me." The look in his eyes showed the triumph he felt.

"One hit does not win the battle." Hana straightened. She was tired of playing cat and mouse. It was time to end this.

She waited until he popped the whip again to attack. Instead of running away, she ran toward him. The move caught Jacob off guard. He did not have time to recover before the nunchaku hit him on the side of his face. She followed it immediately with a punch to the belly. Gasping from the blow, he managed to grab a handful of hair before she could withdraw. He yanked her head back.

She reached over her shoulder and wrapped her hand around his wrist, giving it a wicked twist. He yelped with pain, but continued to hold the hair. He was gaining control and was trying to pin her body against his, thus reducing her ability to fight. She had to do something before that happened.

Bringing her foot upward, she brought the heel down hard on top of his. She did it repeatedly until he let go. Once freed, she spun around, stepped back, and kicked him in the groin. He crumpled. When she tried to kick him again, his arm darted out and grabbed her leg. He jerked it out from under her. She landed with a thud on her back. The nunchaku went flying from her grasp.

Jacob grinned. "I've had that one done before. Since then, I've learned to protect certain parts of my anatomy." He moved quickly, straddling her, trying to pin her arms to the ground.

It was the oldest trick in the book and she fell for it. She knew her freedom, her sanity, and Joseph's life were on the verge of disappearing. This gave her the determination to do what she had to do. She jerked her hand away and hit him square on the end of the nose.

Hana felt the cartilage give. The force of her hit drove it inward into his brain, killing him instantly. Blood oozed from each nostril as he slumped over. His eyes remained open, focused on hers. They were frozen, lifeless. Gagging, she shoved the body off. She hated to kill. It was so unnecessary. Life was too precious, too sacred. In this case, she knew it was necessary. His death meant that many others were saved from being ruined, including her.

The vomiting from earlier had rid her of most of her stomach contents. The dry heaves brought on by killing were worse. Fortunately, they did not last long.

The little woman made her way to Joseph when she was back in control of herself. She wanted to get out of here as soon as possible. "Joseph. Joseph. Wake up." She shook him several times before he responded.

"Wha—," Joseph stammered. He sat up and rubbed his eyes, trying to get the sleep out of them. Seeing the downed combatants, one of them being Jacob, he asked, "What happened here?"

"I solved a problem."

"Why didn't you wake me? I could have helped."

"If the noise of the battle did not wake you, then you would not have awakened otherwise." Hana started toward the open area where the horses were grazing.

"But...."

She suddenly spun around, angry. "No buts. It is over. Move on." She glared at him for a second then continued toward the horses.

"Did I ever tell you that you remind me of a certain cat I know?" Joseph rose to his feet and followed. His gate was weak but steady.

"Thank you."

"I don't think you understand."

"I think he is a very intelligent creature. I'm honored to be compared to him."

"I meant sarcastic till the end—and stubborn too."

"Thank you again."

"I'm not going to win against you, am I?"

"No."

"Hana—you're an incredible woman. When you two meet, my wife is going to love you."

"That's nice," she said as she walked away. "Now, we

need to resume the search for your son. I suggest we head back toward the west. I think we have gone too far east."

Joseph merely shook his head and smiled.

They rode west until it was too dark to see where they were going. Neither one knew for certain where they were. Nothing looked familiar. Finally, Joseph pulled on the reins, halting the forward motion of his horse.

"Hana, we have to stop. I can't see the nose in front of my face."

A little farther. We can go a little farther."

"Hana—no. We stop now. Who knows what we will run into. And we won't even know it's there until too late." He dismounted.

Hana continued a short distance. When she realized Joseph was not following, she sighed and pulled her horse around. "I suppose since you won't move I have to stay with you." She guided her horse to him and dismounted as well.

He let his horse graze on some of grass growing on the edges of the trail they had followed for most of the day. Tall thin trees grew on either side. Their thick tops prevented any light from above reaching them. He was barely able to make out the small woman standing a few feet away.

Frustrated by the inability to see a thing, Joseph said, "I think we need a fire."

"Do you think that wise? It might attract unwanted attention."

"At least we'll be able to see what it attracts before it attacks. Let's get some wood."

The pair soon had a warm glowing fire going. They settled down, hands extended to take in the warmth. Hana remained quiet during the entire process. Joseph knew something was bothering her.

"Hana—are you okay? You've not said three sentences since we stopped."

"It is nothing."

Joseph would not let it go. "Hana, what's eating you?"

"I don't want to talk about it."

"Is it the killing? Are you upset because you had to do it?"

The little woman pulled her legs against her body and

bowed her head. Her hair hid her face from view. Just as Joseph was about to speak, he heard one word spoken barely above a whisper.

"Yes." She raised her head and Joseph saw tears running down her cheeks. "I do not like to kill. I cherish life above all else. To take a life kills a part of me in return."

"But if you hadn't, what would have happened?"

"He would have killed you and enslaved me."

"Then by taking a life, you saved a life." Joseph moved beside her and placed his hand on her shoulder. "I'm glad you did what you did. If you hadn't, I wouldn't be here to look for my son."

She looked into his blue eyes with her sorrowful brown ones. She wanted so much to kiss him, but knew that was impossible. He belonged to another. Instead, she cupped the side of his face, and smiled. "Thank you, Joseph. You have helped me immensely."

"Why don't I take the first watch? I will wake you in four hours. Deal?"

"Alright." She pulled away from his hand and curled up beside the fire, closing her eyes.

Joseph watched her for a few seconds before he rose to his feet. He moved down the trail, out of the firelight. The darkness enveloped him in a matter of steps. It was a good thing. He was starting to have feelings that were reserved only for his wife. If he had stayed there any longer, he wasn't sure what would have happened.

I sure will be happy when this whole mess is finished and my family is back home safe and sound. Shyanne, I miss you...you and that boy of ours.

As promised, he woke Hana in four hours. At the first sign of dawn, they were on the move again. The woman seemed more in control of herself. She even smiled when Joseph glanced back at her. The trail was too narrow for them to ride side by side so he took the lead.

They had gone about five miles when the trail met another. This one ran north and south. Joseph pulled up and turned around in the saddle. "Which way?"

"I think we need to go south. It seems the most logical way."

"South it is."

He tugged the reins to the left and prodded the horse

into motion. This trail was a little larger, but not by much. They continued to travel in a line instead of beside each other.

The area looked like it had rained recently. Puddles of water still in the process of drying dotted the ground. Joseph glanced down at once such puddle and pulled up sharply. Hana jerked her horse sideway to prevent a collision.

"What's the matter?"

On the trail was a hoof print he had not seen in a long time. It belonged to his wife's twin brother, Drayco.

"Bravaro."

"Who?"

"Look—look at that print. It belongs to Bravaro. He's Drayco's horse." He glanced around. Finally, he found what he sought. A paw print was on the trail near the grassy edge. "And there, that's Drizzle's. I'm sure of it. They must be ahead of us." He grinned from ear to ear.

Hana smiled. "That is good. That means you will have help with your quest."

"With the nose on that cat, we'll find Joey in no time."

The fair-haired man faced forward again and in the excitement of finding something good amongst so much bad kicked the horse a little too hard in the sides. It leaped ahead, almost tossing him from the saddle. He frantically grabbed the saddle horn and pulled himself upright, successfully preventing the undesired outcome. Hana shook her head and smiled. Gently prodding her horse, she followed at a calmer speed.

Joseph was almost out of sight when a dark shape moved on her right side. It kept pace with her horse. Within seconds, she saw other dark shapes dart from tree to tree. Sensing something not right, she urged her horse into more speed. The dark shapes stayed with her.

Suddenly, one of the shapes detached itself from the surrounding forest. It stood directly in her path. It was a huge black bear. Its eyes yielded the cunning mind inside the expansive head. Her horse reared. She managed to stay in the saddle on its back.

"Joseph! Joseph! I need you!" She hoped he wasn't too far ahead to hear her cries. "Joseph—help!"

Other bears came into view. She saw they were surrounding her, cutting off any chance for escape. With her hands full, struggling to keep the horse under control, she was unable to reach for her weapon. Hana decided she could not control the animal beneath her and let go of the reins. She grabbed her nunchaku. At least this way she had a chance to survive, if only for a little longer.

One of the bears reared too close for the horse's liking. It flew into a tree when hooves met its chest. A bear close to the first saw an opportunity and moved in. Hana caught the movement in her peripheral vision and brought her weapon down on its nose, forcing it back. Another bear reached out and raked one of the dancing legs. The horse screamed in response.

The smell of the fresh blood caused the bears to get bolder; they moved in for the kill. Just as Hana thought the end was near, a bellow echoed throughout the trees.

Joseph held his sword high as he raced down the path toward the commotion. He arched it in the air at the big one in his way. It leaped off to the side before he could hit it. Another bear was not so lucky. The blade bit into its neck, slicing it open. Blood spurted out of the cut artery.

During the distraction caused by Joseph, Hana failed to see the bear coming up behind her. It reared on its hind legs and sank both teeth and claws into the soft flesh of the horse. Another joined it. Between the combined weights of the two, the horse went down. She leaped off before she was trapped, as well.

Hana ran quickly toward the man thundering toward her.

Joseph leaned over and extended an arm out for her to grab when he passed by. She seized it and threw herself up behind him, wrapping her arms around his waist. He tugged the reins hard, forcing the horse to spin back the way they came and kicked it into motion before the woman behind him had time to settle herself.

The big bear lunged at the couple as they started to move past it. Joseph swung his sword backward in a wide arch, forcing Hana to duck sideway to avoid being sliced. Again, the bear leaped out of the range of the blade. This time it rebounded quickly. It swatted at them with its huge paw, hooking Hana's pants. She hissed in a breath, but said nothing.

Joseph brought the sword forward and this time

struck flesh. He hit the bear on the left ear, slicing it off and sending it flying into the trees. It yanked the paw back, tearing the fabric and the skin underneath it easily. Joseph wasted no time; he urged the horse forward. By the time the bear recovered enough, the pair was moving away, fast. The big monster stayed behind. It decided to show its dominance over the others instead by claiming the screaming horse for itself. The blood flowing from the missing ear was forgotten. The filling of an empty belly took precedence.

Hana buried her face into Joseph's back. She could still hear the screams from the doomed horse. The sound sent shivers up her spine and into the base of her skull, overriding the pain from her right leg. She hugged the fair-haired man tight. Once they were too far for the sound to carry, she relaxed. Unfortunately, the pounding of the wounded leg blended with the pounding of the hooves as they hit the ground. The death grip on Joseph's waist remained.

Joseph continued at the breakneck speed for several miles. When he was certain the bears had not followed, he slowed the horse. Its sides heaved and sweat blanketed its body. He did not stop. He kept it walking to cool down.

"That was close, too close. How are you doing back there?"

Hana kept her face against his back. Her arms stayed around his waist. She did not answer.

"Hana? You okay?" He reached back and placed a hand on her thigh. Something moist and sticky caused his fingers to slide. He brought them forward; it was blood. "Hana! Are you okay?"

She released her grip on him and said, "I am okay."

Jerking the horse to a stop, he twisted in the saddle enough to look at her. She was pale, yet her eyes remained clear. Joseph could tell she was in extreme pain by the expression on her face.

"What happened?" He slid out of the saddle to take a closer look at the skin under the torn fabric. "Did that big bear do this?"

Hana nodded her head yes. She flinched when he manipulated the fabric to see under it. A trio of slashes went across the middle of her thigh. It was deep in some parts, shallow in others.

"We have to get this taken care of. Do you have any

of those medicinal things you used on me?"

"No. Unfortunately, they were with my horse."

"Damn."

"My sentiments exactly." Grabbing the torn pant leg, she ripped it wider. "Can I have some water and a fresh rag? I want to clean this as soon as possible."

Joseph was about to remove the water bag hanging from the saddle when a noise caused him to spin around. He reached over his shoulder and withdrew his sword in one smooth motion. If a bear had followed, he was going to make sure it could not do so again.

He watched a dark shape dart from one tree to another. He was not able to make out what it was due to its incredible speed. Because of the size, he knew it was not the big bear. Maybe it was one of the smaller ones. Either way, he was not going to allow further hindrance to his mission.

Hana looked at where Joseph focused his attention. Being higher, she had a better view of the shape. For some reason, she did not think it was a bear. She had a feeling it was something else. Something familiar.

Joseph saw the shape flash mere feet away. He raised the sword and shouted, "Die you son of a stinking rizbak! You'll not have one of us for your meal!" He started forward, intent on killing the unknown creature before it killed one of them.

"Joseph! Wait!"

His forward momentum faltered because of her shout. Suddenly, the creature leaped from its hiding spot and landed on his chest. He fell onto his back, unable to use his sword at such close quarters. Before he had time to go for his knife, pudgy fingers grabbed his cheeks and a long wet tongue ran across his lips and over his nose.

"Hi, sweet cheeks. Miss me?"

"What the hell...," Joseph stammered. "Drizzle? Is that you?"

"Who else would it be? Ruben?"

"What are you doing here? How in the hell did you find us?"

"Is that how you greet a long lost friend?" Drizzle stepped away from the downed man, which in turn caused the horse to snort and shift its legs. His scent was causing a great deal of discomfort. The cat nodded his head at the excited animal, and said, "You might want to move."

Joseph glanced toward the direction indicated by the cat and saw a hoof rushing at his face.

"Whoa!"

He rolled out of the way just before it landed on the recently vacated spot. His action caused some dirt from the path to waft into the air. It seemed to target his nose. He began to cough and sneeze at the same time.

Hana giggled. The giggle turned into a shriek of surprise when the horse lunged away from the commotion. It tried to turn around and go back the way it came, back toward the bears. She snatched at the reins looped over the saddle horn and managed to grab them before the horse turned fully around. Hopping into the saddle instead of sitting behind it, she pulled back as hard as she could.

The horse fought the bit. It tossed its head and reared. Joseph was on his feet, trying to grab the halter. An occasional cough escaped from him while he avoided the flying hooves. Drizzle sat on his haunches and watched the entertainment through slit eyes.

"Dammit, Drizzle! Hana's hurt. She can't hold on when the horse acts like this."

The horse took that moment to jerk around so the cat could see the right side. Drizzle noticed the torn pant leg and the blood covering it. He moved farther away from the frightened beast. Once he was out of eyeshot, it was easier for Joseph to bring the horse under control.

Concern filled Joseph when he saw the closed eyes and stiff posture. "Are you okay?"

"I am unchanged." She replied through clenched teeth. Opening her eyes, she focused them on the man next to her. "Thank you, Joseph, for your concerns."

"Healer woman, can you travel?" Drizzles words came from down the path. The cat sat watching them.

She shifted her position in the saddle to ease the pain in her leg. "I can. What services do you require?"

"Another needs your help. He lies down this path." Drizzle kept his tone respectful. He had sensed the power in this woman during their first meeting. It had grown considerably since then.

"I do not have any supplies, but I will do what I can."

"What the hell are you talking about, Drizzle?" Joseph

demanded, looking down the path then back at the cat. His tone became more intense, more frantic. "Who's down there? Is it Joey?"

Drizzle ignored him. "Follow me, Healer woman." He turned away from the humans. "Quickly. I'm not sure if he's in the same condition as when I left him."

"Drizzle! Is it Joey?"

Silence was his only answer.

"Drizzle!"

A gentle touch on his shoulder caused Joseph to look away from the cat. Hana leaned over. "Joseph, come. He will not answer you. It only wastes time. Come. We will find out soon enough."

Joseph glared at the retreating form of the big cat. He threw himself up behind Hana, making sure not to touch the wounded leg. "What about you? You haven't had a chance to clean your wound."

"I will live. Another needs me"

Joseph wrapped his arms around the little bit of a woman and held tight as she prodded the horse forward. It resisted, at first, due to the smell of Drizzle. After several soft-spoken words and a few clicks of her tongue, it yielded.

Hours later, at the entrance to a small open area, Drizzle paused. The horse behind him stopped before getting too close. Hana and Joseph heard the cat spat. He was upset about something.

"What's wrong?" Joseph asked, concerned that his son might be ahead, needing him.

"That son of a rizbak's butt is gone."

As a result of those words, Joseph felt the weight of the world lift. He knew the cat would never talk about Joey that way. He had a feeling he knew who the cat talked about, though.

"Was it Drayco?"

Drizzle padded over to the only items visible: a saddle and a blanket. He felt the blanket. It was cold. "He must have left shortly after I did."

"What was the matter with him?" Hana's soft voice carried across to the cat.

"His leg was broken by some bears, maybe the same ones that attacked you. I was able to give him some of what he needed to help in the healing process, but I had to go farther than anticipated to find more." Drizzle hesitated to say more. He wasn't sure how much Hana knew about the dark twin. "That's how I found you two."

Hana sensed Drizzle was holding something back. She ignored it. To pursue the hidden feeling was considered rude by the teachings she grew by. Instead, she asked, "What would lead him to do such a thing?"

"Joey."

Joseph's head jerked toward the speaker. "Did you say Joey?"

"What is it with you human males? Are you all deaf?"

"Answer the question."

"Yes. I said Joey. I found him a short distance from here. He's with Ruben."

"And you couldn't say anything about this before now?" Joseph clenched his hands into fists. He hopped down from the horse and advanced on the cat, his intentions apparent by his mannerism. "That madman has my son...and is doing god knows what to him...and you're more worried about Drayco? Aaarrrr!" He ran toward the cat, swinging his fists at the tawny body when he was close enough.

Drizzle sidestepped the charge. He extended a leg and tripped Joseph. The fair-haired man sprawled across the ground. He immediately jumped to his feet and charged at the cat, angrier than before. Once again, Drizzle avoided the man as he flew past. Compared to the human, the cat was in total control. His moves were calculated, whereas the man was reckless.

Suddenly, Joseph freed his sword and ran at the cat, the blade held high over his head. It was a move Drizzle had not anticipated. He scrambled out of the way before the blade cleaved him in half. Joseph's face was blood red, like the look in his eyes. Drizzle brought a hand up, the claws partially extended, and swatted the wrist holding the sword. Joseph yowled with pain. Four lines appeared across the side on the wrist. The cuts were not deep, but they were effective in causing the out of control human to drop the weapon. Before Joseph recovered, the cat pounced on his back and knocked him down. He grabbed a handful of blonde hair and pulled back. Razor sharp claws brushed against the exposed skin.

"ENOUGH!"

Both combatants stopped. They stared at the woman sitting on the horse. Hana's face was expressionless, resembling stone.

"If you two continue in this fashion, a small child will pay the price. Is that something you want? Is that something that will bring an end to this foolishness?"

"I didn't start this; he did by not speaking up about Joey," Joseph snapped. Due to the sharp claws on his throat, he wasn't able to move his head.

"I will end this with the swipe of my claw if you don't shut up," Drizzle said with a snarl.

Hana's face showed none of the anger boiling inside, but her eyes; they spoke volumes. Instead of speaking, she picked up the reins and prodded the horse forward with her uninjured leg.

Neither man nor cat moved. Neither was willing to give in. Neither wanted to give the other the satisfaction, or the chance, to finish what was started. Hana was half a mile down the path before either realized she was not stopping.

"I don't think she's going to wait for us."

Drizzle pulled Joseph's head back further, forcing the man to lift his chest off the ground. "A truce. When I let go, you will not go after me with that blasted sword. We will focus our energies on hunting for Joey as Hana said. Agreed?"

Joseph glared at the cat. He hated being forced to do something he should have been doing all along: finding his son.

"Agreed?" Drizzle shook the head in his grasp.

"Agreed."

Drizzle let go and leaped away before Joseph could reconsider. His golden eyes watched for a moment. A second later, the cat spun around and raced after Hana. He was not waiting for Joseph to get up. He knew the man would follow.

Joseph sat up and touched the stinging areas on his neck. Frustrated, he wiped the blood off his fingers then rose to his feet. His sword lay a few feet away. He stared at it. The more he thought about what had just happened, the angrier he became. Not at the cat, but at himself. By fighting with Drizzle, he had wasted precious time. Time that could have been spent finding his son. Hana was right; he was foolish. Hopefully, that foolishness hadn't cost him too great a price to bear.

Picking up the sword, Joseph slid it into the sheath on his back. He jogged down the path after his vanished comrades. By the time he caught up to them, the burning anger was nothing more than a smoldering ember. The mission to reunite his family before the eminent birth was once more dominating the forefront.

Sixteen

Drayco had no idea how he made it to the cave, or how he managed to find it at all. The ride was hazy due to the pain wreaking havoc throughout his body. He was forced to keep his splinted leg straight, which made riding awkward, especially without a saddle. His body was tired; he was tired. Finding the cave had rejuvenated him.

He pulled Bravaro up before entering the area surrounding the entrance. Listening, he heard no activity, no movement of any kind. He slid from the horse's back, making sure to put all his weight on his left leg. Bravaro shifted slightly. The action forced the dark twin to catch himself. Pain jarred him. He swore under his breath.

Once he had himself under control, he limped up to the cave. Hugging the rocky face, he listened again. Again, he heard nothing.

They must be gone, he thought. *Now's my change to get in there. Maybe I can find a place to hide. That way I can catch Joey's attention and get him the hell out of here.*

He limped into the darkness beyond. As he drew near an intersection, he caught sight of a glow off to his right, farther down the branch. The branch in front of him remained dark. The light from the entrance did little to penetrate it. Drayco turned right. A few steps down the tunnel, he noticed the chiseled marks on the wall. Reaching up, he felt the irregular patterns. Aware that at any moment Ruben could return, he continued on.

The light grew brighter. A torch rest in a holder attached to the wall. Drayco stared at the wall. Instead of being rough, it was smooth, too smooth to be created by nature. The wall was manmade. He saw a doorway just ahead. Limping to it, he peered inside. The room was circular. It held a single stall, empty at present.

He saw more doorways farther down the hall and moved to the one on the left. It was a storeroom. The room across from it was also used for storage. Both rooms were circular. Something about the place nagged at him. It seemed familiar, as if he knew it from somewhere...but where.

"Well, I'll be damned," he said when it finally dawned on his what he was standing in. "This used to be a bunker."

Drayco moved down the passageway to the main room. It had the same smooth round walls as the others, only larger. Several torches burned bright, chasing away any shadows, showing him no place to hide. The dark man limped across to the only other opening. The room beyond was for sleeping. It had a pad and some clothes too large to be Joey's tossed over a small stool, nothing more.

The only way I can stay undetected is by hiding in a storage room. He returned the way he came until he stood inside one of the rooms.

Crates of various sizes lined one wall. Several more were stacked next to them, making a nice little hiding spot. Drayco worked his way into the small space and stretched out, resting his back against the boxes. The braced leg stuck out. Fortunately, the boxes hid it from the doorway.

Suddenly, he remembered his horse. Muttering several curses under his breath, the dark man struggled to his feet. He limped out of the cave and into the glaring light outside. Blinking away the brightness, he saw Bravaro still standing where he had left him, grazing on some green morsels at the edge of the clearing.

Not wanting to expend more energy than he already had, he whistled softly. Bravaro raised his head at the sound. He pranced to the dark man, rubbing his nose against the outreaching hand.

"Hey, boy, you enjoying yourself?" Drayco moved his hand to the muscular neck and gave it several pats. He spoke to Bravaro similar to how he would a human, knowing full well the horse had no idea what he was saying. "I need you to disappear. Can you do that?" The horse's ears flicked back and forth. "I need you to go find Drizzle. That cat may be a huge pain in my backside, but I need him here. I need backup." A smile creased his face at the memories brought back with that statement.

Drayco grabbed the bridle and turned the horse around. His hand trailed down the body until it reached the back end. There, he rubbed it several times before giving it a hard smack. Bravaro darted forward, but slowed when he got near the pathway. Drayco waved his arms back and forth over his head. He couldn't risk shouting. Ruben might over-hear and be forewarned.

Bravaro continued to slow. In frustration, Drayco picked up several small rocks and threw them, intent on scaring him. One hit the rump, causing the horse to speed up. He disappeared quickly.

"I'm sorry, friend. For the sake of a small boy, I had to do that." With a sigh, Drayco limped his way back to the storeroom.

Resting in the confined space once more, he leaned back and crossed his arms over his chest. He was not sure how long the wait would be. For him, it mattered not; Joey was more important. The throbbing in his leg reminded him that it was not happy with how he had used it lately. By the time an hour had passed, the dark man's mood was foul in-deed.

*　　*　　*

Ruben and Joey were gone for two days. During that time, Sheena had shown little Joey some hand to hand com-bat, her expertise. She took it easy because of his smaller size. Joey was not under such constraints. A couple of times he bested the woman. Ruben suspected she let him, if only to help boost his confidence. Joey relished the attention given to him.

A short while later, Andrew pared swords with Ruben. The fierce swordplay fascinated and thrilled the boy. It was the first time he had seen the big man in action. It reinforced his desire to be just like his new dad.

The mercenary couple had ridden from camp at the

first sign of daybreak. Each told Joey and Ruben they would see them later at the cave. The big man chuckled when Joey shook Andrew's hand vigorously before walking over and punching Sheena in the arm. She scooped him up and planted a wet kiss on his cheek then set him down and tickled him under the arms. He squealed and struggled to break free. A firm kick on the shin accomplished his mission. The hurt look on Sheena's face caused Ruben to roar with laughter.

The sun hung in the midmorning position by the time Ruben rode up to the cave entrance. He and Joey were exhausted. The latter due to playing around with Sheena while the former talked with Andrew.

Ruben pulled Wind Racer to a stop. The horse snorted, jerking his head up and down. Something bothered him. Ruben knew the horse well enough to know the signs. He glanced around the clearing. Nothing appeared out of the ordinary. That didn't mean that nothing was there. It just meant that whatever was upsetting the horse was not visible, or else it was gone already.

Prodding the animal lightly with his heels, Ruben moved toward the cave entrance. He watched the surrounding area, looking for any signs of unwanted company. Again, nothing moved but the gently waving leaves. By the time they reached the opening, Wind Racer had calmed down entirely. The big man shrugged it off. There were too many other things on his mind right now.

Joey sat in front; shoulders drooped from the adventurous last two days. He slid to the ground once they drew to a stop inside the cave. "Dad, I'll put Wind Racer away." He waited for Ruben to dismount.

Ruben beamed at the boy. Even though he was exhausted, he was willing to work. "Of course, son. I'll make sure we have a hearty meal ready by the time you're finished." His feet hit the ground. "Do you need my help getting him to the stall?" He rubbed the horse's neck affectionately.

Joey looked up at the towering beast. Grabbing the reins, he tugged the horse after him. "It's okay, dad. I can do it."

Ruben watched the child pull the huge animal behind him into the gloomy interior. He grinned. His boy made him more and more proud each day. His boy. Those were the best words on the planet.

Feeling the love of a proud father fill his breast, he followed Joey into the cave.

Drayco was roused from his light doze by the distant sound of voices and the heavy clop of hooves on dirt. He listened, trying to make out who was speaking. *That's Joey's voice...and Ruben's. They're coming this way,* he thought. *I'll bide my time. When I know they're apart, I'll make my move. Shyanne's family will be together before the birth if I have anything to say about it.*

"Son, I'll meet you in the main room when you're finished." Ruben's voice retreated farther down the passageway.

"Okay dad." Joey's voice was close.

Drayco bristled. *How dare that person call Joey his son. He's no father. To be a father, one has to show compassion. That monster has no idea what compassion is.* He forced himself to remain calm. To lose control now would most certainly end any chance of getting Joey back to his true family.

He remembered the stable was close. *Maybe now is the time. Maybe while Ruben is distracted, I can get Joey out of here.* He was about to move. Thankfully, he hadn't.

"What do you feel like having?"

Ruben was in the same room as Drayco. The dark twin scrunched himself as far into the recess as he could without making a sound. He heard Ruben moving something close. Too close for comfort. One of the boxes moved. With it gone, he would be visible. He gripped the handle of his sword, ready to bring it upward.

"Dad! I need your help getting the saddle off."

"I'll be right there."

The box disappeared. Drayco peered over the opening to see Ruben walking away, unaware of his presence. He released the breath he was holding once Ruben was gone from sight.

Man, that was almost ugly .In my present state, I don't know if I could have bested him. He glanced at the brace on his leg. *I'll have to get Joey out of here quickly...if I can.*

Ruben walked into the stable room just in time to see Joey struggling with the saddle that was still partially draped over the back of the horse. "Whoa there." He set the box down and rushed over to grab it off the boy. "Couldn't wait, huh?"

"I wanted to try. I wanted to be a man, like you."

The look of defeat nearly shattered the big man's heart. "There'll be plenty of time for that, little man." He shifted the saddle to one arm and ruffled the small head. "Do you think you can put this where it belongs?"

Joey's eyes grew wide. "Do ya mean it?"

Ruben held the saddle out for Joey. The boy brightened. He positioned himself underneath it and held tight to the edges when the full weight lay across his back. He shuffled to the railing for the stall and heaved the heavy object over the top. The saddle almost fell over to the other side. The little hands holding it were the only thing that kept it where it belonged. Joey looked over a shoulder with a triumphant grin.

Ruben leaned back, his hands resting on his hips, and roared with laughter. "Well done, little man. Well done." Turning to leave, he added, "While you brush him down, I'll fix us a nice meal. What do you think of a venison stew?"

"Great!"

The boy ran over and picked up a brush. He moved back to the horse munching on some hay, ignoring the people in the room completely. The sound of heavy exhalations followed the sounds of each brushstroke.

Smiling, the mercenary hoisted the box up off the floor and tucked it under an arm. He moved down the passageway to the main room. In a short time, the scent of stew filled the entire cave.

Drayco watched Ruben move back toward the main room of the cave. He waited until he was certain the man was going to stay there before emerging from the hiding spot. Now was the perfect time to get Joey. The two were separated. Maybe they could get far enough away before Ruben discovered the boy was gone. He hoped so. He was not in any shape to take him on if they didn't.

Limping as quietly as he could, Drayco peered out the doorway. He heard chopping noises followed by a splash. He also heard the sound of a brush as it traveled down the side of the horse. He moved toward the brushing sound. Pausing at the entrance, he looked inside.

Joey stood up on his toes trying to reach the upper back. His young face showed his level of concentration. Drayco felt his heart pull. He had not seen his nephew in over a year. That was far too long; he knew that now.

Nothing I can do about that now. All I can do is make sure it does not happen again.

Drayco moved farther into the room. The sound of his approach caused Joey to look in his direction. His arm froze in mid stroke. His expression went from one of concentration to one of joy.

"Uncle Drayco!"

"Shh. I'm here to take you home to your mom and dad. They miss you very much."

Before the dark twin took three steps, the expression changed again. Confusion replaced the joy. "But they don't want me anymore. Dad, I mean, Ruben, told me so."

"Ruben lied to you." Drayco inched closer to the boy. He had to convince him to leave quickly, or else all would be lost. He reached a hand toward the boy. "Your parents love you very much. They're looking for you right now. Come on, let's go find them."

"But...Ruben is my friend. He wouldn't lie...not to me." Joey inched farther away from the dark man's hand. Tears welled in his eyes. "He wouldn't."

"Joey...."

"He wouldn't! He's my dad now. He calls me little man and lets me do all kinds of fun things."

"Joey...please. We have to go."

"NO!"

Drayco tightened his jaw in frustration. He lunged for the boy, trying to grab him and shut him up before the shouts alerted Ruben. Joey ducked under his arms. He ran around the horse because Drayco blocked the exit. Before he could go after Joey, the sound of running feet forced him to abandon the chase and focus his attention on the doorway

"Dad! Dad! Help me. He wants to take me away from

you."

Ruben appeared with his sword in hand. "YOU!"

Death filled his eyes as the mercenary charged at the dark twin. Drayco knew he was in deep trouble. It was hard enough to handle the larger man when healthy. It was doubly worse with a bum leg.

Ruben ran up and raised his sword with the intent of bring it down on Drayco's head, cleaving him in half. Anger filled his every being. This person, this abomination, was taking his son. That was something he was not going to allow. He brought the sword down hard. It met ground instead of flesh.

Drayco saw the rage boiling within. He hoped to use it to his advantage. If Ruben stayed angry enough, maybe the big man would be careless. Maybe he had a chance to survive this encounter after all. But only if Ruben stayed too angry to think.

He rolled out of the way of the oncoming sword. A wince of pain flew across his face. The sudden movement caused his leg to remind him it did not work as well as it used to.

When Ruben brought the sword upward again, Drayco moved in. He hit the exposed stomach as hard as he could with his fist. He was about to hit the face above when he found himself flying across the room. He landed hard against the railing for the stall. It split in two, nearly impaling him. Before Drayco had time to recover, Ruben was in front of him. Drayco looked up in time to see the sharp blade coming at him. He ducked. The blade buried into the wood mere inches above him.

The dark twin had not had time to drawn his sword because of the charge. Furthermore, he had not wanted to kill in front of Joey. That was unimportant now. The mercenary was not under such restrictions. If he was to survive, Drayco must discard them as well.

He reached for the weapon at his side. As his hand closed on the handle, another hand clamped down over his. He felt his hand pulled forward, drawing the sword out of its sheath. The strength behind the grip was phenomenal. Had he wanted to resist, he couldn't.

Ruben saw the dark twin go for his sword. The anger that had blinded him earlier disappeared. Revenge filled the void left behind. He clamped down on the hand. His own weapon lay embedded deep in the support post for the stall, useless. He pulled Drayco's arm away from his body, withdrawing the sword. The fingers beneath his, shifted. He glared into the dark eyes, expecting to see fear. They were filled with hatred instead, hatred...and something else. Hunger.

For the first time in all his encounters with Drayco, Ruben felt something not experienced often. He felt fear. Fear at what this man would do if he got the upper hand. He had seen if first hand when Drayco was a captive of the Boss.

Drayco glared at the eyes staring into his. For a brief moment, he thought he saw fear. He never had time to reflect on it. Because the next thing he knew, a pain wracked through his body, a pain caused by a fist hitting the side of his head. The world surrounding him went dark, which was lucky for him. He never felt the sword as it sank into the splint wrapped around his leg.

The world rushed back with a vengeance, allowing Drayco to feel every ache, every pain, every ounce of his abused body. He had no idea why he was there. By all rights, he should be dead. With the way he felt, he almost wished he were. Maybe death would be better than what he was experiencing right now.

He was sitting on the ground with his arms wrapped around a firm object behind him. His upper body leaned forward and his chin rested on his chest. Rough edges bit into his arms. Drayco wanted to move. Instead, he remained still and listened. He heard nothing. No Joey. No Ruben. Nothing, He risked peering through slit eyes to see where he was.

He saw he was restrained against a large piece of wood located in the center of a room. The roughness of the wood told him it was used for sparing. He remembered seeing it when he had first explored the cave.

Drayco rolled his wounded leg into a new angle. A pain more intense than the others caused him to focus on his leg. A gouge mark marred the splint near his knee. Fortunately, the depth of the cut had not gone all the way through the wood. He wondered at that, especially with the power the big man possessed. The leg was uncut, but a bruise would be there for sure. The misery caused by the repositioning told him so.

Voices echoed down the passageway. They drew closer. Drayco gave no indication that he was awake, even though his body screamed at him to move.

"But dad, do we hafta?"

"Son...if we don't, he will keep trying to take you back to the ones who don't want you anymore."

"But he's Drayco."

Drayco wondered what they were talking about. What was Ruben up to? He continued to pretend to be unconscious as the pair entered the room.

"Would you feel better if you stayed in the main room?"

"Do ya mean it? You won't be mad at me?"

"Never. You're my son. I will always love you...no matter what. Okay?"

"Okay. Love you dad."

The dark man heard the sound of shuffling feet and pictured Joey throwing his arms around the big man's neck. He wished his arms were tightening around the big neck instead. More shuffling followed. Footsteps receded down the passageway toward the back of the cave. He knew Joey was gone. Only Ruben remained.

"I know you're listening. I can tell by your breathing." Ruben moved closer to Drayco and grabbed a handful of hair. He jerked the prisoner's head up. "I just wanted to let you know why you're still alive."

"Drayco opened his eyes and glared at the monster before him.

"I could have killed you straight off. But that wouldn't have been as much fun. I wanted you to suffer like I did after you killed the Boss. You and that damn sister of yours ruined everything. Now it's my turn to ruin things." Ruben flung Drayco's head back into the support. He stood and smiled at the grimace of pain. The smile held no warmth. It held the promise of unpleasant things to come.

"While Joey and I were gone and you were invading our sanctuary with your foul presence, I ran into a couple of old friends. You remember Andrew and Sheena don't you?"

Shock ran through Drayco. He never thought to hear those names again. Six years ago, he, Joseph, and Drizzle had rescued Shyanne from the Boss. During the rescue, the Boss died. The members separated afterwards when the money ran out. Sheena and Andrew were part of the ruthless mercenaries from Ruben's old group, the group that had captured him and tortured him. Now, they were back.

"We had a fine chat about old times." Ruben leaned forward. "You know what...seems they were just as upset as I was about the loss of steady income. Seems they wanted to thank everyone involved just about as bad as I did. Well, you know, I think we found a way to do so." He straightened and walked several paces away before facing Drayco once more.

"You see, I saw you two at the old couple's house. You know...the ones with that cute little donkey."

Drayco's heart pounded, threatening to come out of his chest. *He was there and we never knew it. How stupid of us. We should have known....*

"Andrew and Sheena never got to meet your sister. So, I told them about her...about where she was...and about her condition." He rubbed his abdomen. "I bet they're almost there by now."

"You low-lying sack of whale scum! How dare you threaten my sister like that!" Drayco struggled against the restraints holding him. "If you or your cronies hurt her in any way, I'll hunt each and every one of you down and make sure you all suffer an agonizingly slow and painful death."

"Tisk, tisk. All these threats from one so unable to follow through with them. And to think, I almost spared you all this wonderful suffering by killing you."

Ruben rushed up to Drayco with a speed unusual for someone his size. He grabbed his shirt and pulled upward, forcing the tied arms into the jagged wood. "Isn't it a good thing I learned to regain control over my anger quickly? Would have missed all this fun otherwise." He let go of the shirt and backhanded the dark twin.

Ruben spun around on his heels and left the room He ignored the angry threats echoing down the passageway. By the time he reached the main room where Joey waited, his step was light and his thoughts were filled with the torturous deaths of the annoying twins.

Seventeen

Shyanne lay in the bed feeling her stomach muscles protest again. *This baby is going to come real soon.* She rolled onto her side and bent her knees slightly, trying to reduce the pull. *Drayco...why did you leave me when I needed you the most? Why did you leave me to deliver this baby without the help of family?*

The spasm eased, allowing her to relax. She knew why Drayco had left almost a week ago. He wanted her family with her when the baby was born. Nevertheless, he was family as well.

A noise by the doorway drew her attention away from the useless pondering. She looked up to see Mini standing there, a tray overloaded with foodstuff before her. She smiled when she saw Shyanne watching her.

"I brought you something to nibble on, dearie."

"I'm not sure if I can, Mini.

"You have to. That baby needs nourishment so she can have the strength to make the hard journey into this world." The older woman moved across the room and set the tray on a small table before taking a seat herself. "Here, try one of these."

Shyanne could not help but smile. An oversized oatmeal cookie hung before her. She took it and bit a small piece off. While chewing, another spasm wrenched through her. It was not as bad as the others were; yet, it stole away the joy of seeing the cookie. She put it down on the bed and rubbed her stomach to loosen the tight muscles.

Min picked up the treat and set it back on the tray. "Oh you poor thing. I haven't seen anyone go through this much before. And I've seen a lot during my time."

"Maybe I can be of some assistance."

The suddenness of another female voice caused Mini and Shyanne to look up sharply. Leaning against the doorframe was a well-tanned woman with long dark hair. Her arms were crossed in front of her and the hint of a smile crooked one corner of her lips. The light shining through the window reflected off the dagger in one of her hands. Behind her, they saw Kilan, a dagger held tight against his throat by a man with dirty blonde hair.

"Who are you? What is it you want?" Mini rose to her feet. She put herself between Shyanne and the unknown female.

Standing straight, the woman said, "Why Mini, or should I call you Minificent. Is that any way to greet your guests?"

"How do you know who I am?"

"A mutual friend of ours told me all about you. He sends his regards, and I'm here to deliver them."

The younger woman strolled over to the older woman and stopped within arms reach. Shyanne watched in horror as the arm holding the dagger shot out. Mini gasped. She stumbled back a step, her hands pressed against her belly. Another step caused her to fall onto the bed. Shyanne saw the dress under the hands was no longer a soft shade of blue. It was a deeper shade of crimson.

Mini glanced down at her abdomen. She saw the red spreading across it far too fast and held out her hand to Shyanne. Blood covered it, making the pale skin seem more ghostly white. Tears welled in her eyes.

"I'm so sorry I won't be here to see the birth of your baby girl." The pain that filled her eyes disappeared. A calmness settled in. She put the bloody hand on Shyanne's swollen belly. "Know that she will be strong and healthy" A tear ran down her cheek. Closing her eyes, she said, "Please, take care of Kilan when I'm gone. He'll be lost without me and will need your help."

"Enough of this, old woman. Die already," Sheena snapped.

Shyanne caught the glint of steel as it sped toward

Mini. She threw her hands up to block the blood that splattered onto her face from the gaping slice through the neck.

Across the room, a man's wail mingled with the laughter from both intruders.

*   *   *

Hana stayed back with the horses to keep them quiet. There were two horses now. The one that Joseph had called Bravaro galloped up to them, riderless, while they were making their way to the cave. Joseph and Drizzle swore at the same time. Both knew the dark man would never leave his horse unless he was forced to. Now they had two people to look for, instead of one.

The cave came into view shortly before dark. The men were there, close to the entrance, watching and waiting.

The oriental woman shifted her weight off her injured leg. The wound itched and it was hot to the touch. It ached, as well. She knew an infection was setting in; and that all her supplies were gone. She also knew that if she did not take care of it soon, the infection would poison her entire system. Her body's defenses were good, but sometimes they needed help.

True to the silence of his breed, Drizzle emerged almost at her heels. To her credit, Hana had not startled. She glanced at the cat. "Did you see anything?"

"Ruben and the boy have returned. I saw no sign of Drayco."

"Maybe he has not come this way yet." The statement rang false, even to her.

"He's here. I can smell him. I think he's hiding in the cave."

"That would be foolish. That's like hiding in the lion's den, hoping the beast doesn't find you and eat you."

Drizzle smirked. "That would be Drayco. Act first, think about it after it's too late."

Hana secured the horse's reins to some trees. She pivoted on her good leg to face the cat. "Where's Joseph?"

"He's still at the cave. He hopes to spot Joey and take him before Ruben finds out. I think both he and Drayco are underestimating the mercenary. I only hope Joey doesn't get caught in the crossfire when everything comes to a head.

"I hope not as well, Drizzle. The boy has been away from loved ones far too long. Let's hope the damage already done can be easily reversed."

Drizzle started back the way he came. Hana followed at a slower pace. He listened to her footfall. It sounded awkward, offbeat, like she was limping. He knew what caused it, but remained silent.

The pair crept up to where Joseph was hiding He was crouched low, his back toward them, watching the opening intently. He was so focused on what lay ahead that he failed to hear their approach.

Hana tapped him on the shoulder and had to throw herself out of the way to keep the dagger in his hand from slicing her midsection open. The sudden move caused pain to shoot up and down her injured leg. It reflected on her face.

"Oh Hana, I'm sorry. I'm so sorry. I didn't mean to hurt you," Joseph whispered. "Did I cut you? Are you okay?" He moved to examine her, but stopped when she waved him off.

"I am fine. You did not cut me. It is only the bear wound, that is all." She saw relief flood over him. She redirected his attention away from her with questions. "What of your son? Have you seen him yet?"

He whirled around to face the cave, her pain forgotten, his pain remembered. "No. I haven't."

"They are in there." She edged closer to Joseph. "See there? See that blur inside the cave? That is not part of the surrounding stone. That has to be something they brought with them."

Drizzle came up behind them, and said, "I'm positive they're in there. Even if I hadn't already confirmed it, I could smell that son of a rizbak's butt a mile away." He looked at Joseph. "Joey's in there too."

The mention of his son's name made Joseph's heart soar. At the same time, it plummeted. *What if Joey doesn't want to come home? What if Ruben has already caused him to hate us? No,* he resolved, *he'll come. He loves us too much not to.*

"Dad! Daaad! Come on!"

Joseph jerked himself out of the depression he was falling into when he heard Joey calling for him. The depression slammed deep into place when he realized whom Joey was calling dad.

"I'm coming, son." Ruben's voice echoed from farther inside the cave, drawing nearer.

Joseph could just make out their shapes close to the white blur Hana had pointed out. He inhaled sharply when the boy stepped into the bright light. *Joey, my boy, how you've grown in such a short time.* Anguish filled him. *God, how I want you back home safe and sound.*

"Find what you were after?"

"Yea. It was right here where you said it was. Thanks dad."

Joseph scowled when he saw Ruben step out and pick up his boy. He tossed Joey over a shoulder and carried him back into the gloomy interior. Both were laughing and enjoying themselves.

The dagger was still in his hand. He looked at it, then at the cave. A small hand came to rest on his shoulder. Joseph glanced over at Hana and saw the love buried deep inside. For the first time, he understood how much she cared for him. Much as he would like to, he could not return that love. His feelings already belonged to another.

The brief glimpse of his son brought the longing for his family to the forefront. Patting her hand, he rose to his feet. It was time to reunite his family.

"Drizzle, it's time to get my son out of there."

The big cat padded up to the Joseph. He looked expectantly at the cave. *Revenge will be so sweet.*

Joseph's hand moved to the sword resting on his back. With a slow determined pull, he withdrew the weapon. His eyes never left the cave entrance when he said, "Hana, I need you to wait here. With your injury, Ruben will see it as a weakness and use it to his advantage."

"I do not think that is wise. I can be of assistance." She reached for the nunchaku hidden in her sleeve.

"Hana, if you want to see this mission succeed, do as I ask. That man in there is a ruthless killer. He will not let the fact that you are a woman stop him. In fact, he would probably get more of a thrill out of it because you are a woman."

She stood her ground. "I can be of help. If you get into a fight with that man, I can take your son away while you keep him busy."

"You are a stranger to him. He may resist you, making the rescue that much harder. Drizzle and I are not." He turned his head and looked at the woman standing next to him. "Either one of us can get Joey out while the other keeps Ruben busy."

"And what of your friend Drayco? Who will help him if he needs it? Or is he now expendable since you know where your son is?"

Hana remained calm. None of the frustration showed on her face, even though Joseph knew it was there. Drizzle sat on his haunches, waiting for the final outcome in the battle of wills.

Seeing her stance, Joseph knew he was not going to win this battle. It reminded him of another female he knew. One he knew very well. She reminded him of Shyanne.

Throwing his empty hand into the air, Joseph rolled his eyes, "Oh, alright. We could use your help to get Drayco out. Who knows what Ruben may have done to him, if he's found him yet." He remembered the last time the dark twin was in the hands of Ruben. It wasn't pretty. "Let's go."

Joseph worked his way through the underbrush toward the side of the cave. Hana walked behind him, being careful to avoid making unwanted noise, and to hide the limp.

Both of them missed the smile that crept onto the cat's face as he followed them. A smile that was filled with humor because of the pair in front of him, and with the promise of things to come for one very unlucky mercenary.

Drayco struggled against the restraints, trying to find a way to loosen them. He had to go to Shyanne. He had to get Joey out of here and back with his family. He had to do so much; yet, because of the restraints and the badly set leg, he was able to do any of them.

Ruben and Joey had passed by the entrance to his room a short while ago. The boy ran past without looking at him. Ruben, on the other hand, slowed and gave him that irritating smile. The one filled with death. The one Drayco wanted to slice off his face with his sword.

It frustrated him. It made him feel helpless. Mostly, it made him angry. More angry than he had ever been in his life.

Nothing on this planet will prevent me from killing that man. He has hurt us for far too long. Drayco struggled to break free again. Again, he was unsuccessful. *Damn these infernal restraints!*

Laughter made him cease his struggling and watch the doorway. Ruben walked past, carrying Joey over a shoulder. He waved and continued down the passage. Drayco grit his teeth to prevent himself from yelling out with frustration.

Joseph edged his way past the unknown piece of machinery. He hated any machine from the past. Especially ones used by Ruben. He remembered the underground complex used by the Boss. He remembered how they had barely escaped from the floating ball with its bright beam of light that killed. He had no use for them. All he wanted...all he needed...was for his family to be together and home.

Hana was a step behind him. He held her eyes for a moment before stepping into the gloomy interior.

Drizzle stayed behind them. He wanted to make sure the big mercenary could not get away this time. He knew Joseph was strong. But he let emotions get in the way when it came to some things...like his son. The cat also knew Ruben was an expert on exploiting those feelings to his advantage.

The trio paused a few steps in, both to adjust to the darkness and to listen. They heard laughter echo from farther back. It was not drawing closer; rather, it remained distant. Joseph nodded his head. They moved as one deeper inside.

They stopped again when they reached the interchange. Ahead, there was only more darkness. To the right, a torch lit the passageway. Gripping the handle of his sword tighter, Joseph led the way to where the laughter came from.

A doorway came into sight. The people hugged the wall and inched forward. The cat crouched low. He waited.

Joseph quickly peeked inside before flattening himself against the wall. That was when he realized the walls were smooth, not rough like natural material. He ran his fingers back and forth. *More stuff from the past,* he thought. His brow furrowed in disgust. *Only Ruben could find another place like this to hide in. The quicker we get out of here, the happier I will be.* Taking his fingers off the wall, he rubbed them on his pants, trying to get the feel of the smoothness off them.

A whinny sounded. Joseph indicated to the others that this was the room where the horse was stabled. He moved past. Hana went next. As Drizzle slid past, the horse snorted. Fortunately, nothing else happened. The occupants ahead remained unaware of their approach.

The torchlight showed two doors this time, one on either side of the passageway. Joseph crept up to the one on the right, while Drizzle glided up to the one on the left. Both took a quick glance into the rooms. Only one gave a sudden inhalation, indicating the surprise at seeing the contents inside.

Joseph slid into the room and rushed to Drayco's side. He looked bad. Almost as bad as he had when he fell off his horse so many years ago. Hana limped in after him. Drizzle remained on guard by the door, in case Ruben showed up.

"Drayco. Drayco. Can you hear me? Are you alright? Drayco!" he whispered.

The dark twin's eyes were closed, his head forward. They flew open when Joseph spoke. He raised his head slowly and locked eyes with the fair-haired man before him.

The look from Drayco's eyes caused another intake of breath, this time from Hana. *So much anger .So much hatred. Will we be safe when we let him go? I hope so.* The moment she saw the splint around his leg, the fears disappeared. Her healer instinct took over.

Hana pushed Joseph out of the way and focused on the wounded leg, removing the straps that held the brace closed. Drayco watched what she was doing and grimaced when she moved the leg.

Seeing what Hana was doing, Joseph worked his way behind the restrained man. He tried to get the rope binding the wrists loosened; they were too tight.

"Drizzle," he whispered. "I need your help over here. I can't get these knots loose. I need those sharp claws of yours."

The cat hesitated. He wanted to stay where he was, watching for the mercenary. He also wanted to help Drayco.

The laughter is still to the right. If I hear it move this way, I'll return to the door. After the short internal debate, he moved next to Joseph.

Unfortunately, the rope was thick. It would take longer than he anticipated to cut through it. A sharp claw sprang from one of his stubby finger. He guided it to the knot pointed out by Joseph. The task at hand forced him to focus on what he was doing. One slip and the dark twin's wrist would be sliced open, causing him to bleed to death.

Everyone was so intent on his or her task that no one noticed the laughter had stopped. When they did, they looked up to see the mercenary standing in the doorway. He held Joey's hand in his. Both had a shocked look on their face.

Before anyone could say a thing, Ruben picked up Joey and ran down the passage toward the flyer. Drizzle was the first to respond; he flew after them and reached them before they could escape. The fork for the passage lay behind the pair. Daylight gleamed through one, darkness through the other.

Ruben had to put Joey down to draw his weapon against Drizzle. Instead of running to the cat, the boy hid behind him. The big man's heart soared.

Drizzle knew better than to attack the mercenary head on. The man had the reflexes of someone forced to live by them a long time. If he wished to succeed, he had to wait for the others to arrive. They would distract Ruben long enough so he could slide inside and kill the big man.

Within minutes, Joseph skid to a stop close to Drizzle. He saw Joey hiding behind Ruben. He saw Ruben facing them with his sword held ready. Like Drizzle, he waited. He yearned to hold his son, but he needed to get to him first. To do that, Ruben had to go.

If I can find out what Ruben told him, Joseph thought, *I can convince Joey that it's all a lie and he'll want to come to me .That way he'll be out of harms way when we fight Ruben.*

"Joey, son, I miss you. I want you to come home with me." He lowered his sword, but did not put it away.

Joey peeked out from behind Ruben. He watched his father. He saw the longing on his face. It matched the longing he felt inside when he first saw him. Then, he remembered how he went to help Drayco before coming for him. To his young mind, that hurt. His new father, Ruben, would never do that. He promised. Besides, when the baby was born, he'd be forgotten again. Ruben said so.

"I don't wanna."

"Joey...please. I miss you. Mom misses you too."

"Mom?" He inched a step toward Joseph. "Is she here?"

"She had to stay back, son. Remember? She's going to have a baby soon."

The moment he uttered those words, the look of yearning on Joey's face disappeared. The fair-haired man wished he could take them back. He had been close, so close. He would try to convince the boy one more time. If that failed, they'd have to grab him forcefully. That was something he preferred not to do, but would rather than lose him again.

"Joey...please...come with me." He extended a hand toward Joey.

Suddenly, Drizzle shot forward. While they were talking, Ruben's attention had been on the speakers, not the cat. He brought his hand up, claws extended, intent on gutting the man. They met air instead.

Ruben caught a glimpse of the cat's rush toward him. He stumbled backward on instinct and shoved Joey out of the way. The move to get the child from harm's reach threw him off balance. Unable to recover in time, he fell against the rock wall. The impact to his head caused everything to go fuzzy. He felt the sword leave his grasp and a sharp object rub against his throat.

Joey screamed, "Dad! You leave him alone! He's my dad...and...and...I love him!"

Joseph made it to his son's side during the melee. As he reached for Joey, the words he shouted caused him to hesitate. The hesitation was long enough for the boy to duck away from his outstretched arm.

Joey ran toward the dark tunnel and spun around when he reached the entrance. He wanted to run toward Ruben. Because Drizzle was in the way, he couldn't. The exit outside was blocked, as well. He would be trapped if he ran back to the main room. Even though he knew it was forbidden, that left only this way.

"I don't want to go with you! I want to stay with my dad!"

"But Joey...I am your dad."

"You don't want me anymore! Ruben said so!" The boy looked at Drizzle. "Go away and leave us alone!"

Drizzle focused his cat eyes on the child. His grip on the big man's shirt never loosened; the claw against the throat stayed where it was. "Joey, you're talking foolishness. Your father...your real father...loves you very much. Why else would he go through all this to bring you home?

"He doesn't love me. He just wants me there til the baby's born. Then he can forget about me...like he did before." Tears welled in the corners of the boy's eyes. "I don't want to go back where no one wants me! I don't want to go back where I have no one to play with!"

"Joseph Jr., that's enough of that," Joseph said, frustrated and hurt by what his son said. "Your mother and I love you very much. I know Ruben has filled your head with all kinds of nonsense. It's all lies." He took several steps toward Joey. "Now come on. We're going home."

"No! I don't want to go there. I want to stay here with Ruben! I want to stay where I can have fun!"

"I said let's go!"

"NO!"

Joey spun around and ran into the darkness beyond. It was the only way he knew of to stay here. If they couldn't find him, they couldn't take him away.

Joseph started after him. A shout stopped him short. Hana limped toward them as fast as she could.

"Joseph! Joseph, wait!"

"What is it? I need to get my son." He moved several steps in the direction taken by the boy.

"Joseph...you need to get to Shyanne. Now."

His step faltered. Dread inched its way into his every being. "Why? What's going on?"

"After you left, I continued to tend to Drayco's leg. He shouted for me to finish untying him first...that he had to go to his sister. After I moved behind him, I heard him muttering about some other mercenaries."

"Other mercenaries?" The dread caused his heart to flip-flop.

"Joseph," Hana gripped his upper arms, "he told me

this man has sent two people to kill Shyanne. He knows where she is. They might already be there."

Joseph paled. "Oh god...."

He turned to face Ruben. Rage pushed the dread aside. He raised his sword, intent on killing the man who had brought so much misery to his family. He put one foot before the other, barely aware that he did so. Before Joseph reached him, Ruben spoke.

"You might want to reconsider that. Only I can help you find your son and end your family problems."

Joseph ignored him. He continued to advance, sword held high. Suddenly, he bellowed and closed the gap in a rush. He brought the sword down.

Drizzle ducked to the side. As the cat withdrew, the claw against the big man's throat left a gouge. It was not deep enough to be life threatening, though blood trickled down the thick neck.

Ruben locked his gaze on the angry man. A faint smile creased his lips. He never flinched when the sword ricocheted off the stone close to his head.

"I knew you couldn't kill me. You need me."

"I promise you this, Ruben," Joseph said between clenched teeth. "When the time comes, I will kill you. And I will enjoy every moment of it."

"If that moment ever comes...," the smile became a grin, "I bet you will."

Eighteen

Joseph was torn. He needed to go after his son so he could bring him home. However, the news given by Hana filled him with an even greater need to go after Shyanne. He gripped the sword handle tighter and contemplated killing Ruben anyway, but the anger he felt moments ago was gone. Reason had replaced it.

Movement beside him brought Joseph out of his reverie. Drizzle shifted his body, the claw once more against the powerful neck. The cat wanted to kill Ruben almost as badly as he did. He too, held back, aware of the unfortunate need to keep the big man alive.

An idea popped into Joseph's mind when he looked at the cat. The more he thought about it, the better he liked it.

"Drizzle, I need you to go to Shyanne."

"But I'm more useful here. I can track Joey faster than this lump of flesh can ever think to find him." The smile vanished on Ruben's face when the cat's sharp claw bit into his neck again.

"Listen to me for a second." Joseph started pacing in a small circle, the sword resting on a shoulder. "To find Joey, that could take hours. In the meantime, the other mercenaries will reach Shyanne and kill her. That is not an option." He stopped pacing and faced the cat. "So, much as I want your nose here to help me find my son, I need your speed more—to save my wife and unborn child.

"He's right, Drizzle. You're the fastest one among us,"

a voice said from behind the group.

Drayco leaned against the rock wall a short distance away. The brace on his leg was gone. He righted himself and limped next to Joseph. "You're the only one who can do it. Joseph is needed here, and I'm incapacitated by this leg." Frustration filled his words.

"As the companion to a humecat, I know of your prowess, of your abilities," Hana stated. "But, the child knows them as well. He may lead you astray simply because he does not wish to be found,"

"He's only five years old. And he doesn't have any blasted pepper with him this time."

"No...but we should not underestimate his intelligence, even though he is so young," Hana added.

Hana's right," Joseph said. "That boy is pretty witty." He put his sword away and moved to the flyer. Much as he hated machines of the past, an item rest upon it that he needed. Picking up the bundle of rope, he carried it over to the cat. "Don't worry; I won't let this curse to humankind get away."

He kneeled behind Ruben and secured his wrists together. Then he wrapped a loop of rope around the mercenary's neck and tied the end around the wrists, as well. Enough of the rope remained to make a leash.

Ruben grimaced when the rope bit into his flesh. Drayco smiled. "Hurts like hell, doesn't it? Get used to it. The next encounter you'll have with a rope will be from somewhere high."

Joseph stood once he made sure the rope was not going to come loose. "You'd better go, Drizzle. Who knows how long those two have been there. Or what they may have done already."

"Do you know where to go?" Hana asked.

"I know the way. I'll be back after I rip out the innards of those rizbak butts." He ran out of the cave without a backward glance.

All eyes followed the cat as he disappeared. All had the same thought: they hoped he got there in time to save Shyanne. All except one.

If I know Andrew and Sheena, they have already arrived and finished that miserable wench off. Ruben looked at Drayco. The smile crept back onto his face. *Oh, do not worry, dark one, I'll get you too before I'm finished.*

Drayco must have felt the big man's eyes burning into him because he rotated his head around and locked his black eyes with his. They mesmerized the mercenary with their endless depth. As he watched, something filled the void. He shuddered and turned away. The smile faded.

Ruben had seen first hand what Drayco was capable of doing. He had brought him victims to drink from so he could heal. He also knew the only thing holding the dark man back from doing the same to him was his usefulness in finding Joey. After that, he suspected nothing would prevent Drayco from following through with what his eyes foretold.

The fact that he was restrained meant nothing to the big man. He remained confident that he and Joey would get away before Drayco lost control. Before the ever-increasing hunger he witnessed in the dark twin's eyes took over and he killed everyone here.

Hana spied the exchange between the men. She saw the darkness, the usugurasa, grow around Drayco. Unlike before, she was not afraid. She wondered if it was because of the healer inside wanting to help him with his injury. Or if it was because the zenryō she felt inside him, the state of being good, was stronger than the usugurasa. Only time would tell her which it was.

Joseph longed to go with the cat and save his wife. Reluctantly, he turned away from the exit. His presence was needed here first and foremost to find his son. With purposeful strides, he walked over to Ruben and yanked on the rope, forcing the big man to fall onto his back. Not waiting for him to get up, Joseph began dragging him across the dirt floor.

"Joseph...stop. You're choking him." Hana limped to his side. She put a hand on his arm, halting his forward progress with the gentle touch. "Please...do not do this. It is wrong to sink to another's level just because he has hurt you. That makes you as bad as him."

Joseph looked at Ruben, then at Hana. "You're right." Frowning, he let the rope slacken. "Get up, you rizbak slime, before I change my mind and sink to your level."

Ruben struggled to his feet. He kept his mouth shut. He was biding his time until they found Joey. When that occurred, he would escape with the boy before anyone knew what happened.

"Hana, grab some torches. We'll need them to light the way. Drayco, can you make it?"

"Don't worry about me. You worry about keeping an eye on him." Drayco jerked a thumb at Ruben. "I trust him about as far as I can throw my horse." He pulled his gaze away from Ruben and focused it on the woman of the group. "Hana, is it? Hana, you are injured. You will slow us down. You need to stay here."

"I wouldn't go there. She has a stubborn streak as long as someone else I know. A couple of you, in fact," Joseph warned.

"I am no more injured than you are. If I should stay behind, so should you. You yourself said you were incapacitated by your leg." Hana met Drayco's glare, refusing to lower her eyes.

"You have no business in this. This is an ongoing battle between this thing and my family."

"I am a part of this now. If I am not, then why am I here?"

Drayco walked slowly over to Hana, trying to make the obvious limp less obvious. "I don't care why you're here. You need to stay out of this, for your own sake." He reached for her arm with the intention on making her leave.

In an instant, she grabbed his hand and spun it around, pinning his arm against his upper back and forcing him to the ground. "Even though I am injured, I can still defend myself. You agree?"

Joseph shook his head. "I told you not to go there, but you wouldn't listen."

Drayco tried to free himself. The way Hana held him down, he was not able to, even though he was larger and stronger than she was. Frustrated at his inability to break free, he demanded, "Why are you so interested in this? What benefit is it to you?"

"It is of no benefit to me. It is for the benefit of the child involved...and for Joseph. The boy needs to be reunited with his family. If he is injured, I can help. If he is not, another set of eyes can make the task of finding him that much easier. That is all." After making her point, Hana released his hand and stepped back.

Drayco sat up. He massaged the sore arm before rising to his feet. "Have it your way. If you get lost, it's on your head. I won't go looking for you."

"Fortunately, if you get lost, I will look for you. I will not lower myself because of your foolishness," Hana quipped in response.

Drayco grabbed a torch and started into the left tunnel branch where Joey had disappeared. He kept his expression blank. Inside, though, he was smiling.

Man, she is so like Shyanne. Takes things with the grace of a woman; yet, can defend herself from the best of them like a man. What a pistol.

Hana grabbed another torch and waited for Joseph. The fair-haired man tugged on the leash and indicated for Ruben to follow Drayco. Hana hesitated after they passed her. She took several deep meditating breaths to ease the pain caused by her leg. By the third one, the pain was under control. With grim determination, she held the torch high and went inside.

After watching Drizzle attack the man he now considered his father, Joey ran into the forbidden tunnel. He had to get away from the people who were trying to take him.

Tears ran down his cheeks. Joey brushed them off with the back of his hand. It was so dark he couldn't see the hand in front of his face. He didn't care. He knew Drizzle was behind him. The cat would track him down quickly. The other father, the one who did not let him have any fun or want him anymore, would force him to leave. He had to keep running. He had to hide before they found him.

Joey lost count of how many times he knocked his shins against a stone outcropping, stubbed his toes, or ran into a wall. He finally slowed his forward momentum when he tripped and landed hard on his knees, making his legs tingle all the way down to the toes before the pain settled in.

He sat on his backside and hugged his legs against him. Sobs silently wracked his little body. He had no idea where he was, or how far into the cave he had gone. He was so scared.

Remembering that the cat might be on his trail, the boy pulled himself together. He reached out with his hand and found the wall, then rose to his feet. Scooting one foot forward, he began moving again.

It felt like an eternity before Joey heard the echo of water as it splashed. It sounded like it was coming from all directions. He stopped. It was not behind him, he had just come that way. So that meant it was up ahead.

He kept his forward pace toward the sound slow. Who knew how deep the water was, or if something might live in it. To go back, though, was worse. Back meant he would never have fun again. Back meant he would lose the only grownup to act as if his opinion counted. He pressed on, using the same slow fashion that had brought him this far.

The rock wall under his hand disappeared. He reached out until it reappeared a short distance later. Joey brought both hands up. The gap in the wall was a littler smaller than he was when he faced it. If he turned sideways, he fit. An idea popped into his head.

I can hide here. They won't be able to follow me. They're too big to fit. The only one who can is Drizzle. And I can use my knife to keep him away.

Joey inched his way into the gap. A few feet into the narrow passageway, the walls widened. Exploring the circumference of the space, his hands told him that the cave was small. When he returned to what he thought was the back, he sat down and pulled out the knife tucked in his boot. He wanted to be ready in case Drizzle showed up.

The boy folded his arms on top of his knees and listened for any sounds. His eyelids slowly drifted shut. He jerked them and his head up. He knew he had to stay awake in case those searching for him found him. The effort from running away and the recent trip had taken its toll on his energy levels, though. He was tired. His eyelids drifted shut again. When his head banged against the rock wall, he rested his chin on his arms. Shortly thereafter, the light sound of snoring filled to darkness.

Joey jerked awake. A noise had caught his attention, bringing him out of his unplanned nap. When he opened his eyes, the darkness remained. As he watched, a faint glow lit the passageway outside his hiding spot. It grew brighter by the moment. Voices followed. It was the voices that had awaken him.

Joey eased onto his feet and inched his way over to

the opening to listen. At first, the words were nothing but jumbled sounds. The closer the voices drew, the easier it was to understand what was said.

"Here's another opening, but it's too small for any of us to search. If only Drizzle were here. He'd be able to check it out." Frustration filled the voice. "Damn. We've been searching for hours now. Where could that boy be?"

Joey ducked back from the opening at the sound of Joseph's voice. He peeked again when another spoke.

"We will search as long as is necessary. Do you want your son with you, safe and sound?"

A woman limped past the opening. She was the same one he remembered seeing before, but had no idea who she was otherwise.

"How can you ask that, Hana? I love my son. I want him home. I want my family together before the baby is born. Joey! Joey!" Joseph shouted. "Where are you, son?"

Joey listened to the words spoken by his other dad and wondered if he really meant them. He missed his mother dearly. If it meant going back to his boring life to see her, he would. He was about to move when a third person spoke, halting him.

"If he believes what this thing has told him, he won't come out."

Joey saw Ruben come into view. He watched Uncle Drayco push the mercenary forward, causing him to trip over some rocks. Since his hands were tied behind him, the big man was unable to catch himself; he landed hard on a shoulder.

The boy saw the rope securing him go taunt. He watched Ruben choking when he was pulled to his feet. He watched his new dad grit his teeth in pain, and gasped. The depth of cruelty delivered by his uncle shocked him.

If Uncle Drayco is that mean now...what would he do to me since I ran away? Fearful of his uncle's punishment, he stayed where he was.

Joseph walked into view. He grabbed the front of Ruben's shirt and pulled him closer. "This lying sack of rizbak dung will never get my son. He flung Ruben away from him. Suddenly, he slapped the prisoner across the face. "Not as long as I have a breath in my body."

"Drayco," Joseph said as he spun around and walked

down the passageway, "bring that stinking rizbak fodder up front. If Joey sees him, he might show himself. Then we can convince him to come home with us, that this trash fooled him with his lies."

Drayco yanked on the rope, jerking Ruben forward out of sight.

Joey watched the light fade. He longed to go after it. On the other hand, the cruelness he had witnessed made him wonder about the people seeking him.

He doesn't care how mean Uncle Drayco is. He's just as mean. There's no way I'm going home with that man...no matter how badly I want to see mom.

A pang filled Joey at the thought of not seeing his mother. He was having fun with Ruben. Nevertheless, he missed her comforting arms.

An image of Ruben's smiling face floated before him. It turned into the one filled with pain.

He remembered how his new father had treated him kindly. He remembered how Drayco and Joseph had treated him. That was something he wasn't going to allow to continue. He may be little, but he was strong. Ruben and the other woman, Sheena, had told him so.

Joey inched out of his hiding spot and followed the dim glow. He stayed far enough behind to hide in the shadows, but close enough to benefit from the glow provided. The light allowed him to see where the rocks were so he could avoid them, reducing the chance of tripping over them and drawing attention his way.

The tunnel was long and straight. Because of that, Joey had to flatten himself against the rock wall several times to avoid detection when members of the party glanced back. These walls, unlike the ones in the living area, were rough and gave the small boy many places to conceal himself.

The dripping sound grew louder the farther into the tunnel they went. Before long, the tunnel opened into a vast cavern. The light from the torches were unable to cut through the darkness.

Joseph squat down and dipped a couple of fingers in the water.

"It's frigid. Too frigid for someone as small as Joey to survive in. And I don't see any kind of path around it." He cupped his hand before his mouth and blew hot air onto the fingers to warm them. Standing up, He faced the others. "I think we should rest here. We've been walking for several hours now and Hana's limping is getting worse, even though she won't admit it." He smiled at the little woman. "So is yours, Drayco."

Hana limped to a small rock and sat down gingerly. She let out a sigh. "I must admit, I am tired. I would benefit from a short rest."

Drayco refused to respond, preferring to keep his level of exhaustion to himself. He shoved Ruben toward a group of stones near the edge of the cave and forced the big man into a sitting position. "It's been a while since I drank. Try to escape and I will enjoy ending my fast with your blood."

Ruben glared at the dark figure standing in front of him. After Drayco moved a few steps away to join the other members, he leaned against the stone behind him and observed the mannerisms of the tiny group.

They're all tired. With any luck, I can use that to my advantage.

Each had their back toward the tunnel recently vacated so they missed the brief glimpse of movement. Ruben kept his face relaxed. He watched for the movement to happen again. When it did, he saw a tiny figure with brown hair. *That is one resourceful kid. And he's all mine.* A plan started forming.

The big man hung his head low, as if he was in pain. Drayco moved over to him and touched a shoulder. The mercenary jerked back. It was the shoulder that had hit the ground.

"What's the matter with you?"

"My shoulder is killing me. The awkward angle of my arms doesn't help any."

"I'm not untying you, if that's what you're after."

"Then can we rest here for a bit longer? If I sleep, it will probably feel better."

Drayco looked around the cave. He returned his gaze on the prisoner. "What are you after, Ruben? You can't escape; there's no place for you to hide."

"I'm not trying to escape, you son of the devil. I just want to rest." He fixed the appropriate glare on his face to match his angry words. "If you force me to move on before the pain in my shoulder has eased, then you've sunk to my level. That would impress the little woman over there, now wouldn't it?"

Drayco's hand shot out. The sound of flesh smacking against flesh reverberated throughout the vast cavern.

Ruben turned his face toward the dark twin. A trickle of blood ran from his mouth where the teeth had cut the flesh inside. "You're causing some of that precious fluid you need to get away. You might want to remember that before you hit again." A slight smile creased his lips as Drayco raised his hand for another swing.

"Drayco. Stop." Joseph moved next to the dark man. "He's right. Hana's practically falling asleep upright."

Upon hearing her name, Hana said, "I'm fine. I can go on."

"No you can't. Too much has happened recently. You're exhausted. If you keep on like this, you'll be useless when the time comes for you to help." He focused on Drayco. "And no matter how much you try and hide it, I know you're exhausted as well. So am I." Glancing at the tunnel, his voice caught with emotion as he continued. "Much as I want to continue looking for my son, I know we can't do that without some sleep." The fair-haired man walked to the water edge and sat down. Hana rose to her feet and sat next to him.

"I see the wisdom of your words. We will rest then."

"What about him?" Drayco asked.

"Use the rope to tie his feet. Make sure there's as little give as possible. I don't want him getting away," Joseph said over a shoulder. "I don't care if he suffers because of the position you have to put him in. I've suffered for a long time. It's about time he did too."

Drayco shoved the mercenary off the rocks, causing him to land once more on the wounded shoulder. He ignored the protests shouted while quickly tying his feet together with the bit of rope used as a leash.

The protests quieted after the last knot was tied. Leaning forward, Drayco goaded softly, "Don't try anything, future meal. Then again, go ahead. I'd love to have an excuse to drain you dry." With a pat on the sore shoulder, the dark twin walked over and joined Joseph and Hana.

All three moved to the opposite wall and huddled together for warmth. Joseph stayed upright to take the first watch. None thought anything would happen so deep inside the cave, but one never knew.

Joey saw Drayco shove Ruben onto the ground and tie his legs, and frowned. After he saw the others huddle together to rest, he moved closer with a stealth that would have rivaled Drizzle. During one of his moves, he noticed that the one he considered to be his father was looking in his direction. He stayed hidden to make sure the others had not noticed. When all remained quiet, he peered at Ruben.

The mercenary leader, his new dad, winked at him. Joey smiled. He knew then that the big man was playing, that he was not really hurt. With renewed determination, he worked his way into the cavern.

Thankfully, his former dad had his chin resting on his chest. Recent events had taken a greater toll than thought. Instead of watching for intruders, he watched the inside of his eyelids. Joey counted to five before moving. He dashed to the cluster of rocks behind Ruben and ducked down.

Inching forward, Joey whispered, "Dad, are you okay?"

I'm glad to see you, son. I was worried for you."

"I'm going to free you. I have my knife." Joey felt the bulk of the wonderful blade hidden in his boot.

"Wait a few minutes. Let them slip into a deeper sleep first. That way they won't hear the cutting sound."

Before the boy could reply, Joseph shifted his position then rose to his feet.

Joey squeezed himself against the rock, trying to make himself as small as possible. If he were discovered, the former dad would take him away. Much as he wanted to see his mother, he had no desire to go back.

Joseph walked over to Ruben and checked on the bonds holding him. He pat on the ropes, satisfied that they had not loosened, and returned to his previous position. Leaning back against the wall of stone, he extended his legs and crossed his arms over his chest. After a few attempts to keep his eyes open, his chin came to rest on his chest.

Ruben waited another ten minutes before allowing the boy to cut at the bonds holding him. No one budged as the steel glided across the rope. In what felt like forever, his limbs were free. The big man eased into an upright position and massaged his wrists.

"Wha...," Joey started to whisper.

A finger shot up to the boy's lips. He quieted immediately. Ruben slowly rose to his feet and grabbed Joey's smaller hand. Watching the sleeping captors, he inched toward the tunnel. Once they were out of eyeshot, the big man turned and picked up the pace. Joey was hard pressed to keep up so Ruben scooped him up in his arms. Within only a few steps, the darkness of the tunnel consumed them completely.

Joey hugged the big neck tight. He was happy to be away, but afraid that they would be lost forever in the dark forbidden section of the cave. He leaned close to Ruben's ear and whispered, "Dad, it's too dark. I'm scared."

"It's alright, son." He hugged the boy closer. "I know this cave like the back of my hand. I've walked these dark tunnels many a day just in case something like this happened. I know right where we are."

Ruben reached out to find the wall. Once his fingers met stone, his forward momentum picked up as his confidence grew. It slowed when the wall disappeared from beneath his fingertips.

"Are we okay?"

"We're fine. I'm just trying to get my bearings. That's all."

In response, the grip around his neck tightened.

Giving the boy a reassuring pat on the back, Ruben said, "We're okay, Joey. All I have to do is reach out until I find the other wall. Once I've found it, I'll be able to get us out of here. Okay?"

"Okay." The grip relaxed, but not much.

"That's my boy."

Shifting Joey to his right hip, Ruben reached out with his left. He took several steps forward until his outstretched hand reached what felt like a corner section.

This is the intersection we turned at. Finally, we're in the main tunnel. All I have to do now is backtrack to where this adventure started. When those fools discover I'm gone and come this way, they'll get mixed up. All the entrances look the same to the unfamiliar eye. And without that cat to track me, it will take them hours to figure the way out, if ever.

"We'll be out of here real soon, Joey. I promise."

"I'm glad you're my dad."

"Me too."

The sounds of footsteps echoed down the tunnel until they disappeared completely. Back in the cavern filled with water, a company of three continued to sleep, unaware that the prisoner had escaped with the much sought after prize.

Nineteen

It took Shyanne a full minute to realize the blood spraying her had stopped. Unfortunately, the laughter continued in an almost manic kind of way. Kilan's wailing mingled with it. She had no time to think about what happen though because another spasm hit, causing her to curl onto her side in agony. By the time it eased, the laughter had too.

"Oh dear. Now look at the mess I've caused." Sheena wiped the knife clean on Shyanne's clothing before putting it away. "It's nothing compared to the mess your going to make real soon." The mercenary walked over to her partner. "I don't think we have to worry about her getting up and leaving any time soon. Let's take this one into the other room and have some fun." She grabbed Kilan by the front of his shirt and led him out of sight. Andrew grinned at Shyanne then followed.

Shyanne rubbed her sore belly, trying to ease the tension. Her hands ran over a wet sticky substance. She looked at the front of her dress and saw a handprint.

Oh, Mini, why did they have to kill you? You were nothing but an innocent bystander in this. Why? Why did they have to take you away?

The table beside the bed caught her eye. A large oatmeal cookie sat on the tray carried in by Mini. A tear rolled down her cheek. It was followed by many more. Before long, the body lying next to the bed and the round object made with love blurred beyond recognition.

That was when the screams started.

Shyanne raised herself up onto her elbows. Before she could get to her feet, a spasm, more like a contraction, put her back down again. Clenching her teeth against the pain, she covered her ears and tried to block out the haunting sound.

Silently, she screamed, *Joseph, Drayco, I need your help. Don't let these people hurt my baby. Oh God, why did they have to come? I don't want to go through this alone.*

Drizzle left the cave and ran the rest of the day. He stopped only when his body insisted he must. During one such stop, a rabbit fell under his claws. The meat helped rejuvenate a severely depleted energy supply.

The moon and sun exchanged places several times before he reached his destination. The faint light of the coming dawn blanketed the inn when it came into view. The cat stayed hidden while he listened for the usual noises that humans made upon rising. The place was too quiet. Something was amiss, and he thought he knew what it was.

They're already here.

He drew closer to the porch and slid up the steps. Stopping by the entrance, he listened again. Still nothing. No sound of movement at all. Upon entering, his nose told him more than his eyes ever would.

Blood. I smell the scent of blood. Death has been here.

Various pieces of furniture blocked his view of the room. Hugging the wall, Drizzle crept past them, making sure to disturb nothing that would give his presence away. He made it to the main part of the room without incident. What he saw there made his heart sad; yet glad at the same time.

The old man sat in a chair near the fireplace. A look of sorrow covered his marred, bloody face and his eyes were looking at the ceiling as if he was able to see what lay beyond the wood. He was dead.

At one time, his shirt had been white. Large sections of red covered it now. Fingers that were once intact lay carved open, revealing the bone underneath. It was the same for his toes. Blood was everywhere. The gaping wound in his exposed chest told the cat how the man died. It appeared he had suffered a long time before the final blow happened.

The sound of a door opening caused the cat to duck behind a cabinet. His hackles went up at the sight of the woman who walked into the room.

Sheena.

It was a name from six years ago. From Ruben's gang of killers.

Sheena walked up to the body and ran her fingers down the slack jaw. "Too bad you didn't last long. I wanted to have more fun today. Oh well, two out of three ain't bad." She turned and departed down the hallway. Drizzle heard a door open and close.

What did she mean by that? Two out of three what?

He crept out of hiding and into the hall. As he neared the first door on the right, nothing but silence greeted him. He neared the next one and heard a soft chucking followed by words.

"I'm looking forward to seeing your baby. Maybe I'll spare you the agony of childbirth and cut it out instead. Wouldn't that be nice? Then I can sell it to the highest bidder. Lots of people want little babies nowadays." More chuckling sounded.

Shyanne.

Suddenly, a cry of pain came from within the closed room. He lunged inside and saw a knife hovering above Shyanne's swollen belly. Sheena had a knee pressed against the pregnant woman's upper chest, preventing her from moving out of the way. Shyanne grimaced as another contraction rippled across her midsection.

She's in labor. Damn.

Drizzle snarled and dove at the mercenary holding Shyanne down. He raked at her with his claws, but met only air. The woman had jumped back before the deadly objects could hit home. Once freed, Shyanne rolled onto her side, grimacing, her hands holding her painful abdomen.

Sheena whipped her sword out of its holder. She knew better than to try taking on an angry humecat with only a knife. She circled the room, keeping an eye on the snarling beast before her. Each time she tried to circle back to Shyanne, the blasted cat got in the way.

Drizzle watched the woman warily. He had witnessed how fast she was and made sure to stay between her and Shyanne. In her present condition, his long time companion would not stand a chance.

Suddenly, the frown on Sheena's face became a smile and her crouched figure straightened. She laid the sword on her shoulder, tempting the cat to attack.

"Why don't you come get me, kitty. Come on. Come and get me. I'm all open." She cocked a hip to the side and waved her fingers, inviting the cat to approach.

"Drizzle! Watch out!" Shyanne managed to shout before she doubled over again.

Wondering what the woman was up to, Drizzle almost missed the movement next to him. A blade hit the very spot he occupied a moment ago. Unfortunately, his leap brought him to the corner of the room. Now he was trapped.

Drizzle flattened his ears and snarled in defiance, claws ready to shred anyone who got too close.

Sheena and her male counterpart, Andrew, advanced on the trapped animal with weapons drawn. "Awww. Now is that any way to treat us? I mean...all we want to do is play."

"Yeah. All we want to do is play Nudge the Cat, that's all." He hefted the tip of his sword at the cat.

"I didn't say how hard we would nudge, though," Sheena guffawed. "Might even nudge so hard blood could leak out." Laughter filled the room. It faded when Sheena continued. "Then we can get back to taking that baby. I have a need for the gold it will bring."

The mercenaries eyed one another and readied themselves to lunge at the cat. A snarl from across the room halted them in their tracks. Sheena spun around and instantly leaped to the side. Andrew was not so luck.

Drizzle sprang forward and sank his teeth into the exposed throat. Clamping down, he used his weight to bring the bigger opponent to the floor. Andrew tried to scream; his airway was cut off. Instead, a gurgling sound reverberated throughout the room.

Seeing what was happening to her lover, Sheena moved toward Shyanne. If she could take the woman captive, she might get out of here alive. If not, she was as good as dead.

She was almost to the bed when a tawny body

mowed into her. Her sword arm hit the wall and the blade fell from her hand. On hands and knees, she struggled to get to it. Her attempt was pointless.

Shyanne watched helplessly as the mercenary advanced. The pain that filled every part of her body gripped her in its vice, preventing her from doing anything but pray. Even if her sword was at hand, she didn't think she had the strength to wield it.

The woman's body blocked the entranceway. She was unable to see what distracted the mercenaries from killing Drizzle. As soon as Sheena hit the floor, Shyanne's eyes opened wide in amazement.

So that's what made the growling sound. Another humecat! But is it friendly, or am I in the same predicament? She didn't have time to ponder over the sudden appearance of the other cat. Another contraction hit. She clenched her teeth and pressed her arms against her belly. *Oh God, I want this to end. I'm so tired.*

Thankfully, her eyes were closed when Chikara ripped Sheena's throat open. After causing the blood of so many to run free over the years, Shyanne wasn't sure if she could handle seeing much more. Not right now. Not with the agony she was enduring.

Having her eyes closed could not stop the overwhelming smell of death that filled the room. Dread coursed through her. *Why is this labor so intense? Is something wrong? Am I going to lose this child as well?*

Once he was certain that Andrew was dead, Drizzle rushed to Shyanne's side. She was drenched in sweat. The wisps of hair surrounding her face stuck to her skin; it looked like tiny lightning bolts covered it. He brushed them aside, wiping her forehead dry with a section of the bedcovering.

Frantic eyes opened and looked into his. She clutched his tawny fur covered arm.

"Drizzle. I need you to go get Joseph. Please. I need him here with me. Something might be wrong with the baby. Please."

Her appeal snatched his heart from his chest. He wanted to leave; but, at the same time, he felt it was his duty to stay. She was going to have the baby very soon. She needed someone close to her when that time came.

"Shyanne…."

"Drizzle, please."

Shyanne, it's several days to where I left them. I won't make it back in time. If what you say is true, I'm needed here."

Chikara came into view and sat next to him. Her bejeweled eyes rested on the woman lying in the bed. An idea came to him.

"Shyanne, what if I sent Chikara? Then I can stay with you and help with the delivery."

"Does she know the way?"

His hopeful expression fell. "No."

The spasm to her swollen belly had eased. She rolled onto her back with her knees bent, and said, "Then it's best that you go, my friend." She reached out and scratched the fur on his cheek. "Besides, I won't be alone. I'll have Chikara with me."

"She doesn't speak like I do. I think Hana communicated with her through her mind. How will you do so?"

"Hana?"

"A long story."

Moving her hand to Chikara's cheek, she continued, "I think us girls will do okay." Shyanne had noticed when the other cat sat next to Drizzle that it was a she, not a he as previously thought.

Chikara rubbed against the hand and emitted a loud purr.

"See. We're hitting it off already."

The smile on Shyanne's face disappeared when another contraction wrecked havoc on her tired body. She grimaced and rolled onto her side. Tears ran from her eyes.

Chikara inched her way past Drizzle and laid her head on the bed next to Shyanne. Her purr took on a reassuring tone, as if to let the woman know all was well; a pink tongue cleansed the wetness from her face.

That solidified it for Drizzle.

"I'll bring Joseph back as fast as I can. I only hope it will be in time."

He turned and ran from the room. With the speed of his kind, the cat started back toward the cave. He only hoped that nothing would get in his way to make the already long trek even longer, for Shyanne's sake.

*   *   *

Drayco jerked awake. It took him several blinks to realize the darkness surrounding him was real and not something else, something far worse.

Another person was snuggled against his body. He felt the small size and knew it was Hana. The warmth emanating from her felt good, especially in the cold, dank cave. He almost fell back to sleep when he realized there was only a small ember of light glowing in the room. Alarm flung his eyes open again.

The dark twin threw himself into a sitting position and looked around. Joseph was against the wall, chin resting on his chest. Hana shifted her position but remained asleep. He looked over where Ruben should have been and saw nothing.

Darkness blanketed that side of the cave. Rising to his feet, he limped to the torches that Hana brought and lit one before the glowing ember faded out. The light erased any doubts. The mercenary leader was gone. Only the ropes that held him remained.

"Damn."

Drayco whipped around and nearly fell when the pain from his broken leg reminded him of the folly of moving too fast. He recovered and shouted, "Joseph! Hana! Wake up. Ruben's gone."

Drayco's outcry registered in Joseph's tired brain, except it seemed more like a dream than an actuality. He shook his head to try to clear the residual sleep. Without warning, his body rocked back and forth like during an earthquake. His eye flew open with fear.

"Dammit all to hell, did you hear me? Ruben's gone. We have to get up and go after him. Wake up, dammit. Wake up!"

"Alright! Alright! I'm awake. Stop shaking me for christ sake."

Joseph stretched his arms wide and heard his back pop several times. That was when Drayco's words finally sunk in. He looked up sharply and saw anger etched on the dark twin's face.

"Ruben's gone?"

"That's what I said, isn't it." Drayco turned away in disgust. "It must have happened after you fell asleep. Who knows how long he's been free." He walked over to the ropes lying on the ground and picked them up. The ends were smooth instead of frayed, and small footprints blended in with the larger ones. "And it looks like Joey helped him get that way."

"Are you sure?" Joseph rose to his feet and moved next to Drayco. He looked down and saw the prints. "Blast it all to hell! What was that boy thinking?"

"He thinks Ruben is his dad now. And we're the ones hurting him."

"But he's not his father. I am."

"Not anymore."

Those words stung. Joseph wondered what he had done to drive the boy away. He considered himself to be a good provider. He made sure the family had everything they needed: food, shelter, clothing. Everything.

Everything except someone to play with. He and Shyanne had sheltered Joey from others in case Ruben found them and tried to take the boy. That happened anyway. Now he may have lost his son in another way, a way far worse. He may have lost him forever to a killer.

Drayco picked up the extra torch and started toward the tunnel. The simple process of walking caused his leg to ache in ways seldom experienced. It made him very grumpy.

"Why the hell did you fall asleep? You must sleep like the dead since nothing woke you. An atom bomb could go off next to you and you would probably sleep right through it."

"Drayco, that's enough." Hana's soft voice carried over his ranting as if it were a shout. "He feels bad enough about what happened. Do not make things worse. Please."

Drayco glanced back at the others. Joseph had his head bowed, his eyes closed. He quieted after becoming aware of the anguish his words had caused. As he watched, Joseph lifted his head and picked up the burning torch. He passed the dark man without a word. Hana followed.

Her gentle fingers brushed against his arm when she came up beside Drayco. "He knows fully well what he has done. Please, he needs our positive words now, not the hurtful ones."

Her brown eyes locked onto Drayco's black ones. He had the feeling of a vast amount of wisdom hidden deep inside the little woman. Of a wisdom far beyond her apparent years. It made him wonder who she really was. He had no time to think on it, though, for the party was moving on, back into the tunnel. They had a killer and a misguided child to find.

The light from the tunnel leading to the outside world showed Ruben where to place his feet. His forward momentum picked up speed. Joey was still in his arms, holding his neck tight. The child's grasp lessened once he saw the light ahead.

"We did it. You're the best, Dad. I knew you would get us out."

"Now we need to get some supplies and get out of here before the others find out I'm gone and track us here. Can you get a pack ready for yourself?" Ruben put the boy down and started into the tunnel leading to their living quarters.

"You bet."

Joey ran ahead of the big man and rummaged through his things until he found a pack. He began filling it with some clothes and other things. Ruben smiled.

The smile faded when he thought about the people still in the cave. He would have loved killing them while they slept, but that was something Joey did not need to see, not yet anyway. Not while a shred of love for his past father remained. He would drive the feelings out of the boy first then kill him. Maybe by then Joey would help. Then his revenge on at least one member of the twin's family would be complete.

Ruben found his own pack and filled it with needed items. By the time he was finished, so was Joey. They met and walked toward the stables.

"Aren't we going to take the flyer?"

"What would we do with Wind Racer?"

Looking perplexed, Joey said, "I hadn't thought about that." A smile creased his young face. "Maybe we could put him on it and go that way."

"Unfortunately, the flyer can't handle his weight. We'll have to leave it."

The smile disappeared but reappeared when they entered the stables. Wind Racer nickered a welcoming and reached his neck over the railing toward the approaching pair.

Joey ran up to the horse and rubbed the head a couple of times before hugging it.

"Let's get a move on, little man."

The big man gave the boy's shoulder a reassuring squeeze before saddling the horse. He plopped Joey onto the strong back and led the animal into the tunnel. As they passed the flyer, he smashed several of the solar panels on the side facing them.

That should prevent them from using it, he thought. He wanted to smash all the panels but time was a factor now. They had to get as far from here as possible.

He was certain Drayco, Joseph and the woman would get out. With any luck, by the time they did, he and Joey would be too far away to follow. Besides, with the pair of mercenaries he had sent to kill Shyanne as a distraction, he was certain Joseph would go to his wife's aid before following him.

Drayco, on the other hand, was another matter. That dark demon spawn from hell might do anything. Ruben knew full well the capabilities of that dark one and he wanted as much distance between them as possible. With those thoughts in mind, he got in the saddle and hugged Joey against him.

"Hold on, son. This is going to be a bumpy ride. You up to it?"

"Yea!"

"Here we go."

Ruben tapped the horse in the ribs and held on as he leaped into the brush ahead. Joey never once looked back.

Drayco led the party down the tunnel to where it branched off in several directions. Joseph had moved to the rear, brooding over the loss of Ruben. Holding the torch closer to the ground, the dark man saw only stone. No footprints indicated which way the mercenary had taken.

"Now what?"

Hana stepped forward. She peered down each tunnel before facing Drayco. "I don't know. Logically, Ruben would have taken the fastest way out. But, if he suspected we would follow, which he knows we would, then he might have gone down any one of these to throw us off, to have us waste time."

"That's just what we're going to have to do. Who knows if there's another exit to this maze. Damn!" Drayco spat out in exasperation.

"Let's get started then. The faster we explore, the faster we find my son," Joseph said. "If we don't see any signs of them within a period of time, we turn back and try another. Agreed?"

"Agreed," both Hana and Drayco piped in at the same time. Drayco added, "But only until this torch holds. Then we move fast to find the entrance."

Without a word, the trio stepped into the first tunnel on the left. Darkness filled the void left behind when the half-burned torch moved deeper into the cave system.

Doing the impossible, Drizzle ran all through the night and the better part of a day without resting. He was exhausted by the time the cave came into sight at dusk. As he passed the flyer, he noticed the broken shards lying on the ground. Ruben's scent was heavy in the area, though it was old. Thinking it was from when they captured the mercenary; he shrugged it off and entered the tunnel system.

Halfway down the tunnel, he stopped and sniffed at the ground. Ruben's scent was stronger, and intermingled with another.

Joey. He straightened. *No time to deal with this now. I have to find Joseph. Shyanne needs him.*

He ran on until he found the part where the tunnels branched into several directions. With his nose to the ground, he discovered that Joseph, Hana and Drayco had been this way recently. Ruben's scent was here as well, but weaker, indicating it was older than the trio overlapping it was. The smells disappeared down several branches. All except one. Ruben's led in only one direction.

What are they up to? It's as if they are randomly searching. If Ruben is with them, why are they doing that? Remembering how he had discovered that Joey's scent was intermingled with Ruben's, he suspected why. *He must have escaped and found the boy. Damn that rizbak stench of a being.*

The urgency of his mission returned full force. He put his nose to the ground once more and found the most recent trail left by the three he hunted. It led to the second tunnel on the right out of the four possible and appeared to be only a few minutes old. The cat followed with as much speed as possible in the darkened conditions.

After only a few minutes, he discovered another entrance that led to the left. The scent trail disappeared down it. *Those fools must be lost. Just like humans, no sense of direction amongst the lot of them. Always stumbling around blindly in whichever direction, even if it's the wrong one.* He shook his head and continued into the new tunnel.

A light appeared a short distance ahead. In silent cat fashion, he crept up on the three standing at the dead-end.

"Now what do we do. We've been searching these tunnels for hours and we're no closer to finding Joey or Ruben." Joseph's tone was laden with irritation. "And we've managed to get lost as well."

Drizzle heard a rock hit the wall and bounce off, landing only a few feet away. Sitting back on his haunches, he said, "Well, if you'd quit running around and just use your senses, you'd find what you're looking for."

"Drizzle!" Joseph yelled.

The trio watched the tawny colored cat as he walk into the light. Instantly, the atmosphere changed. Instead of despair, hope now filled it.

"God am I glad to see you!"

Drayco smashed the enthusiasm of seeing the cat with one sentence. "Why are you here?"

"Just like you, dark one, always cutting to the chase with directness." He focused his gaze on Joseph. "I'm here because Shyanne needs you. Now."

"What? Is Shyanne okay? Did those mercenaries do something to her?" The fair-haired man moved a couple of steps closer. "What the hell is going on?"

"The mercenaries sent to kill her are dead instead. Chikara helped end their mission before it was successful. Unfortunately, we were too late to help the old couple."

"Chikara?" Hana's quiet word broke in. "Just like that cat. Always does what she wants, even if I tell her to stay home."

"Then what's wrong with Shyanne?" Joseph demanded.

"The baby has decided it wants to see the world."

Joseph's mouth hung open.

"There's something wrong, though, isn't there?" Hana asked.

"The labor pains are intense and her water has not yet broken. And the times are not regular."

"We must go to her." Hana moved forward and cupped Joseph's elbow, leading the shocked man toward the cat. "Drizzle, can you lead us out of here?"

"Follow me. Make sure to keep up. I'll be moving fast."

"Don't worry, we will," Drayco said. He came up on Joseph's other side and helped guide him down the tunnel.

Half an hour later, they stood in the sunlight outside the cave entrance. Joseph had recovered enough to walk without guidance. He asked, "How long did it take for you to reach us?"

"A day and a half, the cat replied. "And I didn't stop at any time."

Drayco stood by the flyer. He knelt and examined the broken shards of glass lying on the ground next to it. Glancing over at the others, he asked, "Did Ruben break these?"

Drizzle met his gaze. "I believe he did."

"Was Joey with him?"

"From his scent...yes."

He escaped while we were hunting for him in the cave, didn't he."

"Yes."

Drayco slammed his fist against the flyer. "Damn him. Damn him all the way to hell."

"That is not productive at the moment, Drayco," Hana said. We need to get to Shyanne before another life is lost. A life that has not had the chance to live."

"You're right." The dark man stood. His eyes rested on the flyer. "I wonder..."

"Why are we just standing around?" Joseph blurted out, his tone anxious. "While you're all talking about broken glass and...and..." he choked as he continued, "my son, Shyanne could be dying, along with the baby." He spun around and started toward the horses hidden a short distance from where the party stood. "Well, I'm not waiting any longer. Shyanne needs me and I intend on being there for her."

"Joseph, wait. I have an idea," Drayco shouted.

"I've waited long enough, Drayco. I'm not waiting any longer."

"Joseph, please."

Joseph twirled around and shouted, "Enough! I'm leaving...with or without you!"

He moved toward the horses again, but a growl from Drizzle halted him.

"I think you should listen to him. He might have an idea that will get you there a lot quicker than any horse."

"Drizzle, get out of my way." Joseph tried several times to get past the cat. Each time, the way was blocked with a show of teeth or a sharp claw. Finally, in frustration, he faced Drayco.

"Well, what's this all-wonderful idea you have that's keeping me from my wife?" He crossed his arms in front of his chest and glared at the dark man.

Drayco stepped up on the platform and examined the control panel. A joystick similar to the ones he used while playing video games before the virus sat in the middle. A circular button was located near it. He pushed it, hoping it was what he thought it was. The platform started vibrating; a hum accompanied it.

"I think we can use this to get back quicker than taking the horses. With these panels broken, though, I'm not certain how well it will continue to work."

Drayco grabbed the joystick and gently guided the flyer into the sunlight. The intensity of the vibration increased, but not much.

Joseph's arm slowly fell to his sides. He gaped at the man as if he had just leaped off a mountain and landed on his feet without a scratch. "You expect me to ride on that? Are you crazy?"

"Some might think so, but no, I'm not crazy."

"I'm not riding on that! That's an abomination from hell. That's one of the things that destroyed so much!"

"This didn't destroy a thing. It is a machine that carries a person from one place to another, that's all." Drayco said, frustrated at the man's reaction. He moved toward Joseph.

Joseph backed away. "You'll not get me on that thing. I'll not allow it!" He reached for the sword on his back. "If you try, I'll stop you any way I can."

Before he could pull the sword free, Drizzle plowed into the back of his legs, knocking him over backwards. The sudden landing forced the wind out of him.

Drayco darted forward and hit Joseph on the side of his head. He slumped over like a lead weight, knocked out by the blow.

"Well, that was exciting." Sarcasm laced each word as Drizzle moved toward the flyer.

Hana's healer instincts took over. She limped to Joseph and made sure he was okay before looking at Drayco. "Do you think it will carry all of us?"

"No." He grabbed one of Joseph's arms and flung it over a shoulder. Putting most of the weight of his good leg, he lifted him and carefully carried him to the platform. "But it will carry you and Joseph. Possibly Drizzle as well."

"What about you?"

"I'll come on horseback. Bravaro has been a better companion than any human being will ever be. I'll not leave him."

The small woman eyed Drayco as he gently laid the unconscious man down. A wince of pain appeared as he shifted the wounded leg in the wrong direction during the maneuver; it disappeared just as fast.

That was when she realized the dark one was not as dark as he portrayed. A caring individual lay hidden underneath the gruff exterior.

Standing, Drayco said, "Come over here so I can show you how this works." He pointed at the console and moved up to it.

Making her way next to him, she reached up and placed a hand on his arm then leaned forward to see the console better. He hesitated, surprised by the sudden touch. Within the span of several breaths, he continued.

Once he finished instructing Hana, he stepped off the platform. "Hopefully the battery life will have enough charge to get you there. I don't think you will have any problems since only one side was smashed. Looking up at the sun shining down on them, he added, "You should leave now. That way you will be there before nightfall, just in case the battery isn't working any longer."

"I do not foresee any difficulties. And I will take care of your sister until you arrive. I promise you this." She bowed slightly to Drayco with her hands pressed together.

Drayco held her gaze, then nodded. He peered at the cat sitting a short distance away. "Get on the flyer, Drizzle. After that run-from-hell you just did, you'll only slow me down."

In a manner uncharacteristic of the cat, he padded onto the platform without any argument.

Hana returned to the console and pushed the button to start the flyer. Grasping the joystick with her small hand, she guided it off the ground and into the sky above. The machine was sluggish due to having fewer panels to power it and because of the weight it carried, but it responded better than expected. Before heading toward the ailing sister, she glanced down at the one left behind. He remained near the cave, watching.

Drayco watched the tiny woman guide the flyer into the sky as if she had done it before and disappear. Remembering how she seemed wiser than her years, he began to wonder.

What is it about her that reminds me so much of Shyanne? Her mannerism? Her stubbornness? What?

Shaking his head, he found the horses and removed the saddle from the one ridden by Hana. His saddle was back in the clearing, left behind when the others followed him to the cave. Because of his damaged leg, it was a struggle to get it on Bravaro. But he managed to do so without wasting too much time, or injuring himself further.

With a grimace, he climbed into the saddle and turned the horse in the direction taken by the flyer. He was tempted to go after Ruben. The need to see his sister and make sure she was okay drove that idea to the back of his mind. As before, he would hunt the mercenary down until the man was dead. Then he would return what was stolen, his nephew, to the rightful family.

During the long ride, he thought more about the woman who knew so much, yet seemed so young. By the time he reached the inn, he was no closer to understanding Hana than when he was at the cave.

Twenty

Joseph gradually woke to the feel of air flowing past at a higher than usual rate of speed. He felt the subtle vibrations beneath him and wondered what caused it. With the remembrance of what transpired before the world went black, he sat up abruptly. The ground, or what should have been the ground, rolled from side to side.

That demon spawned twin put me on that contraption from the past!

His heart raced as he frantically reached in several directions, trying to find a handhold to keep from being flung into the unknown. The sudden movement caused the rolling to increase in intensity. The edge of the flyer materialized out of nowhere and he was forced to look down at the trees far below. His heart pounded its way into his throat. He swallowed hard several times, attempting to drive it back where it belonged, unsuccessfully.

He was partway off the platform when a hand grabbed him by the back of his shirt and dragged him back.

"Hold still, you fool, or you'll cause us to tip over and crash into the trees," Drizzle said with a snarl. "Then both your kids will be without their father instead of only one."

The last statement bit deep into his gut. It also forced him to realize the folly of his actions. He froze, lying in the center of the flying machine, afraid to twitch even a finger lest he hastened the hand of death.

"That's better. Now stay there or the next time I grab

you a few claws will be involved."

"It's alright, Joseph. We will be landing in a few minutes. You will not have to endure this much longer."

Hana's soft words did nothing to lessen the terror he felt.

The platform smoothed out and, as promised, the flight lasted about fifteen minutes longer. Those last fifteen minutes were sheer hell, but they allowed Joseph time to think about his family: those here, those missing, and the one about to be born. The second the platform landed, he rolled off it. He was never so glad to see solid ground as he was at that moment.

He had no time to argue with the others over what they had done, though; Shyanne needed him. After this much time, who knew what kind of shape she was in.

Joseph jumped to his feet and ran up the steps to the porch. "Shyanne! Shyanne!" He bolted through the front door and was met by a humecat. "Chikara. Where's Shyanne?"

The cat spun around and ran to a room halfway down the hall on the right. Before he reached it, a scream of pain echoed into the hall.

"Shyanne!"

At the entrance to the room, he saw his wife lying on a sweat covered bed against the far wall. Her hair was matted to her skin and a look of utter pain filled her eyes. Her legs were spread apart with the knees bent. Blood tinged sheets were visible between them. The blood looked fresh.

"Oh God...."

"Excuse me."

Hana pushed the stunned man out of the way and hurried to Shyanne. She moved the sheets and saw a tiny head sticking out. The baby was coming—now. Unfortunately, the woman on the bed was exhausted. She was not able to push any longer.

"Joseph, I need you over here."

Joseph continued to gaze at his wife, unmoving. A sudden shove forced him out of shock and into action. He rushed to Shyanne's side and grabbed her hand. Drizzle materialized at his elbow, purring loud to reassure his lifelong companion.

"Oh God it hurts. It hurts," she panted. "I don't know

how much longer I can take this. Oh Joseph, something's wrong with the baby, I can tell. It's been too long...too long." Her words ended when a contraction caused her to grit her teeth in pain. She fell back when it eased.

"Shhh." It was Hana who spoke. "At present, the baby is okay. But you need to help get it out. I need you to push as hard as you can with the next contraction."

"I don't know if I can do that. I'm so tired, so tired."

"If you want this child to live, you must."

"Lady, you have no idea what I'd give right now for some drugs and a nice cool hospital room."

Before Joseph could ask what she meant, the next wave hit. He lifted Shyanne's shoulders so she could push more effectively, and to feel more useful instead of feeling so helpless.

"That's it. That's it. Keep it up. The baby's almost out," he reassured his wife.

Shyanne had been in the beginning phase of labor when Drizzle left, and was completely exhausted now. Chikara helped comfort her while they waited for help to arrive. The cat wet her dry lips with drops of water from a soaked rag. That was the only thing she had had because anything swallowed during that time came back up.

Now the lack of food and water was working against her. She had nothing left.

"You can do this, Shyanne," Drizzle purred. "You're the toughest person I know."

"Come on, my love. It's only a few more pushes and our baby will be born." Joseph's voice was thick with emotion.

Encouraged by their words, Shyanne clenched her teeth and pushed several times as hard as her tired body allowed. It felt as if the bottom half of her was ripped apart. Sudden relief followed.

She collapsed against Joseph and waited, waited for the crying to start. Nothing happened. Lifting her head, she saw an oriental woman vigorously rubbing something in the sheets. A glance at her husband's face made the pit of her stomach plummet.

"Is my baby alright?"

No one answered. They were all focused on the tiny object in the sheets. Chikara glided next to Drizzle and added her purr to his, as if to tell the new arrival it was okay to cry.

Struggling to sit up, she gripped Joseph's arm and pleaded, "Is the baby alright? Why isn't she crying? Tell me. Tell me!" Shyanne knew with the instincts of a mother that the baby was a girl.

The movement at the foot of the bed stopped. The little woman sat up and gazed into Shyanne's eyes. The frown of concentration left her face. It was replaced with the most wonderful smile. Suddenly, the sound of someone very unhappy filled the room.

"It's a girl, just as your heart foretold."

Tears of joy streamed down Shyanne's cheeks as the wrapped ear-piercing bundle was placed in her arms. As suddenly as the crying started, it stopped. She hugged the tiny girl against her body. Joseph put a finger into the small hand that lay exposed and grinned as it closed.

Drizzle remained where he was, beaming like a proud daddy. Chikara, on the other hand, moved next to the new parents and laid her head on the bed next to Shyanne. As they watched, she rubbed her nose against the baby then licked it.

"Chikara, stop."

"It's okay," Shyanne said. "She only wants to introduce herself."

Joseph laughed. "Hana, if that cat is anything like her companion, we'll have nothing to worry about. And if she's anything like Drizzle, then God help us."

"Thanks. Always open for compliments." He grinned in cat-like fashion.

Hana stood and waved her arms. "Everyone out please. I have to help the new mother clean up."

After giving Shyanne a kiss, Joseph reluctantly got off the bed and started toward the door. Drizzle trailed him. Chikara stayed where she was.

"Chikara...."

The cat looked up at the healer. She returned her head to the recently vacated spot, refusing to leave the baby's side.

Hana laughed. "It seems the baby has a loyal fan." Rubbing the cat's head, she said, "If you're going to stay, you have to help. Joseph, can you fetch some water and some cloths? Chikara can carry the cloths."

"Be back in a second. Come on, Chikara."

Again, the cat refused to move.

"Looks like I'll be doing this job alone. Unless you want to help, Drizzle." The fair-haired man gave the male humecat a sideways glance.

"Like I've said so many times before, I'm not a pack animal. But in this case," he stole a peek at Shyanne, "I'll help. But only this once. So don't go expecting it again."

"Oh, don't worry, your majesty, I know this is menial work for such a cat as yourself."

"And don't you forget it, mister."

The friendly bantering faded as they walked down the hall to complete the task given to them.

Hana searched the room until she found a change of clothes and a brush. She returned to Shyanne and laid the items on a small table. "So, you're the Shyanne Joseph spoke so much about. It's a pleasure to finally meet you."

Shyanne chuckled. "I wish it was under better conditions." She shifted the soiled linens under her, moving them to the end of the bed with her feet since her arms held the baby. "I'm glad you were here to help out. Without you, I don't think we'd be here now." She glanced at the sleeping form in her arms, and smiled.

"I only did what was expected of me, nothing more." Hana picked up the smelly mess and carried it to a corner near the door. "What will her name be?"

"Molly."

"Molly. An utsukushii name for an utsukushii baby."

"That's beautiful. What does it mean?"

"Just that—beautiful."

"Here you go," Joseph said as he and Drizzle entered the room. "Things to help my beautiful wife feel beautiful again."

"Utsukushii wife," Shyanne quipped.

Joseph gave her a quizzical look. "What was that?"

Both women piped in together, "Utsukushii."

"Oh." He shrugged his shoulders and passed the bucket of water over to the oriental woman. Hana and Shyanne chuckled at his reaction.

Drizzle remained in the background, shaking his head at the man. When Hana indicated for him to hand over the cloths, he brought them to her.

"Thank you, gentlemen, your services are no longer required. Please come back at another time when the mother is more presentable." She bowed slightly at the waist and returned her attention to the pair resting in the bed.

Joseph and Drizzle took that as their cue and backed out of the room, pulling the door closed behind them.

"Now what," he asked the cat when they stood outside the closed door.

"I don't know about you, but I'm going to take a nap. I didn't get the luxury of taking one on the way here like someone else."

Joseph frowned. "That wasn't by choice, you know."

Drizzle put a woeful look on his cat face and leaned his head back in a dramatic fashion. "Remember saying this? 'I'm not riding on that! That's an abomination from hell. That's one of the things that destroyed so much!' Those were the words that bought you your nap."

"It is an abomination and should be destroyed." Joseph crossed his arms before his chest.

Straightening, the cat retorted, "It got you here in time, didn't it? And you didn't die in the process."

The new father chuckled. "I'd rather have a good horse under me anytime over so much air."

Drizzle chortled. "You are the true meaning of a country bumpkin, my friend." He started down the hall. "Let's go take that nap in the main room. I saw a comfy chair that has your name written all over it."

"I think I'll check on the horses first. With Shyanne down as long as she was, and the mercenaries dead for I don't know how long, who knows what condition they are in."

"Suit yourself. I'll be asleep if you need anything. Oh, and by the way, the horses are located in the building behind this one. Didn't want you to get lost trying to find them." The cat was gone by the time Joseph realized what he had said.

"Crazy animal," he muttered under his breath while moving toward the back of the house. Almost to the exit, he noticed a bloody trail that led outside. It was too much to be from only one person. *Now I know what happened to the bodies. Chikara must have dragged them out.*

The trail led down the porch and out toward the tree line.

Glad I didn't have to deal with that.

He entered the stable and wrinkled his nose. The stench of several horses living inside for far too many days hit his nose. After letting them out and opening every door and stall in the building, he grabbed a shovel and started in. In a corner stall, he found the body of a small horse like creature with long ears.

Poor little thing. It never stood a chance.

Many hours later, after the stalls were cleaned and fresh water made available, he found his way to the main room and settled into the chair that supposedly had his name written all over it. Within minutes of holding still, his snoring mingled with that of the cat.

Midway through the third day after the birth of Molly, Drayco rode into sight. He was covered from head to toe with trail dust and his mood was somber, having had several days to think about the loss of Joey and Ruben. Instantly, it perked up at the sight of the tiny baby.

"I was beginning the worry," Shyanne said. She sat in a chair on the front porch, gently rocking back and forth.

"You know me, sis, always causing problems."

He limped up the steps and peered at the small form in her arms. He had to watch where to place his feet because Chikara lay close at hand, ever watching over her charge. Shyanne rose to her feet and handed him the sleeping bundle.

"Here, big brother. I need to go to the bathroom. Watch over her like a good uncle." She grinned at the awkward way he took the baby, almost as if she was fine china ready to break with even the slightest touch.

"She's pretty tough, Drayco. You can hold her a little closer without breaking her."

Drayco moved his lanky form to the chair and sat down. He had no desire to drop his new niece. Chikara rose up from the floor and stared at the dark man as if to let him know who the boss was here. As he met her gaze, a shadow of a smile formed.

"Well, I can see my niece will be protected from harms reach." The smile faded as he continued. "Unlike her brother."

Shyanne paused at the doorway and watched her

brother hold the baby. His statement caused her heart to sink.

When she had finished cleaning up after the birthing process, Joseph filled her in on what had transpired since they left their home so long ago. And about how Joey now called the mercenary killer dad.

The news made her angry; it made her cry. Now, seeing Drayco hold the baby, it made her yearn more than ever for the return of her son. With a sigh, she went inside to take care of business.

Later in the evening, after the baby was asleep and all were finished with the excellent meal cooked by Hana, the group sat on the same porch drinking mugs of ale. All except Chikara. She was resting at what was quickly becoming her place, at the baby's side.

Drayco propped his feet up on the railing. It reminded his of how he and Kilan used to do it when the twins were waiting for Ruben to make an appearance. He gazed into his mug, staring at the liquid inside as if it were a mirror to the past.

Shyanne sensed his thoughts and reached out to him. Resting her hand on his arm, she said, "I miss them too."

Raising his eyes to hers, he saw the concern within. He covered her hand with his. "Don't worry, little sis. I won't go off again without letting you know first. Be forewarned, though, once I know that you and the baby are going to be okay, I will be leaving. I don't want Joey corrupted by that monster any longer than necessary."

"I'm right there with you, Drayco. I want my son back more than anyone can imagine." At Shyanne's look, Joseph added, "Except for maybe you, my love."

"Your thoughts may be of your son, but your duty is to your wife and daughter. They need you here."

"Joseph's shoulders fell. "I don't have to like it, but you're right, of course." He stared into the contents of his own mug as if it were a foretelling mirror. "I can't help remembering how much it hurt to hear Joey calling that animal dad." He looked at the dark twin. "I want him to call me dad again, and truly mean it, not just say it to appease me. Do you know what I mean?"

Drayco paused. He understood where Joseph was coming from. Once, a long time ago, he was almost a father.

A madman took his child from him before it had a chance to see the world.

Hana leaned against the doorway listening to the conversation. She watched a sadness settle over Drayco, a sadness long endured, and wondered what had happened to cause it. As the conversation continued, a plan formed. She turned away, leaving the trio to discuss the past as well as things yet to come.

Two weeks to the day from Molly's birth, Drayco paced back and forth in the kitchen. His broken leg had set before he could realign it, giving him a permanent limp.

Hana listened to the sound of his slightly uneven footfall as she stood in front of the stove cooking breakfast, her own wounded leg completely healed. It gave her the impression of a caged animal waiting for a chance to break free.

While she flipped the eggs, Joseph and Shyanne walked into the room with the baby. Each pulled out a chair at the table and sat down. Chikara followed, keeping an eye on the cooing bundle of joy. The cat slid under Shyanne's seat with her upper body poking out so she could see Molly. Drizzle was away hunting for his breakfast.

"That smells absolutely wonderful, Hana. I can't wait to taste it. " Joseph inhaled deeply. "The last breakfast was fantastic too. Where did you learn to cook?"

"My grandfather taught me. He showed me how to use spices and herbs to do many things."

"Is your grandfather still living?"

"No. He died many years ago."

"I bet you miss him. I miss my parents." Shyanne said as she played with the hand poking out of the blanket.

"I do."

"Drayco, sit down. You're wearing me out just watching you," Shyanne emphasized.

"I need to walk." His reply was curt, almost as if it was a bother to answer.

Hana scooped some potatoes, eggs and a slab of ham onto a wooden plate. She halted his pacing by putting the plate in his path. "If you're going to leave tomorrow, you need to eat."

"What? You're leaving?" Shyanne's eyes widened in

surprise. "I thought you were going to tell me before you left."

"I was going to tell you after breakfast." He shot Hana a nasty look.

"I warned you it was coming, love. I could see the signs."

"But why now? Why not wait until after we make it home?"

"That's too long, Shyanne. I told you when I first arrived that I would leave as soon as I knew you and the baby were going to be okay. That time has come."

"We could take the flyer."

"And leave Jack behind? I don't see that happening, sis."

"But…."

"But nothing!" Drayco argued. "Joey needs to be brought home to the family that loves him. I'm tired of waiting for that to happen."

Hana forced the plate of food into the dark twin's hand. "You will have to wait until you are fed to do anything. Sit, before it becomes unfit for even Chikara to eat."

He shoved the plate back into her hands and stormed to the exit. He hesitated before leaving. "I need to refill in other ways before I go. I'll be back later."

The ones remaining in the room watched as the door slammed shut.

"That brother of yours sure is a strange one," Joseph commented.

"He's not strange," Shyanne replied softly. "He's been dealt a rotten hand and is still trying to make the best of it. Sometimes that comes off a bit cold."

Hana set the plate before Joseph and returned to the stove to ready another for Shyanne. When she set it on the table, Shyanne looked up at her.

"What about you, Hana? Are you coming with us?"

"I'm making plans."

Picking up a fork, she inquired, "How is it you came to be with a humecat?"

"She found me, actually. I stumbled into her as a child when I was playing at my grandfather's house. How she came into his possession, I have no knowledge." A slight smile creased her face. "I remember looking into her golden eyes and nearly falling on my backside with fright when her words entered my mind. I fled crying to my grandfather. He comforted me and told me it was okay, then formally introduced me to Chikara. We've been together ever since."

"You two act like you've been together for a long time now."

Gazing down at the cat under the chair, Hana said, "We have." She turned and walked toward the hall leading to the rest of the house. "I have to check on some items. Please, enjoy the breakfast before it gets cold."

Shyanne watched the little woman disappear.

Something about her doesn't seem right. I can't put a finger on what it is...yet, but I will.

Later that evening, after all the chores of the day were completed, husband and wife sat in the main room watching the glowing embers within the fireplace. Shyanne had put the baby down for the night after nursing her. Chikara, as usual, was with her.

Both stared into the flames, refusing to break the silence. Both dwelled on the upcoming events.

For one, it was the safe arrival of his family back at the homestead; all of them except the son who remained in the hands of a ruthless killer. For the other, it was the separation of family the morning would bring.

Shyanne released a heavy sigh.

"I understand. I'll miss him too."

"I wish he wasn't going. At the same time, I'm glad he is. I miss Joey and want him back in my arms."

"I wish I were going with him." He squeezed her hand in reassurance when she glared at him. "But that's not something I'd do to you again, especially with Molly being so young. I'd give anything to be the one to cut that smug grin off Ruben's face though." With a heavy sigh of his own, Joseph added, "And to hear my son call me dad again."

Joseph peered at the woman seated next to him, his voice choked with emotion. "Love you, wife."

She clasped his outstretched hand with hers. "Love you back, husband."

Silence filled the room once more.

Early the next day, Drayco moved about the kitchen

grabbing supplies to take with him. For the first time in weeks, a spring replaced the limp in his step. He was anxious to get going, yet a part of him wanted very much to stay with his sister.

Joseph and Shyanne watched him pack the supplies. Hana was nowhere in sight. With a heavy heart, she asked, "Do you have everything? Enough clothes, blankets, a sharpener, foodstuff?"

"Yes mother, I do." Drayco walked over and ruffled his sister's hair. She ducked away, not in the mood to roughhouse.

Shyanne made her way to the window and looked out. "Seriously, Drayco, do you?"

Matching her somber mood, he replied, "Yes." The dark man walked to his sister's side and leaned against the counter. He tried to get her attention, but she refused to look at him. "Are you going to be okay, sis?"

"I only recently got you back after so long. Now you're going away again." She spun around and crossed her arms before her. "I know why you have to go. I also know that I couldn't stop you if I tried." She looked at everything in the room except her brother. A tear ran down her cheek. Others followed. "I just wish all this had never happened. I just wish I had my family all together."

Drayco lifted her chin and gazed into her eyes. "It happened, Shyanne. And no matter how bad you want thing to be as they were, it's not going to happen, not unless I go find Joey."

Joseph walked up next to his sister and wrapped his arms around her.

"I want you to promise me one thing, Joseph."

"Anything."

"I want you to take care of my sister and niece until I get back. That means you don't go off and leave them. Can you do that?"

"I made that vow when I took her as my wife, Drayco."

"No matter how long it takes, I want you to stay with them. Give me your word that you'll stay."

"You have my word."

Drayco nodded. "Good." Picking up the pack, he started toward the back door. "I'd better get moving. I have a long way to go."

When the trio stepped onto the porch, two saddled and ready horses greeted them: Bravaro and one of the horses belonging to the mercenaries. Hana stood by one in her riding apparel.

"What do you think you're doing?" Drayco demanded.

"I'm going with you."

"No you're not."

"You can not stop me."

"We'll just see about that."

"I wouldn't, Drayco. Remember back at the cave?" Joseph said.

Drayco hesitated. He turned his back on the small woman and walked to his horse. "You are needed here, healer. I do not want you riding with me. You'll only slow me down."

"My services are not required here. As you said, both mother and child are doing fine." She winked at Shyanne. "Besides, with your track record, I think you'll need my services more."

Drayco whirled around to face Hana. He was livid. "Are you dense? What part of I don't want you riding with me do you not understand?"

A chuckle broke out from the side of the porch. In all the excitement, no one had noticed Drizzle's arrival.

"Give it up, Drayco. You're not going to win."

Drayco spun around, "I don't want to hear any comments from the peanut gallery, fuzzball! I said she can't come and that's final!"

Unfazed by the outburst, Drizzle sprawled out to enjoy the morning sunshine. He stated, "That's what you think."

"Why you…." The dark man started toward the cat. A shout halted him.

"ENOUGH!"

All eyes focused on Hana.

She walked calmly over to Drayco and glared up at him. "Enough. I am going with you and that is final."

He glared back, but remained silent.

"Once you find Ruben, and I am certain you will, the boy will suffer greatly over his death. By me being there, treatment can begin immediately."

"Makes sense to me," Joseph threw in.

Drayco gave the fair-haired man a withering look. Again, he remained silent.

"I really think she should go, brother."

Drayco rolled his eyes. "Not you too." Throwing his hands up, he relented. "Oh, all right. But the first time you whine about anything, you'll find yourself alone, got it?"

Hana bowed her head ever so slightly to show she understood and walked over to her horse.

Exasperated, Drayco mumbled, "What about the cat? Is she going along on this little adventure?"

"No. She will stay to watch over the baby."

"But Hana, she needs to be with you. Molly will be fine."

Looking at Shyanne, Hana said, "Chikara has made her choice. She has bonded with the baby and is no longer my companion."

"Oh Hana." Shyanne could imagine what the woman was going through, even though her face remained expressionless. She had felt the same way when Drizzle was a prisoner to Ruben those long years past. It was as if a part of her heart had been ripped out. Coming to her, she hugged the healer tight. "I will watch out for her. When you come back, we'll have a great reunion."

Hana hugged her in return. "You have a special daughter there. With Chikara around, you will never have to worry about her disappearing."

Shyanne let go and moved to Drayco. While they said their goodbyes, Joseph approached the oriental woman.

"Hana, I have a debt to you that can never be repaid."

"I know of no debt," she replied, lowering her eyes from his.

"You've saved my life on several occasions. Now you have saved my wife and child. For that, I will be forever in your debt."

"As a healer, I did what was expected. If I had done nothing, I would have disappointed my grandfather and allowed two people to die."

Pulling her close, Joseph whispered, "Thank you, Grandfather." He stepped back and waited for Shyanne to finish. She joined him a few minutes later, her cheeks wet from tears.

Drayco swung into the saddle and tugged Bravaro's head around. "Okay, let's get this show on the road. Coming Sundance?"

"Right behind you, Cassidy." Hana leaped onto the horse, a mustang she had named Chakotay, and prodded him into action.

Both Shyanne and Drayco stared at her retreating form. They looked at each other as if to say, did you hear what I heard; and if so, what do you make of it?

How does she know about the movie Butch Cassidy and the Sundance Kid? Or was it merely coincidence? She wondered again about the odd feeling she had earlier concerning the oriental woman. *I get the feeling there's more to her than meets the eye.*

"Who are Sundance and Cassidy?"

Joseph's question caused the twins to break out in laughter. Shyanne answered, "I'll tell you all about it later, husband. For now, let's wish them a speedy return."

"Good luck, Drayco. I have a feeling you'll need it." He grinned when Drayco grimaced.

The dark twin urged Bravaro into a lope and followed the healer woman down the road. The couple comforted each other as they watched the departure with dread, as well as anticipation. The riders had gone only a short distance when Shyanne asked Drizzle, "You going with them?"

"Nope. I'm good. Besides, who will look after you two? Molly's set. Hana will do a fine job of keeping Drayco straight. But you two...you two are hopeless." Getting up, the cat padded to the door leading inside. He stopped and tilted his head when he was almost there. "Sounds like someone's calling for you, Shyanne."

The sound of crying wafted outside. Shyanne bolted inside to find out what had upset Molly so. Fortunately, Drizzle knew what her response would be and took the proper precautions by staying off to the side.

Shaking his head, he stated, "Predictable."

"Don't let Shyanne hear you. You'll never hear the end of it." Joseph entered the building ahead of the cat. Glancing back, he questioned, "I'm going to see if that chair still has my name on it. Care to join me?"

"Lead on, McDuff."

"Who's McDuff?"
"Later, Joseph. Much later."
    The door closed behind the pair with a click.

About the Author

Janet started writing while trying to help her son find his own words. Since then, the passion for writing has taken over. When not working as a registered nurse on a busy cardiac floor, she is pounding on the keyboard to her computer creating new worlds. On the other hand, she could be found sitting on the back porch enjoying the gentle breeze while wreaking havoc on her laptop. Sitting inside the local Starbucks or Barnes & Noble is not out of the questions either. Janet resides in the warm state of Florida with her son, furry friends known as cats, and a pair of neurotic dogs.

To learn more about what other books are available from this author check out www.janetdurbin.com.

"I love to keep the story flowing and to keep the reader wanting to see what's going to happen next. When I hear people say 'You're going to go places with this book', 'I loved it', 'When is the sequel coming out?', 'I can't wait for the next book' and so many other nice statements, I feel I have done my job. I have entertained them."

Don't miss the next book in the
Journey of Twins Series,

Vengence

Due to be released in 2008 from
Whimsical Publications, LLC.